Slawter & Bec

Other titles by

DARREN SHAN

Also available on audio

Slawter first published in hardback in Great Britain by
HarperCollins *Children's Books* 2006
Bec first published in hardback in Great Britain by
HarperCollins *Children's Books* 2006
Published together in this two-in-one edition in 2011
HarperCollins *Children's Books* is a division of HarperCollins*Publishers* Ltd,
77–85 Fulham Palace Road, Hammersmith, London W6 8JB

The HarperCollins website address is
www.harpercollins.co.uk

Darren Shan presides over the demons of the internet at www.darrenshan.com

1

ISBN 978-0-00-743643-9

Printed and bound in England by
Clays Ltd, St Ives plc

DARREN SHAN
THE DEMONATA VOL. 3 & 4

Slawter & BEC

HarperCollins *Children's Books*

CONTENTS

Slawter

First assistant director:
Bas "lurhmann"

hair by:
"figaro" Brian

screenwriting muse:
Lynda "minder" Lewis

spliced together by:
Stella "stargate" Paskins

a Christopher Little studios production

PART ONE
VISITORS

LIFE AS WE KNOW IT

→"My eyes! They stabbed out my eyes!"

I shoot awake. Start to struggle up from my bed. An arm hits the side of my head. Knocks me down. A man screams, "My eyes! Who took my eyes?"

"Dervish!" I roar, rolling off the bed, landing beside the feet of my frantic uncle. "It's only a dream! Wake up!"

"My eyes!" Dervish yells again. I can see his face now, illuminated by a three-quarters full moon. Eyes wide open, but seeing nothing. Fear scribbled into every line of his features. He lifts his right foot. Brings it down towards my head — hard. I make like a turtle and only just avoid having my nose smashed.

"*You* took them!" he hisses, sensing my presence, fear turning to hate. He bends and grabs my throat. His fingers tighten. Dervish is thin, doesn't look like much, but his appearance is deceptive. He could crush my throat, easy.

I swipe at his hand, yanking my neck away at the same time. Break free. Scrabble backwards. Halted by the bed. Dervish lunges after me. I kick at his head, both feet. No time to worry about hurting him. Connect firmly. Drive him back. He grunts, shakes his head, loses focus.

"Dervish!" I shout. "It's me, Grubbs! Wake up! It's only a nightmare! You have to stop before you—"

"The master," Dervish cuts in, fear filling his face again. He's staring at the ceiling — rather, that's where his eyes are fixed. "Lord Loss." He starts to cry. "Don't… please… not again. My eyes. Leave them alone. Please…"

"Dervish," I say, softly this time, rising, rubbing the side of my head where he hit me, approaching him cautiously. "Dervish. Derv the perv — where's your nerve?" Knowing from past nights that rhymes draw his attention. "Derv on the floor — where's the door? Derv without eyes — what's the surprise?"

He blinks. His head lowers a fraction. Sight returns gradually. His pupils were black holes. Now they look quasi-normal.

"It's OK," I tell him, moving closer, wary in case the nightmare suddenly fires up again. "You're home. With me. Lord Loss can't get you here. Your eyes are fine. It was just a nightmare."

"Grubbs?" Dervish wheezes.

"Yes, boss."

"That's really you? You're not an illusion? *He* hasn't created an image of you, to torment me?"

"Don't be stupid. Not even Michelangelo could sculpt a face this perfect."

Dervish smiles. The last of the nightmare passes. He sits on the floor and looks at me through watery globes. "How you doing, big guy?"

"Coolio."

"Did I hurt you?" he asks quietly.

"You couldn't if you tried," I smirk, not telling him about the hit to the head, the hand on my throat, the foot at my face.

I sit beside him. Drape an arm around his shoulders. He hugs me tight. Murmurs, "It was so real. I thought I was back there. I..."

And then he weeps, sobbing like a child. And I hold him, talking softly as the moon descends, telling him it's OK, he's home, he's safe — he's no longer in the universe of demons.

→Never trust fairy tales. Any story that ends with "They all lived happily ever after" is a crock. There are no happy endings. No endings, full stop. Life goes on. There's always something new around the corner. You can overcome major obstacles, face great danger, look evil in the eye and live to tell the tale — but that's not the end. Life sweeps you forward, swings you round, bruises and batters you, drops some new drama or tragedy in your lap, never lets go until you get to the one true end — death. As long as you're breathing, your story's still going.

If the rules of fairy-tales *did* work, my story would have ended on a high four months ago. That's when Dervish regained his senses and everything seemed set to return to normal. But that was a false ending. A misleading happy pause.

I had to write a short autobiography for an English assignment recently. A snappy, zappy summing-up of my life. I had to discard my first effort — it was too close to the bone, and would have only led to trouble if I'd handed it in. I wrote an edited, watered-down version and submitted that instead. (I got a B minus.) But I kept the original. It's hidden under a pile of clothes in my wardrobe. I dig it out now to read, to pass some time. I've read through it a lot these past few weeks, usually early in the morning, after an interrupted night, when I can't sleep.

I was born Grubitsch Grady. One sister, Gretelda. Grubbs and Gret for short. Normal, boring lives for a long time. Then Gret turned into a werewolf.

There's a genetic flaw in my family. Lots of my ancestors have turned into werewolves. It hits in your teens, if you're one of the unlucky ones. You lose your mind. Your body alters. You become a blood-crazed beast. And spend the rest of your life locked up in a cage — unless your relatives kill you. There's no cure. Except one. But that can be even worse than the curse.

See, demons are real. Gross, misshapen, magical beings, with a hatred of humans matched only by their taste for human flesh. They live in their own universe, but some can cross into our world.

One of the Demonata — that's the proper term — is called Lord Loss. A real charmer. No nose or heart — a hole in his chest full of snakes. Eight arms. Horrible pale red flesh. Loads of cuts on his body from which blood flows in a never-ending stream. He's big on misery. Feeds off the unhappiness, terror and grief of humans. Moves among us silently when he crosses into our universe, invisible to normal eyes, dropping in on funerals the way you or I would pop into a café, dining on our despair, savouring our sorrow.

Lord Loss is a powerful demon master. Most masters can't cross from their universe to ours, but he's an exception. He has the power to cure lycanthropy. He can lift the curse from infected Grady teenagers, rid them of their werewolf genes, return them to humanity. Except, y'know, he's a demon, so why the hell should he?

"What are you reading?"

It's Dervish, standing in the doorway of my room, mug of coffee in one hand, eyes still wide and freaky from his nightmare.

"My autobiography," I tell him.

He frowns. "What?"

"I'm going to publish my memoirs. I'm thinking of *Life with Demons* as a title. Or maybe *Hairy Boys and Girls of the Grady Clan*. What do you think?"

Dervish stares at me uneasily. "You're weird," he mutters, then trudges away.

"Wonder where I get that from?" I retort, then shake my head and return to the autobiography.

Luckily for us, Lord Loss is a chess addict. Chess is the one thing he enjoys almost as much as a weeping human. But he doesn't get to play very often. None of his demonic buddies know the rules, and humans aren't inclined to test their skills against him.

One of my more cunning ancestors was Bartholomew Garadex, a magician. (Not a guy who pulls rabbits out of a hat — a full-on, Merlin- and Gandalf-class master of magic.) He figured out a way to cash in on Lord Loss's love of chess. He challenged the demon master to a series of games. For every match Bartholomew won, Lord Loss would cure a member of the family. If old Bart lost, Lord Loss would get to torture and kill him.

Bartholomew won all their matches, but future members of the family — those with a flair for magic who made contact with Lord Loss — weren't so fortunate. Some triumphed, but most lost. The rules altered over the years. Now, if a parent wants to challenge Lord Loss, they need a partner. The pair face not only the master, but two of his familiars as well. One plays chess with the big guy, while the other battles his servants. If either loses, both are slaughtered, along with the affected teen. If they win, one travels to Lord Loss's realm and fights him there. The other returns home with the cured kid.

Time works differently in the universe of the Demonata. A year of our time can be a day there, a decade or a century. When the partner goes off with Lord Loss to do battle, their body remains in our world — only their soul crosses over. They become a mindless zombie. And they stay that way unless their soul triumphs. If that happens, their mind returns and they resume their normal life. If they don't fare so well, they stay a zombie until the day they die.

"Are you coming down for breakfast?" Dervish yells from the bottom of the giant staircase which links the floors of the mansion where we live.

"In a minute!" I yell back. "I've just come to the bit when you zombied out on me."

"Stop messing about!" he roars. "I'm scrambling eggs and if you're not down in sixty seconds, too bad!"

Damn. He knows all my weaknesses.

"Coming!" I shout, getting up and reaching for my clothes, tossing the bio aside for later.

→Dervish does a mean scrambled egg. Best I've ever tasted. I finish off a plateful without stopping for breath, then eagerly go for seconds. I'm built on the big side – a mammoth compared to most of my schoolmates – with an appetite to match.

Dervish is wearing a pair of tracksuit bottoms and a T-shirt. No shoes or socks. His grey hair is frizzled, except on top, where he's bald as a snooker ball. Hasn't shaved (he used to have a beard, but got rid of it recently). Doesn't smell good — sweaty and stale. He's this way most days. Has been ever since he came back.

"You eating that or not?" I ask. He looks over blankly from where he's standing, close to the hob. He's been staring out the window at the grey autumn sky, not touching his food.

"Huh?" he says.

"Breakfast is the most important meal of the day."

He looks down at his plate. Smiles weakly. Sticks his fork into the eggs, stirs them, then gazes out of the window again. "I remember the nightmare," he says. "They cut my eyes out.

They were circling me, tormenting me, using my empty sockets as—"

"Hey," I stop him, "I'm a kid. I shouldn't be hearing this. You'll scar me for life with stories like that."

Dervish grins, warmth in it this time. "Take more than a scary story to scar you," he grunts, then starts to eat. I help myself to thirds, then return to the autobiography, not needing the sheet of paper to finish, able to recall it perfectly.

I have a younger half-brother, Bill-E Spleen. He doesn't know we're brothers. Thinks Dervish is his father. I met him when I came to live with Dervish, after my parents died trying to save Gret. (I spent a while in a loony asylum first.)

Bill-E and I became friends. I thought he was an oddball, but harmless. Then he changed into a werewolf. Dervish explained the situation to me, told me Bill-E was my brother, laid out the family history and our link to Lord Loss.

I wasn't keen to get involved, but Dervish thought I had what it takes to kick demon ass. I told him he was mad as a moose, but... hell, I don't want to come across all heroic... but Bill-E was my brother. Mum and Dad put their lives on the line for Gret. I figured I owed Bill-E the same sort of commitment.

So we faced Lord Loss and his familiars, Artery and Vein, a vicious, bloodthirsty pair. I got the better of Lord Loss at chess, more by luck than plan. The demon master was furious, but rules are rules. So I got to return to reality along with the cured Bill-E. And Dervish won himself a ticket to Demonata hell, to go toe to toe with the big double L on his home turf.

I'm not sure what happened there, how they fought, what sort of a mess Dervish went through, how time passed for him, the manner of his victory over Lord Loss. For more than a year I guarded his body, helped by a team of lawyers (my uncle — he mucho reeeech) and Meera Flame, one of Dervish's best friends. I went back to school, rebuilt my life and babysat Dervish.

Then, without warning, he returned. I woke up one morning and the zombie was gone. He was his old self, talking, laughing, brain intact. We celebrated for days, us, Bill-E and Meera. And we all lived happily after. The end.

Except, of course, it wasn't. Life isn't a fairy tale. Stories don't end. Before she left, Meera took me aside and warned me to be careful. She said there was no way to predict Dervish's state of mind. According to the recorded accounts of the few who'd gone through the same ordeal as him, it often took a person a long time to settle after a one-on-one encounter with Lord Loss. Sometimes they never properly recovered.

"We don't know what's going on inside his head," she whispered. "He looks fine, but that could change. Watch him, Grubbs. Be prepared for mood-swings. Try and help. Do what you can. But don't be afraid to call me for help."

I did call when the nightmares started, when Dervish first attacked me in his sleep, mistook me for a demon and tried to cut my heart out. (Luckily, in his delirium, he picked up a spoon instead of a knife.) But there was nothing Meera could do, short of cast a few calming spells and recommend he visit a psychiatrist. Dervish rejected that idea, but she threatened to take me away from him if he didn't. So he went to see one, a guy who knew about demons, who Dervish could be honest with. After the second session, the psychiatrist rang Meera and said he never wanted to see Dervish again — he found their sessions too upsetting.

Meera discussed the possibility of having Dervish committed, or hiring bodyguards to look after him, but I rejected both suggestions. So, against her wishes, we carried on living by ourselves in this spooky old mansion. It hasn't been too bad. Dervish rarely gets the nightmares more than two or three times a week. I've grown used to them. Waking up in the middle of the night to screams is no worse than being disturbed by a baby's cries. Really it isn't.

And he's not that much of a threat. We keep the knives locked away and have bolted the other weapons in the mansion – it's dotted with axes, maces, spears, swords, all sorts of cool stuff – to the walls. I usually keep my door locked too, to be safe. The only reason it was open last night was that Dervish had thrown a fit both nights before and it's rare for him to fall prey to the nightmares three times in a row. I thought I was safe. That's why I didn't bother with the lock. It was my fault, not Dervish's.

"I will kill him for you, master," Dervish says softly.

I lower my fork. "What?"

He turns, blank-faced, looking like he did when his soul was fighting Lord Loss. My heart rate quickens. Then he grins.

"Asshole!" I snap. Dervish has a sick sense of humour.

I get back to wolfing down my breakfast and Dervish tucks into his, not caring that the scrambled eggs are cold. We're an odd couple, a big lump of a teenager like me playing nursemaid to a balding, mentally disturbed adult like Dervish. And yeah, there are nights when he really frightens me, when I feel like I can't take it any more, when I cry. It's not fair. Dervish fought the good fight and won. That should have been the end of it. Happy ever after.

But stories don't end. They continue as long as you're alive. You just have to get on with things. Turn the page, start a new chapter, find out what's in store for you next, and keep your fingers crossed that it's not *too* awful. Even if you know in your heart and soul that it most probably will be.

PRAY AT HIM

→School was strange when I first went back. I'd spent months outside the system, first in the asylum, then in the mansion with Dervish. It took me a while to find my feet. For the first couple of terms I didn't really speak to anybody except Bill-E and the school counsellor, Mr Mauch, better known as Misery Mauch because of his long face. I'd always been popular at my old school, lots of friends, active in several sports teams, Mr Cool.

All that changed at Carcery Vale. I was shy, unsure of myself, reluctant to get involved in conversations or commit to after-school events. On top of the hell I'd been through, there was Dervish to consider. He needed me at home. I became an anonymous kid, one who spent a lot of time by himself or with a similarly awkward friend (step forward Bill-E Spleen).

Things are different now. I've come out of my shell a bit. I'm more like the old me, not quiet in class or afraid to speak to other kids. I've always been bigger than most people my age. In the old days I was a show off and used my bulk to command respect. At the Vale I kept my head bent, shoulders hunched, trying to suck my frame in to make myself seem smaller.

Not any more. I'm no longer Mr Flash, but I'm not hiding now. I don't feel that I have to.

I've made new friends. Charlie Rall, Robbie McCarthy, Mary Hayes. And Loch Gossel. Loch's big, not as massive as me, but closer to my size than anybody else. He wrestles a lot — real wrestling, not the showbiz stuff you see on TV. He's been trying to get me to join his team since I started school. I resisted for a long time, but now I'm thinking of giving it a go.

Loch also has a younger sister, Reni. She's pretty cute, even if she does have a nose that would put Gonzo to shame! I stare at her a lot and sometimes she makes eyes back. I think she'd go out with me if I asked. I haven't. Not yet. But soon… maybe… if I can work up the nerve.

→The end of a typical school day. Yawning through classes, desperate for lunch-time so I could hang out with my friends and chat about movies, music, TV, computer games, whatever. Bill-E joined us for some of it. I don't spend as much time with Bill-E as I used to. He doesn't fit in with my new friends — they think he's geekish. They don't slag him off when I'm around, but I know they do when I'm not. I feel bad about that and try to help Bill-E relax so they can see his real side. But he gets nervous around the others, acts differently, becomes the butt of their jokes.

Thinking about Bill-E as I walk home. I don't want us to stop being friends. He's my brother and he was really good to me when I first moved here. But it's difficult because I don't want to lose my new friends either. Guess I'll just have to work harder to make him feel like part of the group. Try and be like one of those TV kids who always solve their problems by the end of each show.

Dervish is sitting on the stairs when I let myself in. I'm dripping wet — it's been pouring for the last couple of hours. Normally, when the weather's bad, he picks me up on his motorbike. When there was no sign of him today, I figured his mood hadn't improved since breakfast. I was right. He's as blank as he was this morning, staring off into space, not registering me until I'm right in front of him.

"Dervish! Hey, Derveeshio! Earth to Dervish! Are you reading me, captain?"

He blinks, frowns as if he doesn't know who I am, then smiles. "Grubbs. You're alive. I thought…" His expression clears. "Sorry. I was miles away."

I sit beside him. "Bad day?"

"Can't remember," he replies. "Why are you home early?" I hold up my watch and tap it. Dervish reads the time and sighs. "I'm losing it, Grubbs."

My insides tighten, but I don't let Dervish see my fear. "Losing what — your sanity? You can't lose what you never had."

"My grip." Dervish looks down at his feet, bare and dirty.

"I wasn't like this before. I wasn't this distracted and empty. Was I?" He looks at me pleadingly.

"You've been through hell, Derv," I tell him quietly. "You can't expect to recover without a few hiccups."

"I know. But I wasn't this way, right? Some days I can't remember. I feel like it's always been like this."

"No," I say firmly. "It's just a phase. It'll pass."

"All things must pass," Dervish mutters. Then he looks at me sideways, his cool blue eyes coming into focus. "Why are you wet?"

"Took a bath. Forgot to strip." I rap his forehead with my knuckles, then point to the windows and the rain battering the panes. "Numbnuts."

"Oh," Dervish says. "I should have picked you up."

"No worries." I rise and stretch, dripping steadily. "I'm going up to shower and change into dry clothes. I'll stick this lot in to wash. Anything you want me to add?" I did all the jobs around the house when Dervish was a vegetable. Hard to break the habit.

"No, I don't think so. I…" Dervish stares at his left hand. There's a black mark on it, a small 'd'. "There was something I meant to tell you. What…?" He clicks his fingers. "I had a phone call, a follow-up to some e-mails I've been getting recently. Ever heard of someone called Davida Haym?"

"No, can't say…" I pause. "Hold on. Not David A Haym, the movie producer?"

"That's her."

"I thought that was a guy."

"Nope. She uses David A on her movies, but it's Davida. You know about her?"

"Sure. She makes horror movies. *Zombie Zest. Witches Weird. Night Mayors* — that's, like, *Nightmares*, only two words. It's about evil mayors who band together to set up a meat production plant, except the meat they process is human flesh."

"Win many Oscars?" Dervish asks.

"Swept the board," I chuckle. "I can't believe she's a woman. I always thought... But what about her? I didn't think you were into horror flicks."

"She phoned me earlier."

I do a double-take. "David A Haym called you?"

"Davida Haym. Yes." Dervish squints at me. "Have I grown a second head?"

"Hell, it's *David A Haym*, Dervish! That's like saying Steven Spielberg was on the line, or George Lucas. OK, not as big as those, but still..."

"I didn't know she was famous," Dervish says. "She told me the names of some of her movies, but I don't watch a lot of films. She made it sound like she was a cult director."

"She is. She doesn't make films with big-name stars. But her movies are great! Anyone who loves horror knows about David A Haym. Though I'm not sure many know she's a woman."

"That's a big sticking point for you, isn't it?" Dervish grins. "You're not turning into a chauvinist, are you?"

"No, I just…" I shake my head. Water flies from my ginger hair and splatters the wall. "What did she want?"

"She's making a new movie. Asked if she could meet me. She'd heard I know a lot about the occult. Wants to pick my brain." He tweaks his chin, forgetting the beard isn't there. "I hope she didn't mean that literally."

"Did you say yes?" I ask, excited.

"Said I'd think about it."

"Dervish! You've got to! It's David A Haym! Did she say she'd come here? Can I meet her? Do you think—"

"Easy, tiger," Dervish laughs. "We didn't discuss where we'd meet. But you think I should agree to it?"

"Absolutely!"

"Then meet we shall," Dervish says, getting to his feet and heading up to his office. "Anything to please Master Grady."

I tramp up the stairs after him, pulling off my clothes, thinking about how cool it would be if I could meet David A Haym… and also how weird it is that one of the world's premier horror producers is a woman.

→"David A Haym's a woman? No bloody way!" Loch howls.

"You're having us on!" Robbie challenges me.

"How stupid do you think we are?" Charlie huffs.

"Of course she's a woman," Mary says. We gawp at her. "You didn't know?"

"No," Loch says. "You did?"

"Yes."

"How long?"

Mary shrugs. "I dunno. Years."

"And you never told us?" Robbie barks.

"It never came up," Mary laughs. "I've no interest in horror movies. I always tune out when you guys start on that rubbish."

"Then how did you know she's a woman?" I ask.

"There was a feature on her in a magazine my mum reads," Mary explains. "I think the headline was, 'The horror producer chick who beats the boys at their own game'."

They're nearly as excited as I am. Most of my friends don't know what to make of Dervish. In a way he's cool, the adult who rides a motorbike, dresses in denim, lets me do pretty much what I like. On the other hand he sometimes comes across as a complete nutter. Plus they know he was a veg for more than a year.

But now that he's in talks with the slickest, sickest producer of recent horror movies, his cred rises like a helium balloon. They want to know how she knows about him, when she's coming, what the new movie's about. I act mysterious and secretive, giving nothing away, but dropping hints that I'm fully clued-in. In truth, I know no more than they do. Dervish wasn't able to get through to her last night. He left a message and was waiting for her to phone back when I left this morning.

* * *

→"Did she call?"

"Who?"

I groan, wishing Dervish wasn't a complete airhead. "David A Haym, of course! Did she–"

"Oh, yeah, she rang."

"*And?*" I practically shriek, as Dervish focuses on getting dinner ready.

"She'll drop by within the next week."

"Here?" I gasp. "Carcery Vale?"

"No," he smirks. "*Here* — this house. I told her she could stay the night if she wanted, though I don't know if–"

"David A Haym's going to stay in our house?" I shout.

"Davida," Dervish corrects me.

"Dervish… the terrible things I've said about you… the awful names I've called you… I take them all back!"

"Thanks," Dervish laughs. Stops and frowns. "*What* awful names?"

→Everyone wants David A Haym's autograph. They want to meet her, have dinner with us, maybe snag a part in her next movie. Loch auditions for me several times a day, moaning and screaming, pretending bits of his body have been chopped off, quoting lines from *Zombie Zest* and *Night Mayors* — "We elected a devil!" "That's not *my* hand on your knee!" "Mustard or mayo with your brains?" Draws curious stares from teachers and kids who haven't heard the big news.

Bill-E talks up script ideas. Reckons he can pitch to her and become the brains behind her next five movies. "Writers are getting younger all the time," he insists. "Producers want fresh talent, original ideas, guys who can think outside the box."

"You're about as far outside the box as they come," Loch laughs.

"I wouldn't have to write the whole script myself," Bill-E says, ignoring the jibe. "I could collaborate. I'm a team player."

"Yeah," Loch snorts. "Trouble is, you're a substitute!"

I let them scheme and dream. Smile smugly, as if they're just crazy, dreamy kids. Of course, I'm as full of wild notions as they are — I just prefer to play it cool.

→Days pass — no sign of Davida Haym. The weekend comes and goes. I bug Dervish constantly, asking if there's been any further contact. Sometimes he pretends he doesn't know what I'm talking about, just to wind me up.

By Tuesday I'm starting to wonder if it's a gag, if Dervish never spoke to David A Haym at all. It would be a weird, unfunny joke — but Dervish is into weird and unfunny. I'll look a right dope in school if she never shows. I'll have to invent a story, pretend she was called away on an emergency.

Thinking about excuses I could use as I'm walking home. Nothing too simple, like a sick relative or having to pick up an award. Needs to be more dramatic. Her house burnt to the ground? She caught bubonic plague and had to go into isolation?

Warming to the plague theory – can people still get it these days? – when a car pulls up beside me. A window rolls down. A thin, black-haired woman leans across. "Excuse me," she says. "Do you know where Dervish Grady lives?"

"Yeah." I bend down, excitement building. "I'm his nephew, Grubitsch. I mean, Grubbs. Grubbs Grady. That's me." Can't remember the last time I called myself Grubitsch. What a dork!

"Grubbs," the woman says, nodding shortly. "Yes. I know about you."

"You do?" Unable to hide my delight. "Dervish told you about me? Wow, that's great! Uh, I mean, yeah, cool. I know about you too, of course."

"Really?" She sounds surprised.

"Sure. I've been waiting all week for you."

"You knew I was coming?" Sharp this time.

"Yeah. Dervish told me."

She taps the steering wheel with her fingernails. They're cut short, down to the flesh. "Well, may I give you a lift home, Grubbs? That way you can direct me as we go."

"Sure!" I open the door and slide in. Put my seat belt on. Smile wide at David A — I mean, Davida Haym. She smiles back thinly. A narrow, pale face. Moody, if not downright gloomy. Exactly the way I expected a horror producer to look. "Just go straight," I tell her. "The road runs by our house. You can't miss it — only mansion in the neighbourhood."

Silence. Davida is focused on the road. I'm trying to think of something to say that's casual and witty. But my mind's a blank. So I check her out. Thin all over, a long neck, bony hands, straight black hair, dark eyes. Dull white shirt and skirt. Flat, plain shoes. No jewellery, except one ring on her left hand with a large gold 'L' in the middle of a circle of flat silver.

"How have you been, Grubbs?" she asks suddenly.

"Fine."

"I know something of your past. What happened last year with Billy Spleen."

"What do you know about me and Bill-E?" I ask suspiciously, guard rising.

"I know about the lycanthropy. How you fought it."

"Dervish told you *that?*" I cry, astonished.

"How has Billy been? Any recurrences of his old patterns?"

"Of course not! We cured him! He's normal now!"

"And you?" she says quietly, and her eyes flick across, cold and calculating.

"Who the hell are you?" I ask, a tremble in my voice.

"Who do you think I am?" she replies.

"I thought you were David A Haym. But you're not… are you?"

In answer she raises a finger and points. "That must be the mansion."

She pulls into our drive. I have a bad feeling in my gut, not sure who this woman is or how she knows about Bill-E. She kills the engine and looks at me calmly. Her eyes are *really* dark. A robot-like expression. No make-up. Thin lips, almost invisible. A small nose with a wartish mole on the right nostril.

"Shall we go in together, or do you want to go on ahead and tell your uncle I'm here?" she asks.

"That depends. What's your name?" She only smiles in reply. She looks more normal when she smiles, like a teacher — stern, but human. I relax slightly. "You can come with me," I decide, not wanting to leave her here in case she's an old friend of Dervish's and I appear rude.

"Thank you," she says and gets out of the car. She's smoothing her skirt down and studying the mansion when I step out. "Nice place," she comments, then raises a thin eyebrow, the signal for me to lead the way. I start ahead of her, whistling, not letting her see that I'm unnerved, acting like she's an ordinary visitor. In through the oversized front doors. The juicy smell of sizzling steak drifts from the kitchen.

"Goodness," the woman says, looking at the high ceilings, the size of the rooms, the weapons on the walls, the staircase.

"This way," I tell her, heading for the kitchen. "You're just in time for dinner."

She follows slowly, absorbing the surroundings. Obviously hasn't been here before. I keep trying to put a name to her face, thinking of all the people Dervish has mentioned in the past.

I reach the kitchen. Dervish is hard at work on the steak. "No!" he shouts before I say anything. "She hasn't rung and there's been no sign of her. Now stop pestering me or I might—"

"We have company," I interrupt.

Dervish turns questioningly. The woman enters the kitchen. I step aside so he can see her. Instant recognition. His face goes white, then red. He steps away from the hob, abandoning the steak. Eyes tight. Lips quivering. With anger.

"*You!*" He spits the word out.

"It's been a long time, Dervish," the woman says softly, not moving forward to shake his hand. "You look better than I expected."

"I thought she was David A Haym," I tell him.

"She's not," he barks. "She's Prae Athim."

"Pray at him?" I echo.

"Pray Ah-teem," the woman says, stressing the syllables.

"She's one of the Lambs," Dervish says with a sneer.

And the fear which was tickling away at me in the car kicks in solid, like a nail being hammered into my gut.

LAMBIKINS

→In Dervish's study. Like most of the rooms, it's huge. But whereas the others have bare walls, with stone or wood floorboards, the study is carpeted and the walls are covered with leather panels. There are two large desks, bookcases galore, a PC, laptop, typewriter, paper and pens. There used to be five chess sets, but not any more. The swords and axes which hung from the walls are gone too.

Prae Athim doesn't want me here. That's obvious from her disapproving look. Dervish doesn't care. He's seated behind the computer on his largest desk, one hand on the mouse, moving it around in small circles, waiting for his unwelcome guest to speak. Prae Athim is seated opposite. I'm standing close to the door, ready to leave if Dervish tells me to.

Prae finally speaks. "Billy Spleen still lives with his grandparents?" Dervish nods slowly. "I thought you might have moved him in with you. To observe."

"You're the master observer, not me," Dervish says quietly.

"Isn't it dangerous, leaving him there?" she presses.

"Billy's time of turning has passed. There's nothing to fear from him now."

"That's debatable," Prae smiles.

"No. It isn't."

Prae looks at her hands crossed over her lap. Thinks a moment. Then nods at me. "I'd rather not speak in front of the boy."

"Is this about him?" Dervish responds.

"Partially."

"Then you'll have to."

"I really don't think—" she begins.

"Grubbs faced the demons with me," Dervish interrupts. "He fought by my side. I'm not going to keep secrets from him."

"Really?" Prae sniffs. "You tell him everything about your business?"

"No. But I don't hide things from him. When he asks, I answer. And since I'm certain he's going to be asking about this, he might as well stay and hear it first-hand."

Prae sighs. "You never make life easy for us. You've always treated the Lambs like enemies. We're on the same side, Dervish. You should afford us respect."

"I do respect you," Dervish says. "I just don't trust you."

I'd forgotten about the Lambs. They loomed large in my thoughts while Dervish was zombified, especially around the time of a full moon. If I'd found myself turning into a werewolf, I was going to phone them and ask them to put me out of my misery. But since Dervish returned, I haven't had time to brood about my potentially fatal genes or the family bogey men.

The Gradys and their kin have been cursed for a long time. We're talking a *lot* of generations. Over the centuries, family members have tried to figure out the cause of the curse, find a cure for it, and develop ways of dealing with the infected children quietly and efficiently.

The Lambs are the result. A group of scientists, soldiers and I don't know what else, all focused on the problems and logistics of lycanthropy. They spend a lot of time, money and effort trying to unlock the secrets of the rogue Grady-genes. But they also play the part of executioners when necessary.

A lot of parents decide to kill their children if they turn into werewolves. But most can't perform the dirty deed themselves. So they call in the Lambs, who take the transformed child away and do what must be done.

"How did you find out about Billy?" Dervish asks.

"We keep tabs on all the family children," Prae says.

"But Billy didn't leave a trail. There was no evidence that he was turning."

Prae smiles. "You covered up admirably. Gathered the bodies of the animals he slaughtered, disposed of them quietly. But you couldn't be expected to find *every* corpse. And you couldn't do anything about the operative who saw him sneaking out of his house during a full moon."

"You had him under direct surveillance?" Dervish snaps.

"Sometimes, yes."

Dervish's hand goes rigid on the mouse. "You had no right to do that."

"We had every right," Prae disagrees. "If a guardian chooses to deal personally with an infected child, it's not our business. But you didn't. You gave him free reign."

"I was in control," Dervish growls. "He wasn't a danger to anyone. I was waiting for the right moment to act."

"I understand," Prae says. "But we couldn't take any chances. We guessed you would handle the matter this way if he turned, so for some years we'd been keeping an eye on the boy. On your brother's children too."

Dervish starts to retort. Stops and scowls. "Tell me why you've come."

"A few reasons," Prae says. "One — to make sure Billy is normal."

"He is," Dervish says. "We cured him."

"But how certain is your *cure*?" Prae asks. "We know about the demon you deal with, but there's much about the process that's a mystery. You and the others who have faced him keep it a secret. You don't let the rest of us benefit."

"We can't include you," Dervish says stiffly. "He deals with one case at a time, and only with those who have some experience of magic. That's how it works. It's not our choice — it's *his*."

"The demon," Prae nods. "Lord—"

"Don't say his name here," Dervish stops her. "It's dangerous."

Prae looks around nervously. I feel the hairs rise on the back of my neck. Then Dervish catches my eye and tilts his head ever so slightly. It's a gesture I know well — he does that sometimes instead of winking. I realise he's winding Prae up, giving her a scare. I hide a smile behind my hand and wait for her to settle down.

"It's not fair," Prae resumes, less composed than before. "We've never had any contact with the demon. Maybe we could strike our own deal if you put us in touch with him."

"You couldn't."

"But you should let us try. We—"

"We've had this conversation before," Dervish interrupts. "We're not having it again. The Lambs follow the path of science. Demons are creatures of magic. The two don't mix. End of story."

"Very well," Prae says, showing open anger for a second, her pale face flushing. "You choose to lock us out — there's nothing we can do about that. But it means we don't know all that we should about the cure. We have no proof that it works in the long term, or why. So it's natural for us to be suspicious, to run our own checks, to be safe."

"Totally natural," Dervish says sarcastically. "But I don't think you'd have waited until now to make sure Billy wasn't killing. If you were checking on him prior to his change, I'm sure you've monitored him in the year-plus since. So your first reason for being here is a crock — you know Billy's fine. Let's move on to reason two and try to make it a bit more believable this time."

Prae glares at Dervish, then glances at me. "*Two*," she growls. "We wanted to check on Grubbs. He's at a dangerous age. Both his brother–" My stomach tightens another notch. She knows the truth about Bill-E! "–and sister turned. We thought it advisable to have a look at him. We kept out of the way while you were… indisposed, but now that you're back on your feet, we felt it was a good time to have a chat." She faces me and smiles. "How have you been sleeping lately? Any bad dreams? Woken up with dirt under your fingernails or–"

"You know what she's doing, don't you, Grubbs?" Dervish asks.

"Trying to freak me out," I mutter edgily.

"Correct. If they wanted to check up on you, they'd do it secretly. You'd never know they were there. She's saying this to upset you, because I've upset her. So ignore it. And you," he says to Prae, "tell me the real reason you're here or get the hell out."

"Very well." Prae stares at Dervish challengingly. "We want to run some tests on Billy under laboratory conditions."

"You want to turn my nephew into a guinea pig?" Dervish laughs harshly. "You want me to sign him over, so you can prod and poke him and have him urinate into a bottle at your command?"

"It's not like that. We—"

"Get out!" Dervish shouts.

"You're being unreasonable," Prae objects. "Let me finish."

"Oh, you're finished," Dervish laughs. "I've heard enough. Now march back out to your car and—"

"Have you seen a child who's turned?" Prae asks me, raising her voice. "You must have seen your brother, but only in the early stages of his transformation. It takes a few months for the disease to properly set in. They grow hair. Their features distort. Their spines twist. I have some photographs which—"

"No!" I shout. "I don't want to see any photos. I've seen them before."

"Children your own age," Prae says quickly as Dervish stands and strides towards her. "Some even younger. We have an eight-year-old girl. Her parents didn't know about the curse. She killed her mother. Chewed her throat open and—"

"You're so out of here," Dervish snarls, reaching to grab Prae's collar.

"Wait," I stop him, holding up a hand.

"Grubbs, don't listen to—"

"Just wait a minute. Please?"

Dervish breathes out heavily, then takes a step back.

"We're trying to help," Prae says, speaking to me but looking at Dervish. "Your uncle is a man of old science — he calls it magic, but to us it's science by a different name. We're of the new school. Dervish fights one battle at a time. Your mother and father made that choice too. But we're trying to attack the root of the disease. We want everyone to benefit, not just a few. To do that, we have to examine and explore.

"Your brother is one of the very few victims to beat the curse. If we can study him, unlock the secrets behind his remarkable cure, perhaps we can replicate it and save others — without the need for demons or so-called magic."

"You can't," Dervish says wearily. "I've told you before, it's *not* science. It's not of this universe. You can't understand it and you can't mimic it. Do you think I'd stand in your way if I thought there was the slightest chance that you could?"

"You can't be sure," Prae says.

"I am."

Prae mutters something beneath her breath, then tries me again. "We wouldn't hurt Billy. You and your uncle could come and observe. We just want to know more, to understand... to help."

I feel sorry for Prae Athim. Despite her scary appearance and manner, she only wants to do good. But the thought of her taking Bill-E away, locking him up, experimenting on him… I shake my head.

"You should leave now," Dervish says quietly. "We can't help you."

"You're condemning others to change, to die," Prae says angrily.

Dervish shrugs. "We've been condemned a long time. We're used to it."

He lays a hand on Prae's shoulder. She jerks away from him and stands. "My daughter changed," she hisses. "I tried to cure her, but I couldn't. She's still alive. Because I hope and believe. By denying us, you deny her and all the others like her. How will you sleep with that on your conscience?"

"Lousily," Dervish says. "But Billy will sleep sweetly. And to me, that's what matters most, just as your daughter matters most to you." He leans towards her. "If the positions were reversed, would you allow *your* loved one to be taken?"

"Yes," Prae answers immediately. "Without question."

"Well, that's where we differ. Because I always question."

"There are other ways," Prae says, a dangerous tremble to her tone. "We didn't have to ask. We could just take him."

Dervish's expression goes dead. "Try it," he whispers. "See what happens."

"You couldn't stop us," Prae insists, a red flush of anger rising up her throat. "You're powerful, but so are the Lambs. We could—"

"Mess with me and you mess with us all," Dervish interrupts. "Do you really want to do that? Do the Lambs now think themselves the equals of the Disciples?"

"We aren't afraid of your kind," Prae says, but her words ring hollow.

Dervish smiles lazily. "If you lay a hand on Billy or Grubbs, I'll teach you to be afraid. That's a promise."

"You don't want us as enemies," Prae warns him. "Nobody stands alone in this world, not even the Disciples. You may need us one day."

"Yes," Dervish agrees. "But not today." He points at the door.

Prae opens her mouth to try again. Realises she'd be wasting her breath. Shakes her head with disgust. Shoots a look at me. "Pray you never turn. Because if you do, thanks to people like your uncle, we won't be able to help. All we'll be able to do is kill."

She strides to the door, throws it opens and marches out. The front doors slam several seconds later. Then the faint sound of her engine starting, rising, fading.

Dervish stares at me. I stare back. Neither of us says anything. I don't know what my uncle's thinking, but there's only one glaring thought in my head — who the hell are the *Disciples*?

MONSTERS GALORE

→Dervish has another nightmare. Four nights in a row — he must be going for the record. Luckily I'd been expecting this one. Dervish shut himself off from me after Prae Athim left. Kept to his study, pacing around, muttering, brooding. I guessed nightmares would follow. Stayed awake after he went to bed, alert, prepared for a long, active night.

I catch Dervish in the hall of portraits. He snuck past my room without me hearing, even though I'd been listening closely. But a minute ago the screaming started and it was easy to track him down.

The walls of this hall are lined with photographs and paintings of dead family members, mostly teenagers who became werewolves. It's on the first floor, close to my bedroom. When I arrive, Dervish has knocked several photos to the floor and is wrestling with a large portrait, trying to tear it free of its peg.

"Leave me alone!" he screams. "It's not my fault!"

"Dervish," I call, hurrying over to him, grabbing his right hand, trying to prise his fingers loose. "Derveeshio! Derv on a curve — don't lose your verve. Don't roar and bawl — not in this hall."

He ignores the rhymes and jerks free. "Get out of my skull! You're eating my brain!" He collapses to his knees, grips his head hard with both hands, moans with pain and terror.

"Dervish, easy, it's OK, it's coolio, you have to chill. You on the ground — everything's sound."

His eyes fix on a nearby photograph. His breath catches. "I didn't do it!" he gasps. "I didn't kill you! Leave me alone!"

I sweep the photos away, then grab Dervish's hands, pull them down from his head and lock gazes with him. "Wake up, you crazy, bald coot! It's only a dream — no need to scream. None of it's real — fantasy's the deal. You have to snap back. Come on, I know you're in there, I know…"

His expression clears. He looks like a lost child for a few seconds, pitiful, silently begging me for help. Then the real Dervish surfaces and terror gives way to exhaustion and embarrassment. I release him, nodding slowly and repeatedly to show that everything's OK, no damage done.

Dervish looks around at the photos on the floor. Most are ripped, a couple beyond repair. No glass in the frames. We removed all the glass a few months ago, in case something like this happened. Didn't want him hurting himself — or me.

"I thought they'd come back to life," Dervish says. "They blamed me. Claimed I was the cause of the curse. They wanted revenge."

"It was just a dream."

"I know. But still…" He shivers. "I could have done without Prae Athim and the Lambs. I didn't need them now. Not in this state. Why do bad things always come at the worst time?"

"Forget about her," I tell him. "She's gone. You ran her off."

"Maybe I shouldn't have. Maybe…" He coughs, then stands. "No. That's the nightmare talking. The Lambs can't help. They mean well, but in matters like this they're helpless."

"Unlike the Disciples?" I ask, broaching the mysterious subject for the first time, not sure if it's the right moment, but curiosity getting the better of me.

Dervish shakes his head. "I'll tell you about them later. Not now. OK?"

I sniff like it doesn't matter.

Dervish grows thoughtful. "Billy doesn't know about the change, Lord Loss, what we did for him. It's better this way. No point throwing his world into chaos. The Lambs are part of the human world. They've no direct experience of the Demonata or magic. They couldn't learn anything from Billy."

"Then don't worry about it," I mutter. "Go back to bed, get a good night's sleep, kick the nightmares out the window."

Dervish laughs. "If only it was that easy." He checks his watch. Yawns. "But I'll try to snooze, to keep *nurse Grubitsch* happy." He glances at me. "If I drop off, I might go walkabout again. You should lock me in."

"Nah," I smile. "You'd wreck the room. Don't worry about it. I'll sleep with one ear open. I'll see you don't come to harm."

Dervish reaches over, squeezes my hand, then shuffles off for the stairs and bed. I watch until he turns the corner. Stay for a while, thinking about Bill-E, the Lambs, demons, the mysterious Disciples. Then I start clearing up the photos and hanging the less tattered snapshots back on their pegs, knowing I won't be able to sleep.

→Tired. Finding it hard to stay awake. My friends want to know if there are any David A Haym updates, but I only grunt at their questions. Studying Bill-E during lunch. Thinking about him in the hands of the Lambs, strapped to a table, hooked up to banks of electrodes. Can't let that happen. I faced Lord Loss for my brother. If Prae Athim tries anything with Bill-E, she won't just have to worry about Dervish and the Disciples — she'll have to deal with me.

Yeah, I know, she's hardly trembling with terror at the thought of having to go up against a teenager. But I'm big. And I can be nasty. If I have to.

* * *

→A limousine's parked in the drive when I get home. A chauffeur sits behind the wheel, dozing. No prizes for guessing who the limo belongs to.

I hear her as soon as I push open the front doors. She's in the TV room. A loud voice, high-pitched, very theatrical. She's talking about one of her earlier movies – it might be *Zombie Zest* – telling Dervish about the problems she faced trying to get the look of the monsters right.

"...but *every*body's using CGI these days! I don't like it. The audience can tell. They're not afraid. It's psychological. You see a guy in a monster costume, or a cleverly designed puppet, and even though you *know* it's not real, you can trick yourself into believing it is. But if you see something that's the work of a computer, your brain can't accept it. It doesn't scare you. I think..."

I walk into the room and cough softly. Davida Haym looks up from where she's sitting on the couch. A surprisingly normal-looking woman. Fiftyish. Black hair streaked with grey. Pudgy. A warm smile. Purple-rimmed glasses. A bright flowery dress. She looks more like a giggling granny than a horror-movie meister.

"Davida, this is my nephew, Grubbs," Dervish introduces us. He's sitting beside her on the couch, looking a bit overwhelmed — I have the feeling Davida hasn't stopped talking since she came in. "Grubbs lives with me."

"Hello, Grubbs," Davida says, rising to shake my hand. A short woman. Barely comes up to my chest. "Neat name. Is it short for something?"

"Grubitsch," I mutter. "I'm a big fan of yours. I thought *Night Mayors* was the best horror film of the last ten years."

"Why, thank you!" Davida booms, not releasing my hand. "Although, to be honest, my input wasn't so great. The director – Liam Fitz – is a real hardhead. Likes to make the creative decisions himself. I set him off, gave him whatever he asked for, but after that…" She shrugs, still holding my hand.

"And this is June," Dervish says, drawing my attention to a third person in the room, sitting in a chair to my left.

"Juni," she corrects him, getting up. "Juni Swan." Davida Haym finally releases my fingers and I shake hands with the other woman. She's small too, but slightly taller than Davida. Thin. Pretty. White hair, very pale skin, pinkish eyes. An albino. Her hair's tied back in a ponytail. Hard to tell her age because her skin's so white and smooth.

"Juni is Miss Haym's assistant," Dervish says.

"Davida," the producer corrects him. She tuts loudly. "I don't stand on ceremony."

"And I'm not her assistant," Juni says, almost apologetically. She speaks very softly. "Although I am here to assist."

"Let's sit down," Davida says, as if this was her house. She leads us back to the chairs and pats the space on the couch beside her, forcing me to sit with her and Dervish. "I've been telling your uncle about my problems on my other movies. As I'm sure you know – I can tell you're a horror buff – I *love* monsters. *LOVE* them! Fangs, tentacles, bulging eyes, slime… all great stuff, right? Right! But getting them to look real… believable… scare people to the max… that's hard as hell. But I'm telling you nothing new. You've seen loads of terrible monster flicks, I'm sure. Where the creatures are about as scary as a baby in a pram?"

"Yeah," I grin. "Most horror films are crap. That's why they're fun."

"I agree!" Davida shouts. She thumps Dervish's knee so hard that he gasps. "I like this kid! He knows his nettles from his roses!" She turns back to me. "We all love schlocky horror, where the effects are lame and the monsters tame. I grew up on old Universal and Hammer pictures! And that's fine. Sometimes you just want to sit down to a corny bit of hokum and have a laugh."

She raises a finger and lowers her voice. "But there are times when you don't want to laugh, right? When you want to be scared, when you want your world turned upside-down, when you want to sit there in the dark and really feel fear *bite*. Right?"

"Hell, yeah!" There was a period, after my battles with Lord Loss and his familiars, when I didn't enjoy horror. Life was fearful enough. But as the months passed, and the memories of the real horror faded, I rediscovered my love of fictional terror.

"That's where I want to go with my next movie," Davida says, loud again. "I've been off the scene for a while — almost four years since my last film. That's because I've been researching and planning. I want to do something *BIG* with my next one, not rehash an older story. I want screams, not laughs. I want to go for the jugular and shake audiences up, send them home shivering."

"Coolio!" I exclaim.

"Which is where your uncle comes in." Davida smoothes down her skirt and turns her smile on Dervish. "Will we talk business now or do you want to wait?"

"Now's good for me," Dervish says.

"OK." Davida glances around, to be sure nobody's eavesdropping. "I'm about to shoot my new film. Everything's set. I'm not only producing — I've written the script and I'm directing too. Can you imagine? *Me* — a director!" She throws her head back and laughs. Dervish and I laugh too, even though we've no idea what the joke is.

"I've kept the project secret," Davida continues. "I keep quiet about all my films, but I've been especially hush-hush on this one. Everyone connected has signed a lips-sealed contract. The monster designs are locked in a state-of-the-art safe, and only two other people beside myself have seen them in their entirety — everybody else gets a small piece to work on. We won't be shooting in any of the established studios.

I've created my own, far away from prying eyes. Most people aren't even aware that I'm at work again — they think I'm sitting on my ass on a beach, twiddling my thumbs, creatively defunct."

"Sounds like you've given yourself a lot of headaches," Dervish says.

"Are you kidding?" Davida snorts. "I'm having a ball! It's the film I've always wanted to make. I love intrigue, suspense, secrets. It's a game, the best in the world, and I'm the only one who knows all the rules. I wouldn't trade places with anybody right now, not for anything."

"I'm glad you're happy," Dervish says. "But I don't see why…?" He leaves the question hanging.

"Why I'm telling *you*?" Davida looks at me and winks. "Why I'm telling the *two* of you." She lowers her voice again. I don't think she's capable of whispering, but this is as close as she gets. "What I say now has to remain between us. I haven't asked you to sign a confidentiality form yet – you'll have to do it later, if you agree to my offer – but from what I've heard, you're a man of your word. I'm not sure about Grubbs…"

"I can keep a secret," I huff. "You don't have to worry about me."

"Excellent." She gives my right knee a squeeze and almost crushes it. "So, when I ask you to keep what I'm about to say to yourselves, not tell anybody, even your best friends… can I trust you?"

"I won't speak, even under torture," Dervish laughs.

"Me neither," I back him up.

"Great!" Davida beams. "Then listen close and keep it quiet. The film's called *Slawter*."

"*Slaughter!*" I echo. "Brilliant!"

"I think so too," Davida chuckles. "*Slawter* — which is spelt with a 'w' instead of a 'ugh' — is the name of the town in the movie. A bit obvious maybe, but I've always liked a gruesomely OTT play on words. I think it'll look great on the posters — 'Welcome to Slawter!' or 'Let the Slawter commence!'" She squints. "Maybe we'll have to work on the tagline, but you get the picture. Now, here's the good part, the reason I'm here, and the bit I know you're going to love the best. *Slawter* is going to be all about... *demons!*"

She sits back, grinning, and awaits our response, unaware that she's just dropped the mother of all bombshells.

→Davida can't understand why we're not excited. Doesn't know what to make of our shifty glances and awkward silence. She keeps talking about the movie. Tells us that demons take over the town of Slawter. She describes some of the characters and scenes. Dervish and I listen stiffly.

"OK," Davida finally says, "what's wrong?" She sniffs at her armpits. "Do I stink?"

Dervish forces a thin smile. "There's nothing wrong. It's just... We're not fond of demons, are we, Grubbs?"

"No," I grunt.

"Why not?" Davida asks. "Demons are the scariest monsters of the lot."

"Too scary," Dervish mutters, then laughs edgily.

Davida frowns. "But you're supposed to be a demon expert. The more I research, the more your name crops up. I've been told you know all about their ways, their habits, their appearance."

"You're talking about them as if they were real," Juni Swan chuckles.

"Of course they're not *real*," Davida snorts. "But there have been loads of stories and legends about demons, plenty of descriptions and paintings, and Dervish knows more about them than most. He has some of the hardest-to-find demonic books and manuscripts in the world. Right?"

"I know more than many, not as much as some," Dervish answers cagily. "What I can say is, demons aren't to be taken lightly. If you want to make stuff up, go ahead, use your imagination, have fun. But I suspect you want to do more than that."

"Damn straight," Davida huffs. "I want the real deal, the fiercest demons on record. I want this to be believable. I've got most of what I need — as I said, I've been working on this for four years. My demons are ready to go. But I want them to behave realistically. I want to get every last detail right, so even the greatest demon scholar won't be able to find fault."

Davida points at Dervish. "That's where *you* come in. I want your expertise, your insight and knowledge. I want you to come on set as an advisor. Tell us when we make mistakes, steer us right, help us pin the images down."

"You've got the wrong guy," Dervish says. "I know nothing about movies."

"There's a first time for everything," Davida insists. "I'm not saying you look on this as a career move — just a break from the norm. You get to see a film being made... hang out with the actors and crew... tell us what to do when we're messing up... and the money's not bad either!"

Juni coughs politely. "Davida, have you *seen* this place? I don't think money is an issue. Correct, Dervish?"

"I have to admit, I'm not hard up," Dervish says, smiling at the pretty albino.

"So don't do it for the money," Davida shrugs. "Do it for the experience. This is the chance of a lifetime. You could bring Grubbs along too. You'd like to see a movie being made, wouldn't you, Grubbs?"

"You bet!" I reply enthusiastically. Then I remember what the film's about. "But demons... they're... it sounds silly, but..." I pull a face.

"This is incredible," Davida snaps. "I thought you guys would be dying to get in on this. There are others I can ask if you're going to be ridiculous about it. I'm not–"

"Davida," Juni interrupts calmly. "You won't convince them to get involved by antagonising them. If they don't want to do it, you'll have to accept their decision and move on."

"I know," Davida mutters. "I just don't get why they're turning me down!"

"It's nothing personal," Dervish says, then looks at Juni. "What's your role in this, Miss Swan?"

"I'm a psychologist. There are lots of children involved in this movie. I've been hired to look after them on set."

"Do you do a lot of this type of work?" Dervish asks.

Juni shakes her head. "This is my first time."

"I brought Juni along because we're going to interview a young actor later," Davida says. "I like her to be involved with the kids as early as possible. She can spot a problem child a mile off."

"What about problem adults?" Dervish asks.

"I don't think you'd be any problem," Juni responds with a shy smile.

"I'm not so sure about that," Davida grumbles. Then she suddenly turns the full force of her smile on Dervish. "Hellfire, Grady! I don't care if you're a problem or not. I want you on my team. What can I do to convince you?"

Dervish starts to say there's nothing she can do, then hesitates, glances at Juni and frowns. "Do you have a copy of the script?"

"No," Davida says. "And I wouldn't show it to you if I did. But I've got some excerpts on disc, along with a rough plot outline and descriptions of some of the demons — I needed *something* to grab the interest of potential investors. But I don't like revealing even that much, especially to someone who hasn't signed a contract."

"I understand," Dervish says. "But if I could have a look, I'd be able to tell you whether or not you need me. I don't want to waste your time or mine. If there's no reason for me to be there – nothing I can help you with – then…"

Davida doesn't look happy. "I have a few copies of the disc," she says, nodding at her handbag on the floor. "They're digitally protected, so you shouldn't be able to copy the material or send it to anyone by e-mail. But…"

She thinks it over, then reaches into the bag and produces a boxed disc. "I don't know why I'm trusting you with this. You're not *that* important to me. But you're the first person to turn me down on this movie and I don't like it. People aren't supposed to say no to the fabulous Davida Haym." She laughs shortly, then rises.

"You can have it for twenty-four hours. Juni and I have that interview tonight. We'll be passing back this way tomorrow. We'll drop in to collect the disc. I'll ask – just once – if you've changed your mind. If you don't want to do it, fine." She beams at Dervish, nods at me, then heads for the door like a person of noble birth.

Juni gets up, smiling. "She's a drama queen, isn't she?" Juni says when Davida is out of earshot.

"And then some!" Dervish laughs.

"But she's sweet," Juni says. "And a natural with the children. She treats them like a mother. Not a bad bone in her body, despite the horrible films she makes."

Juni starts for the door. Pauses. Looks at Dervish. "I hope you change your mind. I…" She stops, clears her throat, smiles quickly and exits.

Dervish hurries after her, to see the pair out. I remain in the TV room, staring at the disc on the couch, sensing trouble of the very worst kind, though I'm not sure why.

DON'T GO DOWN THE CELLAR

→Dervish is humming when he returns. "Nice people," he says.

"Especially Juni," I note drily.

"Yes." He picks up the disc and looks at it silently.

"What made you change your mind?" I ask.

"I haven't," he says.

"But you're thinking about it, aren't you?"

"Yes. This is probably nothing to worry about, just a film-maker conjuring up the usual smorgasbord of hysterical fakes. But I got the feeling Davida knows too much for her own good. She wants the film to be realistic. Maybe she plans to dabble where she shouldn't, use old rites that might backfire. I'm a hard man to find. I'm worried that she was able to root me out. It makes me wonder what else she might know."

"So you want to check the plot and demon descriptions, make sure there's nothing dodgy going on?" I ask. Dervish nods. "Except I got the impression you only agreed to think it over when Juni smiled at you."

"Don't be ridiculous!" Dervish protests. "She had nothing to do with it."

But by the strength of his reaction, and the way he storms out of the room in a huff, I'm sure she did!

→Having shrugged off my foolish sense of unease, I try convincing Dervish to let me have a look at the disc. I want to know what a David A Haym film looks like at this early stage. But he refuses and locks himself in his study. Back downstairs, I fall asleep on the couch. Wake some time during the night, cold, shivering. Think about hauling myself up to bed, but I'm too lazy. Instead I grab a few pillows and stack them around me for warmth. Starting to drift off to sleep again when I suddenly snap wide awake.

Dervish is in trouble.

Not sure how I know — gut instinct. I slide off the couch, scattering the pillows, and race upstairs. Dervish isn't in his bedroom or study. Nowhere on the second floor. Or the first. I wind up back on the ground floor. A quick scout — no sign of him. That means he either went out... or down to the cellar.

Before descending, I go to the kitchen and make sure Dervish hasn't broken into the cutlery cupboard and stocked up on knives. Then I head down the stairs, automatic lights flickering on as I hit the bottom steps. The cellar's where

Dervish stores his wine. I don't come down here much. Nothing of interest for me.

Listening to the hum of the lights, watching for shadows, trying to pinpoint Dervish's position. After a minute I take the final step and explore the rows of wine racks, fists clenched, anticipating an attack.

I don't find Dervish in the cellar. Search complete, I want to go back upstairs and try the area outside the house. But there's one place still to look. It's the last place I want to try — which makes me suspect that's where Dervish is.

One of the walls houses a secret doorway. I make for that now. It's covered by a giant wine rack, mostly containing normal bottles. But one's a fake. I find it and press hard on the cork with a finger. It sinks in. The rack splits in two and both halves slide away from each other, revealing a dark, narrow corridor.

"Dervish?" I call. My voice echoes back to me, unanswered.

I start down the corridor, breathing raggedly. The halves of the wine rack slide back into place. I'm plunged into darkness. But it's temporary. Moments later, lights flicker on overhead, the glow just strong enough to see by.

The corridor runs to a secret underground cellar. It's where Dervish keeps his most magical and dangerous books, where he goes if he wants to practise magic. It's where we fought Lord Loss all those months ago. Where I almost died.

I come to a thick wooden door with a gold ring for a handle. The door stands ajar and there's a pale light coming from within. "Dervish?" I call again. No answer. I *really* don't want to go in, but I must.

I push the door all the way open and enter, heart pounding.

A large room. Wooden beams support the ceiling. Many torches set in the walls, but none are lit. A steel cage in one corner, the bones of a deer lying on the floor within. Two broken tables. A third in good repair. Chess pieces, books, charred pages and other bits of debris brushed up against the walls. A stack of weapons close to the rubbish, lined with dust, riddled with cobwebs.

And Dervish, squatting in the middle of the room, a candle in one hand, a book in the other.

I approach cautiously. Freeze when I catch sight of the book. There's a painting of Lord Loss on the cover. Just his face. And it's *moving*. His awful red eyes are widening, his lips spreading. Dervish is muttering a spell, bending closer to the book. Lord Loss's teeth glint in the light of the candle. His face starts to come off the page, like a 3D image, reaching for Dervish, as though to kiss him.

I hurl myself at Dervish. Knock him over and punch the book from his hand. The candle goes out. We're plunged into darkness. Dervish screams. I hear him scrabbling for the book. I thrash around, find Dervish, throw myself on top and pin him to the floor, yelling at him, keeping him away from the book, calling his name over and over, using all my weight to keep him down.

Finally he stops fighting, pants heavily, then croaks, "Grubbs?" I don't reply. "You're squashing me," he wheezes.

"Are you awake?" I cry.

"Of course. Now get off before…" A pause. "Where are we?"

"The secret cellar."

"Damn. What was I…?"

"You had a book about Lord Loss. You were chanting a spell. His face was moving. It looked like he was coming alive — coming *through*."

"I'm sorry. I… Let's get some light. I'm awake. Honest. You can get off me. I promise."

Warily I slide aside. Dervish gets to his feet. Stumbles to the nearest wall. I hear him rooting through his pockets. Then he strikes a match, finds the nearest candle and sets it aflame. The room lights up. I see the book, lying facedown. No movement.

"Could you have brought him here?" I ask, not taking my eyes off the book.

"No," Dervish says. "But I could have summoned part of his spirit. Given him just enough strength to… hurt me."

"And me?"

"Absolutely not. You were safe. The spirit couldn't have got out of this room."

"But when I came in?"

Dervish says nothing. A guilty silence. Then a deep sigh. "Let's get out of here. There are things we must discuss."

"And the book?" I ask.

"Leave it. It can't do any harm. Not now."

Standing, I stagger out of the room. Dervish follows, leaving the candle burning, shutting the door on the past, trailing me back up the corridor to the safety of the normal world.

→"The Disciples fight the Demonata and do what we can to keep them out of our universe."

We're in Dervish's study. We both have mugs of hot chocolate. Sitting facing one another across the main desk.

"We're all magically inclined," Dervish continues. "Not true magicians, but we have talents and abilities — call us mages if you like. In an area of magic – the Demonata's universe, or a place where a demon is crossing – our powers are magnified. We can do things you wouldn't believe. No, scratch that — of course you'd believe. You fought Lord Loss."

"How many Disciples are there?" I ask.

"Twenty-five, thirty. Maybe a few more." Dervish shrugs. "We're loose-knit. Our founder is a guy called Beranabus. He *is* a true magician, but we don't see a lot of him. He spends most of his time among the Demonata, waging wars the rest of us couldn't dream of winning.

"Beranabus sometimes gives orders, sets one or more of us a specific task. But mostly we do our own thing. That's why I'm not sure of our exact number. There's a core group who keep in touch, track the movements of demons and work together to deal with the threats. But there are others we only see occasionally. In an emergency I guess Beranabus could assemble us all, but in the usual run of things we don't have contact with every member."

"So that's your real job," I say softly. "Fighting demons."

He smiles crookedly. "Don't misinterpret what I'm telling you. This isn't an organisation of crack magical heroes who battle demons every week. There are a few Disciples who've fought the Demonata several times, but most have never gone up against them, or maybe only once or twice."

"Then what do they do?" I frown.

"Travel," he says. "Tour the world, watch for signs of demonic activity, try to prevent crossings. Demons can't swap between universes at will. They need human assistants. Wicked, power-hungry mages who work with them from this side and help them open windows between their realm and ours. Usually there are signs. If you know what to look for, you can stop it before it happens. That's what we do — watch for evidence of a forming window, find the person working for the demon, stop them before it gets out of hand."

"*You* don't travel around," I note. "Is that because of me?"

"No," Dervish smiles. "I used to travel a lot, but I do most of my work here now, at the command of Beranabus. It's my job to... well, let's not get into that. It's not relevant."

Dervish sips from his mug, looking at me over the rim, awaiting my reaction.

"What happens when a demon crosses?" I ask.

"It depends on the strength of the demon. Most of the truly powerful Demonata can't use windows — they're too big, magically speaking. They need a tunnel to cross – a wider, stronger form of window. They're much more difficult to open. It's been centuries since anyone constructed a tunnel."

"Lord Loss is a demon master," I note. "He crosses."

"He's an exception. We don't know why he can cross when others like him can't. He just can. There are rules where magic's concerned, but those rules can be bent. Anything's possible with magic, even the supposedly and logically *im*possible.

"The other demons who cross are nowhere near as powerful as Lord Loss," Dervish continues, "We drive back the lesser specimens, but we leave the stronger demons alone and try to limit the damage."

"You let them get away with it?" I cry. "You let them kill?"

Dervish lowers the mug. "It's not as heartless as it sounds. There's far less magic in our universe than theirs. When they cross, they're nowhere near as powerful as they are in their own realm. And most can only stay here for a few minutes.

Occasionally a window will remain open longer, for an hour or two, but that's rare. Thankfully. Because if they could cross with all their powers intact, and stay as long as they liked, we'd have been wiped out long ago.

"We stop maybe half of all potential crossings," Dervish goes on. "Which is pretty good when you consider how few of us there are. Although we're only talking six or seven attempts to cross in any given year."

"So three or four get through?" I ask.

"Apporximately. We aren't always there when one crosses. When we are…" He sighs. "If it's a weaker demon, we try to drive it back. A single Disciple will engage it, occasionally a pair. We don't like to risk too many in any single venture."

"And when you don't think you can stop it?" I ask quietly.

Dervish looks away. "A demon will normally kill no more then ten or twenty people when it crosses."

"Still!" I protest. "Ten *people*, Dervish! Ten *lives*!"

"What do you want us to do?" he snaps. "There are battles we can't win. We do what we can — we can't do any more. We're not bloody superheroes!"

"Sure," I say quickly. "Sorry. I didn't mean to sound critical. I just…"

"I know," he mutters. "When I first heard about the Disciples, I was like you. I didn't want to admit the possibility of defeat or make concessions. But when you see enough people die, you realise life's not like the movies or comics. You can't save everyone. It's not an option."

Dervish falls silent. We never talked much about his past. To be honest, with all the problems I've faced over the last couple of years, I haven't had time to think about anybody else's troubles. But now that I consider it, I realise my uncle must have seen a lot of bad stuff in his time. We got lucky against Lord Loss. We beat him at his own game and walked away relatively unharmed. But Dervish told me there are more failures than successes when humans battle demons. And if he's been around for even a few failures... seen people die like I saw my parents and sister die... had to stand by and let it happen because he didn't have the power to stop it...

"I'm telling you this because of Davida Haym," Dervish says, interrupting my thoughts. "I went through her disc earlier. From the outline it sounds like fun – demons run wild and take over a town – but I don't like it. The few demons she described are *very* realistic. She mentions rituals you can use to summon them. She's gathered information cleverly but I don't think she knows how dangerous that information is.

"I'm going to accept her offer to work on set as an advisor. I want to make sure she doesn't accidentally summon a demon or supply others with the means to. The chances of that happening are slim, and in the normal run of things I wouldn't bother with her.

"But I need to get away from here for a while." His eyes are dark, haunted. "I haven't been the same since I came back. The nightmares... fear... confusion. Maybe my brain will never properly recover and I'm doomed to live like this until I die. But I'm hoping I can shrug it off. I've been living the quiet life — too quiet. I need something to focus my attention. A challenge. Something to sweep away the cobwebs inside my head."

"But you're protected by spells here," I note. "You might not be safe outside Carcery Vale. Lord Loss…"

"Remember the book in the cellar?" Dervish says. "Unless I dig myself out of this hole, I don't think I'm safe anywhere."

I nod slowly. "How long will you be gone?"

"However long the shoot lasts," Dervish says. "I'll ask Meera to keep an eye on things while I'm away."

"Meera's going to be staying with me?" I ask, not minding the sound of that one little bit — Meera Flame's hot stuff!

"No," Dervish says. "You won't be here either. Unless you object, I want to take you with me. Billy too."

"You want to take us on set?" I yelp.

"Davida said I could," he reminds me. "Well, she didn't mention Billy, but I'm sure that won't be a problem."

"Brilliant!" I gasp, face lighting up. Then doubt crosses my mind. "But why?"

"Two reasons," Dervish says. "One — I need you to look out for me at night, to help me if the nightmares continue." He stops.

"And the second reason?"

"I don't trust Prae Athim and the Lambs. They might pull a fast one if I'm not around."

"You think they'd kidnap Bill-E?"

"It's possible. Right now I want Billy where I can protect him, twenty-four seven. I'll rest easier that way."

"So we're going into the movie business," I laugh.

"Yep." Dervish laughs too. "Crazy, isn't it?" He checks his watch. "Three-thirty in the morning. Ma and Pa Spleen would hit the roof if we phoned Billy at such an ungodly hour." He cocks a wicked eyebrow at me. "Do you want to ring or shall I?"

PART TWO
LIGHTS... CAMERA... DEMONS!

FILM FOLK

→"I've always wanted to eat human flesh. I mean, it's not an obsession or anything. I wouldn't go out of my way to kill, skin and cook somebody. But I've always been curious, wondered what it would taste like. So, when the opportunity dropped into my lap, yeah, I took it. Does that make me a bad person? I don't think so. At least, not much badder than—"

"Worse than," Bill-E interrupts.

"*Worse!*" Emmet winces. "I keep tripping on that. 'Not much *worse* than, not much *worse* than, not much *worse* than…'"

I feel sorry for Emmet, watching him struggle to learn his lines. It's not easy to keep a load of words that aren't yours straight inside your head, then trot them out in a seemingly natural fashion. I used to think actors had a great life. Not any more. Not after a week on the set of *Slawter*.

Slawter, as Davida told us when she visited Carcery Vale, is the title of the movie and the name of the fictional town which features in it. It's also what they've called the huge set which Davida's crew has constructed. It's an amazing place. They found a deserted town in the middle of nowhere. Rented the entire area and set to work restoring the buildings, clearing the streets of rubble, putting in fake lamps, telephone wires, signs for restaurants, hotels, bars, etc. They also erected a lot of fake buildings which look real from the front but are entirely empty on the other side. Walking down the streets, it's hard to tell the real buildings from the fake ones — until you open a door.

There are trailers on the outskirts of Slawter – the movie veterans refer to them as the circus – where many of the cast and crew sleep, but a lot of us are staying in the old, real buildings. Since we're so far from any other town, Davida decided to turn some of the buildings into makeshift hotels, so everyone could stay in one place, in comfort. The 'hotel' where Dervish, Bill-E and I are staying looks like a butcher's shop out front, but it's cosy inside.

I've been told this isn't the way films are normally made. Usually the crew does a bit of location work, then heads back to the studio to shoot the interior scenes. But Slawter *is* the studio. There are huge warehouses, built beyond one end of town, where the interiors can be shot. And since all the outdoor action in the film is set in the town, everything can be done on site. They even do the editing here, and the special effects. Often, on a big budget film, there might be several teams around the world working on effects at the same time. But Davida wants to keep total control over this project. She refuses to farm out any of the work, even though it makes life much harder for her. This is her baby, the jewel in her movie crown, and she's doing it exactly the way she wants — damn the inconvenience!

She even insists on keeping the cast together for the duration of the shoot. Emmet's worked on a couple of films before and explained how, if you have a small part in the movie, you only turn up for a few days, shoot your scenes, then head off. Even the big stars don't hang around the set the whole time.

Well, here they do. All the actors, cameramen, artists, carpenters, caterers – *everyone* – had to agree to stay here until filming is finished. Davida kept everything secret in the build-up to shooting. Now that we're all on set and the cameras are rolling, most of the secrets have been revealed. Copies of the full script have been circulated and we've seen some of the demon costumes. To make sure none of the secrets leak to the outside world, Davida arranged for everyone to remain in Slawter until the entire film has been shot.

It costs a fortune to keep us here – food and drinks are free, games have to be organised to keep people amused in their spare time, two swimming pools have been built, tennis courts, a football pitch and so on – but Davida doesn't care. Her other movies made a load of money and she's managed to convince her backers that this one is going to be a mega blockbuster, so she's free to spend whatever she likes.

Not having any jobs to do, Bill-E and I have been enjoying the filming. We wander through Slawter, watch scenes being shot, check out the old buildings and fakes, hang out with some of the other kids and generally just have fun. It's great. Reminds me of when I first moved to Carcery Vale, when Bill-E and I spent pretty much all our free time together. We're best buddies again, breezing along in a little world of our own, no Loch Gossel or other friends of mine to complicate the situation.

You can divide the children of Slawter into three groups. There are the actors, twenty or so. Most haven't much experience, or have only been in a few films, like Emmet Eijit, who's our best friend here.

Then there are the actors' relatives. It's a big deal being a child actor. There are all sorts of rules and regulations. They can only work so many hours a day. They have to be schooled on set. At least one of their guardians – normally a parent – has to be with them all the time. And there have to be other children for them to play with. Juni's in charge of that side of things. She makes sure the kids are being looked after, having fun, not feeling the stress of being part of such a costly, risky venture.

Finally there's the likes of Bill-E and me, children of people working on the film. Because everyone involved had to move to Slawter for the duration of the shoot – at least three months – they were allowed to bring their families. Davida likes the relaxed family atmosphere.

We don't have much personal contact with Davida Haym. Or with Dervish. He's been working closely with Davida since we arrived, advising, censoring, subtly guiding her away from the workings of real demons wherever possible. He's one of the few people to have seen inside the D workshops. That's where the demon costumes are being created. The demons are to be a mix of actors in costumes and mechanised puppets. There will be some CGI effects, but Davida's trying to keep the computer trickery to a minimum.

The costumes and puppets are housed in a giant warehouse, the biggest in Slawter, and access is granted only to a chosen few. Some of the costumes have been given a public airing, but most are still locked up within the D. Dervish said it's a maze of corridors and sub-sections in there. He's only been allowed into a couple of rooms so far, but he's trying hard to gain access to the rest, to check out all the demonic details.

"I've always wanted to eat human flesh," Emmet says again, running through his big lines for the fiftieth time today. He plays a minor villain in the film, a kid who becomes a cannibal and works for the demons. He dies about a third of the way through, having been discovered by one of the heroes while eating the corpse of their headmaster.

Davida is shooting the film in sequence as much as possible, although as on any movie, certain scenes from later in the script have to be shot early. Which means Emmet is getting to 'die' a couple of weeks earlier than he should have. He's super excited about it.

"This is my first death scene!" he raved yesterday. "Most kids don't get to die on screen — how many films have you seen where a child bites the big one? And it's the first visible killing of the movie!"

Later, excitement gave way to nerves. He's been fussing ever since, worried he'll blow his lines or not be able to scream convincingly when the demon turns on him and rips him to pieces.

"At least, not much badder than– Hellfire! I did it again, didn't I?"

"Afraid so," I laugh.

"Take it cool," Bill-E advises, mimicking Davida's on-set mannerisms. He's been even more impressed by the whole movie-shooting experience than me. He now wants to be a director when he grows up.

"*Cool!*" Emmet snorts. "That's easy for you to say. You're not the one up there on display."

"You know the lines," Bill-E murmurs, then laughs like Davida when she's trying to calm a nervous actor. "You probably know your lines better than anyone on the set, even Davida. You're a professional. They'll come when you're filming. And if not, who cares? Nobody gets it right the first time. And even if they do, Davida reshoots it anyway. You'll nail it the fifth or sixth time."

Bill-E's not exaggerating about the reshoots. Every scene is played out at least six or seven times, from various angles, the actors trying out different expressions and tones. Repetition is part and parcel of the film-maker's life. I don't know how they stand it. I'd go cuckoo if I had to do the same thing over and over, day after day.

"He's quite the expert, isn't he?" Emmet remarks cuttingly.

"Hey, man, I'm just trying to help," Bill-E says, unruffled.

"For someone with no real experience, you certainly know a lot about it."

Bill-E laughs Emmet's criticism away. "I'm just calling it like I see it. If you'd rather I removed myself, no problem. Come on, Grubbs, let's go and—"

"No!" Emmet pleads. "I'm sorry. I'm just all wound up. One last time, please. If I don't get it right, we'll quit and all go play foosball. OK?"

"OK," Bill-E says. "But don't forget — *coooooollllllllll*."

Emmet shoots him an exasperated glance, then shares a grin with me. Focusing, he repeats his lines silently to himself, then tries them out loud and all too predictably blows them again. As soon as he breaks down, we drag him off to the foosball table and keep him there, though we can't stop him muttering the lines as he plays.

* * *

→Dinner with Dervish, Juni and some others, in the ginormous catering tent at the heart of Slawter. Everybody talking at once, a nice buzz in the air. A mime artist signals to me that he'd like the salt and pepper. His name is Chai and he's a bit of a nutcase. He never speaks, although he's not mute. Apparently he's perfectly chatty when he's not working. But throughout the duration of a shoot, he keeps his lips sealed. It doesn't matter that he has a tiny part in the movie and will only be filming for a few days. Chai considers himself a *method actor*.

"How are you two faring?" Juni asks Bill-E and me. "Enjoying yourselves?"

"Totally!" Bill-E gushes. "It's great. Incredibly invigorating and inspiring. I think I've found my calling in life."

"Not getting into any trouble, are you?" Dervish grunts.

"As if!" Bill-E smirks.

"I was discussing your situation with Dervish earlier," Juni says hesitantly.

Uh-oh! It's never good when an adult says something like that.

"I'm worried that you'll fall behind in your schoolwork," Juni goes on. "Things have been a rush lately — Dervish accepting our offer, bringing you two with him, a crazy first week of shooting. Schooling arrangements have been made for the other children, but we overlooked you and Bill-E. I think it would be a mistake to let things continue as they are and Dervish agrees, so…"

"No!" Bill-E cries dramatically. "You're going to stick us in a class? Say it ain't so, Derv!"

"It's so," Dervish laughs. "Juni's right. We're going to be here three months, maybe longer. If you go that length of time without lessons, it'll mean repeating a year when we get back to Carcery Vale."

"You won't have to do full days," Juni promises. "We keep classes flexible, to fit in around shooting, so it'll be a few hours here, a few hours there, just keeping you in line with what your friends are doing back home. That doesn't sound so awful, does it?"

"Too bad if it does," Dervish interjects before we can reply, "because you don't have a choice."

"Slave-driver," Bill-E mutters, but he's only pretending to be grumpy. We both knew this was coming. The freedom couldn't last forever.

Juni and Dervish start talking to each other again. Juni's been with my uncle most times that I've seen him recently, which is strange since they can't have a lot of business together. Dervish is part of the inner technical circle, whereas Juni's job revolves around the children. There must be another reason why he's sticking to her like superglue and I think I know what it is — good old-fashioned physical attraction!

It seems incredible. If asked a week ago, I'd have laughed and said the bald old grump didn't have a romantic bone in his body. But something's stirring in the hidden depths of Dervish Grady. There's a gleam in his smile which was never there before. He's switched to a pungent new aftershave. His clothes are freshly ironed. He's even started combing the wisps of hair dotted around the sides of his head into place. There's no doubt about it — he's trying to impress the cute albino!

→Juni knows that Bill-E and I are friends with Emmet, so she places us in his class. Most of the other students are actors. There's the Kane twins, Kuk and Kik, a boy and girl, small and slender, very alike in looks. They don't speak much to anyone, going off by themselves whenever there's a free period. They have big roles in the film as eerie, psychic twins.

Salit Smit is the main child star of *Slawter*. He's a bit older than the rest of us. A nice guy but not the brightest spark. He just smiles and nods a lot in class, not bothering to apply himself, convinced he's going to be the biggest movie draw since Tom Cruise.

I absolutely despise the other three. A clique of snobs presided over by the dreadful Bo Kooniart, a girl who was born solely to annoy. She's been in a few commercials and thinks she's God's gift. Always dresses stylishly, like a model. Sucks up to Davida and anyone else with power and influence. Ignores the rest of us, treating us like simpletons or servants.

Her brother, Abe, is almost as bad. A scrawny, miserable excuse for a child. He's not an actor but his father – the loud, obnoxious Tump Kooniart, a movie agent – insisted he be cast if they wanted to hire Bo. From the rumours,

Davida resisted, but finally caved in and gave him a small part as a kid who raises the alarm when the demons are about to break through *en masse*. I don't think Davida gives way too often so Tump must be good at his job. Which is just as well, because from what I've seen of Bo and Abe, they're awful at theirs!

The third mini-tyrant is Vanalee Metcalf. Her parents are multimillionaires. Too busy to waste time with their daughter on set, so she came equipped with her own bodyguard-cum-servant, who glares at anyone who doesn't grovel at her feet.

Bo, Abe and Vanalee took one look at Bill-E and me when we were introduced to them this morning, smirked at each other in a snide, superior way and turned their noses up to let us know we weren't worthy of direct notice.

Our tutor's a sweet but nervous woman called Supatra Jaun. I can tell within ten minutes that she can't handle Bo and her posse. She lets them talk to each other while she's teaching and doesn't ever try to assert her authority. Sometimes she'll murmur, "Now, now, Bo, please pay attention," but without any real hope that the blonde, pony-tailed, stick-thin brat will obey.

Miss Jaun seems genuinely pleased that Bill-E and I have been added to her class, probably because we're polite and show some interest. She chats to us warmly, finds out what we've been studying, takes a few notes, promises to haul us up to scratch in next to no time.

"I bet those scruffbags know a lot about scratching," Bo sniffs.

"Meaning?" I growl at her.

"*Lice*, you moron!" she screeches, and Abe and Vanalee burst out laughing.

"We've found our nemesis," Bill-E mutters in my ear, pegging it dead-on. "Hate her, Grubbs. Hate her good and proper."

"Does her character die in the script?" I ask Emmet.

"No," he says. "She ends up saving the town, along with Salit."

"A pity," I sigh.

"But she does fall into a pit full of demon manure at one stage," Emmet says, and my day lights right up.

→Our first session lasts two hours, a mix of history, biology and maths. Miss Jaun seems to be confident in all subjects — a smart cookie. Then an assistant director pops in and says they need Bo and Salit. Miss Jaun checks her watch, says we might as well all take a break and asks those of us not involved in filming to return in an hour. It's certainly a lot more laid back than our school in Carcery Vale.

Emmet wants to practise his lines on Bill-E and me again, but we don't have the patience, so we leave him with his mum in his trailer. We grab sandwiches from one of the many mobile canteens, then go see if anything exciting is happening. There's not much to keep us amused today.

Davida and her crew are setting up a tracking shot on a street, trying to get lots of actors in place and working in sync with each other. Fairly boring to watch. A lot of filming is.

"I still can't believe we're here," Bill-E says as we go for a wander. "Maybe this will become Dervish's full-time job and we'll travel around the world on film shoots with him."

"I doubt it," I laugh. "Your gran and grandad wouldn't allow it. I'm surprised they agreed to let Dervish have you for this long. Did he work some magic spells on them?"

"Nope," Bill-E says. "They were happy to let me come. Gran loves movies, especially old flicks starring the likes of David Niven and Ingrid Bergman. She thought this was a great opportunity for me. I think she's hoping I'll fall in love with a beautiful blind cellist or some such guff. She believes a lot of those old films were based on true stories, that the world's really like that."

"Mind you, a girl would have to be blind to fall in love with you," I comment.

"Your face," Bill-E snorts. "My flabby nether regions. Spot the similarity?"

I get Bill-E in a headlock and rub my knuckles into his skull, but it's all in fun. He has no idea of the real reason why he's here. He thinks Dervish is his father, that he didn't want to spend a few months parted from his darling son. He doesn't know about Dervish wanting to make sure Davida doesn't raise hell, or about Prae Athim's interest in experimenting on him.

"I can't wait to see the demon tomorrow — or it might even be tonight," Bill-E enthuses once I've released him. "Emmet says it depends on how shooting goes today. If they finish that shot on the street in time, they'll do his scene later. It'll be coolio!"

"Hmmm," I say neutrally.

"What are you moaning about, Goliath?" Bill-E frowns. Then, studying me carefully, his expression clears. "Oh. I'd forgotten. Your parents and sister…" He trails off into silence. Although Bill-E doesn't know about his lycanthropic genes, or the battle Dervish and I fought with Lord Loss, he knows demons killed my family.

"Are you going to be OK with all this?" Bill-E asks awkwardly. Sympathy isn't something that he does well.

"Sure," I grunt.

"Really?" he presses. "Because they can't keep us here. I know Dervish signed those contracts saying we'd stay until the end, but *we* didn't. If you want to leave, I'm sure there's nothing they can do about it. I've watched lots of courtroom movies. I know what I'm talking about."

"No," I smile. "I'll be OK. I mean, we're talking movie demons here — rubber, wire and paint. How scary can they be?"

* * *

→Emmet's nervous all afternoon, practising his lines even in class. Davida popped in to see him during lunch and told him they'd definitely be shooting his death scene tonight. The way he's behaving – pale, shivering, mumbling to himself – I think it might take quite a few attempts to get it right!

Near the end of class, Emmet's summoned to the make-up trailer. He won't be required on set for a few hours yet, but they want to run some tests. It's going to be a gory scene – Davida wants blood spurting every which way – so they need to make sure everything's set up smoothly before they stick him in front of the cameras.

Salit and Bo return as Emmet's leaving. "I can't believe they're letting you go through with this farce," Bo says, blocking the doorway. "You'll choke, Eijit. You know it, I know it, everybody knows it. So why don't you just–"

"Leave him alone!" Bill-E shouts. "Meddling cow!"

"Now, Bill-E, that's not–" Miss Jaun begins.

"Shut up, pipsqueak!" Bo defends herself, spitting venom at Bill-E. "If I want advice from a fat geek with a dodgy eye, I'll let you know. Otherwise…"

I stand up, flexing my muscles, stretching aggressively. "You're going to apologise," I tell Bo flatly.

"Says who?" she retorts, but I've unnerved her. It's not often that I threaten anyone, but when I do, I can make quite an impression.

I step out from behind my desk and crack my knuckles,

staring at Bo levelly. "*Now*," I say firmly.

Bo glares at me, then sneers and says mockingly, "I'm so sorry, Billy One-eye. I won't point the truth out to you again." Her gaze flicks back at Emmet. "But you're still going to mess up. Let me know when you do. It's not too late for Abe to step in and do the job properly."

"Ignore her," Bill-E says, his left eyelid fluttering furiously. "You'll be great. Davida wouldn't have picked you if she didn't believe you could do it."

"Thanks," Emmet says hollowly, then pushes past Bo, visibly upset. Bo smirks and takes her seat.

"That wasn't very nice," Miss Jaun says disapprovingly.

Bo looks up at our teacher as though just noticing she's there. "Excuse me?"

"You shouldn't–" Miss Jaun begins.

"What was that?" Bo asks loudly, cutting Miss Jaun off. She tilts her head and pushes her lower lip out with her tongue, daring Miss Jaun to challenge her. For a moment it looks as though she will and I ready myself to cheer the timid teacher on. But then her shoulders sag and she looks away.

"Let's get on with our lessons," she says meekly. "I'll finish up with the others, then take you and Salit for a couple of hours. Now, where were we…?"

→"Someone should sort her out," Bill-E storms when class has finished. "Bo bloody Kooniart! Davida should put that little monster over her knee and spank her till her hand turns blue!"

"I agree," I say grimly, "but it's not going to happen. She's a star. She can get away with crap like that. To be honest, I thought they'd all be like her. I'm surprised how normal most of the others are."

"A pity the demons aren't real," Bill-E grumbles. "We could feed Bo to them, and her horrible little brother. Vanalee too."

"It would certainly make life easier," I agree. "But they're not real. There's nothing we can do except ignore her. Come on." I slap his back. "Let's go see what Emmet looks like in his make-up."

→Emmet's covered in fake blood. He's spitting it out and wiping it from his eyes. "The bag exploded early," he moans.

"You squeezed too hard," a props person says, sliding a hand up inside Emmet's jumper, removing an empty plastic bag which had been filled with the red, sticky liquid. "You have to be more gentle. Don't worry — you'll get the hang of it soon."

Emmet goes off to be cleaned, before trying on a fresh costume and having his make-up applied again. Rather him than me. Sometimes an actor can spend most of the day sitting in a chair, having make-up dabbed on, cleaned off, dabbed on, cleaned off, dabbed...

Bill-E and I go for a swim, then head for dinner. We spot Dervish dining with Davida and Juni, but they're talking shop so we don't disturb them. After that we check on Emmet again. This time he's managed not to burst the bag of blood and is ready to face the cameras.

"She's been trying to unsettle me all week," he says about Bo. "She thinks Abe should have had this part. Her dad does too. He told my mum I was an amateur and shouldn't be here."

"Charming!" Bill-E huffs.

"Mum hit the roof," Emmet chuckles. "Told Tump Kooniart what she thought of him and to keep out of our way for the rest of the shoot. She complained to Davida, but he's an agent for several of the actors so there's not much Davida can do. In an argument, if it's us or him, she has to take his side. I could be replaced easily, but if Tump walked off and told his gang to follow…"

"Never mind," Bill-E says encouragingly. "There's nothing they can do about it now. This is your scene. Go out there, strut your funky stuff, and leave Tump Kooniart and his brats to stew."

Emmet laughs, then asks if he can run through his lines with us. This time we let him, and say nothing as he makes his customary mistake and grinds to a miserable halt. Then, before he can practise again, his call comes and we have to leave.

Showtime!

*   *   *

→This is the first big action shot of the movie, so a large crowd of curious bystanders has gathered. Thanks to modern technology, scenes with monsters aren't normally interesting to watch being filmed. More often than not, an actor will play out their part against a blue-screen background. The monster effects are added later, using computers.

But Davida wants the demons to look as lifelike as possible, for the action to play realistically. That means taking a less flashy approach than in her other movies, keeping it gritty and believable, using almost no computer effects.

Bill-E and I find a good place to watch, next to Dervish and Juni. The scene's being filmed on one of the smaller, darker alleys of Slawter. There's a manhole on the left side of the street, from which the cover has been removed. The demon will spring out of the manhole, grab Emmet and drag him underground.

"This is going to be fun," Dervish says warmly. "Hardly anyone here has seen the demon costume. I think people will be really scared."

"Nonsense," Bill-E says. "How can you be scared of a guy in a monster suit?"

"Trust me," Dervish grins. "This doesn't look like a guy in a suit. There are engines and wires within the costume, so it can pull expressions, ooze slime like you wouldn't believe, even…" He lowers his voice. "It smells."

"Come again?" Bill-E blinks.

"Emmet doesn't know this, so don't say anything, but Davida wants to wring as much genuine terror out of him as she can. So she created a demon-type stench, to throw him off guard. She has a few other tricks up her sleeve too. I feel sorry for the kid — he doesn't know what's going to hit him!"

"I don't think that's fair," I mutter. "He's nervous enough as it is."

"Don't worry," Juni smiles. "We talked it over with his mother. She gave us the all-clear. He'll enjoy the joke when he recovers. It will make the scene more believable, which will make his acting seem all the more professional. That will stand him in good stead when he's looking for his next big role."

I'm a bit worried about Emmet despite Juni's reassurances. I'd hate if he got so freaked out that he couldn't finish filming the scene and had to hand the part over to Abe. I can see the moody Master Kooniart standing across from us, with Bo and their fat, leering father, Tump. I wonder if the stench idea was theirs to begin with.

I'd like to warn Emmet, but Davida is talking with him and Salit, explaining the dynamics of the scene. This is where Salit finds Emmet eating their headmaster and realises he's working for a demon. Emmet starts to give a long speech about how the demons are going to take over the town and why he's working for them. In the middle of it, his demonic ally pops out of the manhole and makes off with him.

"It's important you don't look like you know what's going to happen," Davida tells Emmet. "As far as you know, this demon is your best buddy and Salit's the one in trouble. You'll hear some rumblings, feel a few tremors. Ignore them and concentrate on your lines."

"About that," Emmet cuts in. "I've been having a few problems."

"Oh?" Davida smiles and waits for him to continue.

"It's the line, 'At least not much worse than a guy who gives in to temptation and steals a bar of chocolate.' I *know* the line, but I keep coming out with 'badder' instead of 'worse'. If it happens, can we do it again straightaway? I'll try to get it right, but I might…"

Davida holds up a hand. "Emmet, as far as I'm concerned, there's not one line in the script that isn't open to negotiation. I should have made that clear earlier. It's *your* voice I want to hear, not mine. If 'badder' is what comes naturally to you, then 'badder' it is."

"I can change the line?" Emmet gawps.

"Absolutely."

A big smile works its way across Emmet's face. Across from us, Abe and the other Kooniarts are glowering. They couldn't hear the conversation, but they can see the fear fade from Emmet. They've lost their chance to bump Abe up the pecking order. I want to thumb my nose at them and stick out my tongue. But that would be childish, so I settle for a smug wink when I catch Bo's furious eye.

They shoot the early exchanges several times, from a variety of angles. A fake corpse is placed in the alley, close to the manhole cover. Emmet starts the scene crouched over it, pulling bits off and stuffing them in his mouth. He's so convincing it's hilarious, and Salit keeps laughing when he comes upon him.

"'Matt!'" he cries, calling Emmet by his screen name. "'What are you doing with Mr Litherland's nose in your...' Sorry!" he shouts, doubling over. "I can't help it! He looks so crazy!"

"Don't worry," Davida says, smiling patiently. "We have all night. Keep trying. The joke will wear thin eventually." She grimaces at a cameraman. "I hope!"

→Salit finally gets through his lines without laughing and they move on to the next scene. The cameras and lights are redirected, the make-up artists make sure Salit and Emmet are looking the way they should, Davida has a last few words with Emmet, then they're ready to go.

"OK, people," an assistant director yells. "We're going to try and get this right first time, so we want *absolute* quiet!"

When everyone settles down, the technicians do their final checks, Davida looks around slowly from one member of the crew to another, then nods. A man calls out the title, scene and take, and snaps the traditional clapperboard shut.

"And... action!" Davida roars.

"'How could you do it?'" Salit cries, in his role as Bobby Mint, boy-hero.

"'What?'" Emmet protests. "'It's not as if anyone liked Mr Litherland.'"

"'But he's human!'" Salit cries.

"'He *was*,'" Emmet corrects him. "'He's yummy for my tummy now!'" Emmet rubs his stomach with a sick laugh. "'I've always wanted to eat human flesh. I mean, it's not an obsession or anything. I wouldn't go out of my way to kill, skin and cook somebody. But I've always been curious, wondered what it would taste like. So, when the opportunity dropped into my lap, yeah, I took it. Does that make me a bad person? I don't think so. At least, not much badder than a guy who gives in to temptation and steals a bar of chocolate. It's not like I killed him myself.'"

"'But you let it happen!'" Salit cries. "'You knew about the demon!'"

Emmet shrugs. "'What's done is done. No point crying over spilt milk — or a butchered headmaster.'" He holds out a severed, bloodied arm to Salit. "'You should try some, Bobby. You might like it. It...'"The ground begins to rumble. A foul stench fills the air. For a second, Emmet falters and his gaze flicks to the open manhole. Then he recovers and continues like a true professional. "'It goes down super sweet, especially if you add a dollop of ketchup. Tastes a bit like–'"

That's when the demon bursts out of the manhole and grabs him.

It happens in a blur and is so fast, so violent, so shocking, that several people in the crowd gasp aloud.

The demon is green, slimy, with fierce yellow eyes, four long arms with claws at the ends, a mouth full of fangs. There's something wolfish about its face, long and lean, with patches of hair here and there.

The demon whips Emmet off the ground. He screams, not having to fake it, caught off-guard. Salit falls backwards, yelling with genuine horror.

My world goes red with fear. I'm thrown back in time… that night in the cellar… earlier… my old home… walking into my parents' bedroom to find Lord Loss, Vein and Artery at work. Feeling the exact same thing in my gut now as I did then.

The demon screeches and vanishes back underground, carrying Emmet with it. There's a moment of hush. Then Emmet's face appears, sheer terror in his expression. "Help!" he cries. "For the love of–"

Blood erupts around him, shooting up through the hole like a geyser. The howl of the demon drowns out his final words. His eyes go wide, then dead. As his head slumps, the demon pulls and Emmet disappears again, this time forever.

It all happened so swiftly, I'm in a state of shock. So's everybody else. Stunned silence. People with hands over their mouths and disbelief in their eyes. I sense screams building in a dozen throats, ready to erupt at once, a chorus of terror.

"Now that's what I call a death scene!" Davida Haym roars triumphantly, shattering the spell of fear. "Cut! Did you get that? You'd better have! We'll never top that take!"

And suddenly everybody's laughing, relief flooding through them. They thought for a few seconds that the demon was real, that Emmet was really being attacked. Now the moment has passed and they've remembered — this is make-believe, horrific fun, a movie. They're embarrassed at having been caught out, but since so many of the others reacted the same way, they're not left feeling *too* red-faced.

"I told you!" Dervish laughs, clapping loudly. "Wasn't that the most vicious, coolest thing you've ever seen?"

"My heart!" Juni gasps, fanning her face with one hand. "I didn't expect it all to happen so fast!"

"That was amazing!" Bill-E exclaims. "Did you see it, Grubbs? That spray of blood — like it was coming from a fireman's hose! It was... Grubbs? Are you OK? Hey, Dervish, I think there's something wrong with Grubbs. He looks like..."

I block out Bill-E's words and the other sounds. I experienced the same sense of terror that many of the people around me felt. The same jolt of fear. The same moment of belief that this was real. But whereas they've got over that moment, I can't.

Because I'm remembering the look of the demon. Its movements. The hate in its eyes. The effect it had on me.

And I'm staring at the open manhole, all the blood around it, no sign of Emmet or the monster.

And I'm thinking... every part of me is insisting...

That was no damn guy in a suit.

That demon was *real*!

THE LAUGHING STOCK

→"It was just a movie monster," Dervish says.

"No. It was real. It killed Emmet."

We're still in the alley. The blood's being washed away and people are chattering about the big scene with the demon. I grabbed Dervish as soon as I could move. Told him what I thought. He thinks differently.

"Grubbs, come on, I said it was going to be realistic. You're–"

"I know what I saw!" I retort, voice rising. "That was a demon, like Lord Loss! It killed Emmet!"

Juni looks at me oddly. Bill-E is gawping openly. Dervish smiles crookedly at them, takes hold of my elbow and marches me out of earshot. "Are you insane?" he hisses as we turn a corner. "We're on a film set. That was a guy in a costume. A very convincing costume, but just–"

"Don't tell me you thought that wasn't real," I moan. "Didn't you feel it in your gut, the same thing you felt when we faced Lord Loss? The magic in the air?"

Dervish glares at me. Starts to say something. Stops, his

expression softening. "I've been a fool. I thought you'd got over the Lord Loss incident, but I guess you haven't."

"Of course I haven't 'got over' it!" I snort. "You don't 'get over' demons murdering your parents and sister! But I've dealt with it. Moved on. This isn't delayed shock. I know what I saw and that was a real bloody demon."

"You're hysterical," Dervish says.

"No," I snarl. "Look at me. Look into my eyes. I'm not being a big kid. That. Was. A. Demon. Nobody can mimic the look and movements – the aura – of a real demon. I don't care how many special-effects artists work on it. Some things can't be replicated, by anybody, ever."

"Grubbs…" Dervish can't think of anything else to add.

"Where's Emmet?" I challenge him. "If he was acting, why didn't he come out when Davida yelled 'cut'?"

"They took him away to wash the blood off," Dervish says.

I shake my head. "I bet you're wrong. I bet we can't find him."

Dervish sighs impatiently. "OK. Let's go look for Emmet. But!" He raises a finger. "When we find him and you see that he's unharmed, I want you to accept it. I don't want you saying it's not really Emmet, it's a changeling, or any nonsense like that. OK?"

"Fine," I smile bitterly.

Grumbling sourly, Dervish leads me away in search of Emmet Eijit, even though I know in my heart that the only place we'll find him now is amidst the bones and scattered shreds of skin in some dirty demon's den.

→Emmet's not in any of the trailers. Nobody's seen him. I shoot Dervish a meaningful look, but he waves it away and goes looking for Davida. She's still in the alley, talking with a technician. We wait for her to finish, then Dervish nudges forward and asks if she knows where Emmet is. Says we want to congratulate him on his performance.

"Of course!" Davida cries. "Hell, I want to too. I plain forgot about him. That was amazing. I loved the final touch — the scream for help. It worked perfectly. No need for a second take. He'll be getting the blood cleaned off, so—"

"No," I interrupt. "We checked. He isn't in make-up."

"Oh. Then I guess… Hey, Chuda! Where'd Emmet get to?"

A tall, thin man without eyebrows steps forward. Chuda Sool, the first assistant director and Davida's closest confidant. They've worked together on her last four films. He's a quiet sort, keeps to the background, makes sure everything's running smoothly, tries to head off problems before they bother Davida.

"There's been a flare-up," Chuda says softly. "Perhaps we should speak about it in private."

"What are you talking about?" Davida growls. "What happened?"

"Nora — Emmet's mother — ran into Tump Kooniart after shooting," Chuda says. "They had a huge argument. Tump said some very nasty things. He upset her. Nora grabbed Emmet, demanded a car, collected their belongings and…" Chuda shrugs.

"They left?" Davida barks. "Are you mad? Nobody leaves until shooting finishes. It's in their contract. Get them back!"

"I can't," Chuda says. "When Nora calms down, maybe we can convince her to return, but—"

"She has no choice!" Davida insists. "She signed the contract. They have to stay on set for the duration."

"You're absolutely correct," Chuda says patiently. "But she went anyway. You can withhold Emmet's payment and maybe force them back that way, but for the time being…" He shrugs.

"Told you," I mutter, glancing up at Dervish. Then I turn and walk off, not wanting to waste my time on more ridiculous excuses. Emmet's dead, slaughtered by a demon. And if his mum's missing, that means she was probably killed too. Time for Grubbs Grady to make an ultra-quick exit from Slawter!

→"You can't just walk off," Dervish argues as I pack my bag.

"Watch me." I turn to Bill-E, who's standing by his bed, blinking like a startled owl. "You're coming too. I'm not leaving you to end up like Emmet."

"It looks bad, especially as there's no sign of Emmet," Dervish says. "But we need to make sure. Chuda could have been telling the truth. Emmet's mother—"

"Bull!" I snort. "There was no argument with Tump Kooniart. Chuda made that story up. Emmet was killed by a demon. His mum's dead too, I guess. Chuda must be working for the demon, since he lied to cover up the truth. And I doubt if he's the only one."

"Wait a minute," Bill-E splutters. "You believe that was a real demon? You think Emmet was really killed? Are you mad?"

"Maybe," I laugh shortly. "But if I am, I'm going to be mad far, far away from Slawter. And you're coming with me. I won't leave you behind." I look hard at Dervish. "I *won't*."

"OK," Dervish sighs. "I won't keep you here against your will. But you're overreacting. Until we know for sure, we should—"

There's a knock at the door. Juni Swan. "Can I come in?"

I go stiff. Is Juni working with Chuda Sool and the demon? Has she been sent to convince me that my imagination has run wild? I like Juni. I'd hate to think that she's evil. But if she backs up Chuda's story...

"I wanted to check that everything's all right," Juni says, eyeing the bag which I'm in the middle of packing.

"Did Chuda send you?" I ask tightly.

"No. I came because I heard you telling Dervish that Emmet had been killed by a real demon. I wanted to know what you meant."

"I'd have thought that was obvious."

"You can't truly believe that was a real demon," Juni says. "Demons don't exist, do they, Dervish?"

Dervish clears his throat. "Well, I wouldn't say that exactly."

"But... we're making a film about demons. That was just an act. Emmet—"

"—has mysteriously disappeared," I cut in.

Juni frowns. "Excuse me?"

"Nora had a fight with Tump Kooniart," Dervish explains. "The way we heard it, she lost her temper, grabbed Emmet, demanded a car and took off."

"But she can't have," Juni says. "Their contract..."

"They tore it up," Dervish says softly. "Allegedly."

Juni's frown deepens. Then she looks at me, expression clearing. "That explains the bag. You think this confirms what you suspected. You're getting out before the demons kill you too."

"Damn straight."

Juni nods slowly. "And if I try to convince you that Emmet hasn't been killed... that demons aren't real... would you think I was part of a conspiracy?"

I hesitate, not wanting to offend her if she's innocent.

"I don't know anything about a fight between Nora and Tump, or why Nora would have been allowed to leave," Juni says steadily. "And it's strange that it happened so quickly, without them saying goodbye to anyone. You might be right. The demon could have been real. Maybe it did kill Emmet."

Juni reaches inside the light jacket that she's wearing and pulls a pink mobile phone out of a pocket. She holds it towards me. As I take it, suspicious, she says, "I have contact numbers for everyone connected to the children working on this film. Nora's number is in there. I'd like you to call her."

I glance up sharply. "No tricks," Juni says. "I don't know what will happen when you dial that number. I'm making no promises. I think Nora will answer, or if she doesn't, you can leave a message and she'll phone back shortly. But short of us getting a car and tearing after them in hot pursuit, I think this is the only way to determine the truth."

I stare at the buttons. I don't want to do this. I want to pass the phone back to Juni, finish packing and get the hell out.

But I can't. Because maybe — just maybe — I called this wrong. Maybe the fear dates back to my fight with Lord Loss and my mind's playing tricks on me. I'm pretty sure it isn't. But if I refuse to dial, I'll look like a crackpot.

I unlock the phone. Thumb up the list of names. "Is it under E or N?" I ask.

"N for Nora," Juni says.

I search for the Ns. There's a lot of them. I scroll down. There it is — Nora Eijit. I hit the dial button. It rings. Once. Twice. Three times. Four. Fi-

"I don't want to talk about it!" a woman's voice snaps. "Kooniart can fry in the fires of hell! You tell him—"

"Mrs Eijit?" I interrupt.

A pause. "Who's this?"

"Grubbs Grady. Emmet's friend."

"Oh. I'm sorry. I saw Juni's name come up, so I assumed…"

"I'm ringing from her phone."

"I see. Do you want to speak to Emmet?"

"Yes please." Speaking mechanically, figuring this could be any woman — I don't know Mrs Eijit's voice well enough to make a definite identification. Waiting for the kicker, for her to say he's asleep, or he doesn't want to talk to me, or –

"I'll pass you over."

The sound of her phone being handed across. The noise of a car engine in the background. Then — Emmet. "Hi, Grubbs," he says quietly, miserably.

"Hi," I reply weakly.

"I can't talk now. I'm sorry I split without saying goodbye. I'm hoping we can come back later, when–"

"No way!" Emmet's mum shrieks. "Not unless that fat fool Kooniart gets down on his knees and–"

"I'll have to call you back," Emmet says quickly and disconnects.

I look at the little red button on Juni's phone. Slowly, reluctantly, I press it. Hand the phone back to Juni. Raise my eyes. And smile like a fool, silently admitting to Juni and the others that I was wrong — even though, inside, part of me still insists the demon was real.

→"I can't believe you thought Emmet had been killed," Bill-E chuckles. It's the morning after. We're on our way to class.

"I don't want to talk about it," I mutter.

"I just don't see how you could—"

"Enough!" I snap. Then, softly, "Remember what I told you about my parents? How they died?"

"Oh. Yeah." Bill-E's face drops. "Grubbs, I didn't mean—"

"It's OK. Just don't say anything about it. Please? To the others?"

"Of course not," Bill-E smiles. "This stays between us. I'll never breathe a word of it to anyone, especially not Bo Kooniart and her mob. They'd have to torture it out of me."

"Thanks. Because if they knew..."

"Like I said, your secret's safe with me," Bill-E promises. "Dervish won't say anything either, or Juni. Nobody will ever find out. It'll be coolio."

→"Look out!" Bo screams as we walk into class. "It's a demon!"

Bo, Abe, Vanalee, Salit – even Kuk and Kik – howl theatrically, then burst out laughing. Miss Jaun blinks at them, astonished. I groan and raise my eyebrows at Bill-E, who can only shrug, bewildered.

"My dad was in the corridor outside your room," Bo says smugly. "He heard you talking. He heard *everything*." She laughs again and I know I'm in for a *long* few months.

MISSING

→The joke doesn't wear thin for Bo. Every day she drags it out, mocking and ridiculing me, keeping the story of my hysterics alive. She tells anyone who'll listen, the other actors, the crew, Davida. Most smile and dismiss it, too busy to bother about such trivial matters. But knowing they know causes me to blush fiercely every time somebody even glances at me.

Emmet never rang back and I'm too shamefaced to call him. I doubt if he'll have heard about my panic attack, but there's no telling how far Bo might have decided to spread the joke.

The person I'm angriest with — apart from myself, for being such an idiot — is Tump Kooniart. I can't blame Bo for wringing such wicked pleasure out of my embarrassment — it would be hard for any kid to ignore such a juicy bit of bait if it fell into their lap. But why was her father sneaking around outside our room? And why didn't he keep his big mouth shut? If Dervish had heard something like this about Bo, he wouldn't have told me.

Tump Kooniart should have kept quiet. He didn't. So now it's payback time!

→I spend a lot of hours thinking about ways to get even with Bo's father. Itching powder in his clothes? Rat droppings in his soup? Human droppings in his stew or chocolate ice cream?!? Shave him bald or glue his lips together while he sleeps?

All good stuff, but basic. I want something that'll give him a fright, that I can use to humiliate him. Like, if he's scared of rats, borrow one of the trained rats which are being used in the film, drop it down the back of his shirt when there's a crowd around, laugh my head off as he writhes and screams. But to do that, I'll have to find out more about him and what he's scared of.

So I start shadowing him. I do it when I'm not in class. I don't tell Bill-E. He'd happily join in if he knew what I was up to, but I don't want him getting into trouble if this backfires. Tump Kooniart's a powerful player. If I humble him in public, I might end up being booted off the set. I don't mind that, but there's no need for Bill-E to suffer too.

Tump's easy to follow. Tall and wide, always dressed in a drab brown suit. He walks with a slow waddle, mopping sweat from his forehead with a handkerchief which rarely leaves his hand. He usually talks loudly as he strolls, to himself if no one's with him. He doesn't seem to be able to keep silent, except when a scene is being filmed. I bet he even talks in his sleep. If I was blind, I could probably follow him by sound alone.

I don't learn much about Tump, except he loves to talk and eat. He has a trailer on the western edge of Slawter, separate trailers beside it for Bo and Abe. Three of the biggest trailers on the set. When he's not on the prowl, making sure his actors are happy or pigging out in one of the canteens, he spends most of his time in the trailer. He makes lots of phone calls. There are no personal computers allowed in Slawter – no video mobiles either – so he has to work from a huge Filofax in which he keeps all his contact details and other info. I think about stealing the Filofax and burning it, but that's hardly going to leave him a trembling wreck!

→Close to Tump's trailer, nearly a week after I began shadowing him. Waiting for him to emerge, sitting in the shade of another trailer, reading a movie magazine — always plenty of those around. Starting to tire of the detective work. Bo's still annoying me, but her insults have grown stale. Nobody really laughs at her jokes any more. Maybe I should quit this game and forget about vengeance.

Someone knocks on Tump's door. I look up and spot Chuda Sool entering the trailer. I haven't spoken to Chuda since the day of the 'demon' attack. I'm sure Bo told him about my hysterics. He must think I'm a right nutter. He might even feel insulted that I didn't believe him when he told me about Nora and Tump.

"Look what the cat dragged in," someone says behind me. I jump, but it's only Bo, on her way back from filming. "Discover any demons today, Grady?"

"No. Discover any new jokes?"

"Don't need them. Not when the old ones are still funny." She flashes her teeth and growls demonically. I yawn and focus on my magazine until she loses interest and goes away. I wait for the sound of her trailer door locking, then get up, angry, sick of hanging around. I could be playing foosball with Bill-E, not sitting here like a third-rate substitute, wasting my –

Tump steps out of his trailer, followed by Chuda Sool. Tump's talking loudly, mopping away busily at his forehead. Chuda never seems to sweat, which is handy — without eyebrows, sweat would flow straight into his eyes. The pair set off in a northerly direction, looking a bit like Laurel and Hardy from the rear. Since I'm here, I decide to follow. But this is the last time. I've had enough.

Tump and Chuda head for the D workshops. The huge warehouse dominates the northern part of Slawter. I haven't spent much time up here — no point, since access to the workshops is strictly prohibited. As Tump and Chuda show their passes to a security guard on the western door – one of four doors leading into the warehouse – I hang back and take a long look at the building.

Three storeys high, 70 or 80 metres wide, maybe 120 metres long. Large, unplastered block walls. A flat roof. No windows. Grey and featureless, apart from a big red D painted on the wall above the door. A small guard's hut to the right of the entrance.

I'd love to have a look inside, at the monster costumes and puppets. A small part of me still believes the demon was real. If I could check out the costumes perhaps it would help convince me of the truth. But hardly anyone is allowed to enter the hallowed halls of the D workshops. Even Dervish has only seen a small section of the complex.

I wait impatiently for Tump and Chuda to come out. Then I figure, stuff them! I'm through with this crap. I decide to find Bill-E and hang out with him for the rest of the afternoon. But before departing, I wander around the warehouse on the off chance that one of the doors is open, its guard asleep in his hut. That won't happen, of course, but I might as well give it a shot while I'm here.

The guard on the southern door studies me suspiciously as I approach. Though he doesn't openly carry any weapons, it wouldn't surprise me if he had a gun hidden on him somewhere. I smile politely and don't stray any closer. Walk to the eastern end and turn left. The door on this side is shut too and although the guard's in his hut, he isn't asleep — I spot him through the window as I walk past, leafing through a magazine with pictures of tanks on the cover.

I reach the northern end and turn left again. The guard here is standing next to the door, leaning against the wall. He smiles as I go past. I think about stopping to chat, maybe try to blag my way inside, but his smile isn't *that* inviting.

Back to the western end. Heading south, thinking about where Bill-E might be. As I come up to the guard's hut, the door to the workshops opens. I hear Tump's voice and stop behind the hut, where he and Chuda can't see me, to wait until they pass.

"…not going to like it," Tump is booming.

"They're not meant to like it," Chuda replies in a much softer voice.

"But the boy will be hard to keep quiet. They're so close to each other. Maybe we should take them both."

"One will be enough," Chuda says. "Now all we have to…"

Their voices fade. I remain where I am, frowning, wondering who and what they were talking about.

→The next day, Kik goes missing.

Kuk turns up for class by himself, looking lost. "Have any of you seen Kik?" he asks, eyes darting around the room as if his twin sister might be hiding behind a desk. "I can't find her. I don't know where she is. Kik? Are you here?"

Miss Jaun sits the agitated Kuk down, tries to soothe his nerves and coaxes the story out of him. It's not complicated. He woke this morning and Kik's bed was empty. He couldn't find her. Their dad wasn't too concerned – said she'd probably gone for a walk – but Kuk smelt a rat immediately.

"We don't go anywhere without telling each other. She wouldn't have slipped out without saying anything."

"Maybe she just needed to be alone for a while," Miss Jaun suggests.

"We don't like being alone," Kuk says, shaking his head vigorously. "Alone is bad. Alone is scary."

When Miss Jaun fails to calm Kuk's nerves, she calls security and asks a guard if he can put the word out to look for Kik. "It's no big deal," she tells him. "We'd just like to know where she is."

Class proceeds as normal, except for Kuk, who fidgets behind his desk, eyes wide and searching, staring out the window. He unnerves the rest of us. Even Bo is discomfited by him and remains quiet, no jokes or digs.

Towards the end of class, Miss Jaun summons the guard again. He says nobody has seen Kik but they're still looking.

I raise a hand. "Have you tried the D workshops?" I ask innocently.

The guard frowns. "She wouldn't be there."

"She might have snuck in."

The guard grins. "Into the D? I don't think so. Even I haven't been inside — I don't have clearance."

"But she *might* be there," I insist. I'm holding a steel ballpoint pen, gripping it tight, remembering the conversation I overheard yesterday, Tump saying "the boy will be hard to keep quiet".

"I'll check with the guys who were on duty this morning," the guard says, rolling his eyes slightly. "If they've seen her, I'll let you know."

"Thanks."

The guard leaves. Class ends. Kuk hurries out to search for his sister.

"What was that about the D warehouse?" Bill-E asks, hanging back.

"Nothing. I just thought they might not have looked there."

Bill-E squints suspiciously. "I know you too well, Grubbs Grady," he says in a bad Bela Lugosi accent. "You wouldn't have said something like that without a reason. What are you hiding from me?"

I consider telling him what I heard Tump Kooniart say. But I'm still smarting from my previous humiliation. I don't want to reveal my fears, only for Kik to turn up, leaving me looking like a paranoid maniac.

"It's nothing," I say, unclenching my fist to lay my pen down. "Let's…"

Grey liquid drips from my hands on to the table. Bill-E pulls a face. "What's that?" he asks. "It looks like mercury."

I don't reply. I'm staring at the liquid, the last few drops dripping from my fingers, black ink bubbling on my palms. It's the remains of the pen. The steel ballpoint which I was holding.

I melted it.

*   *   *

→Night falls. Kik hasn't been seen all day. Kuk's not the only one worried about her now. Her father's frantic. The search has intensified. The security forces have been deployed in earnest. Davida even suspended shooting so everyone could join the search parties and help.

I'm with a group exploring the eastern end of town, going through all the real buildings, checking behind the façades of the fakes. Trying to focus on the search. Trying not to think about the pen and how I melted it. But I can't *not* think about it. There *could* be a scientific explanation. But I'm certain the melting had nothing to do with science. It was *magic*.

I'm not a natural magician. Dervish told me that only one or two real magicians are born every century. There are others like Dervish and Meera Flame – mages – with the potential to perform acts of magic, usually with the aid of spells. I could maybe do that. But I never have. I'm not keen on magic. Plus, there hasn't been time. Dervish was a zombie for more than a year and he's not been up for teaching duties since he recovered.

So how did I melt the pen?

There's only one answer I can think of. When demons enter our universe, they affect the area where they cross. They're creatures of magic and that magic infects the world around them. When my parents were killed, I was able to tap into the magical, demonic energy and use it to escape. I did it again later in the secret cellar, when I fought Artery and Vein.

I think that's happening now. There's magic in the air — the magic of demons.

→We don't find Kik. The search concludes after midnight. Everybody turns in. Most people reckon she ran away. The guards say they'll search for her beyond Slawter tomorrow, take Kuk and his father with them.

I haven't told anyone about my fears. No point — I'd only be laughed at. But I can't sit back and do nothing. I have to try to help Kik, assuming she *can* still be helped. So I track down Dervish. He's been searching with Juni and a few others. Him and Juni aren't an item yet, but they've been spending more and more time together, and she's with him now. He says she's helping him cope with his nightmares, that she's taught him how to control his dreams, to keep the monsters of his subconscious at bay. But I think he's more lustful than grateful — he's practically bathing in that new aftershave now!

I get my story straight before I hit Dervish with it. I say I saw Kik yesterday, near the D workshops. Tell him I think she found a way in, that she's hiding inside, possibly trapped. "Maybe something fell on her. She could be pinned to the floor, crying out for help, nobody around to hear."

Dervish doesn't think she could get in — security's too tight. But Juni says they should check it out. "It's the one place we haven't explored. If she did somehow sneak in and had an accident..."

Neither Juni nor Dervish has the authority to enter the D workshops, so we go to Davida. We find her in her office, discussing the next day's shoot with Chuda Sool. Davida's tired and irritable — the delay has put the company behind schedule. She hears us out, then shakes her head. "We already checked. Grubbs mentioned the D earlier, so the guards who were on duty this morning – and last night – were questioned. They all said they hadn't seen her."

"But they wouldn't have if she snuck in," Dervish presses.

"Impossible," Chuda says and I catch him shooting a glare at me. "There's no way into the D warehouse other than through the doors. We constructed it to be impenetrable."

"But—" Dervish begins.

"No!" Chuda snaps, staring at Dervish directly.

Dervish stares back at Chuda, his pupils widening. Then he smiles and shrugs. "Guess we were wrong."

Chuda nods, his eyes still fixed on Dervish. "I guess you were."

My stomach tenses. It's not like Dervish to back down so easily. Is Chuda controlling Dervish's thoughts? Was I right about the browless assistant director? Is he in league with demonic forces?

Before I can challenge Chuda, Juni speaks up. "We need to search there," she tells Davida. "Or, if you won't allow us in, send in a team of guards and tell them to fine-comb the place. Because if Kik is in there – and a determined child can always find a way in, no matter how tight the security – she might be in trouble. If we ignore that and something bad happens to her..."

Davida sighs. "Chuda, assemble a team of guards and–"

"I think you should oversee this personally, Davida," Juni interrupts. She smiles sweetly at the glowering Chuda. "No offence, Mr Sool, but you're too convinced the girl isn't there. You might just take a cursory glance around, then quit."

Chuda bristles angrily and squares up to Juni. Before he can start an argument, Davida says, "We'll have no in-fighting, thank you. Chuda, please assemble a team for me. I'll go with them into the D workshops and make sure every room and cupboard is scoured methodically. Is that acceptable, Miss Swan?"

"Perfect," Juni smiles and we file out. I walk just behind Dervish, studying him carefully, worried about what might be going on inside his head.

→We wait outside the warehouse while Davida and the guards search for Kik. Juni is concerned about Dervish. She asks if he feels all right, if he has a headache. She saw it too, the exchange between him and Chuda. I doubt if she understood it the way I did, but she knows – or senses – something isn't right.

It's after 2:30 in the morning when a yawning Davida and her guards emerge. She shakes her head, exasperated. "No sign. We checked everywhere."

"You're sure?" I ask.

Davida doesn't answer. "We'll search the surrounding countryside tomorrow," she tells Juni. "The girl probably had an argument with one of the other children and took off in a huff. Maybe she'll turn up by herself."

I smother a snort. "I doubt it!"

→I set the alarm back an hour and sleep in late. Stare at the ceiling when I wake, tired and grumpy, finding it hard to get out of bed. Wondering what to do about Kik. Ideally I'd like to tell Dervish what I heard Tump Kooniart and Chuda Sool saying. Insist that Emmet *was* butchered by a demon, and Kik…

But I spoke to Emmet. He wasn't killed. Unless…

You can do just about anything with movie technology or magic. Maybe Chuda Sool was also eavesdropping with Tump Kooniart when I told Dervish and Juni my fears. Perhaps he intercepted the call and faked Emmet's voice, using either a mechanical or magical vocal distorter. Difficult — but not impossible.

I grab my trousers from the chair at the foot of my bed, dig my mobile out of the pocket and dial Emmet's number. There's no dial tone at his end. His phone's turned off or he's somewhere without a signal.

I get up, dress and head for class. I think about asking Juni for alternate phone numbers for Emmet and his mum, but she'd probably want to know why I was looking for them now. I don't want to reveal my suspicions to anyone in case I end up a laughing stock again. So, at the end of lessons, I casually ask Miss Jaun if she has Mrs Eijit's number. I say I've been trying to contact Emmet on his mobile but haven't been able to get through. Miss Jaun searches her list of names, then calls the number out to me. I thank her and dial it as I head for lunch. Dead, like Emmet's. I try his number again — the same as earlier.

It might not mean anything. Then again, it might.

→I try the two numbers several times over the course of the day. Not a peep out of either. I dial directory enquiries and get their home number. Ring it, only to find that the line has been disconnected.

One last try. I remember Emmet telling us about his local school. Again I use directory enquiries, then call and ask if I can speak with Emmet Eijit. I say I found his mobile phone and want to return it. The secretary says Emmet's not at school, he's making a film. I say I thought he'd finished and returned. No, she says, he hasn't. I ask if she's sure, if maybe he's back home, just not at school. She says definitely not, she knows his mother.

I stare at my phone a long time after that, certain I've been tricked. Emmet and his mum are still here, along with Kik — but not necessarily alive.

* * *

→Night. Kik hasn't been found. The search teams return at seven. Kuk and his father aren't with them. The searchers say Mr Kane and his son have gone home, in case Kik heads there. I groan when I hear that. I hope it's true. I pray that it is. Not just because I don't want Kuk and his dad to be dead — but because if it's a lie, it means the guards who were with them are part of a cover-up. It means it isn't just Chuda Sool and one or two others I have to be wary of. I might not be able to trust anybody in the entire cast and crew.

→Filming resumes in the morning. Davida's still worried about the missing Kik (or claims to be — *who can I trust?*), but life must go on. A film costs a fortune to make. Every day is vital. She can't afford to have her team sitting around idle. So, while a selection of guards took off to search the land around Slawter as the sun rose, the cameras rolled as normal.

They're filming the second big demon scene tonight. No carnage or loss of life this time. It's a scene from the third act, in which a demon appears to Bobby Mint and his friends. It predicts doom, warns them of the destruction to come, then tells them they can't leave, it's too late, they're destined to die, along with everyone they care about and love.

I've lost interest in filming but I have to go watch tonight's shoot, to check out the demon. I've heard it's different to the one that killed Emmet. I wonder if this creature will be real or a model? I know what I'd put my money on!

→A large crowd gathers for the shoot, but not as many as at the first demon show. This scene's being shot outside a church, one of the fake buildings in Slawter. In the script, the heroes have gathered inside to discuss the demons and what they can do to alert others to the danger. Those scenes have been filmed – or will be – on an interior set. This scene is set at the end of their debate. They've just come out. As they're heading down the steps, the demon appears out of the church behind them, laughing, saying it's overheard their entire plan.

Davida sets the scene, runs the actors through their paces, makes sure all the cameras and lights are correctly positioned, then takes her seat. Action!

I watch nervously, holding my breath, as Salit Smit and the others spill out of the church, faces bright and determined. There are eight steps down from the doors. As they hit the second from bottom step, laughter echoes from within.

"Poor, foolish humans," the demon crows. Salit and his crew whirl, gasping. "You think you know so much. But, like all mortals, your knowledge of the world is pitiful. It would be amusing, were it not so sad."

I start to shiver at the first syllable. There's no mistaking that voice, the low, mournful tone. I know what's coming next. I'd give anything to be wrong but I know I'm not.

The demon appears, gliding out of the shadows. He's lit perfectly. I hear murmurs of approval from the people around me. They were caught by surprise with Emmet, but they're ready this time, in control of their emotions. Besides, although this demon is more horrific in appearance than the first, he moves so fluidly and gracefully that they have time to appreciate his design, the months of hard work which must have gone into creating him.

"You cannot defeat me or my kind," the demon says, looking from one so-called hero to another, then beyond, to the crowd watching the filming. "We can go anywhere you can and to places where you can't. We see all, hear all, know all. And we will *kill* all."

A tall demon, pale red skin with lots of cracks in it, from which blood continually oozes. Dark red eyes. No hair or nose. Grey teeth and tongue. A hole where his heart should be, filled with dozens of tiny snakes. Mangled hands at the ends of eight arms. No feet, just fleshy strips dangling from his waist, giving the appearance of thin, misshapen legs. He doesn't touch the floor, but hovers a few centimetres above the ground all the time.

"This is our town now, or soon will be," the demon says. "There is nothing you can do to stop us." His eyes fall on me and he smiles widely. "There is nothing *any* of you can do — except be *slaughtered*."

Then he laughs and drifts back into the church. The doors slam shut. A boy in the group of heroes screams. Davida yells, "Cut!"

Everyone pours forward, cheering, congratulating the actors, remarking on how realistic and creepy the demon was, questioning how the effects team got it to hover so believably, what mechanics were involved.

But there were no strings or engines. It wasn't a model or costume. The few doubts I had up to this point vanish. We're in seriously deep trouble. The demon wasn't speaking from a script. His words weren't meant for the fictional characters — but for those of us watching.

There *are* real demons here. Emmet *has* been killed, and probably Kik and her relatives too. And it's going to get worse. Because the monster who wowed the crowd a minute ago is the one who killed my parents and sister, who vowed to kill Dervish, Bill-E and me… the majestic, terrible demon master himself… lowly *Lord Loss*.

D

→Incredibly, impossibly, Dervish doesn't believe me.

"It was just another guy in a costume," he says. "You have to stop seeing demons everywhere you look. I know—"

"Don't!" I snap. I've got him by himself, out of earshot of everybody. "That piece of scum killed my Mum and Dad. He slaughtered Gret. Don't tell me I could ever confuse a movie prop for the real thing. Don't you dare."

"Grubbs, I know this is hard, but you've got to believe—"

"That was Lord Loss!" I cry.

"It looked like him," Dervish says soothingly, "but that's because Davida did a lot of research. She knows what real demons look like. Actually, I helped her out on this one. She had some of the details wrong. She didn't know about the cracks in his skin, the colour of his eyes or that he didn't have real feet."

"Really?" I sneer. "And you filled her in on the facts?"

"Yes," Dervish says, trying to sound modest.

"And her technicians were able to make the changes—" I click my fingers —"*like that*? They were able to take elaborate, mechanised costumes they'd been working on for months and alter them within the space of a few days?"

"Yes," Dervish says evenly.

I stare into my uncle's eyes but I don't find him there. The Dervish I know wouldn't smile at me glibly like this and dismiss my fears so carelessly. Chuda Sool has brainwashed him, I'm sure of it. I'll have to look elsewhere for allies.

"Where are you going?" Dervish asks as I turn my back on him and march off.

"To find someone who'll believe."

→I ask Juni to visit Bill-E and me in our room. I say it's about Bo Kooniart, that I'm having problems with her and would like Juni's advice. Naturally Juni's only too happy to help. Promises to drop by within the next half hour.

Bill-E knows something big is up. He doesn't know what it is, but he's delighted to be involved, proud that I'm including him. He wasn't happy when I skulked around the set without him, not saying why, but now I'm bringing him in on the secret, all is forgiven.

I say nothing until Juni arrives, getting things clear in my head, deciding how much to tell them, what to say and what to keep to myself. When she's finally here, sitting on a chair, hands clasped on her knees, I begin by confessing that I lied. "I didn't really bring you here to talk about Bo."

"I guessed," she smiles. "You're not a good liar. Which is a positive thing — don't think I'm criticising you!"

"Before I get down to the crazy stuff, have either of you noticed anything strange about Dervish?" I ask.

"What do you mean?" Bill-E frowns.

"I'll take that as a no. Juni?"

She pauses. "I don't know your uncle very well, but he's seemed a little… unfocused recently."

"You saw it when he was talking with Chuda about the search for Kik, didn't you?"

"I saw… something," Juni says cagily. "Dervish has been through a lot these last two years. The responsibility of having to look after you, the temporary loss of his mind, trying to readjust to normal life, the nightmares."

"Nightmares?" Bill-E asks. We never told him about Dervish's bad dreams.

"He's had trouble sleeping recently," Juni explains.

"That's the first I've heard of it," Bill-E grumbles.

"He finds it easy to share his secrets and fears with me," Juni says. "He's able to tell me things he finds hard to discuss with others. I've been trying to help him sort through his problems. We were making good progress but now he seems to have regressed."

"Chuda's messing with his mind," I tell her. "Controlling his thoughts."

"You can't be serious," Juni laughs. But her laughter dies away when she sees that I am.

"I'm going to tell you something that will sound insane," I begin. "Bill-E knows some of it but not all. I need you to hear me out and at least try to believe me."

"Of course," Juni says, leaning forward, intrigued.

I take a deep breath. Glance at Bill-E, knowing what I say is going to hurt him, then launch straight in. "Demons killed my parents and sister…"

→I fill them in on most of the details. My early encounter with Lord Loss. Escape. Madness. Recovery. Moving to Carcery Vale. The curse of the Gradys. Then the big one — Bill-E turning into a werewolf.

"So that's it!" Bill-E cries. He's trembling, his lazy eyelid quivering wildly. "I never bought your story that Dervish locked me up to protect me. I knew there was something you weren't telling." He glares at me accusingly. "You lied to me."

"We didn't want to hurt you," I sigh.

"I can take hurt. Not lies. You should have told me."

"Maybe," I mutter miserably.

"So, am I cured?" Bill-E snarls.

"Yes."

"For real? Forever?"

I nod glumly, then outline the deal which certain members of our family had going with Lord Loss, the chess matches, the battles with his familiars. I tell them how Dervish and I challenged Lord Loss on Bill-E's behalf. The only part I leave out is the truth about Bill-E's father. I don't tell him we had the same dad. This isn't the time to open that can of worms.

Bill-E's rage dwindles as he hears what Dervish and I risked to save him. He's staring at me with awe now, tears trickling down his cheeks. I find that more unsettling than his anger. He's gawping at me as if I'm some kind of hero. But I'm not. I only did it because he's my brother, but I can't tell him that, not now. He thinks Dervish is his dad. If I told him the truth, I'd be hitting him with the news that his real father's dead.

I finish quickly with the last few months, Dervish defeating Lord Loss in his demonic realm and regaining his senses, the nightmares, coming here to try and sort himself out, the demon which killed Emmet, overhearing Tump Kooniart and Chuda Sool talking, the appearance of Lord Loss.

"It was definitely him," I tell them. "I wasn't a hundred per cent sure before, but now I am. There are real demons in Slawter. Chuda and Tump are working for them, along with some of the crew. Davida might be one of their allies too. Lord Loss swore revenge on me, Dervish and Bill-E. So the three of us are for the chop, no doubt about it. Probably the rest of you as well."

Silence. Bill-E is staring at me, torn between hero-worship, terror and doubt. Juni doesn't know what to think or say. She's probably heard all sorts in her time, but nothing like this. She's trying to think of a gentle way of denying what I'm saying, without insulting or enraging me.

"It's OK," I smile. "You can say I'm crazy. I won't mind."

"People roll out that word too swiftly," Juni objects. "It's an easy fall-back. I try never to make such gross generalisations. But…"

"…in this case you'll make an exception," I finish for her.

She grins shakily. "I wasn't going to say that."

"But you were thinking it, right?"

She tilts her head uncertainly. "We have a lot to discuss. This goes back a long way. You have deep-rooted issues which we'll have to work through, one at a time. To begin with—"

"Do you believe in magic?" I interrupt.

"No," Juni says plainly.

"What if I could convince you?"

"How?"

I've been thinking a lot about this. I knew words alone wouldn't be enough. I haven't done anything magical since melting the pen, but I'm sure magic is still in the air, surrounding me, waiting to be channelled. It had better be or else I really will look like a loon!

"Is that worth a lot?" I ask, pointing at the watch on her wrist.

"No," she frowns.

"Does it matter to you? Would you miss it if you lost it?"

"Not really. Where is this going, Grubbs?"

"You'll see." I fix my gaze on the watch, willing it to melt. I'm anticipating a struggle, but almost as soon as I focus, the watch liquidises and drips off Juni's hand.

"Ow!" Juni yelps, leaping to her feet and rubbing her wrist. "It's hot!"

"Sorry!" I jump up too. "Are you OK? Do you want me to get some ice or–"

"I'm fine," Juni snaps, then quits rubbing, stares at the red mark left behind by the melted metal, then at the puddle on the floor, then at me. "Grubbs… what the hell?" she croaks.

"That was just for openers," I beam, confidence bubbling up. "Have you ever wanted to fly?"

→In the end we don't fly. Juni isn't ready to open the window and soar over the buildings of Slawter. I'm not either, really. But we levitate a bit, to prove that the melting watch wasn't a hoax, that this is real magic, not some stage trick.

"This is incredible!" Juni laughs as I make the light switch on and off just by looking at it, while juggling six pairs of balled-up socks without touching them.

"Bloody amazing is what it is!" Bill-E gasps. "Could I do that too?"

"Maybe," I say, flicking the light on and off a few more times, then letting the socks drop. "Dervish said lots of people have magical potential. They just don't know it. The magic's thick in the air around us here, but you and the others aren't aware of it. I am, because I fought demons and part of my mind – the part that's magic – opened up. If you could open that part of *your* mind, I bet you could do everything I can."

"I need to get me a demon to whup," Bill-E mutters.

"Of course, it could all be in my head," Juni says. "You could have slipped me hallucinogenic substances. I might be imagining the watch, floating, the socks."

Bill-E wrinkles his nose. "You couldn't hallucinate the smell of Grubbs's socks!" he says and we all laugh.

"You don't really believe that, do you?" I ask Juni.

"No," she sighs. "But I want to keep an open mind, like you advised. That means not accepting your story about demons even if the magic is real." She looks at me earnestly. "One doesn't verify the other. I haven't seen any evidence of demons yet."

"You don't need to!" I groan. "If demons aren't real, where am I getting my power from?"

"I have no idea," Juni says. "You might be generating it naturally, subconsciously. The demons might simply be your way of rationalising your powers." She holds up a hand as I start to argue. "I'm not saying that *is* the case — just that it *might* be."

Juni sits back, a troubled look on her face. "Actually I can't tell you how much I hope that the demons *are* a product of your imagination. For Emmet's sake, Kik's and the others."

"I know," I mutter. "I wish they weren't real too. But they are."

She licks her lips, frowning deeply, trying to get her head around what I'm telling her. "I need proof," she finally says. "I'm not sure what you want me to do, but I can't do anything until I've seen direct evidence."

"I want you to help Dervish," I tell her. "Chuda Sool has some sort of mind lock on him. I want you to help me break it. You can do that without believing in demons, can't you?"

"Perhaps," she says. "But I don't want to go anywhere near your uncle's mind until I know for sure what I'm dealing with."

"I think I *can* prove it," I say softly, lowering my gaze. "But it could be dangerous. The sort of dangerous where we all die horribly if things go wrong."

"I'm prepared to take that risk," Juni says evenly.

"Me too," Bill-E pipes up bravely, though the squeak in his voice betrays his fear.

I nod reluctantly. "Demons don't appear out of thin air. They have to be summoned. Their universe has to merge with ours. A window or tunnel between worlds has to be opened. If Lord Loss and the other demon were real, there has to be a place where they crossed. A secret place. A place where nobody but their human partners can get into."

"The D workshops," Bill-E and Juni say at the exact same time.

"Got it in one," I chuckle bleakly.

*   *   *

→Juni keeps saying she must be crazy for going along with this, it's a mad plan, she should have her head examined. But the magic unnerved her. She's confused, not in complete control. I should give her a day to think things over and clear her head. But she might not play ball if I did. She might start rationalising and analysing, and decide nobody in her position should break into a building. Worse — she might tell Davida what I believe and tip our enemies off. So I rush her along, allowing her no time to think.

It's impossible to sneak up on the D warehouse, no matter what time you come. Large, powerful lamps are trained on all sides of the building at night. You can't approach it without your shadow preceding you, growing like a giant's the closer you get.

But I've got magic on my side. I could have performed any number of miracles in our room to convince Juni of my power. I didn't randomly choose to experiment on the light bulb.

Studying the lamps from the shelter of the closest building to the warehouse. Juni and Bill-E are quiet behind me. I can't see all the lights from here, but I can imagine them.

Not sure if I have the strength to do this. Just have to try and hope for the best. Focusing, I close my eyes, keeping the picture of the lamps vivid in my thoughts. I visualise the lamps flaring and going out, all at once, like a flashbulb on a camera. Call on the magic. Try to extend it to the lights. Doubting if I can really—

"Bloody hell!" Bill-E gasps. Then a chuckle. "Coolio!"

I open my eyes to darkness. "Let's go," I hiss, starting forward, not sure how much time we'll have.

"Oh my," Juni says breathlessly. But she runs after me with Bill-E, along for the ride even if she doesn't truly want to be.

→The guards come out of their hut with strong torches. We drop to our stomachs as their beams sweep the surrounding area. I think about quenching the torches but that would really stir up their suspicions.

Lying on the cool ground, head down. I hear one of the guards on his walkie-talkie, checking if the lamps are out all over. He doesn't sound worried. The guards sweep the area a few more times with their torches, then return to the hut. One keeps his torch beam trained on the door of the D. There's no way we could get in through it without being seen. So it's just as well I didn't plan on entering that way.

Rising, I hurry forward, trying not to make any noise, heading for a point about three-quarters of the way along the side of the warehouse, where it's nice and dark, where we can't be easily seen by the guards.

I rest when I get to the wall, panting heavily, more from fear than the run. Juni and Bill-E arrive moments later. Bill-E's puffing hard — he's not as fit as me. I can see their faces in the light of the moon and stars. Bill-E looks scared but excited. Juni's just scared. Funny, but I feel like the adult here.

"What now?" Bill-E asks when he gets his breath back.

"The Indian rope trick," I grin, then try to make a length of rope appear, dangling from the roof. Nothing happens. I try again, this time demanding the rope to simply appear on the ground. Nothing.

I frown, wondering if I used up all my magic quenching the lights. But then I recall my fight with Artery and Vein. Dervish supplied the weapons, laid them on the floor of the secret cellar, axes, swords, etc. He wouldn't have gone to all that effort if we could have simply made weapons appear. Maybe magic doesn't work that way and objects can't be created out of thin air.

So the roof's out. Fine. Time for Plan B.

I focus on the wall. Bare blocks, cemented tightly together. No chinks. Can't tell how thick they are, but I imagine the wall's more than a single block deep. I place my left hand on the nearest block and concentrate. Not sure if I can melt stone like metal, but I give it a go.

The block doesn't melt. I try again but still it holds. I sigh — looks like I've run out of ideas. But as I lean forward, trying to think of some other way in, my fingers gouge into the stone. It's like putting my hand in mud. I make a half-fist and scoop out a handful of mushy material. I smile at the muck, then at Juni and Bill-E. "You two clear the mess away," I tell them. "I'll get to work on the rest of the blocks."

"Be careful," Bill-E whispers. "We don't want the wall collapsing."

"No worries," I snort. "Grubbs Grady's on top of the situation!"

"This is madness," Juni mutters, but digs her fingers into the semi-melted block and begins scooping it out.

→It takes fifteen minutes to gouge a hole big enough for us to fit through. It feels like hours. All the time I'm aware of the threat of the lamps snapping back on, the guards sighting us, everything coming undone.

But the darkness holds and at last I melt through the third and final layer of blocks. I poke my head through the gap and switch on the torch I brought with me. This looks like an ordinary props room — puppets and moulds lying around, tools, mannequins, bits of material, tubes of glue. I switch off the torch and slide forward. Juni follows, then Bill-E.

Bill-E's frowning when he steps in. He looks back at the hole. "What are we going to do about that?" he asks. "If they see it when the lamps come on..."

"We just have to hope they don't."

"And when we leave?" he persists. "They'll know we've been here."

"I'll try to make the stones solid again and put them back," I tell him. "But if I can't, don't worry. If I'm right and we're dealing with demons, we're not going to hang around like horror-movie victims, waiting for them to get wise to us."

"And if you're wrong?" Juni asks. "If there aren't any demons?"

"Then we'll wind up in a heap load of trouble," I chuckle. "But it'll be trouble of the ass-kicking, job-losing kind, and trouble like that I don't mind so much."

"So what now?" Bill-E asks, glancing around.

"We wander. Explore as much of the building as we can. Keep going until we find something strange or run out of rooms."

"Perhaps one of us should remain here, to alert the others if the guards find the hole," Bill-E suggests.

"How?" I grunt.

"Phone." He roots out his mobile, flicks it on, frowns, shakes it, then scowls. "No signal. Damn."

"It's probably better if we stay together anyway," Juni says, then lets out an uneasy breath. "I've never done anything like this. I never even stole sweets from shops when I was a child. I've always respected the law."

"Welcome to the underworld, baby!" Bill-E chortles, trying to sound like a 1930s gangster.

"No more talking," I whisper.

We advance.

FRESH MEAT

→We don't spot any security cameras. I guess Chuda Sool or his superiors thought the armed guards outside would provide enough protection. Or there are hidden cameras which we can't see. Or they didn't think anyone who found their way in would be able to get out.

Winding through the building, one ordinary room giving way to another. Lots of weird, demon-shaped puppets on display, but the work of human hands. Cleverly constructed, but hardly hewn in the fires of hell. Plastic, metal, rubber — not flesh, bone, blood.

I try not to lose confidence as we push further into the warehouse. It's logical that they'd have an outer ring of genuine workshops. While this place is off-limits, some of the crew – like Dervish – have been allowed into parts of it. This is camouflage. Things will be different further in.

I hope.

I fear.

* * *

→We come to a massive steel door unlike any of the others we've encountered. The full height of the ceiling and three metres wide. There's a small digital screen on the right-hand side, the outline of a hand printed on it.

"Fingerprint controlled," Bill-E notes, rapping the door with his knuckles. He reaches out to press his hand on the screen.

"Wait," I stop him. "It might sound an alarm if an intruder touches it."

Bill-E lowers his hand. "We gonna melt our way through the wall, boss?"

"Reckon so, kemosabe."

I lay my fingers on the blocks to the right of the door. Focus my magic and tell the stone to melt. Push forward to scoop out the first handful of molten rock.

It's solid.

I try again — no joy. Rubbing my fingers together, trying to figure it out. It can't be that I'm running low on juice — there's more magic in the air here than outside. I can feel it practically crackling around me. Just to be sure, I make myself rise half a metre off the ground. No problem.

"Something wrong?" Juni asks, eyeing me nervously as I float in the air.

"The wall's protected," I tell her, smoothly descending. "It's been charged with magic, or there's magic pushing out from within. I can't melt it."

"We could try somewhere else," Bill-E says. "There might be another door or a part of the wall that isn't…"

I shake my head. "It's going to be like this all the way round. I can sense it — literally. There's an inner structure, a building within the warehouse. If there are other doors, they'll be like this. The wall will be the same everywhere too. And the roof."

"Then we can't go on," Juni notes with relief. "Let's get out, plug up the hole we made, and discuss a new—"

"No," I cut her short. "I'm not stopping. Not until I've convinced you."

"But if we can't get through…" she protests gently.

"I didn't say that. We just have to be a bit smarter."

I move back to the screen and study the outline of the hand. My magic's not strong enough to combat the magic of the wall, but maybe I can outfox the technology of the door.

I place my right hand on the screen, tensing in case alarms sound. But there's no klaxon squeal. Lights don't flash. Breathing softly, thinking hard, trying to direct magic into the screen. It's set up to recognise certain fingerprints. I want to tell it that my prints are among those it accepts. But how do you talk to a computer which only understands binary code?

I ignore the complications. Send a simple message, over and over, letting magic flow all the time. "You know me. My prints are in your database. *Open*."

Nothing happens. Bill-E and Juni keep quiet, but I sense their lack of belief. Ignoring them, I keep talking to the computer, trying to trick it. I don't ackowledge the possibility of failure. Change tack. Start telling it I'm Chuda Sool. "You *will* open — I'm Chuda Sool. You *must* open — I'm Chuda Sool." Picturing his long, thin face, his browless eyes and cold gaze.

There's a click. Another. A whole series of clickings and whirrings.

The door opens inwards, silent as you please.

I remove my hand and glance back smugly at the astonished faces of Juni and Bill-E. "Oh ye of little faith," I murmur.

We enter.

→Darkness. The other rooms were dark too, but I was able to light them with my torch. This room's too big. The beam is like a pin, showing us almost nothing of the space around us. We can tell that it's huge, but no more than that.

"This feels wrong," Juni says as we stand a few metres from the open doorway, reluctant to press ahead any further.

"It's like we're surrounded," Bill-E agrees, squinting into the darkness.

I flash the torch left, then right. We can't see anyone. But that doesn't mean that people – or other creatures – aren't there. Or that they can't see us.

"Maybe we should come back with stronger torches," Juni says.

"If we quit now, we'll never return," I mutter.

"But we can't see anything."

"Give me a minute. Let me think."

I can't make objects appear out of nothing. But magic is a form of energy. Maybe I can convert that energy into a different form.

Concentrating. Speaking to the magic within me. In a weird way it feels like I'm two people, the one I've always been, and Grubbs Grady — magician.

"I want to make light," I tell my magical half. "I'd like a big ball of light to appear just above my head. Is that possible?"

In response, I feel energy stream from my hands. It gathers overhead, pulses a couple of times, then transforms into a ball of blinding white light. I gasp with pain, covering my eyes with an arm. "Not so bright!" I hiss, then squint with one eye over the top of my arm. The light has dulled slightly, but is still painful to look at. "Keep dimming. More... more... Stop."

I remove my arm. Bill-E and Juni have both covered their eyes. "It's OK," I tell them. "You can look now."

Their eyes are watering when they lower their hands. Juni looks like she's going to be sick. "How did you do that?" she whispers.

"Easy-peasy," I grin.

"You're a freak," Bill-E says. "But a useful one to have around."

"Thanks. Now let's see what we've walked into..."

I send the ball of light forward, letting it brighten the further away from us it moves, until it lights up the entire room. Only it's not really a room. It's a huge, single, cavernous chamber. A bare earth floor. Brick walls which rise up the full height of the building, all three storeys of it. No props, furniture, nothing… except a tall stone in the centre… and lots of shapes around it.

Bodies.

"This isn't good," Bill-E says nervously.

"Those look like…" Juni croaks, then starts forward.

"Wait!" I cry.

Juni shakes her head. "I have to be sure. They could be old bags or mannequins. I must check."

"We don't know what's in here with us," I say, losing my nerve slightly.

Juni pauses, looks around, then shrugs. "There's nothing. We're alone. Except for *them*."

She carries on. Bill-E and I glance at each other. We can't be outdone by a woman. The shame would be too much to bear. So we set off after her, away from the door and the possibility of a quick retreat.

→Juni sinks to her knees a few metres from the bodies, staring hopelessly, jaw slack, disbelief in her pinkish eyes. There are twenty or twenty-five of them encircling the stone, the head of one body lying on or under the feet of the next. Emmet's one of the dead. His mother. Kik and Kuk Kane. Their father. Others I don't recognise.

Some of the bodies have chunks ripped out of them or limbs torn loose. Others have cut throats. A few look like they're asleep, but I'm sure if we turned them over we'd discover fatal wounds.

Bill-E reels away and vomits, groaning over the mess, shaking his head, trying to deny the reality of this dreadful scene. This is the first time my brother's seen anything like this. It's hard. Not like what you see in the movies. On the silver screen, corpses mean nothing. You know they're not real, just models or actors faking death. You can admire the staging, the special effects, the pools of blood. The grosser it is, the cooler.

But in real life it's sickening. The most distressing sight in the world. Death's always hard to take, but murder… slaughter… people killed in the name of some disgusting demonic cause… spread out like sacks of meat and bone…

Juni's taking *deep* breaths. I'm sure she wants to vomit too, but she's keeping the bile down. Just.

Me, I'm a veteran of atrocity. As bad as this is, as much as it hurts seeing Emmet lying there with his throat and stomach slit open, it's nowhere near as bad as when I walked in on my parents and sister and found them torn to shreds. I'm not saying I'm cool with this, or it's water off a duck's back. I'm just better prepared to deal with it than Bill-E or Juni.

I turn my attention away from the bodies, not wanting to dwell on the pain they must have suffered, the tragedy of dying in this callous manner. I study the stone, the focal point of the room. It looks like a Stonehenge monolith. A big chunk of rock jutting out of the ground, mostly smooth, but with a few jagged knobs poking out of it in various places. No writing, at least not on this side. But several gouges run across the middle and near the top, different lengths and depths.

"Some of the bodies have been here a long time," Juni says. She points to a couple of corpses in an especially bad state. Flesh rotting, inner organs dried up, bones jutting through the dry and brittle skin. "This hasn't all happened in the last few weeks."

"No," I agree. "I think this goes back months, maybe longer."

Juni looks around at me. "What the hell's happening?" she sobs. "*Why?*"

Before I can think of an answer, there's a scratching noise behind the rock. Then a sniffing sound, followed by raspy chuckling. Something sticks its head out. Studies us. Then steps into view.

It's a demon. Five long, spindly legs. The body of a giant ant. A long neck and the head of some sort of rabid monkey. No arms, but several small mouths in addition to its main one, sticking out of its body, set on mushroom-like stalks. The mouths are filled with blood-red, dagger-sharp teeth.

The demon gurgles at us. I can read its thoughts — "Fresh meat!"

Juni and Bill-E scream. I scream too, but there's magic in my cry. It hits the demon like a cannon ball, knocks it backwards, clear of the stone and bodies. Sends it tumbling across the floor.

"*Run!*" I roar.

Bill-E and Juni don't need to be told twice. They race for the door, howling, terror overriding their other senses. I want to run too. I try to. But the magic stops me. *Not yet*, a voice within me whispers. *You can't let it attack from behind. You'll die if you turn your back on it.*

The demon finds its feet and snarls. It has several bright green eyes, set above and under its main mouth. Some look at the light overhead. The others stay pinned on me. The demon's lips move fast. Inhuman mutterings. I sense magic and prepare myself for an assault, teeth chattering, inching away from the monster, keeping it in sight the whole time.

The ball of light dims, then is quenched, plunging us into blackness.

Bill-E and Juni's screams get louder. The demon shrieks triumphantly. The sound of scampering feet. My first instinct — turn and run for dear life. But my magic half holds me in place. Makes me listen. The scampering sounds come closer. Closer. Any second now, those teeth will be ripping into my flesh and tearing off chunks of...

Sudden silence.

Down! the voice barks.

I drop instinctively and, in response to a second command, stick my legs up in the air. I force magic down to my feet, transforming them, directed by the voice.

The demon hits. A wet stabbing sound. My knees buckle, but I hold them straight. There's weight pressing down on me, more than I could naturally bear. I use magic to steady my legs and support the heavy load. The demon's struggling, screeching. Something splashes over my face and neck — blood or bile, maybe both. I scream with fear and hate, then force my feet up higher. The demon chokes, writhes a few more times, then goes still.

I hold my position, wary, in case the demon's faking. But when, after several long seconds, there's no movement, I allow myself to relax a bit and summon a fresh ball of light.

My legs are rigid above me. The demon's impaled on them. I can see two grey, metallic prongs sticking out of the monster's back. My feet, transformed into blades. How cool is that!

"*Grubbs!*" Bill-E yells.

I tilt my head and look behind me. Bill-E and Juni are standing in the doorway. I see panic in Bill-E's face. He can't see the blades from there. He thinks the demon's feasting on me.

"It's OK," I call, lowering my legs, using my hands to try and push the demon off. When that fails, I use magic to propel it clear, then turn my legs back to their normal form. I stand.

"Grubbs?" Bill-E says, softly this time, uncertain.

I smile at him and Juni. She looks suspicious too. "I killed it."

Bill-E takes a step forward. I increase the brightness of the light so he and Juni can see me clearly, as well as the motionless demon.

"You killed it?" Bill-E echoes, walking cautiously towards me, staring at the dead monster. "How?"

"Magic." I feel weird. I've never killed anything before, apart from flies and other insects. I know this is a demon and it was trying to kill me, but it's still a strange sensation. I don't feel guilty – I'm glad as hell that I'm not the one lying dead! – but I'm not thrilled either.

Juni steps up beside Bill-E. She's trembling. Brushes strands of white hair out of her eyes. "I've never seen anything like that before," she mumbles. Takes a step towards it. Stops. "Are you certain it's dead?"

"Yes. But others might come. We can't afford to hang around."

"I have to examine it," she says.

"This isn't the time for an autopsy!" I snap.

"I have to make sure there are no wires or engines inside."

"You think that thing's a fake?" Bill-E exclaims. "Are you insane?"

"No," Juni says. "To both questions. But I have to be *sure*. If this is real, it changes the entire way I think about the world. Before I accept that, I have to be certain this isn't a clever movie prop that got out of control."

Juni crouches next to the demon. Studies it closely, hands raised defensively in case it leaps back to life and attacks. I move up behind her, also worried about the demon, no longer positive that I killed it. Remembering when I fought Vein and Artery. I could cut them up into bits, but I wasn't able to kill them. This might be a lesser demon, or I might be more powerful than I was before. Or it might only be wounded, faking death to lure us closer.

Juni kicks one of the demon's legs — no response. She kicks a mouth stalk. It wobbles from side to side, but only from the force of her blow. Slowly, carefully, she prises its main mouth open and peers down its throat. I tense. If the demon's faking, this is the perfect moment to strike. I see the teeth start to come together and prepare a ball of energy to hurl.

But I'm stressing for nothing. The mouth's only moving because Juni is fiddling with the demon's neck.

"I need a knife," Juni mutters, running her hands over the demon's ant-like shell. She looks up. "Either of you?"

Bill-E fishes in a pocket and passes her a small Swiss army knife. Juni pauses, grimacing, then cuts into the demon's flesh. It's softer than it looks, or else Juni is stronger then she appears, because the blade plunges in up to her hand. She shudders, then carves downwards along the length of the demon's side. Worm-like guts ooze out as she slices, as well as a greyish substance which might be blood. Remembering the spray I caught earlier, I wipe a hand across my face and it comes away wet and sticky with the same grey liquid.

"I'd kill for a shower," I mutter, chuckling darkly at the sick joke.

Juni cuts a long, jagged line through the creature's flesh, ignoring the grey blood and guts, then hands Bill-E his knife. He grimaces and tries to wipe the muck off on his trousers. Juni looks at me and grins shakily. "I wanted to be a vet when I was younger," she says — then drives her right hand deep into the demon's stomach.

"This is *so* gross," Bill-E moans.

"It hasn't put you in the mood for liver and kidneys for breakfast?" I ask.

Bill-E's face goes green and he almost throws up again.

Juni searches with her fingers for a minute, then draws her hand out. All sorts of horrible bits and pieces come with it — fleshy and slimy, no wires or mechanisms. Juni stares at her fingers, rubs them together, then tries to clean them by digging her hand into the earth.

"Convinced?" I ask.

"It's impossible," she sighs. "Demons are creatures of myth, the phantasmagorical creations of primitive superstition."

"They're the Demonata," I correct her. "Mankind's greatest enemies. They've existed since before the dawn of our species. They hate us and love to kill. Sometimes they break through into our universe and the bloodshed starts. That's what happened here." I lock gazes with her. "They've already killed some of us. If we don't warn the others, they'll slaughter us all."

Juni nods slowly. "I thought I was so clever," she whispers. "I knew so much about the mind, people, behaviour. Now..."

Her eyes clear and she gets up, businesslike. "Who can we trust?" she asks.

"Dervish," I answer promptly. "But he won't believe us."

"He'll believe *me*," Juni growls and her face is beautifully stern.

KIDNAP

→I keep expecting the worst as we reel back through the warehouse, anxiously retracing our steps, making mistakes and having to backtrack. I'm sure the lamps will come on outside, the hole will be discovered, guards will pour into the building to block our escape. Chuda Sool will appear and summon an army of demons. We'll die miserably and be added to the pile of corpses around the stone.

But none of that happens. Apart from the wrong turns, our journey back to the hole in the external wall passes unremarkably. And when we get there, the lights are still dead outside, the guards in their huts, nobody aware of our presence.

"Will we try and fill in the hole?" Bill-E asks.

"That would take too much time," Juni says. "We should just—"

I point at the mud-like mess on the ground. Draw upon the magic. Snap my fingers. "Ubsacagrubbsa!" I quip. And the molten rocks flow upwards, defying gravity. They fill the gap, solidifying within seconds. It's not perfect — there are no individual bricks now, just one large patch of unbroken block

— but it should only be noticeable if one of the guards passes up close.

"Nice work," Bill-E says.

"You're growing more powerful by the minute," Juni notes.

"Let's not waste time on compliments," I grunt, then lead the way through the welcome, night-time darkness of Slawter in search of my uncle.

→ Even though I'm soaked from head to toe in demon blood, Dervish doesn't believe us. Rather, he doesn't *want* to believe.

"This is a movie set," he insists. "The D workshops are full of amazing demon facsimiles. It wasn't real, just a—"

Juni curses crudely, surprising us all, then points a finger at the startled Dervish. "Don't give me that rot!" she snarls. "You weren't there — *I* was. You didn't see it — *I* did. It was no piece of movie magic. It was a demon. It would have killed us all if not for Grubbs."

I feel pride welling up inside. Bill-E gives me a dig in the ribs and sticks his tongue out, making sure my head doesn't get too big.

Dervish stares uncertainly at Juni, finding it harder to dismiss her protests than mine. That's a positive sign. Chuda Sool hasn't fried Dervish's brain completely.

"It was a real demon," Juni says slowly, keeping her eyes on Dervish's. "I don't know how these things can be real but they are. It killed Emmet, Kuk and Kik, a lot of others. It—"

"No," I cut in. "That demon wasn't the killer. I think it was just a guard, set there to protect the stone in case anybody got through the rest of the building. There are worse demons than that around — Lord Loss, for one."

"I told you that wasn't—" Dervish begins.

"Shut it!" Juni stops him. "If Grubbs says he saw the demon master, he did. I believe him now. Totally."

Dervish sighs, confused. "What do you want me to do?" he grumbles. "If you've already killed the demon..."

"There are more!" I hiss. "The one that killed Emmet. Lord Loss." I glance at Juni and Bill-E. "That was an awfully large room. Why make a room that big for just a few demons? I think more are planning to cross. A *lot* more." I face Dervish again. "You have to stop them. Call the Disciples. Destroy that stone and get all the actors and crew out of here."

"Who are the Disciples?" Juni asks, but I wave the question away, glaring at my bemused-looking uncle.

"I still think it was only..." Dervish mutters, then pulls a face. "But I'm not going to argue with all three of you. Let's go back to the warehouse. Show me the demon. If you're right, we'll—"

"If you think we're going back inside that place, you're certifiable," Juni says, beating Bill-E and me to the punch. "Run the risk again? Give them another chance to discover what we're up to, so they can trap and murder us? No way!"

She points at the door. "We're out of here. We'll get to safety, call in help — soldiers, police, whoever the Disciples are — then have this place evacuated. I'm not happy leaving the others behind, but it will be safer to help them from the outside."

"That's the sort of plan I like," Bill-E beams. "Run for the hills, tails between our legs — excellent!"

"You're asking me to believe this and flee with you — breaking our contracts, by the way — without any proof, purely on the strength of your word?" Dervish asks sullenly.

Juni stares at him straight. "Precisely."

"That's crazy and insulting," Dervish says coolly. Then winks, looking like my real uncle for the first time in weeks. "Last one to civilisation's a rotten egg!"

→We take Juni's car. She and Dervish sit up front, me and Bill-E in the back. We drive through the heart of Slawter, heading for the connecting road to the motorway. Everybody's silent, staring out the windows. We've seen enough movies to know that this is the part where the bad guys are supposed to rumble us, block off the road, stop us from leaving.

But we see nobody except a few technicians working on the sets and they pay no attention to us. Moments later we pass the last building — an old hat store that's been designed to look like it did a hundred years ago — and are on the road to freedom.

"I bet they'll come after us," Bill-E whispers, gazing out the back window.

"No," I say. "By the time they realise we're gone it'll be morning and we'll be too far away for them to catch up."

"A pity," Bill-E sighs. "I always wanted to be part of a high-speed car chase."

Juni accelerates once we're in sight of the motorway... then slows to a stop, though she leaves the engine running. She and Dervish are staring hard ahead.

"What's wrong?" I ask, peering over Dervish's shoulder.

"There's something in the middle of the road," Juni says. "It might be rubbish sacks."

"Or a body," Dervish murmurs.

I squint but I can't see anything. "Are you sure?"

Dervish nods slowly, then looks at Juni. "Can we circle around?"

"Yes." She licks her lips. "But if it's a person in trouble..."

"No way!" Bill-E gasps. "You can't even be *thinking* about getting out!"

"It doesn't sound like the best of moves," Dervish agrees.

"I know," Juni says. "It feels like a trap. But I can't see anybody else. And if there are demons lurking, why wait for us to get out of the car? If they meant to attack, they'd have hit us as soon as we slowed."

Dervish stares out the windows, then checks the rear-view mirrors. "I'll go," he decides. "Keep the engine running. If anything happens – *anything* – slam your foot down on the accelerator and forget about me. Do *not* play the hero. Grubbs?" He glances at me, trusting me to know about life and death situations, and how to deal with them.

"We'll do what we have to," I tell him.

"Wish me luck," Dervish mutters and opens his door. Just as he's stepping out, the car shakes wildly. Dervish falls. The rest of us shriek. The engine cuts out. Juni fumbles for the key. The lights go dead. Something hits the car. A cloud of gas. Coughing, I reach for the door handle. Before my fingers find it, gas fills my mouth and nostrils. My eyes close. I groan softly. Then slump over, senses shutting down, figuring the next thing I see when – *if* – I awake will be the jaws of a ravenous demon.

→I was wrong about the demon. Instead I wake to Juni slapping my cheeks and calling my name. A far more pleasant sight than one of the Demonata!

"What happened?" I moan, sitting up, shaking my head, ears ringing, the taste of the gas still thick on my tongue.

"We were knocked out," Juni says, going to check on Dervish. I'm lying outside the car, on the road. Dervish is close by, sitting upright, massaging the back of his neck, looking around woozily. No sign of Bill-E.

"Where's Bill-E?" I ask.

"We've been unconscious for forty minutes," Juni says. "I'm not sure what they used on us. It might have been—"

"*Where's Bill-E?*" I ask again, sharply this time.

Juni looks at me steadily. "I don't know. He wasn't here when I regained consciousness."

I try to stand. Dizziness hits me hard. I stagger and sit down again.

"That happened to me too," Dervish says sluggishly.

"Why are we alive?" I ask. "Why did they spare us and only take Bill-E?"

"I don't know," Dervish says. "It doesn't make sense. This is… confusing."

"They might be playing with us," Juni says. "They could have taken Bill-E to use as bait, to lure us back to town, so they could torment us."

"If they did," Dervish says, standing slowly, groaning, "they're smart as hell. I'm not leaving him behind."

"It would be madness to return," Juni says. "We can help him more by–"

"No," I say, standing up like Dervish, fighting the dizziness. "We aren't going without Bill-E."

"But you can leave," Dervish tells Juni. "In fact it would be better that way. Us on the inside, you on the outside. You could spread the alarm and fetch help — if not for us, then for the rest of the people here."

"But…" Juni starts to argue, then stops. "No. I can see your minds are made up. I'm not going to waste time trying to talk you out of it. I'll leave, like you suggest. You can give me the names and numbers of anyone you think I should contact. I'll return as quickly as I can and just pray that's quick enough."

"I like your style," Dervish smiles, reaching out, gently touching her right cheek.

Juni smiles back. Then blinks. "Oh, here, I don't think this has anything to do with Bill-E, but..." She picks a small object off the front passenger seat and hands it to Dervish. "I found it when I came to."

Dervish stares at the object. I see his mouth tighten at the corners. A new cloud of anger rises in his eyes. His fingers clench, then relax. He holds his hand out to me. There's a silver ring nestled in his palm. A flat, circular piece on top, with a gold 'L' inscribed on it.

My eyes shoot up. Dervish and I stare at each other, more astonished than furious. If this ring is what I think it is, demons didn't kidnap Bill-E. He was taken by the *Lambs!*

PART THREE
THE LABORATORY

DISCIPLES

→We get back in the car and tear out of Slawter as fast as Juni dares drive, Dervish busy on his mobile. He makes a series of calls and speaks with six or seven different people. Juni and I listen silently, not understanding everything that he says.

When Dervish finally lays the phone down, he shuts his eyes and massages his eyelids. Juni gives him a few seconds, then says quietly, "I assume the plan is for us to go after Bill-E?"

"Yes," Dervish says.

"And those we left behind? I don't want to be insensitive, but we're talking about the lives of hundreds of people. Is Bill-E *that* important?"

"He is to me." Dervish opens his eyes and sighs. "I'm not forgetting the others. I've convinced two of my colleagues to help us get Billy back. And I'll find another couple to send to the film set."

"Only two?" Juni frowns. "Shouldn't we alert the authorities? Send in more than just a pair of your friends?"

"My *friends* have devoted their lives to dealing with the Demonata," Dervish growls. "The Disciples are people with magical abilities, accustomed to handling messes like this. They'll know what to do."

"But surely, the more back-up we provide…"

Dervish looks at Juni with a wry smile. "OK. Call the police. Tell them demons are on the loose. Draw little pictures of Lord Loss and—"

"Don't," Juni snaps. "I won't stand for sarcasm, not in my own car."

"Sorry," Dervish says. "But you have to understand, we're on our own, just us and the Disciples. That's the way it's always been. Even if you convinced the police to send in troops, they wouldn't achieve anything. Demons can only be killed by magical means. Human weapons don't affect them, not unless they're wielded by a mage. If the Disciples can't stop the massacre, nobody can."

"But—"

"No more talk," Dervish says, letting his seat back.

"You're going to sleep?" Juni snorts with disbelief.

"I'm going to try," Dervish says. "Unless you want me to drive?"

"No."

"Then wake me when we hit the airport."

And with that Dervish shuts his eyes and dozes.

Juni looks at me in the mirror, astonished. I shrug. "At least he's not acting like a brainwashed simpleton any longer," I say with a smile.

"I think I preferred him when he was!" Juni huffs.

* * *

→We have to wait four hours for a flight, then three hours in the next airport. Dervish makes more phone calls, recruiting a couple of Disciples to go to Slawter, while Juni and I use the restrooms.

I spend several minutes at one of the sinks, splashing water over my face, enjoying the coolness. As I'm dripping dry, I study my reflection in the mirror and frown. Something's not right, but I don't know what. I look much the same as always, skin a touch paler than normal, eyes a bit wider. Yet I can't shake the feeling that something's wrong. Is it my hair? I run a hand through my ginger mop — nothing amiss there.

Unable to put my finger on the problem, I go see how Dervish is getting on, then Juni and I grab a bite to eat.

"You shouldn't worry," Juni says as I nibble with disinterest at a BLT. "We'll get your brother back."

"Thanks." I start to smile, but again I'm struck by an uneasy feeling. I glance around nervously — are we being followed? But nobody's watching us. I'm just being paranoid, imagining threats that aren't really there.

→A long second flight. Seven hours in the air. Dervish fills Juni in on what's happening. Tells her about the Lambs, the visit from Prae Athim, her interest in Bill-E. Explains about the Disciples, their efforts to stop the Demonata from crossing into our world and slaughtering at will.

Dervish says he knows where the Lambs' main laboratory is situated. It's part of a vast security complex. Lots of armed guards. Breaking in will be very dangerous. He won't blame her if she doesn't want to get involved. Juni waves that away, but she's not entirely happy with the plan.

"You can't know for certain that they'll take Bill-E to this laboratory," she says. "What if they place him somewhere less obvious?"

"Then we'll find out," Dervish says flatly. "But this is as good a starting point as any."

I can't shake the edgy feeling I've had since the restroom at the airport. This feels wrong. How did the Lambs know where we were? How did they know we'd be leaving, that they could hit us outside town? And why should Prae Athim kidnap Bill-E in such a dramatic fashion? She must have known Dervish would come after her. She was scared of the Disciples the last time we spoke. Why do something guaranteed to turn them against her now?

I discuss my fears with Dervish but he dismisses them. "Prae Athim always had a chip on her shoulder about the Disciples. The Lambs don't like playing second fiddle to anyone. Maybe she sees this as their chance to test us. Or perhaps she figured we wouldn't suspect the Lambs, that we'd blame Billy's disappearance on the Demonata. If we hadn't found the ring, we'd never have guessed the Lambs were involved. We were ready to face down the demons. Maybe she hoped they'd kill us."

I remain unconvinced. That doesn't explain how Prae Athim knew about the demons in Slawter. Or how she judged her moment so finely. Or why her people would leave us for the demons to kill, instead of murdering us themselves while we were helpless. This is more involved than it seems. There's a conspiracy afoot. The Lambs in league with the Demonata? Maybe. If Lord Loss or one of his crew offered to give the Lambs the power to reverse lycanthropy, in exchange for a little help getting rid of the meddling Grubbs and Dervish Grady...

But that's crazy. We were knocked out. At their mercy. If they'd been working with the demons, they'd have simply handed us over. We'd be dead now, not flying after them in hot pursuit.

Something's wrong, but I can't pin it down and it's driving me mad.

→The plane touches down. The two Disciples meet us in the arrivals hall of the airport. A man and woman. The man's tanned, tall and bulky, with short grey hair, dressed in army fatigues. There are letters tattooed on his knuckles – S H A R K – and a small picture of a shark's head on the flesh between his thumbs and index fingers. No surprise when he tells us his name is Shark.

The woman is Indian, dressed in a colourful sari. Old. A kindly face. She walks slowly, with a pronounced limp. Hugs Dervish hard, kisses his forehead, then introduces herself to us as Sharmila Mukherji. She looks familiar, and I realise after racking my brains that Dervish and I watched a documentary about her a while ago.

"I never did like Prae Athim," Shark barks. "I'm looking forward to cutting her down to size."

"But we will have to be careful," Sharmila warns. "The Lambs should not be underestimated. They might not be able to repel us with magic, but they are well versed in other forms of warfare."

"Against us three?" Shark snorts. "They don't stand a chance! It's just a pity Kernel and Beranabus aren't here — it'd be a proper reunion."

Dervish, Sharmila and Shark smile at each other, while Juni and I share an uncertain look. Then the Disciples quickly discuss their plans and how to proceed. Before setting off, Dervish again gives Juni the option of pulling out.

"To be honest," Juni says, "I'm not comfortable. I'd rather we focused on the problems in Slawter. But if this is where you think the battle is, I'm with you. I won't quit now."

"Fighting words," Shark grins. "You're my kind of gal!" He looks around the airport, sniffs, then nods towards the exit. "Let's go round up some Lambs."

→A four-hour drive. Dervish, Shark and Sharmila discuss the past for the first hour. From what I gather, the three only fought together once before, many years ago, but kept in touch and are close friends. As we progress, talk turns to the present and tactics. Shark has seen the plans of the building and knows the layout of the laboratory, its weak points, where the greatest obstacles will be.

I fall asleep as Shark and Sharmila are discussing the plans, exhaustion catching up with me. I don't dream.

→When I wake, we're in the middle of nowhere. Dry, arid land stretches out in all directions. A huge metal and glass building stands ahead of us, ringed by a security fence, dotted with armed guards, sporting a massive antenna on the roof. It reminds me of something. I think I've seen it before, but I can't have. I've never been here.

The feeling that something's wrong sneaks up on me again, but I ignore it and focus on the conversation.

"—electrified, but that won't bother us," Shark is saying. "Once inside the perimeter, we head left. There's a small, disguised door that opens on to a corridor that cuts past a lot of the building — an emergency exit."

"What about the guards?" Juni asks.

"We'll fight them with magic," Shark says. "I would have brought a few weapons along – fight fire with fire – but Dervish vetoed the idea."

"I don't want to harm anyone," Dervish says quietly. "Most of the staff here are just ordinary people doing their job. They won't know about the kidnapping or that we only want to rescue Billy. We mustn't kill them. A person shouldn't be killed just because they're ignorant of the truth."

"You're too soft," Shark grunts, then throws his door open and smacks his right fist hard into his left palm. "Let's do it!"

→We stand outside the electrified fence, in plain sight, watching as more guards gather. They cock their weapons, eyeing us critically.

"We're here for Billy Spleen," Dervish shouts. "Tell Prae Athim we know she took him. We'll settle for his safe return. If she gives him back to us, or tells us where he is, we'll leave without a fuss. We don't have to go to war."

A high-ranking guard speaks into his headpiece. Listens to the response. Nods and addresses us through an amplifier. "This is private property. If you try to come on to our grounds, we'll use all available force to halt you."

"War it is then," Dervish sighs. He extends a hand and snaps his fingers at the fence. The wire splits and unfurls, leaving a gap wide enough to drive a bus through. The guards around it yelp with surprise and fall back a few metres. At a signal from Dervish we press ahead, marching but not running. The officer shouts a command. A group of guards raise their weapons and aim at us. Shark and Sharmila mutter a spell. The weapons melt and distort and the guards drop them, crying out that they're too hot to hold.

Gunfire from our right. Much louder than in the movies. Terrifying. I yell and duck, covering my ears with my hands, expecting to be ripped apart by bullets. Juni ducks too. But the Disciples only pause, concentrating hard. After a few seconds I realise the bullets aren't striking. Looking up, I see them dropping to the ground half a metre away. We're surrounded by a magical energy shield which the bullets can't penetrate.

"You could have told me about that!" I snap at Dervish as I stand.

"You'd have known if you'd stayed awake in the car," he retorts.

We press on.

→Shark finds the secret door and we slip inside. I'm delighted — the air was red with bullets around us, and I heard Sharmila grumble that she wasn't sure the shield was going to hold much longer. Shark shuts the door once we're all in and uses magic to seal it in place, so the troops will have to blast through to enter.

We hurry down a long, brightly lit corridor. As with the outside of the building, there's something familiar about it. I'm sure I've seen it before. This is *déjà vu* of the highest order. It's really starting to bug me.

Guards spill into the corridor as we come to the end. Shark roars as they fire upon him, then throws himself at them, scattering them like a bowling ball knocking apart a set of pins.

We slip through the gap and race down a staircase. Guards are firing at us from all directions but the shield holds. At the bottom of the staircase we wait for Shark to catch up. The volume of gunfire increases. "We could use some help," Dervish grunts at me. He's sweating.

"What do you mean?"

"Break those up," he says, nodding at the guards. "Stop them all firing at once."

"How?" I frown.

"Magic, dummy!"

"But I can't—"

"Of course you can," he snaps. "Just focus."

I feel uneasy about it, but I do as Dervish says, set my sights on a group of guards and direct a ball of magic at them. Seconds later, unnatural energy floods through me, smashes into the middle of the group of guards and sends them flying in all directions.

"Way to go!" Juni whoops.

I grin at her, pleased with myself, then disrupt more of the guards, causing as much chaos as I can, careful not to seriously injure anybody.

We advance through a series of corridors, up and down staircases, Shark leading, the rest of us – apart from Juni – providing cover from the guards. Eventually we come to a door which is operated by fingerprint recognition.

"This is your field of expertise," Sharmila says, winking at me.

"No problem." I step forward, lay my hand on the panel and trick the computer into believing I'm Prae Athim, much like I did back in the D workshops. The door slides open. We enter a large, dimly lit room. Grim brick walls. Lots of cells, cased off by hard glass panels, like those in the movie *The*

Silence of the Lambs. Several lab technicians in white jackets. A handful of guards.

And Prae Athim.

The scientist is scowling at us, her dark eyes like a couple of drill bits. "You're trespassing on private property," she growls.

Dervish laughs. "Sue us!"

"This is outrageous," Prae Athim says. "You have no right to come in here."

"*You* have no right to steal my nephew," Dervish retorts.

"I don't know what you're—" she starts to say, but before she can complete the denial, we hear a voice shouting from one of the cells.

"Dervish! Hey, Dervish, I'm in here! Help!"

Prae Athim glares at one of the technicians close to her. "I told you to dope him so he couldn't speak!"

"I did," the underling whimpers.

"Magic is stronger than drugs," Sharmila laughs. She smiles at me. "I thought they might try something like that, so I sent out a wake-up call when we came in, guaranteed to raise just about anybody who was not dead."

I race to the cell where the call came from. Bill-E's inside, smiling shakily. "What took you so long?" he says flippantly.

"We weren't going to bother coming at all," I reply, turning the glass in front of me to water, stepping back as it splashes over the floor and washes away. "But Dervish said every family needs its simpleton."

"Charming!" Bill-E huffs, then steps through the puddles of water and hugs me hard. "Thanks for not leaving me here," he whispers. I can hear tears in his voice.

"I'd never leave you behind," I whisper back, then push him away before things get any more mushy.

"Did they harm you?" Dervish asks, standing where he is, keeping a wrathful eye on the quivering Prae Athim.

"Hark at our old maid of an uncle!" Bill-E sniffs, winking at me. "Nah, they gave me some nasty injections, but they didn't have time to do much else. You came too quickly — ruined their well-laid plans."

"That's a habit of mine," Dervish laughs. He stares coolly at Prae Athim. "Now, we just have to decide what to do with—"

"No," I say softly, interrupting. Dervish glances at me, one eyebrow raised. "No," I say again, shaking my head, staring at the cells, the technicians, Prae Athim, Bill-E. My head's clearing. All the little bits that didn't add up... that seemed out of place or too familiar... I'm starting to see it now. Bill-E helped me make the breakthrough. Provided the jolt that shattered the spell. He called Dervish his uncle. Nothing wrong there — Dervish *is* his uncle. Except Bill-E doesn't know that.

"What's wrong?" Dervish asks.

"Wait," I mutter, waving his question away. Thinking hard. Cutting through the web of lies and crapola.

These cells don't just *look* like the set from *Silence of the Lambs* — this *is* Hannibal Lecter's institution. And now I realise where I've seen the building before. In James Bond movies. There are elements from several of the films, all jumbled roughly together.

I step away from Bill-E, dizzy, fighting to hold on to my train of thought. "Grubbs," Juni says, concerned, stepping towards me. "Are you OK? Can I help? Is there—"

"Shut up!" I shout, breaking through the labyrinth of untruths, rapidly, one lie falling after another, mental dominoes toppling quickly.

I'm a mage, not a true magician. I was only able to draw upon my potential in Slawter because of all the magic in the air. There's no magic in this laboratory, so how come I'm able to unleash great energy bursts and turn glass into water? The same goes for the Disciples. They shouldn't have so much power here.

All the logical hiccups and flaws reveal themselves in quick succession. The Lambs turning up at just the right moment to knock us out and kidnap Bill-E. Dervish handily knowing the location of the main laboratory. Prae Athim taking Bill-E there. Shark so conveniently having seen the plans of the building.

Sharmila knew that I'd opened the fingerprint-operated door in the D workshops — but we hadn't told her about that. In the second airport, Juni referred to Bill-E as my brother — but she doesn't know we're related.

And in the restroom, the first time I became aware that something was wrong. I get it now, what I saw but couldn't make connect. My reflection was *clean*. It had been all the time, even before I washed my face. Clean skin, hair, clothes. No grey demon blood. But I got soaked in the D chamber. I never washed the blood off. It should have been caked on at the airport, just as it should be now. But it wasn't and it isn't, because...

"None of this is real!" I scream, startling everyone around me.

"Grubbs," Juni says softly. "Calm down. You're losing control."

"You're not real!" I shout. "None of you are!"

"What's wrong with him?" Dervish snaps at Juni.

"I don't know. Maybe he—"

The magic part of me whispers something. It's been quiet all this time, even while I thought I was working magic. But now it breaks its silence and tells me what to say. Ignoring the chatterings of the figures around me, I bellow out loud, words of magic and power. Prae Athim's face contorts with hatred. Demon eyes glare at me. She shrieks, as do all the scientists and guards — but it's too late.

The walls of the cells bubble. The human Lambs turn into demons, then fade. A red haze comes down around Dervish and the others. Magic phrases trip off my tongue. Pain washes over me. I fall to my knees but keep on shouting, ripping the vision to pieces. The redness thickens. Fills the room, blocking out everything, humans, demons, all.

I utter the final words of the spell and wearily close my eyes.

Everything goes silent.

PART FOUR
DEMONS-A-GO-GO

WAKEY WAKEY

→Dervish snoring. When I hear that, I know I'm back in the real world — there's no mimicking a dreadful, pig-choking noise like that! I open my eyes and sit up, groggy, head pounding, utterly confused but no longer ensnared by the dream reality of the laboratory.

I'm in a small, dark room, chinks of light sneaking in around the edges of a dusty old set of blinds. Propped up on a bare wooden floor. Dervish and Bill-E spread out next to me. Both asleep.

"Dervish," I mumble, shaking him hard. No answer. I shake him again, hissing his name in his ear, not too loud in case anybody's on the other side of the door. Still no response. I roll up his eyelids with one hand and snap my fingers in front of his eyes with the other. He carries on snoring.

You were all dreaming the same thing, the magic part of me whispers. *They're still trapped inside it. They can't wake themselves. You'll have to use magic to bring them back.*

It tells me the words to use. I murmur them softly, feeling magic flow out of me, into my uncle and brother. They stir.

Bill-E moans. Dervish grunts something about an armadillo. Their eyelids flicker and they struggle awake.

"What's happening?" Bill-E groans.

"Where are we?" Dervish asks. "Where's Prae Athim? Sharmila? Shark? The—"

"That was bull," I cut in, steadying him as he tries to stand. "Easy. Don't make any noise. We're probably under guard."

"I don't understand. What...?" He stares around, forehead creased.

"It was a dream. The kidnapping, meeting up with the Disciples, the lab. None of that was real. It was all fantasy."

"Don't be crazy!" Dervish snaps. "I know the difference between..." He stops. Thinks about it. His jaw drops. "Bloody hell. It had me fooled completely."

"Me too, for a while. But bits didn't add up. There were mistakes."

"The lab," Dervish says slowly. "It looked familiar. Now I know why — I got the image from Franz Kafka's book, *The Trial*."

"Kafka?" I frown. "It looked like buildings from James Bond movies. And the cells were straight out of *Silence of the Lambs*."

"What are you talking about?" Bill-E says. "The cells were like something in a sci-fi flick, all those control panels and lasers."

"We provided our own dream variations," Dervish says wonderingly. He rises, panting, and leans against a wall until his legs support him. He staggers to the blinds and parts a few slats. Peers out. Then looks at us. "We're still in Slawter. We never left. Grubbs is right — it was all an illusion."

Dervish walks around the room, giving his head time to clear, flexing his legs and arms. "I forgot how cunning the Demonata are. They're masters of deception. They found out we were leaving, or they had a barrier in place to stop anyone getting out. Blocked us with magic. Created an insane scenario which seemed logical to us. Since our minds were active and focused on the dream – thinking that was reality – we couldn't wake up."

"Why not simply drug us?" Bill-E asks.

"They're demons. They don't work that way." Dervish chuckles. "I can't believe I fell for it. Walking on to the planes without tickets. Breezing through customs, nobody asking to see our passports."

"I didn't spot that," I wince.

"What about you, Billy?" Dervish asks. "Notice anything out of place?"

"No," Bill-E says, scratching his head. "Although I did think it strange that some of the nurses weren't wearing any…" He coughs and blushes.

"They wanted us out of the way," Dervish says, "so they subdued us. They could have killed us, but I guess they want us around for the finale. If Lord Loss is masterminding this, he won't want to slaughter us while we're sleeping. He'll want to make us suffer first, so he can feast on our pain and gloat."

"We have to get out of here," I pant, getting up, fighting off a wave of dizziness. "We have to stop them. Get everybody out. Call the Disciples."

"What about Juni?" Bill-E asks, and Dervish and I flinch, only now realising that she isn't with us.

"They're probably keeping her in another room," Dervish says.

"Why?" Bill-E frowns.

"I don't know. It doesn't matter. There isn't time to think about it."

He strides to the door and presses an ear against it. I can tell by Bill-E's expression that he's going to push Dervish about Juni. I slip up beside him and whisper, "Dervish didn't say it because he didn't want to freak you out, but Juni's probably dead. That's why she isn't here."

Bill-E stares at me, ashen-faced. "But she was in the laboratory…"

"So were a lot of people. That doesn't mean anything." I squeeze his arm. "Dervish cares about Juni a lot, but he can't think about her now. We can't either. We can hope for the best, and if we're lucky we'll find her, sleeping like we were. But if she's not… if the worst has happened… we have to overlook it. We have ourselves to worry about. And all the others."

Bill-E trembles, but nods reluctantly. I squeeze his arm again, then help him to his feet. When he's able to walk, we edge up behind Dervish, who's still listening intently at the door. "Anything?" I ask.

"No. But that doesn't mean there's no one there. Or no *thing*."

"We can't wait in here forever," I note.

"True." Dervish looks over his shoulder at me. "Ready to fight?"

I crack my knuckles. "Damn straight."

"Then let's go for it."

He turns the handle and slams open the door.

Nobody's outside. We creep along a damp, musky corridor. We're in one of the town's original buildings. It hasn't been renovated. Holes in the walls, rotting floorboards, broken windows.

"How much of that dream world was real?" I ask Dervish, trying to calm my nerves by focusing on something other than the possibility that we might run into a team of demons any second. "Sharmila and Shark — do they really exist?"

"Yes," Dervish says. "And pretty much the way we saw them — or at least the way *I* saw them. From your viewpoint, was Shark wearing army fatigues? Sharmila a sari?"

"Yes."

"Then that much we shared." Dervish pauses and looks at me. "How did you know it wasn't real? What tipped you off?"

"Lots of little things. But it was when…" I glance at Bill-E. "What did you say to Dervish when we broke you out?"

Bill-E thinks a moment. "I'm not sure. Something like, 'Hey, neighbour, what took you so long?'"

"I heard you say something else, something you shouldn't have said. That let me draw the different pieces together."

"What did I say?" Bill-E asks.

"It's not important," I lie, not wanting to tell him that in my version he knew Dervish was his uncle.

"You were clever to break the illusion," Dervish says. "Even if I'd twigged, I'm not sure I could have woken up. A spell like that will normally divert you down another path when you start to suspect something, lead you into the middle of another dream."

"Maybe it has," I laugh edgily. "Maybe this isn't real and we're still lying on a floor somewhere, asleep."

Dervish grunts dismissively. "I'm not *that* gullible. This is the real world. We're awake. I'm sure of it." But he looks around nervously all the same. Then his gaze settles on me again. "If we come through this, you and I need to have a talk."

"What about?"

"Magic. You're doing things you shouldn't be able to. I want to know how."

"No big mystery," I shrug. "I'm just drawing magic out of the air, putting it to good use, like when we fought Artery and Vein."

"Hmm," Dervish says, unconvinced. He licks his lips and focuses. We're almost at the back door. I can hear voices outside. But they're human voices and they fade quickly — people walking past.

"What now?" Bill-E asks. "Do we try driving out of town again?"

"No," Dervish says. "We have to alert the others. Tell people what they're up against. They might not believe us, so we'll have to be firm. Get them out of here, even if we have to force them. Fight if necessary — and I expect it will be. If we're lucky, we'll only have to worry about Chuda and his human accomplices."

"And if we're unlucky?" I murmur.

"Let's not think about that," he says, then opens the door and walks out to face whatever hell awaits.

ASSEMBLY CALL

→On the outskirts of Slawter. Proceeding slowly, Dervish slightly ahead of Bill-E and me, one hand held palm up, trying to determine whether or not there's a barrier in place. He said we should determine the lay of the land before raising the alarm. No point trying to herd dozens of people out of town if they're going to be knocked out by a magically enforced shield.

"Why aren't we hungry?" Bill-E asks, checking the date on his watch. "We've been asleep for... hell on a Harley! Six days! We should be ravenous but I don't even feel peckish."

"Trust you to be thinking about your stomach at a time like this!" I snort.

Dervish laughs gently. "No, it's a good question. The answer's simple — magic. We were cocooned from the demands of the real world. Hunger and thirst will hit us later, if we make it out, but right now we're still operating by the magical rules of Slawter."

"Is there anything magic can't do?" Bill-E asks.

"Not much," Dervish says, then draws up short. His fingers are trembling. He moves his hand left, right, left again. "Can you feel it?"

"No," Bill-E frowns.

"Yes." I take a step forward, sniffing the air. It doesn't smell different, but it feels wrong. I raise a hand like Dervish, slide it forward, sense power building against it.

"No further," Dervish says. "We don't want to disturb the fabric of the barrier — it might tip off our enemies."

"What is it?" I ask.

"In non-technical terms, a bubble of magic. They've sealed off the town. Enclosed it within a magical sphere, like putting a giant glass bowl over everything." He frowns. "No demon is powerful enough to create a barrier this size, not in our universe. They're using the stone you saw in the D workshops. It must be a functioning lodestone, a reservoir of ancient power. There aren't many left in the world. The magic drained from most of them centuries ago. Others were deliberately destroyed, to prevent them falling into the hands of demonic mages.

"This is worse than I thought. With the power of a lodestone at their disposal, they can build a tunnel. Dozens of demons can cross and run riot within the barrier. Stay as long as they like. Nobody will be able to escape."

"We have to stop them!" Bill-E gasps. "We can, can't we, Dervish?"

"Of course," Dervish says wearily, lowering his hand. "If we shatter the lodestone, the bubble will burst. But now that we know about it, the Demonata will have increased security around the warehouse. They're not stupid."

"We have to try," I say quietly. "We can't stand by and let people die."

"You're forgetting our earlier conversation," Dervish says with a bitter smile. "The Disciples often let people die. In a situation like this, we'd normally sit back and let the Demonata run their course. We don't have the power to stop them. Better to conserve our strength and fight them when we have a chance of winning."

"But this is different," I growl. "We know these people."

"That's not enough of a reason to get involved. I've had to sacrifice friends to demons before."

"Don't tell me you mean to—" I start to explode.

"Easy," Dervish calms me. "We won't stand by idly. We can't. Because you're right, this *is* different. We're caught up in it. If we don't find a way out, it's not just the cast and crew of *Slawter* who'll perish — we'll die too."

→Heading into the heart of town. Dervish says there might be another way out of this mess — burst through a small section of the bubble, creating a temporary gap through which we can flee. But we're not powerful enough to do it ourselves. We need to pin a demon against the bubble, then explode it with magic. By focusing the energy generated, we should be able to blast a hole through the barrier, which we can keep open for a while, allowing people to slip out.

Should. No guarantees.

One of our main problems will be getting a demon in the right place, at the right time. We can't just march into the D Workshops and ask one of them to come to the barrier with us.

But before that, we have to figure a way to convince the rest of the crew and cast that we're not crazy, their lives are in danger, demons are real, they have to trust us if they want to live. To that end, we're heading for Davida Haym's offices. If she's innocent – bloody unlikely! – Dervish hopes to recruit her and use her to issue a general alarm. If, as we suspect, she's in league with the Demonata, he plans to make her confess in public, to persuade the others to trust us.

It's hair-raising stuff, sneaking through town, ducking down side-alleys, keeping out of sight. We don't know who our enemies are. Dervish doesn't think many humans will be working for the demons, that most of the people here are innocent. But we can't be sure who to trust. We know a few of the traitors — Chuda Sool and Tump Kooniart, the guards who were with Kuk and his father when they disappeared, probably Davida. But there will be more. We can't expose ourselves and risk raising the alarm.

I suggest making ourselves invisible. Dervish vetoes the idea. "Powerful demons can sense magic being used. We've been lucky so far, but every time one of us draws on the power in the air, we risk pinpointing our position."

So we steal through town unassisted by magic. Luckily, although it's afternoon, Slawter is quiet, not many people about. We make it to Davida's offices unnoticed and let ourselves in. One of her secretaries is usually stationed at the front desk, but our luck holds — the chair is vacant. We slip past and into the main office, the hub of operations, from which all orders flow.

Davida isn't here. The office is empty. Lots of papers, small demon models, a miniature set of the town, maps on the walls with scores of dates, names, times, schedules. But no Davida Haym.

"Go through the drawers," Dervish says, hurrying to one of the many file cabinets in the room. "Look for anything that might give us an advantage — plans, a list of demons, spells, whatever."

"You think she'll keep details like that in unlocked cabinets?" Bill-E asks.

"No," Dervish sighs. "But it'll keep us busy. And you never know — we might strike lucky."

Rooting through drawers, pulling out folders, glancing through the pages, then discarding them, scattering them across the floor, not caring about the mess we're making.

I'm halfway through a drawer when Bill-E makes a shushing sound and hurries to the door. He listens for a second, then nods — people are coming. Dervish and I move up next to him, taking cover behind the door, crouching low so as not to be visible through the upper panels of glass in the office wall.

Footsteps. Two people talking. The door opens.

"...*have* to get it right," Davida Haym says, stepping into the office. "This is a one-time deal. If we blow it, we won't—" She spots the mess and stops.

"What the hell?" Chuda Sool says, stepping up beside her.

Dervish springs to his feet. His right hand comes flying up, fingers curled into a fist. He punches Chuda's jaw like a professional boxer. Chuda grunts and spins aside, smacking hard into the glass of the upper wall, cracking it. Bill-E and I leap on Davida as she screams. We pull her down and cover her mouth with our hands. She tries to bite but we jam our hands down more firmly.

Dervish closes in on Chuda, who's dazed but still on his feet. Chuda tries to block Dervish's next punch, but it penetrates, grazing the side of his head, not connecting as firmly as the first blow, but knocking Chuda back a few more centimetres. I always knew Dervish was stronger than he looked but I've never seen him in this sort of kick-ass mode before. It's cool!

Chuda grabs a paperweight from Davida's desk and swings it round, but Dervish blocks his arm and knocks it aside. Chuda roars and gets the fingers of one hand on Dervish's throat. Dervish lets him squeeze, cool as ice, sizing him up.

Then he pummels a fist into Chuda's stomach. Chuda grunts. His fingers loosen. Dervish takes a step back, judges the angle, then takes one final crack at his opponent's jaw. Chuda's head snaps back, his eyes flutter shut and he slumps to the floor.

Dervish turns away from Chuda, panting lightly. His eyes fall on Davida, still struggling beneath Bill-E and me. He jerks his head at us. We slide off. Davida starts to sit up, spluttering furiously. Before she completes the move, Dervish puts a foot on her chest and pushes her back down. Stands over her like a triumphant gladiator, fixing her with a glare which is evil in its intensity.

"Now, lady," he snarls, "it's time for you to talk. And you're going to tell me exactly what I want to hear." He moves his foot up to her throat. "Or I'll do things to you that would make a demon blanch."

→You have no right to do this," Davida says sourly. Dervish has allowed her to rise. She's sitting in her plush leather chair, glaring at us. "When I tell security what you've done, you'll be in so much—"

"We know about the Demonata," Dervish snaps. "Lord Loss and his familiars. The barrier and the lodestone in the D workshops. You can't fool us any longer. So talk."

Davida pinches her lips shut. We think she's working with the demons, but we're not sure. I guess Dervish figures it's best to assume the worst and treat her harshly. He can apologise later if she's innocent.

"Don't think I won't do terrible things to you," Dervish says softly. "I obey human laws when it suits, but break them without hesitation when I must. The only reason I haven't gone to work on you is the boys. But I'm five seconds away from sending them out to the next room and doing whatever I have to to get answers."

"You don't know what you're interfering with," Davida snarls, betraying herself, confirming our worst suspicions. "This is way beyond anything you can imagine."

"You underestimate my imagination," Dervish smiles icily.

"These are real demons, you fool! They can do things you wouldn't believe. If you mess with them, you'll wind up—"

"I've been messing with the Demonata for decades," Dervish interrupts. "Now tell me your story. How deep are you in this? What did they promise? Power? Magic? Eternal life?"

"They promised nothing except what I asked for — a great movie."

Dervish frowns. "We're past that stage. Your lousy movie cover is blown. I want to know the real reason why—"

"*Cover?*" Davida laughs contemptuously. "It was never a *cover*. I'm making the greatest horror film ever. A movie with real demons, doing what real demons do, captured on film — what better reason could there be than that?"

Dervish's frown deepens. "You're telling me that was the trade-off? You helped the demons cross to our world, provided them with all the victims you could and they agreed to be filmed? It was as shallow as that?"

"You know nothing about movie-making," Davida sneers. "Life is shallow. It's meaningless. Life passes and is forgotten within minutes. But movies endure. A film outlives everyone involved. If it's good enough. If it's magical."

She leans forward intently. "You think I'm evil and you're probably right. I brought all these people here, knowing they'd die. But we all die in the end. Pointless, forgettable deaths. We fade and it's like we never existed. We come, we live, we die, and that's that. Not much of a story, huh?

"But that's about to change for you, me, everybody here. We'll become part of history. I'm making a movie which will survive as long as the human race itself. Demons will attack... kill hundreds of people in unimaginable ways... and I'll capture it all on camera. Splice it in with the other scenes I shot. Make the most shocking horror film ever. I'll be notorious, yes, feared and despised. I'll be imprisoned, maybe executed. But I'll be *remembered*. And so will the others. And that's the most any of us can hope for."

She stops, breathing heavily, face flushed.

"She's loco," Bill-E says. "How come she wasn't locked up years ago?"

Dervish shakes his head in wonderment. "You planned to let these people be butchered in the name of art, so you could film the massacre and turn it into entertainment. That's a new one. I've seen crazy mages bring the Demonata into our world for all sorts of reasons — but never to break box-office records."

"You don't get it," Davida laughs. "This is immortality. It will put us up with the ranks of the great. We'll mingle with the giants of history — Caesar, Alexander, Napoleon. The world will always want to see this film, to experience true terror, to get as close as they can to the reality of the demonic."

"You're deluding yourself," Dervish says. "There won't be a film. Even if you capture the footage, you won't live to edit it. The Demonata will kill you along with the rest of us. You'll be a brief news item — nothing more."

"No," Davida insists. "We have a deal. I give them you, they let me make my film."

"Do you have that in writing?" Dervish chuckles, then stops. "What do you mean, you give them *us?*"

"I've spent the last several years recruiting demons," Davida says. "I got a few lesser demons involved once I laid my hands on the lodestone and they saw that I was serious, but I needed a demon master. By myself, I could only use the stone to create a brief window between universes. I knew a demon master could help me use it to build a tunnel, letting many more demons cross and giving them plenty of time to cavort.

"The trouble is, demon masters are hard to contact. I managed to find one – Lord Loss – but he wasn't interested. I pushed ahead anyway, determined to make the best of what

I had. Then, a few months ago, Lord Loss sent one of his most trusted servants to me and offered his services — *if* I could lure you and the two boys to the set. Lord Loss hates you. He wanted you to be here, to suffer horribly before he personally ripped you to pieces."

"So you came to Carcery Vale to ensnare me," Dervish says bitterly. "Did you cast a spell? Mess with my mind?"

"Of course," Davida smirks. "It wasn't that difficult, or so I've been told — I didn't do it myself. Your brain was all over the place. Quite easy to manipulate. You fell into our trap without any complications. I'm just surprised you recovered your senses now. You weren't supposed to wake until tomorrow, when the bloodshed was in full flow. Still, it doesn't really matter. Your timing's slightly ahead of schedule, but only just. It's far too late for you to make a nuisance of yourself."

"What do you mean?" Dervish growls.

"You don't know?" Davida giggles with delight. "I did think it strange that you were here, grilling me instead of… I thought you hoped to use me as a shield, to bargain your way out. But you really don't know, do you?"

"What the hell are you—" Dervish starts to shout, but is cut short by a voice outside, amplified by a loudspeaker.

"Ten minutes," the voice says. "Will everyone please assemble immediately outside the D workshops. Ten minutes to showtime, folks!"

Dervish stares at Davida, face whitening. She giggles again. "It's the final scene, Grady. When the demons break through and hell erupts. We brought it forward once you found out the truth — we couldn't keep you comatose indefinitely. The actors and crew think the heroes in the movie will save the day. But that's not how it's going to work. I've a surprise up my sleeve. Dozens of demons who aren't playing by the rules of monster movies, who don't have weak spots, who aren't going to be thwarted by a clean-cut movie brat with a cool haircut and a dazzling smile."

Davida looks at her watch and smiles serenely. "Nine more minutes. Then Lord Loss and his familiars burst out of the D warehouse and kill just about every living soul in town." She brings her hands up and claps slowly, to emphasise each word. "Lights! Camera! *Slawter*!"

THE REAL STARS
OF THE SHOW

→Dervish rushes out of the office, leaving a laughing Davida and unconscious Chuda Sool behind. Bill-E and I hurry after him. "Shouldn't we have tied Davida up or knocked her out?" I pant, running fast to catch up with Dervish.

"No time," he barks.

We race through the mostly deserted streets of Slawter. Dervish spots a group of people making their way to the assembly point. He roars, "Get out! Go back!" They stop and stare at him oddly.

"There's been an explosion!" Bill-E yells, lurching up behind us. "They think it's a gas leak. The entire gas system's been compromised. There could be further detonations anywhere within town. We have to get out. *Now!*"

"Good one," I compliment him as the panicked group turns and heads west.

"We need to think about this logically," he gasps, face red

from running. "If we tell people that demons are going to kill them, they'll think we're mad."

"So we make it a gas leak instead," I nod. "Get them moving away from the danger zone. You hear that, Dervish?"

"Whatever," he grunts. "But in another few minutes we won't have to tell them anything — they'll see the demons themselves."

→We round a corner and approach the gigantic D warehouse. A huge crowd has gathered outside. Most of the people are at the southern end, but some spill around the east and west wings of the building. There are cameras everywhere, on tripods and cranes, in the hands of cameramen mingling with the crowd, a couple on top of the warehouse roof. I guess the cameramen are part of Davida's inner circle, wise to the Demonata, otherwise she couldn't trust them to man their posts when the chaos erupts.

Several of the crew have megaphones and are directing the crowd. Dervish storms over to the nearest one – a young man with a ponytail – grabs the megaphone and shouts into it, "Gas leak! There have been explosions! Everybody out! We have to evacuate *now!*"

Uncertain mutterings among the crowd. People stop talking and stare at Dervish. He's running up and down, repeating his message, gesturing in all directions, telling people they have to make for the outskirts of town immediately.

Before anyone can move, a large man steps forward with a megaphone of his own. It's Tump Kooniart. "Ignore that lunatic!" Tump roars. "It's Dervish Grady. We fired him last week. He's trying to disrupt proceedings to get his own back. Guards — seize him! The boys too!"

Security guards move forward. Dervish curses and tosses his megaphone aside. "Enough of this gas-leak crap," he mutters. "Time to open their eyes."

Dervish says something magical and points at the guards closing in on him. They float up several metres into the air with yells of alarm and fear. All around us, jaws drop. Eyes fix on the floating guards, then on Dervish, who looks like a man charged full of electricity.

Dervish touches a couple of fingers to his throat and addresses the crowd, his voice far louder than it was with the aid of the megaphone. "You're all going to die. Davida Haym has struck a deal with demons. *Real* demons. They're going to break out of the warehouse in a couple of minutes and kill everyone. Unless you flee now, you're doomed."

"Ignore him!" Tump Kooniart screams. "He's lost his mind!"

I see Bo and Abe close behind their father. They look worried, scared, incredulous, like most of the people around us.

"Real demons?" Tump snorts. "Madness! He's trying to wreck the shoot. He—"

Tump Kooniart chokes, drops the megaphone, falls to his knees, face purple, hands clawing at his throat and mouth.

"Don't kill him," I whisper in Dervish's ear.

"He deserves to die," Dervish snarls, looking completely unlike the gentle man I've lived with all these months.

"Maybe," I say, voice trembling. "But we don't have the right to kill people. We're trying to save them, even those who don't deserve it."

Dervish snorts, but breaks the spell. Tump Kooniart breathes again.

"Listen to us," I shout, using magic to amplify my voice. "I know it's hard to believe, but you can see the guards floating overhead. You can hear our voices, even though we're not using any equipment. Your lives are in danger. You have to run now or else—"

"Enough!" Davida Haym screams, her voice even louder than mine or Dervish's. The guards fall back to earth, some injuring themselves badly. Davida's standing behind us, a groggy Chuda Sool by her side. Her eyes are blazing. "You're not going to ruin my movie! Cameramen — are you ready?" Dozens nod and shout that they are. "Sound?" Davida cries.

Dervish raises a hand to stop her. Before he can, he's spun aside by a magical force. It's not Davida's work. Doesn't look like Chuda's doing it either. There must be a powerful, hidden mage somewhere in the crowd.

"Sound?" Davida shouts again and this time there's an answering bellow. "All right. Let's dispense with the countdown and cut to the chase. You lot inside the warehouse — it's time to make your grand entrance.

"*Action!*" she roars, and the hounds of hell are unleashed.

→The giant door in the middle of the southern wall of the warehouse explodes outwards. Those nearest it are caught by flying splinters, some as long as my arm. Most go down screaming, though a few are torn apart and killed instantly by the shrapnel.

Stunned silence from those not struck by the debris of the blast. Everybody's staring at the wounded and dead. Wondering if this is real or part of the movie. They live in a make-believe world where anything can happen and nobody is ever really hurt. Their senses tell them this is different, it's not part of a script, they should run. But the movie-making part of their brain is trying to figure out how the explosion was arranged and how the scattering of the splinters was timed so as not to harm anybody — struggling to convince themselves that those on the ground are acting, the blood isn't real, it can't be.

Dervish is back up on his feet. Staring at the hole in the wall like the rest of us. The explosion created clouds of dust around the doorway. As they clear, a figure glides forward from within the warehouse. Pale red skin, lumpen, no heart, eight arms — who else but the ringmaster himself, Lord Loss?

"Alas," he sighs, looking around sadly. "Here we all are. Bound by chains of blood and death. No way out. Doomed.

Dervish tried to warn you, to save you, but he failed. Here you are trapped. Here you will die."

One of the cameramen moves in for a close-up. "Yes," I hear Davida murmur. I glance back. She's speaking into a microphone, directing the cameraman. "His face first, then pan down to the hole in his chest. I want to see those snakes slithering."

Lord Loss gazes without much interest into the camera. He smiles slightly, then runs his eyes over the crowd, judging their mood, taking in their expressions, most more confused than terrified. "Ah," he notes. "You do not believe. You think this is part of the film. That I am a movie prop." He chuckles. "It is time to burst that bubble of misperception."

He moves to one side. I glimpse other shapes behind him. Eyes. Tendrils. Teeth. Claws. Fangs. "Now, my darlings," Lord Loss whispers.

The demons spill out in their dozens, each one more misshapen and nightmarish than the last. A variety of vile monsters, spitting bile, oozing pus and blood, screeching and howling with malicious glee. They collide with the shocked members of the cast and crew closest to the building. Cut into and through them, severing limbs and heads, disembowelling, biting and clawing.

Realisation hits the masses swift and hard. A single scream rings out. Then a volley of them. Panic sweeps the crowd. A stampede develops, everyone wanting to get away from the demons, trampling over one another, the weak going down in the crush, dying beneath the feet of their workmates. Anarchy at its most destructive and terrifying.

Lord Loss laughs and his laughter carries over the sounds of the screams. I'm rooted to the spot, unable to react, heart jackhammering, not wanting this to be happening, wishing I could be anywhere in the world but here.

I see the cameraman who moved forward turning away to capture the scenes of mayhem. "Not yet!" Davida snaps. "Stay on the hole. Give me a close up."

The cameraman steps right up to Lord Loss's chest, manoeuvring his camera to within a few centimetres of the writhing, hissing snakes. He moves his head from behind the camera to check something — and one of the snakes strikes. It lashes out from within the hole where Lord Loss's heart should be. Sinks its tiny fangs into the cameraman's left cheek. He yelps, drops his camera and tries to pull away. But the snake has a firm hold. It yanks him closer so his face plunges into the hole. And now all the snakes are biting. The cameraman's arms and legs thrash wildly, then go still. He falls away a few seconds later, his face a blood-red map of bites and rips, skin flailed, bone cracked, brains dribbling down his chin.

"No!" Davida gasps. "He hadn't finished the shot! They shouldn't have…"

She stops and studies the demons tearing into the humans. They're drawing no distinction between the intended victims and the collaborators, dragging down cameramen and other technicians as well as the unsuspecting members of the cast and crew.

"*No!*" Davida screeches. "We had a deal!"

Lord Loss looks at her sneeringly. "I do not make deals with fools. I promised you chaos, which you and your underlings could film, but I never said I would spare any of you. You simply assumed — and assumed wrong." He smiles at me. "Greetings, Grubitsch. Such a pleasure to see you again. I will take much satisfaction from your long, slow, painful death."

"Not today!" Dervish bellows and suddenly he's by my side, right hand raised. He fires off a bolt of energy at Lord Loss. The demon master deflects it, but is knocked sideways. "Come on!" Dervish snaps at me and Bill-E. "We have to get out of here."

"But what about...?" I gesture at the fleeing people.

"We'll summon them when – if – we blast a way out," Dervish says. "The best thing they can do for now is flee. That will delay the demons and buy us some time."

"But–" Bill-E begins.

"No arguments!" Dervish barks. "Follow me now or, so help me, I'll leave you for the bloody Demonata!"

With that he turns and flees south, sidestepping the stunned, frozen Davida Haym. There's no sign of Chuda, who must have deserted her when he realised they were going to perish along with those they'd planned to sacrifice. I'm not sure where he thinks he can run to or hide, but he fled anyway.

Davida can't move. She's weeping, seeing all her dreams of immortality go up in flames. I'd like to say I feel sorry for her, but I don't. All I can think right now is, "Serves you right, you mad old cow!"

Then Bill-E and I are past the desolate producer, following Dervish through the warren of streets and alleys of Slawter, the screams of the dying and yowls of the demons rising all the time.

→Twisting and turning, Dervish in the lead, no apparent route in mind. He stops in the middle of a street. There are doors on either side of us. Handy for a getaway if we're attacked. "Are you OK?" he asks us.

"Any reason we should be?" I reply calmly, hiding my terror as best I can.

Bill-E says nothing. He looks like a shell-shocked soldier. As awful as I feel, I think Bill-E feels a hell of a lot worse.

"Billy?" Dervish says softly. "Are you with us? Are all the lights on in there?" He taps the side of Bill-E's head.

"They killed them," Bill-E wheezes, his lazy left eyelid snapping open and shut at great speed. "I saw a thing with… it looked like a tiger… but bits and pieces sticking out… it killed Salit. He tried to stop it. He didn't know it was real. He was acting his movie part, where he was a big hero. But it cut him down the middle and—"

"We don't have time for hysterics," Dervish growls. "Be a man and help us fight, or go and babble somewhere until the demons find and kill you."

I hate him for saying that, but I know he's only doing it for Bill-E's sake. Cruel to be kind and all that guff.

Bill-E glares at Dervish, anger driving the fear away. "I'm not hysterical," he says stiffly.

"Glad to hear it," Dervish says. "Now listen and listen good. Lord Loss is the only demon master. The rest are his familiars or others Davida roped in. Some are stronger than us but most aren't. We need to capture one of the weaker demons and use it to get out."

"And the other people?" I ask quietly.

"We'll take as many as we can," Dervish promises. "If we're successful, I'll send a telepathic signal and let all the survivors know where we are."

"Why not do that now?" I ask. "Arrange a meeting place and tell them to go there. It would give them more time, a better chance."

Dervish shakes his head. "Those who were working for the Demonata would receive the message too. They'd go running to Lord Loss — try to save their own foul lives by selling out the rest of us."

"OK," I mutter. "So how do we catch a demon?"

Dervish scratches his left cheek nervously. "Bait," he says softly. And his gaze settles on Bill-E.

* * *

→I don't like it. Hell, I hate it! But it's the quickest, easiest way. We're up to our eyeballs in trouble. We have to take risks.

We leave Bill-E standing in the middle of the street, twisting his hands, face crumpled with fear. He trusts us but he's terrified. I would be too in his shoes.

"If anything happens to him…" I whisper to Dervish.

"It won't," Dervish says solidly. "Now don't talk — watch."

A minute passes. Two. Screams fill the air, a chorus of agony and anguish. Every hair on my body is standing upright. I have to keep my teeth parted, afraid I'll grind down to the gums if I don't take care. Part of me wants to run, make for the barrier, force a way through, forget everybody else. *Save your own skin*, it whispers. *Dervish and Bill-E are the only ones who matter. Convince them to leave with you. Let the others look after themselves.*

I ignore the treasonous, selfish voice — but only with an effort.

Movement at the end of the street. Several figures come racing around a corner. Dervish and I tense, ready to unleash a burst of magic, then hold it back when we see that the figures are children. Bo Kooniart, Vanalee Metcalf, three others.

"Run!" Bo screams at Bill-E. "We're being chased! Get the hell out of here, you moron, before—"

"Bo!" I yell. "Over here." She stops, panting, eyes wide with terror. "Quick!"

"But there's—"

"I know. Trust us. We can stop it. But you have to—"

"Here it comes," Dervish interrupts.

I look left. A demon with the body of a giant bee is humming through the air after Bo and the others. As it gets closer I see that it has a semi-human face, except with bee eyes and more teeth than any human I've ever seen. Magic flares within me. I stretch out a hand in the direction of the bee demon.

"Not yet," Dervish says. "Let it get closer… closer… *Now!*"

Together we channel magic and unleash it. Twin bolts of energy strike the demon sharply, knocking it across the street, away from the children. It smashes into the wall on the opposite side. As it slumps to the ground, Dervish runs towards it. I follow, caught up in the moment, acting instinctively.

The bee shakes its head and starts to rise, buzzing angrily. Dervish grabs a wing before it gets out of reach. Yanks it down. The bee lashes out at him with a stinger the size of a large kitchen knife. He ducks. I scream and smash an elbow into the bee's semi-human face. Its teeth bite deep into my forearm, but I jerk my arm free before it can do serious damage.

As I grab the bee with my uninjured arm, I feel Dervish's magic burn into the demon. It makes wild buzzing sounds. Thrashes, trying to break free, snapping its teeth, stabbing at him with its stinger. He holds on tight. I do too. I head-butt the bee, letting magic shoot through my forehead, intent on sizzling the demon's brains.

"Not too much!" Dervish pants as the demon goes slack. "We want it alive." He stands, sliding both arms around the bee. "Let's keep it like this and—"

"*Monster!*" a voice screams and suddenly there's someone beside us. A hand shoots by my head. A fist buries itself deep in the demon's chest, then comes ripping out, dragging guts and yellow blood with it. Stunned, I fix on the face of the assailant — and my heart leaps joyfully.

"*Juni!*" I yell, releasing the bee's head, throwing my arms around her.

Juni Swan hugs me hard, then steps away, staring at the demon, then her fist. "How did I do that?" she croaks. "I felt something inside me. It was power, but I don't know where…"

"Hi," Dervish says quietly, letting the dead demon drop to the floor. He smiles crookedly, then slips his arms around Juni and buries his face in her neck. "We thought you were dead," he half sobs.

"I was… dreaming, I think," she says. "Bill-E was kidnapped. We rescued him. Then we were attacked by ninjas and had to go to a mountain in search of their lair." She shakes her head. "I woke up in a small room. I came out and saw demons. I fled. Then I saw you. I thought the bee was going to kill you. Something exploded inside me. Before I knew it…"

She stares at her fist again, a look of astonishment on her face.

"Seems you have a talent for magic after all," Dervish chuckles, then sighs. "But you timed it badly. We wanted this one alive." He quickly explains his plan to her and the children, who've crept across. Bo seems to be less shaken than the others. She's trembling fiercely and her face is white with fear, but she's in control of her senses and listens intently.

I use magic to heal my wounded arm and watch Bo cautiously. Her father was one of the collaborators but that's not her fault. I'm pretty sure she didn't know about his pact with the Demonata. Bo was never anything worse than a spoilt brat. You don't deserve to be killed for that.

Dervish finishes outlining his plan. "So Grubbs, Juni and I will pull back, leave you kids here, wait for another demon to come along, then… kablooey!"

"*Kablooey?*" Juni repeats, raising an eyebrow.

"I liked comics when I was a kid," Dervish says with a shrug.

"How are we going to get the demon to the barrier?" Bo asks, and though her teeth chatter, her voice sounds normal.

"Grubbs and I will drag it there," Dervish says. "Juni can help."

"But—"

"Here she goes," Bill-E groans. "Always has to have her say!"

"Shut up, shrimp-breath!" Bo snaps, then appeals to Dervish. "I don't want to be a trouble-maker. I just want to get out of this alive. But it's what you said about how you were going to alert everybody and tell them where to come." She pauses.

"Go on," Dervish says kindly, though if I was in charge, I'd tell her to put a sock in it. She's being a drama queen, trying to grab the attention. Typical Bo.

"Well," Bo says hesitantly, "if you're able to use telepathy, I was wondering… can demons do the same?"

Dervish stares at Bo, then nods slowly. "Some can."

"So," Bo continues, "if you catch a demon and it realises you're dragging it off to the edge of town to kill it, won't it call for help? And bring a load of other demons down on top of us?"

Dervish scowls. "She's right. It'll take several minutes to get to the barrier from here. If the demon summoned help, we'd never make it."

"Can't we knock it unconscious?" Juni asks.

"Perhaps. But if it gets out a shout…"

He falls silent. Bo looks at me smugly, but I'm too impressed to bear her any ill feelings. She's not entirely brainless, I'm reluctantly forced to admit.

"I have a suggestion," Bo says. She's stopped trembling. Confident. On a roll.

"I'm all ears," Dervish says with a wry smile.

"Why don't we lure a demon to the barrier before you go messing with it? Trick it into chasing after us. It wouldn't call for help if it didn't know its life was in danger."

"We have a genius in our midst," Dervish says, smile widening. Bo beams like an angel. Despite myself, I have to laugh. She'll be more unbearable than ever after this, but right now that doesn't seem like such a bad thing.

"There's only one problem with your proposal," Dervish says.

"Problem?" Bo frowns.

"Running's dangerous. If there's a demon hot on your heels, you can't concentrate on what lies ahead. Very easy to run into another demon, or a pack of them. We can't control the situation if we do what you suggest. And control is vital. Grubbs and I *must* reach the barrier. If we don't, everybody dies. We can't risk running into a trap."

Bo mulls that over, starts to speak, goes silent, then says very quietly, "What if the rest of us did the running? What if you and Grubbs went to the barrier and we tried to lure a demon to you?"

I blink, astonished. I never thought I'd hear the spoilt Bo Kooniart make a suggestion like that. What she's proposing is close to self-sacrifice. Without us, she and the others won't stand much of a chance against the demons.

"You know what you're saying?" Dervish's voice is grave. "You know the risk you'd be taking?"

"Of course. But it doesn't seem like we have much of an option, does it?"

"I'm not doing it!" Vanalee protests, bursting into tears. "I want to come with you, Mr Grady! Please don't make me go after demons!"

"I won't make anybody do anything," Dervish says. He looks at the other children. "Bo's risking a great deal for us. Will anyone volunteer to help her or does she have to face the demons by herself?"

The three children look at one another. Two raise shaky hands. The third hangs his head.

"OK," Dervish says. "Now all we have to do is arrange a meeting place, so you know where—"

"I'll go too," Bill-E interrupts.

"No!" I yell.

"I have to." He smiles thinly. "I'm not magical like you and Dervish. There's no benefit in me coming with you. I can do more good with Bo and the others."

"But—"

"He's right," Dervish says. I look at my uncle, unable to believe he'd let Bill-E go like this. But his eyes are dark and firm. This isn't easy for him but he's going to let Bill-E go anyway. I start to protest, but then I realise why Dervish is doing this — it wouldn't be fair to let Bo and the others volunteer and not put forward one of our own.

"I'll go," I whisper. "You take Bill-E."

"No," Dervish says. "I need you at the barrier."

I shake my head. "You can kill a demon without me. And you have Juni to help. The others will stand a better chance if I go with them."

Dervish hesitates.

"We can both go," Bill-E says.

"No. You're sticking with Dervish, no arguing." I lower my voice so only Bill-E can hear. "I don't want him to lose us both. And you're his son — you're more important to him than I am." I hate lying to Bill-E, but if it saves his life, it will be worth it.

"OK," Bill-E says miserably, after a moment of tormented consideration. "But I'll kill you if you don't come back alive."

"All right," Dervish says. "We're wasting time and we don't have much of it. Grubbs can go with the others. Now, you know the old hat store we passed when we tried to drive out of here?" I nod. "Make your way to that, then head due west. We'll be waiting. Come as fast as you can." He looks at Juni. "Ready?"

"Don't you think I should go with the children?" Juni says nervously.

"No. They're as safe with Grubbs as they would be with you. Safer."

"Well… I don't like it… but if you think that's best…"

"It is." Dervish looks at me steadily. "See you soon — and that's an order."

Then he, Juni, Bill-E, Vanalee and the boy head west to safety. Dervish is the only one who keeps his sights set firmly ahead. The others all look back, faces dark with doubt. They think they won't ever see us again.

I want to call after Bill-E and tell him we're brothers. I don't want to die without telling him the truth. But my mouth's dry. My throat's tight. I can't.

I stare at Bo and the others. One's a boy a year or two older than me. The second's a girl a few years younger. I don't know either of them. I think about asking their names, then decide it's better not to know.

"Are you ready?" Bo asks, taking control, even though I'm the one who should be in charge. We nod silently and turn towards the sounds of bloodshed and mayhem. Pause a terrified moment. Then silently jog back into the death den of the Demonata.

THE CHASE

→I want so much not to be doing this. One half of me is screaming bloody murder at the other half, telling me I'm mad, I should run, protect my own neck and damn the rest. But how could I leave Bo Kooniart to save the day? I'd never be able to live it down.

We pass from one street to another. No sign of the Demonata, though the cries of the dying and the roars of demons are everywhere. I'm sweating buckets. Can't stop shivering. I never knew I could be this scared. After all, I've faced Lord Loss before. But it's even scarier this time. I'm starting to understand that fear is like cancer —you can beat it back, but if it returns it can be worse than ever.

We turn a corner and find three demons feasting on a dying man, tearing into his flesh, gulping down bloody chunks as if they were marshmallows. One of the demons is shaped like a short elephant, another a giant cockroach, the third a huge slug that's been partially melted. Sick rises in my throat, but I force it back.

As the elephant-shaped demon moves aside to chew on a

piece of gristle, I recognise the unfortunate victim. It's Chai, the mime artist. Even in his death throes he's remained true to his role. He isn't screaming aloud, but is instead miming weakly. It would be hilarious if it wasn't so tragic.

I want to help Chai, but it's too late. Even as I take a step forward, he stiffens, makes a few last feeble gestures, then goes still.

I study the demons again as they continue to strip the corpse of flesh. They don't look like they're especially swift on their feet. I check with Bo and the others. They're terrified, but each nods to show they're ready.

"Hey!" I try to shout, but the word comes out as a squeak. I try again, but my mouth is as dry as a lizard's arse.

"Some hero you are," Bo mutters. Then she cups her hands over her mouth and bellows, "*Hey!*" The demons look up. "Come and catch us, uglies!"

She turns and runs. The rest of us follow. The demons shriek and give chase.

→Running as fast as I can. With my long legs, I quickly pull ahead of the others. Start to leave them behind. Feeling good, like I'm going to survive. Even if the demons catch up, they'll have to chew through the other three before getting to me. Maybe they'll stop there, happy to have one human each, leaving me free to race to safety and…

But that's not the plan. I'm supposed to be helping, not outpacing the others. I keep the speed up for a few more seconds, wrestling with my conscience. Then I curse and slow down, letting Bo and co catch up with, then slightly overtake me.

I look back. The demons are close, only ten or twelve metres behind. They can move a lot faster than I thought. If I don't stop them, they'll be on us long before we make it to the edge of town, never mind the barrier beyond.

I stop and force magic into my fingers. Trying to think of the best way to stall them, when they suddenly stop, stare at me hatefully, then turn and shuffle off.

"What the...?" I squint at them, thinking this must be a trick, but they keep going.

"What's happening?" Bo asks. The three of them have stopped. They're staring dumbly at me and the departing demons.

"I don't know," I mutter. "Maybe they sensed my magic and decided there were easier pickings elsewhere. Or—"

Something barrels into the boy whose name I don't know. He screams once, then is silenced. The girl and Bo leap away from him. I see a squat, long demon, like a dog, but with spikes sticking out all over and no legs. It's munching on the boy's head. I start towards them. Come to a halt when I hear a familiar voice high above me.

"You did not think I would leave you to the whims of my familiars, did you, Grubitsch?" I look up and spot Lord Loss, hovering above the roof of the building to my left. He descends slowly, gracefully. "I gave orders for you, your uncle and brother to be spared. I plan to finish you Grady boys off by myself."

Lord Loss comes to within half a metre of the ground and stops, his eight arms extended, smiling viciously. "What now, poor Grubitsch?" he murmurs. "Have you the strength of character to fight a demon master or will you run like a cowardly hyena?"

"*Run!*" I roar, then race away from him. Bo and the other girl hurriedly join me.

Lord Loss laughs and sets off in pursuit of us, savouring our fear and flight. He doesn't have the slightest clue that I'm running for a reason other than sheer terror, that I'm trying to lure him into a trap. He glides along after us, calling to me, the usual crap, telling me how desperate the situation is, how I'm going to let myself down, the pain I'll suffer, the tears I'll shed. He says I'll betray Dervish and Bill-E, abandon my friends, beg for mercy.

I know he's messing with my mind, trying to stoke up my fear, to wring more misery out of me. But it's hard to ignore him. I feel myself losing hope, seeing the future through the demon's eyes. Part of me wants to surrender and accept a swift, painless death. And perhaps I would — except I remember his look of hate when I beat him at chess, his vow to make me suffer before he killed me. There will be no quick, easy death if I fall into Lord Loss's hands.

A strange skittering sound. I look over my shoulder. The dog demon is chasing us too. It's almost upon us. It uses its spikes to move, a bit like a centipede crawling, only a hell of a lot quicker. It has a head like a dung beetle's, but dog-sized.

"Go, Malice," Lord Loss says, and the demon leaps high into the air, coming down on Bo's head, mouth opening wider than its narrow body, fangs glinting.

I shoot a bolt of magic at the demon called Malice and knock it sideways. It squeals, hits the ground, twists sharply, launches itself at my face. Without thinking, I turn my right hand into a blade, drop to one knee and slash at the demon's underbelly. Malice sees the threat but can't change direction. My hand slices its stomach open from neck to tail. It's finished by the time it hits the ground, entrails spilling out, whining feebly as it flops into the dust.

"Fool!" Lord Loss snorts at his dying familiar. "I am ashamed that one of my servants should be despatched so pitifully." He spits on the dying demon, then looks at me and smiles. "You are stronger than the last time I saw you fight. You were unable to kill Vein or Artery then, yet here you have killed two just as powerful. You must be feeling confident, like you could even defeat *me*?"

"Maybe," I growl, magic bubbling up within me, picturing the demon master dead at my feet, tasting the triumph of revenge.

Lord Loss chuckles. "Do not delude yourself, Grubitsch. You are not *that* strong. A demon master will always outrank and outpower a human."

"Dervish beat you," I sneer. "He fought you on your own turf and won."

Lord Loss's features darken. "That was not a fight to the death. He had only to get the better of me in battle. He could not have killed me. Just as you cannot kill me now."

Lord Loss reaches out with all eight arms, pauses, twists slightly and beckons. The girl whose name I didn't ask for goes flying towards him, screaming. I try to pull her back, but before I can, she's in the demon master's embrace.

"Poor little Karin," Lord Loss sighs. "You had such fine dreams. A movie career, marriage, children." The girl screams, struggling to break free. I try to pry her out of Lord Loss's grasp, but he deflects my magic easily, then kisses her. She goes quiet. Stiff. Her skin turns grey as he sucks the life out of her. I hear bones cracking. Her feet jerk a few times, then stop.

Bo's crying. She sinks to her knees, defeated, staring at the demon master as he drains the girl of the last vestiges of life. I want to give up too. But I know I won't be killed as smoothly as this if I do.

"Come on!" I roar, grabbing Bo's arms, yanking her to her feet.

"I can't," she sobs.

"You can!" I shout, pushing her ahead of me. "Run! Now! Or I'll kill you myself!"

Bo curses me but does as I command, lurching forward, running blindly, wiping tears from her eyes. I look back at Lord Loss. He casts the girl's ruined body aside and smacks his lips. "Karin was a tasty little girl," he says with relish.

"I hope you choke on her!" I scream in retort, then wave a hand at the building above him and cause the outer wall to explode. It showers Lord Loss with bricks and chunks of cement, taking him by surprise, driving him to the ground. I know I haven't killed him, but I've delayed him and that's all I wanted. Turning, I race after Bo, screaming at her to run faster, trying to judge how much further is left and what our chances are of making it to the barrier alive.

→Lord Loss is soon on our trail again, scratched and bruised but otherwise unharmed. He congratulates me on the way I brought the wall down on him, but adds that if I'd thought of it a bit earlier I could have saved poor Karin. Making me feel guilty, as though I'm to blame for her death.

I ignore the demon master. Turn corners wildly. Race through the streets of Slawter. I stumble occasionally, fall hard twice and scrape my hands and knees. But I keep ahead of our hunter and force Bo on, making her stay ahead of me so I can see when she falters and roar at her for support.

Two more of Lord Loss's familiars join him. One is the giant cockroach I saw earlier. The other is even more familiar. A young child's body but with an unnaturally large head. Pale green skin. Balls of fire instead of eyes. Maggots for hair (it used to be cockroaches). Small mouths set in both its palms. The hell-child, Artery.

"No need to introduce you two," Lord Loss says.

"Although, if you are interested, this fine specimen—" he nods at the cockroach —"is called Gregor."

"Very amusing," Bo snorts, but I don't get the joke so I just keep on running, saving my breath for a scream of triumph. Or a death cry. Whichever proves more appropriate.

→Finally, as I'm starting to think we've lost our way, I spot the old hat shop. Seconds later we dash past it and are out of town, racing across soft, grassy ground. Lord Loss and his familiars pursue us casually, taking their time, confident we can't escape.

"You should have tried to hide," Lord Loss taunts me. "You stood a better chance that way. This was a poor call, Grubitsch. It will cost you your life. Bo's too. I will make you watch while Artery eats her from the inside out. That will be the last thing you see in this world."

Looking for Dervish and the others, but there's no sign of them. My heart sinks like the Titanic. I'd be able to see them if they were here. No trees or bushes for them to hide behind. It's open ground. Maybe I got the meeting place wrong, but I doubt it. I think they've fallen. They didn't make it out of town. They ran into some bad-ass demons and are dead now. Just like Bo and I soon will be.

"Where… are… they?" Bo gasps. She looks more petrified than ever.

"Keep going," I reply. "Find the barrier."

"But—"

"Do it!" I roar, then whirl and yell a spell at Lord Loss and his familiars, prompted by my magical half. The ground in front of the demons bursts upwards. Blades of grass thicken, lengthen and entwine. They form a net which wraps around the startled demons, tightening, choking them, holding them in place.

I look for Bo. She's still running. I jog after her, keeping one eye on the Demonata, hardly daring to hope. And I'm right not to. The grass around them turns brown... red... burns away. Seconds later, Lord Loss is free and his familiars are soon clawing their way out. There are blades of green jammed into many of the cuts on Lord Loss's body, but unless they turn septic and he dies of disease much later – some hope! – he's going to be fine.

I try the same spell again, but this time Lord Loss is ready and with a wave of two hands the blades of grass bend downwards and spread out, flattening, not getting in the way of the demons.

"Fool me once, shame on you," Lord Loss says. "Fool me twice..." He pulls a smug expression. "But nobody has ever fooled me twice, Grubitsch. And you will not be the first."

Bo yells with pain and surprise. My gaze snaps forward. She's come to a halt and is struggling with an unseen force, arms and legs jerking slowly, as if caught in a web. Moments later she frees herself and falls backwards.

We've reached the barrier. Nowhere else to run. With an empty feeling in my gut, I stop and face the approaching demons.

Showdown.

BATTLE

→Artery and Gregor spread out to the left and right of their master, falling a couple of metres behind. They're here to make sure we don't escape and perhaps they'll get to kill Bo as a bonus. Neither will be allowed to harm me. Lord Loss is keeping me for himself.

"Grubbs," Bo whimpers.

"I know," I say softly.

"What are we going to do?"

"Be brave. Fight."

"But I don't know any magic."

"Just do what you can." Eyes on Artery and the cockroach. Trying to believe it's not hopeless. If I can pin one of them to the barrier and kill it, Bo and I can escape. Gutted that we can't take anyone with us, but I mustn't think of that now. I have to focus on getting us out alive.

"Did you forget about the barrier, Grubitsch?" Lord Loss sniggers. "You are slow to learn. I would have thought, after running foul of it once, you would have had more sense than…" He stops, frowning. "But you are not stupid. A cunning boy, as I learnt to my cost the last time we clashed. Might you have had another motive for coming here?"

He's close to the truth. I have to act now, before he makes the connection. My eyes flick from Artery to Gregor. I settle on the baby — smaller, hopefully easier to manipulate. With a magical cry, I unleash my power. Artery shoots forward, into the air, wailing with alarm, propelled towards the barrier. I step closer to the spot where he's going to hit, readying myself to kill the hell-child.

But then he stops mid-air. I feel a force working in opposition to mine. I scream a phrase of magic and tug harder. Artery jolts forward another metre, stops again, then falls to the ground. He scuttles back to his master, hiding behind him like a child seeking shelter behind a parent.

"That was a very nice attempt, Grubitsch," Lord Loss murmurs. "You had me foxed until almost the very end. I should have known you had an ace up your sleeve. Dervish must have told you how to create a rip in the barrier. You planned to kill my sweet Artery and skip out of the party early." He tuts mockingly. "That was rude. I shall have to..."

I hear noises in the background and spot people running towards us from the town. Lord Loss looks around, casting his eyes over the various faces, searching – as I am – for Dervish. But my uncle isn't part of the crowd. He's not racing to my rescue. These are just ordinary, terrified movie folk. They won't be any help.

"More victims," Lord Loss laughs. "See how they run towards me? Perhaps, from a distance, I look like an angel. Should I pretend to be good? Sweep them to my breast, shower them with kisses, only to turn vile and make my true intentions known when it is too late for them to escape?"

I focus on the cockroach. I try to pitch him at Lord Loss, hoping to knock the demon master off guard, then hurl Gregor or Artery at the barrier. But the demon doesn't even slide a centimetre off balance.

"No, Grubitsch," Lord Loss says. "We will have no more of that. Leave my familiars alone. Your battle is with me, not them."

"Then come on!" I scream. "Step up if you think you can take me! What are you waiting for? Do you want to reduce me to tears before you attack? Afraid to fight me on even terms?"

Lord Loss's face goes dead. The snakes in the hole in his chest stop hissing. "So be it," he whispers, rising a metre higher into the air, arms spreading outwards with a slow, dreadful, majestic grace.

"Grubbs," Bo mutters.

"Not now!" I hiss, trembling all over, preparing myself for whatever Lord Loss is about to launch against me.

"But… over there… it's… I think I can see… *Dervish*!"

That startles me so much, I look away from the threat of Lord Loss. Thankfully, the demon master is also caught by surprise, and instead of piercing my defence and finishing me off, he too glances to the side.

Bo is pointing off to my right. At first I don't see what she's gesturing at. The land looks devoid of life, just grass and weeds. But then I notice the air shimmering slightly. The shimmer intensifies, thickens, then fades to reveal... Dervish! And just behind my uncle, between him and the barrier — Bill-E, Juni, Vanalee and the boy whose name I don't know.

"An invisibility shield," Lord Loss groans. "I don't believe I—"

A wind blows up out of nowhere. It smacks hard into Lord Loss, driving him backwards, bowling him and Artery over.

"Grubbs!" Dervish yells, focusing on the wind, veins stretched across his face like ridges of blue putty. I know instantly what he wants. Pointing at Gregor, who has been unaffected by the gale, I shout a word of magic. The demon flies forward, mandibles gnashing together in a mixture of hate and fear. He strikes the invisible barrier. Sticks. Dozens of tiny legs kick at thin air as he tries to tear himself free.

"Juni!" Dervish shouts. "Kill it like I showed you!"

Juni steps up to the struggling cockroach. She makes a fist and takes aim at the brittle shell of its stomach. Then she pauses and half turns away, lowering her fist. She's smiling. She starts to say something, but before she can, one of Gregor's hairy, spindly legs strikes the back of her head. She falls with a startled cry, tries to rise, then slumps, dead or unconscious.

My first instinct is to rush to her aid, but I ignore it. Instead I look for Artery. Concentrating on the fire in the hell-child's eye sockets, I magically rip the flames out. As Artery squeals and slaps blindly at his eyes, I transport the flames to inside Gregor's stomach — like cutting and pasting on a computer!

I hold the flames tight for a second, letting them increase in strength but keeping them compact. Gregor is frothing at the mouth, glowing from the inside out. I flash the cockroach a wicked grin. Then, clicking my fingers for emphasis, I release the flames and they erupt in a ball of destructive red and yellow fury.

The demon explodes with a cry of delicious agony. There's a crackling, throbbing sound. Then a jagged line appears in the air around the demon's remains, a rough semi-circle of discoloured light — a hole in the barrier!

"Get out!" Dervish barks at Bill-E and the others. The wind is still blowing, but Lord Loss and Artery have stopped tumbling backwards and are facing into it now, the demon master furious, Artery confused, waving his childish hands at his empty sockets, trying to ignite fresh flames.

As Vanalee and the boy race to safety, Bill-E hurries to Juni's side. He turns her over, checks quickly, then shouts, "She's alive!"

"Then take her with you!" Dervish roars, struggling to maintain the wind.

Bill-E hesitates — I can see he wants to stay and help — then grits his teeth. Propping Juni up, he slides his hands under her armpits and drags her through the hole. As they exit, the quality of light changes and it's as though I'm looking at them through a thin, semi-translucent veil.

Bo scrambles to the opening but stops and looks back at the crowd racing towards us. She's panting hard, squinting. "My father and brother. I can't see them."

"Forget them," I growl.

"I can't."

"You must. They're—"

"I'm going back for them!" Bo cries.

"No!" I shout, but she sets off regardless.

My left hand rises. Magic flows. Bo comes to a forced stop. She turns her head and looks at me pleadingly. "Grubbs," she whimpers. "Let me go. I have to do this."

"But you'll die if—"

"Probably," she interrupts, "but not necessarily. Maybe I'll find and rescue them." She shrugs helplessly. "I have to try."

"But your father was working with the demons. He helped bring this upon us."

"He's still my dad. And Abe did nothing wrong. Apart from get on your nerves, like I did," she grins.

I grin back and reluctantly release her, knowing I don't have the right to deny her, figuring I'd probably do the same in her place. "Don't spend too long looking for them," I warn her.

"I won't," she lies. And then she's gone, racing past the people fleeing the town, leaving me to marvel at how poorly I judged her.

I wish Bo silent luck, then blank her from my thoughts and step up beside Dervish. I want to bolt through the hole in the barrier after Bill-E and the others, but my uncle needs me. My magical half shows me how to link up with my uncle. As I add my power to his, the force of the wind increases. Lord Loss slides backwards again, straining against the wind, but – momentarily at least – losing ground.

"You could have let me know you were here," I growl.

"Couldn't risk tipping Lord Loss off," Dervish disagrees. "We were lucky. You normally can't fool a demon master with an invisibility spell, but he was so focused on you he didn't see through it."

People from the town spill past us, then through the hole, called to safety by Bill-E, who's laid Juni to one side and is now directing the survivors.

"You sent the message to everyone?" I ask.

"Yes. As soon as I saw you coming."

"How come Bo and I didn't get it?"

"I excluded you. I–"

"–didn't want to tip Lord Loss off," I finish for him.

"Sorry," Dervish says.

"Don't worry about it."

The wind suddenly dies away. Lord Loss straightens himself.

"What does that mean?" I ask.

"We should get the hell out of here."

There are still people running and limping towards us from the town, chased by demons, some missing limbs, many bleeding and screaming, all terrified but hopeful. Because Dervish told them to come. He said this was their way out. He promised.

"You're staying," I note.

"Until the hole starts to close," Dervish nods.

"You'll know when that's about to happen? You'll escape in time?"

"I'll know. As for whether or not I'll be able to escape…" He jerks his head at Lord Loss, who's started to glide back towards us.

"OK," I decide, proud of my courage but at the same time dismayed. "I'll stay too. We'll buy the survivors as much time as possible."

Dervish smiles. "Did I ever tell you I loved you, Grubbs?"

"No."

"Good. I hate sentimental crap like that."

Then Lord Loss shrieks and fire engulfs us.

→ Dervish spits out words of magic and the flames evaporate before they have time to burn through our skin. But Lord Loss uses those few seconds to sweep across. With a cry of hate, he propels himself at Dervish, whips him off the ground and drags him high up into the air, all eight hands lashing and ripping at him.

No time to worry about my uncle. Artery is only seconds behind his master. Races at me on his tiny feet, flames in his eyes bright and vicious again, the teeth in his three mouths gnashing menacingly.

I wait until Artery's upon me, then drop to one knee and shoot a hand out. I grab his throat. Squeeze the cartilage hard. Crush it. Toss him aside. Choked gurgling sounds. Artery brings up his hands to repair the damage. I step towards him, set on finishing him off. Before I can, another demon bursts on to the scene. It's shaped like a monkey with several heads and has been chasing humans out from town. When it sees the hole in the barrier and spots me battling with Artery, it comes barrelling at me.

I glimpse claws and fangs. Whirl away. A blast of magic hits my left shoulder. My arm goes numb. When I look down, I realise it's been cut clean off. It lies on the ground nearby, singed and twisted.

"Grubbs!" Bill-E screams as the monkey demon closes in for the kill.

"Stay where you are!" I yell, kicking the demon away, magically stopping the blood pumping from the gash where my arm should be. I bark a command and the earth at the demon's feet explodes, throwing it backwards. While it's recovering, I grab my arm and stick it back in place, blasting magic at it. Severe pain as flesh, muscles and bone knot together, but I use more magic to dull it.

I'm able to do so much more than when I first fought

Lord Loss's familiars. It's frightening. I'm not in control of myself, just reacting, doing things without knowing how. The magic part of me isn't even giving me instructions now. It's bypassing the conscious part of my brain, working by itself.

More of the cast and crew stumble through the hole. Several of the demons in pursuit try to tear through after them. I scatter the monsters, then quickly establish a second barrier around the hole, which allows humans through but not demons.

A heavy thudding sound. Dervish and Lord Loss have crashed to earth. Still struggling with each other, both wounded and bruised, roaring spells and curses.

The familiars make a coordinated attack, ganging up on me. They close from all angles, encircling me. I try backing up to the wall of the barrier, to guard myself from sneak attacks, but a few have already got in behind me. Artery – neck fixed and hot for revenge – snickers. I sense the confidence of the demons. They have me trapped. My situation should be hopeless. But the magic part of me only sees this as a way to deal with them all at the same time.

I find myself rising into the air, then turning, slowly at first, then at great speed, 360 degree spins, around and around, creating a vortex. The demons are sucked towards me, collide and are thrown clear. I'm not injured by the collisions — my skin has automatically toughened.

A couple of demons try to fight the bite of the wind and drag me down, but all are repelled. Eventually they quit and return to harassing and killing other humans. I drift back to the ground. Slightly dizzy but otherwise fine, I do what I can to protect the fleeing crowd, trying to shepherd through as many as I can.

There aren't many coming now. The stream has died away to a trickle. No sign of Bo returning. I wonder how long we have left, if she'll have time to make it back. As if in answer, Dervish bellows, "We have to get out! It's going to close!"

"You'll never leave!" Lord Loss screams, digging a couple of hands deep into Dervish's flesh. The snakes in the demon master's chest are spitting at Dervish's face, trying to bite him.

"Go!" Dervish shouts. "Save yourself!"

"As if!" I snort, eyeing up Lord Loss. I focus on his lumpy, writhing arms. With a cruel smile, I gnash my teeth together — and all eight of his limbs are abruptly severed. Stunned, he topples backwards, yelping with pain and shock, his disconnected limbs flopping to the ground.

Dervish crumples up into a weary ball. I hurry to my uncle, grab him and toss him through the hole in the barrier as if he was a frisbee, using magic to soften his fall. A quick glance at Lord Loss. I can't resist the opportunity to toss a final movie-style quip his way. "Some people say you're a bad-ass — but I think you're pretty 'armless!" Then I skip out before he recovers and rips me to pieces.

BITTER SWEET

→I feel the difference as soon as I step through the hole. Magic drains away from me instantly. Tiredness sets in. My left arm and shoulder ache like no pain I've experienced before. But I'm not completely powerless, not yet. I face the gap in the barrier, summon the final dregs of my magic and prepare myself to fight any demon that tries to follow us through.

Dervish groans and forces himself up, helped by a trembling Bill-E. One of Lord Loss's hands is embedded in the flesh of his stomach. He prises it out and tosses it away. It twitches for a few seconds, then disintegrates into an ash-like substance.

I see humans running towards the barrier. "Faster!" I scream. "You don't have much longer! You've got to—"

Lord Loss glides across the face of the hole, blocking my view. His face is a mask of hatred and fury. Snarling, he starts to come through... then pauses, looks around and drifts backwards.

"He doesn't dare cross," Dervish mutters. "His magic would fail him out here. He'd have to fight on our terms."

"You will suffer for this," the demon master snarls. "Your deaths would have been horrible, but now they'll be far worse. I will find new ways to—"

"Yeah, yeah," Bill-E says, stepping up beside us. "Go blow it out your rear, you pathetic waste of space."

Lord Loss hisses and starts to spit out a spell. Before he completes it, there's a sharp cracking sound and the hole in the barrier seals itself. Lord Loss looks up and down, in case there's any crack remaining, but it's been completely repaired.

"I will answer your insults later," he vows, new arms forming from all eight stumps. "You will die at these hands eventually. Only now it will be much slower and far more excruciating than I had originally planned."

Glancing backwards, the demon master flexes his fresh fingers and points at the people still fleeing Slawter, those trapped within the bubble of magic. "Your day of reckoning will arrive sooner than you imagine, Grady scum. For now, watch as I content myself with this sorry lot and consider it a taste of the horrors to come."

Having delivered his threat in a manner any movie demon would be proud of, the eight-armed, heartless monster floats towards the doomed humans, warding off his familiars, saving these last few victims for his own warped pleasure.

"Look away," Dervish says wearily to those of us on the safe side of the barrier. "This is going to be ugly. You don't want to watch."

"We have to get them out!" a woman wails. "My son's still in there. You have to go—"

Dervish looks at her darkly. Puts a finger to his lips. She falls silent. Then my uncle turns his back on the town, sits on the ground, and very slowly and deliberately closes his eyes and places both hands over his ears — blocking out the sights and sounds of the inhuman, bloody *slawter*.

→Dervish is right. It's not something that should be seen. Yet I have to watch, at least for a while, as Lord Loss savages and slaughters one person after another, dragging them kicking and screaming up close to the barrier so we can see and hear more clearly. It's dreadful, the ways he finds to torture and kill them. I want to reach through and stop him, but my powers are swiftly fading. Even if there was some way of breaking through the barrier, I no longer have the strength to harm him. I'd have to go back in, but that would be suicide.

Juni regains consciousness while Lord Loss is hard at work. Groans, sits up, looks around groggily, then leaps to her feet, eyes wide. "It's OK," I tell her. "We made it. They can't—"

"What happened?" she shouts, striding up to the barrier, stopping just short of it, studying the bloody scenes within, astonished, on the verge of tears.

"You were knocked out," Bill-E tells her. "We pulled you through."

"But… the barrier…" She touches it. Pulls her hand back quickly when she feels the power.

"The hole's gone," I explain. "It was only temporary. We got out as many as we could. The rest…" I shake my head sadly.

Juni stares at Lord Loss and his victims, her pale skin flushed, dried blood caking the back of her head where she was struck. She's trembling with confusion and fear, like the rest of us. I think about giving her a hug but I'm too tired. So I just stand and stare with her.

Gradually we all turn away from the horrific scenes, sickened, weeping and shaking, grasping each other for support and comfort. I'm one of the last to look away, watching for Bo, hoping against hope that she'll show, that another hole in the barrier can be opened, that I'll be able to get her out.

But she doesn't appear. She's either still looking for Tump and Abe or — more likely — has been killed by a demon. If the latter, I hope it was quick and painless, though I don't suppose it was. Who'd have thought that of all the deaths today, Bo Kooniart's would hit me hardest.

Eventually, I look around and do a quick head count. Thirty-four. Of all those working on the film… hundreds of people… only thirty-four remain.

I'm about to sit, when one of the faces catches my attention. Slowly, incredulously, I march across and glare with contempt and hatred at a bruised, dazed but very much alive Chuda Sool.

"*You!*" I snarl. He looks up timidly. "How dare you? So many dead because of your treachery, but you sit here among the living, meek as an innocent child. You should have stayed behind with your masters!"

"Please," Chuda croaks. "I didn't know… they said… I thought…"

"You knew!" I scream. "They said they'd spare you — that's the only thing you got wrong. That's your only complaint." I grab his head and force him to look at the destruction on the other side of the barrier. "You made this happen! They're dying – dead – because of *you!*"

Chuda starts to cry — but with fear, not regret. "Don't hurt me. Please… I can help you… I know spells. They promised me a long life, hundreds, maybe thousands of years. How could I say no? Davida convinced me. She set this up. She's the one you should blame."

"Davida's dead," I growl. "She got her comeuppance. Now you will too."

I reach deep within myself for the dwindling flames of magic, intent on destroying this traitor.

"No, Grubbs," Bill-E says quietly, laying a hand on my right arm.

"He deserves it!" I yell.

"He probably deserves a whole lot worse," Bill-E agrees. "But it's not for you or me to pass judgement. We don't have the right to take his life. You'll become a killer, no better than any of those demons, if you murder him."

"It's execution, not murder," I growl.

"Different word, same thing," Bill-E says. "It's wrong. You'd hate yourself."

"He's right," Juni says, leaving the barrier and stepping up on my other side. "You're a child, Grubbs. No child should ever kill." Chuda smiles at her pitifully, but her eyes are hard. "Especially when there are plenty of capable adults around," Juni whispers, then grabs Chuda's head with both hands. His eyes fly wide open — then fill with a white light. He gibbers madly, trying to knock her hands away, but Juni holds firm, pumping magic into Chuda's brain, frying the circuits, her mouth twisted into a wicked leer.

Chuda falls back when she releases him, jerks a few times, then dies, face contorted, skin black at the sides of his head. Bill-E and I gawp at Juni, shocked. Dervish is staring at her too, along with most of the people around us.

"I did what I had to," Juni mutters, looking away to hide her shame. "We couldn't let him walk away, not after..." She gestures at Slawter.

"B-b-b-but..." Bill-E stutters.

"Don't," Juni stops him. "The last thing I want right now is a child lecturing me about ethics." She walks off, rubbing her hands up and down her arms.

"Leave her," Dervish says sadly. He looks over his shoulder and spots Lord Loss finishing off another of his playthings. Sighs and stands. "Let's gather everybody together and get out of here. I've had enough of bloody demons."

*   *   *

→How do you explain away a massive demonic killing spree? Easy — by covering it up and pretending it was an accident.

Dervish spends the rest of the evening making calls, to the Disciples, police, politicians, journalists, firemen, doctors and nurses. The Disciples have a network of contacts, ready and waiting to smooth over the cracks when something like this happens. It's how they've managed to keep previous crossings quiet in the past. They come in their droves, the first arriving late at night, setting up camp close to the barrier around Slawter, so they can move in swiftly and mop up when the time is right.

They keep the survivors together for four days, in vans and tents brought to the site by more of Dervish's contacts. Nobody's allowed to leave or make a call. Counsellors work hard, making the most of the time, trying to help people stave off nightmares and come to terms with the deaths of relatives and friends.

Waiting for the demons to finish off the last few victims and return to their own universe. I often feel like going back to the barrier, to view the devastation, to curse Lord Loss or just stand there and let him curse me. But I don't.

The barrier finally dissolves when the last of the Demonata take their leave. Dervish and a team of volunteers enter the town and demolish the magical lodestone in the D warehouse, closing the tunnel between universes. When the threat of a follow-up invasion has been averted, they retrieve the bodies and body parts, stack them in buildings around the town, then set the place alight. It's a gruesome end for the unfortunate victims, but necessary to mask the demonic marks and trick the outside world into believing they died in a ferocious fire.

That's the official story, built on the bones of Bill-E's gas leak rumour — there was a massive explosion and a wave of fire swept through the town with brutal speed, killing most of the cast and crew. I doubt if all the survivors will stick to it. I'm sure a few will protest in the months and years to come, tell their friends, go to the media, try to spread the truth. But who'll believe them? If anyone goes on a TV show prattling about demons, the audience will think they're a crank.

The teams destroy the film reels too. Davida's notes. The models, props, costumes. A thorough job, leaving nothing behind, removing every last trace of the Demonata, planting fake evidence in its place. The only people who knew what the film was about were all in Slawter. As far as the rest of the world will ever know, Davida Haym's last film was going to be a departure from her earlier movies — a love story with a touch of science fiction.

I think, if Davida's watching in some phantom form, that will hurt the most. Not the deaths, the betrayal by the demons, her own grisly slaughter. But that her film was destroyed and all traces of her masterpiece removed.

Good! I hope her ghost chokes on it.

* * *

→Standing beside Dervish as the fires rage, the night sky red and yellow, thick with smoke. Watching Slawter disappear forever. Most of the survivors and emergency crew are with us. Silence reigns.

"It's over," Dervish says as the roof of a large building — maybe the D warehouse — caves in with a raucous crash, sending splinters of flames flickering high up into the sky. "In the morning we can leave. Everyone can go."

The sweetest words I've ever heard.

→Juni is gone before we wake. She leaves a note for Dervish. She's been quiet and withdrawn these past few days, not saying much, refusing to discuss the mayhem or her killing of Chuda Sool.

In the note she says she's confused. She knows Chuda was guilty, deserving of punishment, but she can't believe she acted so callously. Her whole world has changed. She knows about demons now and she's seen a side of herself that she doesn't like. She needs time alone, to reflect, consider, explore. She says she has strong feelings for Dervish, but doesn't know if she ever wants to see him again. Tells him not to look for her. Promises to visit him in Carcery Vale one day — *if*. That's the last word — *if*. I think she meant to write more, but couldn't.

Dervish doesn't say anything when he reads the note. Just hands it to me and Bill-E once he's done, then goes for a long, lonely walk. I'd help him if I could, say something to make him feel better. But I don't know what to say. Bill-E doesn't either. So we don't say anything when he returns, only stay close in case he needs us.

→The evacuation proceeds smoothly, people leaving without a fuss, driven home or to train stations, airports, wherever. Some of the counsellors travel with the worst affected, not only to comfort them, but to make sure they don't harm themselves or wind up in trouble.

I think some of the survivors won't be able to live with what they've witnessed. This will haunt all of us, but it will hit some harder than others. I think there will be a few more deaths in the years to come.

I'd like to do something to help the worst afflicted, but I can't. It's not possible to save everybody. Even heroes have their all-too-human limits.

→By four in the afternoon the last cars are leaving. The press has been told of the supposed fire and news teams begin to arrive, eager to scour the ashes of Slawter — renamed Haymsville for the benefit of the rest of the world. They're angry to find none of the survivors here, and they hit the roof when they learn that the emergency crews were on the scene so long before them. But there's nothing they can do about it except moan.

I watch with little interest as the reporters circle the skeletal remains of the town. I've had enough of the place.

I just want to forget about it. Put it behind me and move on.

Bill-E is beside me, silent as a corpse. He's kept himself busy in the aftermath, spending a lot of time with the other children who made it out alive, talking about what happened, trying to help. That's been his way of dealing with the tragedy. He doesn't want time alone to think about it, to remember, to fear. At night he wakes screaming, but in the day he fights the memories. What will he do when we're home and he has nothing but ordinary life to occupy his time? What will *I* do?

"They didn't find all the bodies," Bill-E says. "I heard Dervish talking about it with another Disciple. The demons took some people back to their universe. Maybe Bo was one of them. Maybe she'll escape and return. I'm sure it's possible. I mean, Dervish did it, right?"

I grunt negatively in reply, knowing in my heart that Dervish would have told us if there was even the slightest glimmer of hope.

I turn to face Bill-E. I instinctively know that this is the right moment, the one I've been waiting so many months for. Time to tell him we're brothers.

"Bill-E…" I begin, but before I get any further, Dervish appears.

"Hey," he says with forced good humour. "You want to stay here all night or are you coming with me?"

"Coming where?" Bill-E asks, turning, and the moment is

lost. I won't make the great revelation, not now. Later. When another good time comes around.

"Yes — where?" I ask, turning like Bill-E, so we're both looking at our uncle.

"Home," Dervish croaks. And as soon as he says that, for reasons I don't quite understand, all three of us smile shakily and then start to cry.

A LITTLE CHAT

→It's strange, trying to settle back into everyday life, not telling anyone about Slawter, acting like normal people who've merely survived a very human tragedy. Bill-E and I lie to our friends, make up stories about the filming, describe the fire and how we were lucky to escape. Not a word about demons.

Bill-E stays with us the first few nights, despite the objections of Ma and Pa Spleen. Nightmares galore, both of us. Remembering. Screaming. Crying. Talking with each other and Dervish, trying to cope. Ironically – considering how this all started – Dervish sleeps like a baby. The confrontation with evil was a tonic for him. It blew the cobwebs from his head, helped him out of the bad patch he'd been stuck in. The fighting, the cover-up, getting in touch with the other Disciples, discussing ways to keep the truth secret... All of that was nectar to my uncle. It fired up his engines. He was in his element dealing with the demonic fallout. I'm not saying he enjoyed it, but he needed it. That's his real work.

I wish it was so easy for me, that I could go off, find a demon, have a scrap, purge myself of the bad memories and fears. But I took nothing positive out of what happened in Slawter. I'm just disgusted, tired and afraid. I'm sure it will be years before I can sleep properly. If ever.

But the show must go on. The charade has to be maintained. So Bill-E returns to Ma and Pa Spleen. We go back to school. We force ourselves to focus on homework, friends, sport, TV, music, day-to-day life. We pretend that's all there is to the world, that there's nothing more frightening in life than a surprise test or saying something stupid in front of your friends and having them laugh at you.

And sometimes – just sometimes – I almost believe it, and for a little while I forget about Lord Loss, Davida Haym, Bo Kooniart, Emmet, the demons, the dead. And life is the way it should be, like it is for most people. But the sensation never lasts. It can't. Because I know the truth. I've seen behind the curtain of reality. I know that monsters *are* hiding underneath a billion beds across the world. And I know that sometimes… more often than we imagine… they come out.

→"Time for that talk."

We've been home for nearly three weeks. I'm in the TV room, some comedy show playing on the big screen, not really concentrating. When Dervish sits beside me and speaks, I'm not sure what he's talking about. Then, as he switches off the TV, I remember. In the middle of the madness he said that if we got out alive, we'd have to have a chat about my magical prowess.

"You were amazing in Slawter," Dervish says. "Magic was pumping through you and you had complete control over it."

"I just tapped into the power in the air," I shrug uneasily. "No biggie."

Dervish smiles. "Modesty's becoming, but let's not bull ourselves — you were on fire. You did things I can't even comprehend. When I was fighting Lord Loss, I noticed some of the demons trying to get through the hole in the barrier. You kept them back. How?"

"I established a second barrier around the hole. Demons couldn't get through it but humans could."

Dervish chuckles. "Do you realise how difficult that is? I couldn't do it. Even when I was in Lord Loss's realm, at my most powerful, I couldn't have pulled off something like that. I don't know many who could."

"It wasn't like I planned it," I say, for some reason feeling edgier the more he praises me. "I reacted to what was going on around me. The magic told me what to do. I wasn't in control. I couldn't do any of it again. I don't even remember most of what I did."

Dervish studies me closely, his expression serious. I sense his reluctance to continue — and with a jolt, I guess the reason why and instantly understand why I've been so nervous.

"The Disciples are few in number," Dervish says quietly. "We're always on the lookout for new recruits, but most mages never realise their magical potential. It lies dormant unless they have an encounter with the Demonata. Even then there's no guarantee that it will develop, that we'll be able to make use of them."

"No," I say softly.

Dervish frowns. "I haven't asked you anything."

"I know what's coming. And the answer's no. Please don't ask me." I look away, trembling, fighting hard not to cry. "I hate it, Dervish — the demons, the battles, the madness. I don't want to face Lord Loss or anything like him again. I don't want to become a Disciple."

A lengthy silence. Finally Dervish sighs. "I'd spare you if I could. But there are so few of us and we're so limited. From what I saw in Slawter, you could be one of the most powerful Disciples ever. You might even..." He clears his throat. "You might even be a true magician. Like Bartholomew Garadex."

"No way!" I cry. "You told me I wasn't. You said magicians are born that way, that their powers are obvious from birth."

"I know. But the way you handled yourself... Maybe I was wrong. Maybe there are late-developing magicians. But even if you're not a magician," he says quickly as I start to protest, "you *are* part of the world of magic. No normal person could have done what you did. You have a very powerful, important talent and it would be a crime to deny it. I know you don't want to involve yourself with the Disciples, but you have to.

Some of us believe that the universe creates champions, that a few humans in each generation are given the gift of magic in order to protect this world from the Demonata. If you've been chosen by the universe..." He smiles shakily. "You can't say no to a calling like that, can you?"

"Just watch me," I snap.

Dervish's expression darkens. "You're acting like a child."

"Well, duh! Haven't you noticed? I *am* a child! Big for my age, but don't let size fool you. Try me again when I'm old enough to vote."

"I can't wait that long," Dervish says. "Magic must be nurtured. Every day we hesitate is a day wasted. When you face your next demon, you might–"

"There won't be a next!" I shout. "Weren't you listening? I don't want to join your band of do-gooding Disciples! I said *NO!*"

"Unacceptable," Dervish replies flatly. "You have a responsibility. I know it's hard – I've gone through it myself – but you have to be who you are."

"You don't know anything!" I hiss. "You didn't lose your family to demons. You didn't have to fight Lord Loss when you were my age. You haven't felt the terror of... of..." I'm breathing hard, hands clenched, tears in my eyes.

"You can't let fear rule your life," Dervish says. "Everyone's afraid when they face a demon. We learn to mask our fear, but it's always there, chewing away at us. Fear... doubt... wishes that we weren't magical, that we didn't have this cross to bear. I can help you overcome that fear. I can show you the way."

I stare at him heavily. There's no point arguing. He really doesn't understand. I'm not just afraid — I'm horrified. In Slawter I did what I had to. It was an unreal situation and I had no choice but to let the magic wash through me and use it to fight my way out. But I hated the whole experience and I've no desire to repeat it. I'm through with the universe of demons. I've done more than my fair share. Got the better of them — and saved lives — twice. That's enough.

I start to tell Dervish this, to try to make him see it from my point of view. But all that comes out is a sigh, then a sullen, "Anyway, it's irrelevant. I'm not a magician or a mage. It was just a Slawter thing."

"You're wrong. The power is there. We have to develop it. You can't–"

"What if it isn't?" I interrupt. "What if I'm just an ordinary kid who did something weird and wild, but is back to normal now? Would you leave me alone then?"

He frowns. "Yes, of course. If the talent isn't there, obviously we can't fan it into life. But it is. It must be."

"Look for it," I challenge him. "Can you find out if a person has magic in them or not?"

Dervish nods. "We can't in people who haven't tapped into it, but once someone unleashes their power, it's always there. I can search for it, find it, prove it to you. I should have done it before, after you fought Vein and Artery, but I wasn't thinking straight when I returned from my battle with Lord Loss."

"Go on then." I face him directly. "You won't find anything, but if you want to look, feel free."

Dervish puts his hands on my shoulders. My left arm's still sore from when it was cut off. I wince, but steel myself and grunt for him to continue. I'm not sure why I'm so confident that he won't find anything. But I am.

Dervish's eyes close. "Relax," he says. "You'll feel a force… an intrusion. Try not to fight it. I'll get out as quickly as possible."

I let my eyelids flutter shut. Seconds later I sense a presence, a soft probing, like fingers creeping through the corridors of my brain. I tense against it.

"Relax," Dervish murmurs. "It's OK. I won't hurt you. Trust me."

It's hard, but I do as Dervish says, opening myself up to him, letting him probe deep… deeper. I feel him closing in on a part of myself which I wasn't aware of a few months ago. I know that if he finds it, he'll continue pestering me to become a Disciple. He won't give up. He'll keep on and on, and eventually I'll cave in and let him train me. And that will mean facing the Demonata again. More pain, craziness, terror.

Something moves within me. A pulse. A shiver. Hard to define. Like when you think you catch a movement out of the corner of your eye, but you're not sure, and when you look closely, nothing's there.

My eyes open. Dervish's forehead is creased, his lips moving. I close my eyes again. Smile faintly and let him continue. Warm now, safe, at ease.

Finally Dervish releases me. When I look at him, he's shaking his head, confused. "I don't understand. I was certain. You shouldn't have been able to... if there was nothing there... if you're not a mage... It doesn't make sense!"

"I assume that means no magic," I grin.

"Not even a trace. I thought I was zooming in on it, but then... nothing. I carried on looking, went deeper than necessary, because I was so sure..."

"You can try again if you want," I tell him.

"No point." He manages a brief smile. "It's either there or it isn't. I'd have found it if it was. You can't hide magic, not from those who know what to look for. I was wrong. You were right. You're clean."

"So I don't have to sign up? The Disciples can struggle on without me?"

Dervish pulls a face. "I don't know. The magic isn't there now, but I suspect, if we placed you in an area of magic again or took you into the universe of the Demonata... Our leader, Beranabus, is more powerful than any of us. He spends a lot of time among demons. Perhaps..."

I feel fear creeping back, but then Dervish scowls. "No. I'm not going to sign away your life to him. Maybe you'll choose to go down that path when you're older. But I haven't the right to pass that sort of a sentence on you. Beranabus plays rougher than the rest of us. I've seen how he treats those closest to him, and I wouldn't wish it on anyone."

"Then I'm free?" I say hopefully. "I don't have to…?"

"No." Dervish smiles, warmly this time, pleased for me, even though he's disappointed not to have found a powerful new recruit. "Congratulations, Grubbs. You're ordinary. I hope you enjoy a long, happy, boring life."

"Coolio!" I laugh. Then the pair of us settle back, turn the TV on and spend a few hours surfing channels, chatting about things deliciously unimportant.

→In my room. Dark. I haven't turned the light on. Sitting on the end of my bed. Thinking about what happened earlier, Dervish's probe, what it would have meant if he'd found magic, how awful my life might have been. I should be celebrating the fact that I'm not one of the magical breed. Rejoicing. But I can't. Because I know that's a crock.

I rise, walk into the bathroom and stand in front of the basin, facing the mirror above it, even though I can't see it in the darkness. I don't want to do this. But I have to be sure.

I think I outfoxed Dervish. I think there *is* magic inside me, but it responded to my wishes and hid itself or deflected my uncle's probe. He said that wasn't possible, but if you're powerful enough, maybe it is. I could be wrong – I'm praying that I am – but I'm not sure. And I have to be. Even if nobody else ever knows, I need to.

I focus on the light bulb overhead. For a long second nothing happens. The darkness holds. I begin to hope.

Then the light comes on. A warm, steady, unnatural light. And the hope dies away as quickly as it was born.

I look at my scared reflection in the mirror. Make it disappear, so only the wall behind me is reflected in the glass. Then I let my reflection reappear and the light fade. I stumble back to bed. Lie down on top of the covers. Silent. Shaking. Terrified. Unable to sleep. Certain now — I'm not normal. I tricked Dervish, but I'm part of the world of magic. I can't escape. The universe of the Demonata will call to the magic within me and suck me back in. I know it will. This isn't over, not by a long shot.

There are no happy endings.

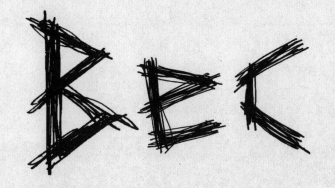

BEGINNING

→Screams in the dark.

Mother pushes and after a long fight I slip out of her body on to a bed of blood-soaked grass. I cry from the shock of cold air as I take my first breath. Mother laughs weakly, picks me up, holds me tight and feeds me. I drink hungrily, lips fastened to her breast, my tiny hands and feet shivering madly. Rain pelts us, washing blood from my wrinkled, warm skin. Once I'm clean, mother shields me as best she can. She's weary but she can't rest. Must move on. Kissing my forehead, she sighs and struggles to her feet. Stumbles through the rain, tripping often and falling, but protecting me always.

→Banba never believed I could remember my birth. She said it was impossible, even for a powerful priestess or druid. She thought I was imagining it.

But I wasn't. I remember it perfectly, like everything in my life. Coming into this world roughly, in the wilderness, my mother alone and exhausted. Clinging to her as she pushed on through the rain, over unfamiliar land, singing to me, trying to keep me warm.

My thoughts were a jumble. I experienced the world in bewildering fragments and flashes. But even in my newborn state of confusion I could sense my mother's desperation. Her fear was infectious, and though I was too young to truly know terror, I felt it in my heart and trembled.

After endless, pain-filled hours, she collapsed at the gate of a ringed, wooden fort — the rath where I live now. She didn't have the strength to call for help. So she lay there, in the water and mud, holding my head up, smiling at me while I scowled and burped. She kissed me one last time, then clutched me to her breast. I drank greedily until the milk stopped. Then, still hungry, I wailed for more. In the damp, gloomy dawn, Goll heard me and investigated. The old warrior found me struggling feebly, crying in the arms of my cold, stiff, lifeless mother.

"If you remember so much, you must remember what she called you," Banba often teased me. "Surely she named her little girl."

But if she did give me a name, she never said it aloud. I don't know her name either, or why she died alone in such miserable distress, far from home. I can remember everything of my own life but I know nothing of hers, where I came from or who I really am. Those are mysteries I don't think I'll ever solve.

* * *

→I often retreat into my early memories, seeking joy in the past, trying to forget the horrors of the present. I go right back to my first day here, Goll carrying me into the rath and joking about the big rat he'd found, the debate over whether I should be left to die outside with my mother or accepted as one of the clan. Banba testing me, telling them I was a child of magic, that she'd rear me to be a priestess. Some of the men were against that, suspicious of me, but Banba said they'd bring a curse down on the rath if they drove me away. In the end she got her way, like she usually did.

Growing up in Banba's tiny hut. Everybody else in the rath shares living quarters, but a priestess is always given a place of her own. Lying on the warm grass floor. Drinking goat's milk, which Banba squeezed through a piece of cloth. Staring at a world which was sometimes light, sometimes dark. Hearing sounds when the big people moved their lips, but not sure what the noises meant. Not understanding the words.

Crawling, then walking. Growing in body and mind. Learning more every day, fitting words together to talk, screeching happily when I got them right. Realising I had a name — *Bec*. It means 'Little One'. It's what Goll called me when he first found me. I was proud of the name. It was the only thing I owned, something nobody could ever take from me.

As I grew up, Banba trained me, teaching me the ways of magic. I was a fast learner, since I could remember the words of every spell Banba taught me. Of course, there's more to magic than spells. A priestess needs to soak up the power of the world around her, to draw strength from the land, the wind, the animals and trees. I wasn't so good at that. I doubted I'd ever make a really strong priestess, but Banba said I'd improve in time, if I worked hard.

I discovered early on that I'd never fit in. The other children were wary of the priestess's apprentice. Their mothers warned them not to hurt me, in case I turned their eyes into runny pools or their teeth into tiny squares of mud. I was sad that I couldn't be one of them. I asked Banba where I came from, if there was a place I could go where I'd be more welcome.

"Priestesses are welcome nowhere," she answered plainly. "Folk are pleased to have us close, so they can call on us when the crops fail or a woman can't get round with child. But they never truly trust us. They don't take us into their confidence unless they have to. Better get used to it, Little One. This is our life."

The life wasn't so bad. There was always plenty of food for a priestess, from people eager to win her favour and avoid a nasty curse. And there was respect, and gifts when I made spells work. People wondered how powerful I'd become and what I could do to make the rath stronger. Banba often laughed about that — she said people were always either too suspicious or expected too much.

A few treated me normally, like Goll of the One Eye. Chief of the rath once, now just an ageing warrior. He didn't care that I was a stranger, from no known background, studying to be a priestess. I was simply a little girl to him. He even spoilt me sometimes, since in a way he felt like my father, as he was the one who found and named me. He often played with me, put me up on his broad shoulders and gave me rides around the rath, grunting like a pig while others laughed or sneered. All the children loved Goll. He was a fierce warrior, who'd killed many men in battle, but he was still a child secretly, in his heart.

Those were the best days. Dreaming of the magic I'd work when I grew up. Harvesting the crops. Herding cattle and sheep. I wasn't supposed to do ordinary work, but if a child was lazy and I offered to help, they usually let me. Some even became friends over time. They wouldn't admit it in front of their mothers or fathers, but when nobody was looking they'd talk to me and include me in their games.

Playing… working… learning the ways of magic. Good times. Simple times. Life going on the way it had since the world began, like it was meant to.

Then the demons came.

CASUALTIES

→A boy's screams pierce the silence of the night and the village explodes into life. Warriors are already racing towards him by the time I whirl from my watching point near the gate. Torches are flung into the darkness. I see Ninian, a year younger than me, new to the watch... a two-headed demon, pieced together from the bones and flesh of the dead... *blood*.

Goll is first on the scene. An old-style warrior, he fights naked, with only a small leather shield, a short sword and axe. He hacks at the demon with his axe and buries it deep in one of the monster's heads. The demon screeches but doesn't release Ninian. It lashes out at Goll with a fleshless arm and knocks him back, then buries the teeth of its uninjured head in Ninian's throat. The screams stop with a sickening choking sound.

Conn and three other warriors swarm past Goll and attack the demon. It swings Ninian at them like a club and scythes two of them down. Conn and another keep their feet. Conn jabs one of the monster's eyes with his spear. The demon squeals like a banshee. The other warrior — Ena — slides in close, grabs the beast's head and twists, snapping its neck.

If you break a human's neck, that person will almost surely die. But demons are made of sturdier stuff. Broken necks just annoy most of them.

With one hand the demon grabs the head which Goll shattered with his axe. Rips it off and batters Ena with it. She doesn't let go. Snaps the neck again, in the opposite direction. It comes loose and she drops it. She pulls a knife from a scabbard strapped to her back and drives it into the rotting bones of the skull. Making a hole, she wrenches the sides apart with her hands, digs in and pulls out a fistful of brains. Grabs a torch and sets fire to the grey goo.

The demon howls and grabs blindly for the burning brains. Conn snatches the other head from its hand. He throws it to the ground and mashes it to a pulp with his axe. The demon shudders, then slumps.

"*More!*" comes a call from near the gate. It's late — later than demons usually attack. Most of the warriors on the main watch have retired for the night, replaced by children like me. Our eyes and ears are normally sharp. But this close to dawn, most of us are sleepy and sluggish. We've been caught off guard. The demons have snuck up. They have the advantage.

Bodies spill out of huts. Hands grab spears, swords, axes, knives. Men and women race to the rampart. Most are naked, even those who normally fight in clothes — no time to get dressed.

Demons pound on the gate and scale the banks of earth outside, tearing at the sharpened wooden poles of the fence, clambering over. The two-headed monster might have been a diversion, sent to distract us. Or else it just had a terrible sense of direction, as many corpse-demons do.

Warriors mount ladders or haul themselves up on to the rampart to tackle the demons. It's hard to tell how many monsters there are. Definitely five or six. And at least two are real demons — Fomorii.

Conn arrives at the gate, shouting orders. He bellows at those on watch who've strayed from their posts. "Stay where you are! Call if clear!"

The trembling children return to their positions and peer into the darkness, waving torches over their heads. In turn they yell, "Clear!" "Clear!" "Clear!" One starts to shout "Cle—", then screams, "No! Three of them over here!"

"With me!" Goll roars at Ena and the others who fought the first demon. They held back from the battle at the gate, in case of a second attack like this. Goll leads them against the trio of demons. I see fury in his face — he's not furious with the demons, but with himself. He made a mistake with the first one and let it knock him down. That won't happen again.

As the warriors engage the demons, I move to the centre of the rath and wait. I don't normally get involved in fights. I'm too valuable to risk. If the demons break through the barricades, or if an especially powerful Fomorii comes up against us — that's when *I* go into action.

To be honest, I doubt I could do much against the stronger Fomorii. Everybody in the rath knows that. But we pretend I'm a great priestess, mistress of all the magics. The lie comforts us and gives us some faint shadow of hope.

The younger children of the rath cluster around me, watching their parents fight to the death against the foul legions of the Otherworld. Their older brothers and sisters are at the foot of the rampart, passing up weapons to the adults, ready to dive into the breach if they fall. But these young ones wouldn't be of much use.

I hate standing with them. I'd rather be at the rampart. But duty comes at a price. Each of us does what we can do best. My wishes don't matter. The welfare of the rath and my people comes first. Always.

One of the Fomorii makes it over the fence. Half-human, half-boar. A long jaw. A mix of human teeth and tusks. Demonic yellow eyes. Claws instead of hands. It bellows at the warriors who go up against it, then spits blood at them. The blood hits a woman in the face. She shrieks and topples back off the rampart. Her flesh is bubbling — the demon blood is like fire.

I race to the woman. It's Scota. We share a hut sometimes (I'm passed around from hut to hut now Banba's gone). Her usually pale skin is an ugly red colour. Bubbles of flesh burst. The liquid sizzles. Scota screams.

I press my palms to her forehead, ignoring the heat of her flesh and the burning drops of liquid which strike my skin. I mutter the words of a calming spell. Scota sighs and relaxes, eyes closing. I tug a small bag from my belt, open it and pour coarse green grains into the palm of my left hand. Dropping the bag, I spit over the grains and mix them together with a finger, forming a paste. I rub the paste into Scota's disfigured flesh and it stops dissolving. She'll be scarred horribly but she'll live. There are other pastes and lotions I can use to help the wounds heal cleanly. But not now. There are demons to kill first.

I look up. The boar demon has been pierced in several places by the swords and knives of our warriors, but still it fights and spits. I wish I knew where these monsters got their unnatural strength from.

Screams behind me — the children! A spider-shaped Fomorii has crawled out of the hut over the souterrain. The beast must have found the exit hole outside the rath and made its way up the tunnel, then broke through the planks covering the entrance.

Conn hears the screams. He looks for warriors to send to their aid. Before he can roar orders, two brothers hurl themselves into the demon's path. Ronan and Lorcan, the rath's red-headed twins, barely sixteen years old. Their younger brother, Erc, was killed several months ago. The twins were always strong fighters, even as young children, but since Erc fell, they've fought like men possessed. They love killing demons.

Conn refocuses on the demons at the gate. He doesn't bother sending other warriors to deal with the spider. He trusts the teenage twins. They might be among the youngest warriors in the rath, but they're two of the fiercest.

Ronan and Lorcan move in on the spider demon. Now that it's closer, I see that although it has the body of a large spider, it has a dog's face and tail. Demons are often a mix of animals. Banba used to say they stole the forms of our animals and ourselves because they didn't have the imagination to invent bodies of their own.

Ronan, the taller of the pair, with long, curly, flowing hair, has two curved knives. Lorcan, who cuts his hair close and whose ears are pierced with a variety of rings, carries a sword and a small scythe. They're both skilled at fighting with either the left or right hand. But before they can tackle the dog-spider, it shoots hairs at them. The hairs run all the way along its eight legs and act like tiny arrows when flicked off sharply.

The hairs strike the brothers and cause them to stop and cover their faces with their hands, to protect their eyes. They hiss, partly from the pain, but mostly with frustration. The Fomorii moves forward, barking with evil delight, and the twins are forced back, chopping blindly at it.

I could call Conn for assistance, but I want to handle this on my own. I won't place myself at risk, but I can help, leaving the warriors free to concentrate on the larger, more troublesome demons.

I hurry to the beehives. We kept them outside the rath before the attacks began, but certain demons have a taste for honey, so we moved them in. The bees are at rest. I reach within a hive and grab a handful of bees, then prise them out, whispering words of magic so they don't sting me. Walking quickly, I place myself behind Ronan and Lorcan. Taking a firm stance, I thrust my hand out and whisper to the bees again, a command this time. They come to life within my grasp.

"Move!" I snap. Ronan and Lorcan glance back at me, surprised, then step aside. I open my fingers and the bees fly straight at the dog-spider, attacking its eyes, stinging it blind. The Fomorii whines and slaps at its eyes with its legs, losing interest in everything except the stinging bees. Ronan and Lorcan step up, one on either side. Four blades glint in the light of the torches — and four hairy legs go flying into darkness.

The demon collapses, half its legs gone, sight destroyed. Ronan steps on its head, takes aim, then buries a knife deep in its brain. The dog-spider stiffens, whines one last time, then dies. Ronan withdraws his knife and wipes it clean on his long hair. His natural red hair is stained an even darker shade of red from the blood of demons. Lorcan's stubble is blood-caked too. They never wash.

Ronan looks at me and grins. "Nice work." Then he runs with Lorcan to where Conn and his companions are attempting to drive the demons back from the fence.

I take stock. Goll's section is secure — the demons are retreating. The boar-shaped Fomorii has been pushed back over the fence. It's clinging to the poles, but its fellow demons aren't supporting it. When Ronan and Lorcan hit, blades turning the air hot, it screams shrilly, then launches itself backwards, defeated. Connla – Conn's son – fires a spear after the demon. He yells triumphantly — it must have been a hit. Connla picks up another spear. Aims. Then lowers it.

They're retreating. We've survived.

Before anyone has a chance to draw breath, there's a roar of rage and loss. It comes from near the back of the rath — Amargen, Ninian's father. He's cradling the dead boy in his arms. He had five children once. Ninian was the last. The others – and his wife – were all killed by demons.

Conn hurries across the rampart towards Amargen, to offer what words of comfort he can. Before Conn reaches him, Amargen leaps to his feet, eyes mad, and races for the chariot which our prize warriors used when going to fight. It's been sitting idle for over a year, since the demon attacks began. Conn sees what Amargen intends and leaps from the rampart, roaring, "No!"

Amargen stops, draws his sword and points it at Conn. "I'll kill anyone who tries to stop me."

No bluff in the threat. Conn knows he'll have to fight the crazed warrior to stop him. He sizes up the situation, then decides it's better to let Amargen go. He shakes his head and turns away. Waves to those near the gate to open it.

Amargen quickly hooks the chariot – a cart really, nothing like the grand, golden chariots favoured by champions in the legends – up to a horse. It's the last of our horses, a bony, exhausted excuse for an animal. He lashes the horse's hind quarters with the blunt face of his blade and it takes off at a startled gallop. Racing through the open gate, Amargen chases the demons and roars a challenge. I hear their excited snorts as they stop and turn to face him.

The gate closes. A few of the people on the rampart watch silently, sadly, as Amargen fights the demons in the open. Most turn their faces away. Moments later — human screams. A man's. Terrible, but nothing new. I say a silent prayer for Amargen, then turn my attention to the wounded, hurrying to the rampart to see who needs my help. The fighting's over. Time for healing. Time for magic. Time for Bec.

REFUGEES

→No clouds. The clearest day in a long time. Good for healing. I take power from the sun. It flows through me and from my fingers to the wounded. I use medicine, pastes and potions where they're all that's needed. Magic on those with more serious injuries — Scota and a few others who were struck by the Fomorii's fire-blood.

The warriors are tired, their sleep disturbed. They'll rest later, but most are too edgy to return to their huts straightaway. It takes an hour or two for the battle lust to pass. They're drinking coirm now and eating bread, discussing the battle and the demons.

I'm fine. I had a full night's sleep, only coming on watch a short while before the attack. That's my regular pattern on nights when there isn't an early assault.

Having tended to the seriously wounded, I wander round the rath, in case I've missed anybody. I used to think the ring fort was huge, ten huts contained within the circular wall, plenty of space for everyone. Now it feels as tight as a noose. More huts have been built over the last year, to shelter newcomers from the neighbouring villages in our tuath. Many of those who lived nearby were forced out of their homes and fled here for safety. There are twenty-two huts now, and although the walls of the rath were extended outwards during the spring, we weren't able to expand by much.

The use of magic has wearied me and left me hungry. I don't have much power, nothing like what Banba had. The sun helps but it's not enough. I need food and drink. But not coirm. That would make me dizzy and sick. Milk with honey stirred in it will give me strength.

Goll's sitting close to the milk pails. He looks downhearted. He's scratching the skin over his blind right eye. Goll was king of this whole tuath years ago, the most powerful man in the region, with command of all the local forts. There was even talk that he might become king of the province — our land is divided into four great sectors, each ruled by the most powerful of kings. None of our local leaders had ever held command of the province. It was an exciting prospect. Goll had the support of every king in our tuath and many in the neighbouring regions. Then he lost his eye in a fight and had to step down. He's not bitter. He never talks of what might have been. This was his fate and he accepts it.

But Goll's in a gloomy mood this morning. He hates making mistakes. Feeling sorry for the old warrior, I sit beside him and ask if he wants some milk.

"No, Little One," he says with a weak smile.

"It wasn't your fault," I tell him. "It was a lucky strike by the Fomorii."

Goll grunts. That should be the end of it, except Connla is standing nearby, a mug of coirm in his hands, boasting of the demon he hit with his spear. He hears my comment and laughs. "That wasn't luck! Goll's a rusty old goat!"

Goll stiffens and glares at Connla. Eighteen years old, unmarried Connla's one of the handsomest men in the tuath, tall and lean, with carefully braided hair, a moustache, no beard, fashionable tattoos. His cloak is fastened with a beautiful gold pin, and pieces of fine jewellery are stitched into it all over. Unlike most of the men, who wear belted tunics, he favours knee-length trousers. He was the first man in the rath to wear them, although several have followed his lead. His boots are made from the finest leather, laced artistically with horse-hair thongs. He looks more like a king than his father does, and when Conn dies he'll be one of the favourites to replace him. Most of the young women in the tuath desire him for his looks and prospects. But he's no great warrior. Everyone knows Connla's an average fighter. And far from the bravest.

"At least I was there to make a mistake," Goll growls. "Where were you, Connla — combing your hair perhaps?"

"I was in the thick of the fighting," Connla insists. "I struck a demon. I think I killed it."

"Aye," Goll sneers. "You hit it with a spear. In the back. While it was running away." He claps slowly. "A most courageous deed."

Connla hisses. His hand goes for a spear. Goll snatches for his axe.

"Enough!" Conn barks. He's been keeping an eye on the pair. He always seems to be on hand when Connla's on the point of getting into trouble. The king steps forward, scowling. "Isn't it bad enough that we have to fight demons every night, without battling among ourselves too?"

"He questioned my courage," Connla whines.

"And you called him an old goat," Conn retorts. "Now shake hands and forget it. We don't have time for quarrels. Be men, not children."

Goll sighs and extends a hand. Connla takes it, but his face is twisted and he shakes quickly, then returns to the small group of men who are always huddled close around him. As they leave, he starts to tell them again about the demon he speared and how he's certain the blow was fatal, boasting of his great skill and courage.

→Later. The gate of the rath is open. The cows and sheep have been led out to graze. Demons can only come at night, gods be thanked. If they could attack by day as well, we'd never be able to graze our animals or tend our crops.

I go for a walk. I like to get out of the ring fort when my duties allow, stretch my legs, breathe fresh air. I stroll to a small hill beyond the rath, from the top of which I'm able to look all the way across Sionan's river to the taller hills on the far side. Many of the men have been to those hills, to hunt or fight. I'd love to climb the peaks and see what the world looks like from them. But it's a journey of many days and nights. No chance of doing that while the demons are attacking. And for all we know, the demons will always be on the attack.

I feel lonely at times like these. Desperate. I wish Banba was here. She was more powerful than me and had the gift of prophecy. She died last winter, killed by a demon. Got too close to the fighting. Struck by a Fomorii with tusks instead of arms. It took her two nights and days to die. I haven't learnt any new magic since then. I've worked on the spells that I know, to keep in shape, but it's hard without a teacher. I make mistakes. I feel my magic getting weaker, when it should be growing every day.

"Where will it end, Banba?" I mutter, eyes on the distant hills. "Will the demons keep coming until they kill us all? Are they going to take over the world?"

Silence. A breeze stirs the branches of the nearby trees. I study the moving limbs, in case I can read a sign there. But it just seems to be an ordinary wind — not the Otherworldly voice of Banba.

After a while I bid farewell to the hills and return to the rath. There's work to be done. The world might be going up in flames, but we have to carry on as normal. We can't let the demons think they've got the beating of us. We dare not let them know how close we are to collapse.

*   *   *

→After a quick meal of bread soaked in milk, I start on my regular chores. Weaving comes first today. I'm a skilled weaver. My small fingers dart like eels across the loom. I'm the fastest in the rath. My work isn't the best, but it's not bad.

Next I fetch honey from the hives. The bees were Banba's. She brought them with her when she settled in the rath many years ago. They're my responsibility now. I was scared of them when I was younger, but not any more.

Nectan returns from a fishing trip. He slaps two large trout down in front of me and tells me to clean them. Nectan's a slave, captured abroad when he was a boy. Goll won him in a fight with another clan's king. He's as much a part of our rath now as anyone, a free man in all but name.

I enjoy cleaning fish. Some women hate it, because of the smell, but I don't mind. Also, I like reading their guts for signs and omens, or secrets from my past. I haven't divined anything from a fish's insides yet but I live in hope.

The women grind wheat in stone querns, to make bread or porridge. Some work on the roofs of the huts, thatching and mending holes. I'd love to build a hut from scratch, draw a circle on the ground and raise it up level by level. There's something magical about building. Banba told me that all unnatural things – clothes, huts, weapons – are the result of magic. Without magic, she said, men and woman would be animals, like all the other beasts.

Most of the men are sleeping, but a few are cleaning their blades and still discussing the night's battle. It was one of our easier nights. The attack was short-lived and the demons were few in number. Some reckon that's a sign that the Fomorii are dying out and returing to the Otherworld. But they're dreamers. This war with the demons is a long way from over. I don't need fish guts to tell me that!

Fiachna is working by himself, straightening crooked swords, fixing new handles to axes, sharpening knives. We're the only clan in the tuath with a smith of its own. That was Goll's doing when he was king. Most smiths wander from clan to clan, picking up work where they find it. Goll figured that if we paid a smith to settle, folk from nearby raths, cathairs and crannogs would come to us when their weapons and tools needed repairing, rather than wait for a smith to pass by. He was right. Our rath became an important focal point of the tuath — until the attacks began. The demons put paid to a lot of normal routines. Nobody travels now, unless it's to flee the Fomorii.

When I get a chance, I walk over to where Fiachna is hammering away at a particularly stubborn blade. I watch him silently, playing with a lock of my short red hair, smiling shyly. I *like* Fiachna. He's shorter than most men, and slim, which is odd for a smith. But he's very skilled. Stronger than he looks. He swings heavy hammers and weapons with ease. If I could marry, I'd like to marry Fiachna. If nothing else, we're suited in size. Maybe it's because of the name Goll gave me, or perhaps it's coincidence, but I'm one of the smallest girls in the rath.

But it's not just his size. I like his kind nature and gentle face. He has a short beard – dark-blond, like his hair – which doesn't hide his smile. Most of the men have beards so thick you can't see their mouths, so you never know if they're smiling or frowning.

I often dream of being Fiachna's wife, bearing his young, fighting demons by his side. But it won't happen. I'm almost of marrying age – my blood came a couple of years ago, earlier than in most girls – but I can never wed. Magic and marriage don't mix. Priestesses and druids lose their power if they love.

Sometimes it makes me sad, thinking about not being able to marry. I find myself wishing I could be normal, that the magic would fade from me, leaving me free to wed like other girls my age. But those are selfish thoughts and I try hard to drive them away. My people need my magic. It's not the strongest in the world and I'm in dire need of a teacher to direct me. But it's better than having no magician in the rath at all.

Fiachna looks up and catches me staring. He smiles, but not in a teasing way, not like Connla would smirk if he saw me looking at him. "You did well with the bees last night," Fiachna says in his soft, lilting voice, more like a fairy's than a human's.

I feel my face turn red. "It wasn't much," I mutter, sticking my big right toe out over the lip of its sandal and stubbing the ground.

"You're getting stronger," Fiachna says. "You'll be a powerful priestess soon."

We both know that's a lie but I love him for saying it. I give a big smile, like a baby having its tummy tickled. Then Cera calls me and tells me to give her a hand dyeing wool. "Do you want me to help you with the weapons?" I quickly ask Fiachna, hoping for an excuse to stay with him. "I can bless the blades. Put magic in them. Make them stronger."

Fiachna shakes his head. "There's no need. I'm almost finished. I'll work on farming tools in the afternoon."

"Oh." I try not to let my disappointment show. "Well, if you need me, call."

Fiachna nods. "Thank you, Bec. I will."

Simple words, but as I dip strands of wool in a vat full of blue dye, they ring inside my skull for ages, making me smile.

→In the afternoon, while the men are stirring in their sleep and the women are working on the evening meal, a lookout yells a warning. "Figures to the north!"

The rath comes on instant alert. Demons have never attacked this early – there's at least two hours of daylight left – but we've learnt not to take anything for granted. Men are out of their huts and reaching for weapons within seconds. Female warriors throw away their looms, combs, tools and pots, and hurry to the rampart. Those outside the rath are summoned in. They come hastily, anxiously driving the animals ahead of them.

Conn emerges from his hut at the centre of the village, eyes crusty, looking less worried than anyone else. A king should never look scared. He climbs the rampart and strides to the lookout. Stares off into the distance. Connla shouts at him from the ground, "Demons?"

"Doesn't look like it," Conn grunts. "Human in shape. But maybe they're dead."

The dead often come back to haunt us. The demons get the bodies from dolmens or wedge tombs. They use dark magic to fill the corpses with evil life, sometimes stitching bits from various victims together. We're not sure why they do it. Maybe some of them can't make bodies of their own and have to steal the bones of our dead. We've gone to all the local tombs that we know of over the last year, burning the corpses. But there are many hidden and forgotten tombs. The demons are always finding new bodies. At times, it seems like there's more dead than living in the world.

Conn watches for several minutes, more of the clan joining him, shading their eyes with their hands, studying the approaching shapes. I see the more hawk-eyed among them — Ronan, Lorcan, Ena — relax and I know it's all right. But nobody says anything before Conn. It's his place to give the all-clear.

Finally, Conn smiles. "Not to worry," he says. "They're human. Alive."

Calm settles over the rath and everyone returns to their normal routine. We're curious about the strangers but we'll find out all about them in good time. No point standing around guessing, when there's work to be done.

* * *

→They arrive half an hour later, ragged and weary from battle and the road. Four men, three women and four children. We know them — the MacCadan. When the demons first attacked, Conn sent an envoy to Cadan and asked if he was open to an alliance. There had been bad blood between us but Conn wanted to make peace, so we could fight the demons together. Cadan refused. He said his people could stand alone. We haven't heard from them since then.

Cadan's not among the eleven. The leader's an old warrior – even older than Goll – who limps awkwardly and trembles pitifully when he's not on the move. He announces himself at the gate as Tiernan MacCadan and requests entrance. The eleven trudge into the rath and present themselves miserably, heads low.

Conn goes straight to Tiernan and clasps his arms warmly, welcoming him. He asks if they're hungry or thirsty. Tiernan says they are and Conn gives orders for a feast to be prepared. The women set to the task immediately.

Conn leads our guests to the area in front of his hut and lets them settle. They haven't brought much – spare clothes, a few weapons, some tools – but it's plain this is all they have. I know what's happened, just as Conn and everybody else knows, but nobody says anything. We let Tiernan explain.

The demons overwhelmed them. The end had been coming for a long time but they held out stubbornly, even past the point where they knew it was folly. Their best warriors had fallen to the foul Fomorii, their children had been taken, their animals slain, their crops destroyed.

"Many argued against staying," Tiernan sighs. "We said it was madness, that we'd perish if we didn't join forces with our neighbours. But Cadan said we'd lose face if we retreated. He was a proud man, not for bending. But eventually, like all who refuse to bend, he snapped. The Fomorii took him last night, along with three others. This morning, before the sun had risen, we packed our goods and marched here. We hope to fight with you, to offer whatever aid we can, to…"

He trails to a halt. Two of the men are seriously injured and Tiernan's no chick. One of the women is a warrior but the other two aren't. And the children are too young to fight. Tiernan's trying to make it sound like we need them, that they can make a difference. But really they're just looking for sanctuary. Taking them in would be a mercy, not a merger.

The men of the rath are sitting in a circle around the newcomers. I'm on the outskirts, only allowed this close in case any magical matters arise. I see doubt on the faces of most. We're already cramped. We'd need to expand the fort again to comfortably hold eleven more people. That's hard to do when you're under attack from demons most nights.

Tiernan senses the mood and speaks rapidly. "We could build our own huts. Our women are skilled, the children too. We'd depend on your hospitality for a few weeks but we'd work every hour we can to set up on our own. We wouldn't be a burden. And when it comes to fighting, we're stronger than we look. Even the youngest child has drawn blood. We—"

"Easy, friend," Conn interrupts. "We're pleased you came to us when there are so many other clans you could have gone to. It's an honour to receive you. I'm sure you will be of great help."

Tiernan blinks. He hadn't expected such a gracious welcome. After the years of feuding, it's more than he dared hope. Tears well in his eyes but he shakes them away and smiles. "You're a true king," he compliments Conn.

"And, I hope, a true friend," Conn replies, then barks orders for beds to be made for the MacCadan. Some don't like it — Connla's face is as dark as a winter cloud — but nobody's going to argue with our king, certainly not in front of guests. So they obey without question, shifting beds, clothes and goods from one hut to another, bunching up even closer than before, squashing together, making room for the new additions to our demon-tormented clan.

THE BOY

→Preparations for the feast are at an advanced stage, and the sun is close to setting, when there's a call from another lookout. "I see someone in the distance running towards us!"

Conn raises an eyebrow at Tiernan. They've been talking about their battles with the demons. I've sat in close attendance. Our seanachaidh fled not long after the attacks began, so I've been charged with keeping the history of the clan. I'm no natural storyteller but I've a perfect memory.

"It's not one of ours," Tiernan says. "We brought all our living with us."

"Is it a demon?" Conn shouts at the lookout.

"It doesn't look like one," comes the reply. "I think it's a boy. But the speed at which he's running... I'm not sure."

Conn returns to the rampart with Tiernan and a few of our warriors. I slip up behind them. I normally avoid the exposure of the higher ground, but a lone demon in daylight can't pose much of a threat.

As the figure races closer, we see that it's a boy, my age or slightly older, running incredibly fast, head bobbing about strangely. He lopes up to the gate, ignoring Conn's shouts to identify himself, then stops and looks at us dumbly. Dark hair and small eyes. He smiles widely, even though Conn is roaring at him, threatening to stick a spear through his heart if he doesn't announce his intentions. Then he sits, picks a flower and plays with it.

Conn looks angry but confused. "A simpleton," he grunts.

"It could be a trap," Tiernan mutters.

"Demons don't send humans to lay traps," Conn disagrees.

"But you saw how fast he ran," Tiernan says. "And he doesn't look tired. He's not even sweating. Maybe he's not human."

"Bec," Conn calls, "do you sense anything?"

I close my eyes and focus on the boy. Demons have a different feel to humans. They buzz with the power of their own world. There's a flicker of that about this child. I start to tell Conn but then something strange happens. I sense a change in the boy. Opening my eyes, I see that the light around him is different. It's like looking at him through a thick bank of mist. As I squint, I realise the boy is no longer there. Instead, I'm staring at my mother.

There's no mistaking her. I've seen her so many times in my perfect memories. She looks just like she did on the day she gave birth to me — the day she died. Haggard, bone-thin, dark circles under her eyes, stained with blood. But love in her eyes — love for me.

As I stare, numb with wonder — but no fear — my mother turns and points west, keeping her eyes on mine. She says something but her words don't carry. With a frown, she jabs a long finger towards the west. She starts to say something else but then the mist clears. She shimmers. I blink. And I'm suddenly looking at the boy again, playing with his flower.

"Bec," Conn is saying, shaking me lightly. "Are you all right?"

I look up, trembling, and think about telling Conn what I saw. Then I decide against it. I've never had a vision before. I need time to think about it before I discuss it with anyone. Focusing on the boy, I control my breathing and try to calm my fast heartbeat.

"I th-think he's hu-human," I stutter. "But not the same as us. There's magic in him. Maybe he's a druid's apprentice." That's a wild guess, but it's the closest I can get to explaining what's different about him.

"Does he pose a threat?" Conn asks.

A dangerous question — if I answer wrongly, I'll be held responsible. I think about playing safe and saying I don't know, but then the boy pulls a petal from the flower and slowly places it on his outstretched tongue. "No," I say confidently. "He can't harm us."

The gate is opened. Several of us spill out and surround the boy. I've been brought along in case he doesn't speak our language. A priestess is meant to have the gift of tongues. I don't actually know any other languages but I don't see the

need to admit that, not unless somebody asks me directly —
and so far nobody has. I keep hoping he'll change and
become my mother again, but he doesn't.

The boy is thin and dirty, his hair thick and unwashed, his
knee-length tunic caked with mud, no cloak or sandals. His
eyes dart left and right, never lingering on any one spot for
more than a second. He's carrying a long knife in a scabbard
hanging from his belt but he doesn't reach for it or show
alarm as we gather round him.

"Boy!" Conn barks, nudging the boy's knee with his foot.
No reaction. "Boy! Who are you? What are you doing here?"

The boy doesn't answer. Conn opens his mouth to shout
again, then stops. He looks at me and nods. Licking my lips
nervously, I crouch beside the strange child. I watch him play
with the flower, noting the movements of his eyes and head.
I no longer think he's a druid's assistant. Conn was right —
he's a simpleton. But one who's been blessed in some way by
the gods.

"That's a nice flower," I murmur.

The boy's gaze settles on me for an instant and he grins,
then thrusts the flower at me. When I take it, he picks
another and holds it above his head, squinting at it.

"Can you speak?" I ask. "Do you talk?"

No answer. I'm about to ask again, when he shouts
loudly, "Flower!"

I jump at the sound of his voice. So do the men around
me. Then we laugh, embarrassed. The boy looks at us,

delighted. "Flower!" he shouts again. Then his smile dwindles. "Demons. Killing. Come with." He leaps to his feet. "Come with! Run fast!"

"Wait," I shush him. "It's almost night. We can't go anywhere. The demons will be on the move soon."

"Demons!" he cries. "Killing. Come with!" He grabs my hand and hauls me up.

"Wait," I tell him again, losing my patience. "What's your name? Where are you from? Why should we trust you?" The boy stares at me blankly. I take a deep breath, then ask slowly, "What's your name?" No answer. "Where are you from?" Nothing. I turn to Conn and shrug. "He's simple. He probably escaped from his village and—"

"Come with!" the boy shouts. "Run fast! Demons!"

"Bec's right," Connla snorts. "Why would anyone send a fool like this to—"

"Run fast!" the boy gasps before Connla can finish. "Run fast!" he repeats, his face lighting up. He tears away from us, breaks through the ranks of warriors as if they were reeds and races around the rath. Seconds later he's back, not panting, just smiling. "Run fast," he says firmly.

"Do you know where you're from, Run Fast?" Goll asks, giving the boy a name since he can't provide one himself. "Can you find your way back to your people?"

For a moment the boy gawps at Goll. I don't think he understands. But then he nods, looks to where the sun is setting and points west. "Pig's trotters," he says thoughtfully.

For a second I see my mother pointing that same way again, but this is just a memory, not another vision.

Goll faces Conn. "We should bring him in. It'll be dark soon. We can question him inside, though I doubt we'll get much more out of him."

Conn hesitates, judging the possible danger to his people, then clicks his fingers and leaves the boy to his men, returning to the fireside with Tiernan, to discuss this latest turn of events.

→Run Fast isn't big but he has the appetite of a boar. He eats more than anyone at the feast but nobody minds. There's something cheering about the boy. He makes us all feel good, even though he can't talk properly, except to explode every so often with "Demons!" or "Come with!" or – his favourite – "Run fast!"

As Goll predicted, Run Fast isn't able to tell us any more about his clan, where he lives or how great their need is. Under normal circumstances he'd be ignored. We've enough problems to cope with. But the mood of the rath is lighter than it's been in a long while. The arrival of the MacCadan has sparked confidence. Even though the eleven are more of a burden than a blessing, they've given us hope. If survivors from other clans make their way here, perhaps we can build a great fort and a mighty army, keep the demons out forever. It's wishful, crazy thinking, but we think it anyway. Banba used to say that the desperate and damned could build a mountain of hope out of a rat's droppings.

So we grant Run Fast more thought than we would have last night. The men debate his situation, where he's from, how long it might have taken him to come here, why a fool was sent instead of another.

"His speed is the obvious reason," Goll says. "Better to send a hare with half a message than a snail with a full one."

"Or maybe the Fomorii sent him," Tiernan counters, his bony, wrinkled fingers twitching with suspicion. "They could have conquered his clan, then muddled his senses and sent him to lure others into a trap."

"You afford them too much respect," Conn says. "The Fomorii we've fought are mindless, dim-witted creatures."

"Aye," Tiernan agrees. "So were ours to begin with. But they've changed. They're getting more intelligent. We had a craftily hidden souterrain. One or two would find their way into it by accident every so often, but recently they attacked through it regularly, in time with those at the fence. They were thinking and planning clearly, more like humans in the way they battled."

Conn massages his chin thoughtfully. Our one great advantage over the demons — besides the fact they can only attack at night — is that we're smarter than them. But if there are others, brighter than those we've encountered...

"I don't think it's a trap," Fiachna says quietly. He doesn't normally say much, so everyone's surprised to hear him speak. He's been sitting next to Run Fast, examining the boy's knife. "This boy doesn't have the scent of demons on him. Am I right, Bec?"

I nod immediately, delighted to be publicly noticed by Fiachna. "Not a bit of a scent," I gush, rather more breathlessly than I meant.

"He's telling the truth," Fiachna says. "His people need help. Run Fast was the best they could send. So they sent him, probably in blind hope."

"What of it?" Connla snorts. I can tell by the way he's eyeing Run Fast that he doesn't like him. "We need help too. Our plight's as serious as theirs. What do they expect us to do — send our men to fight their battles, leaving our women and children at the mercy of the Fomorii?" He spits into the dust.

"He puts it harshly but there's wisdom in what my son says," Conn murmurs. "Alliances are one thing, but begging for help like slaves… asking us to go to their aid instead of coming to us…"

"Perhaps they can't travel," Goll says. "Many might be wounded or old."

"In which case they're not worth saving," Connla laughs. Those who follow him laugh too — wolves copying the example of their pack leader.

"We should go," Goll growls. "Or at least send an envoy. If we ignore their pleas, perhaps ours will also be ignored when we seek assistance."

"Only the weak ask for help," Connla says stiffly.

Goll smiles tightly and I sense what he's going to say next — something along the lines of, "Well, it won't be long before *you* ask then!"

Luckily Conn senses it too, and before Goll utters an insult which will demand payment in blood, the king says, "Even if we wanted to help, we don't know where they are, and I don't trust this empty-headed child to find his way back."

"If the brehons were here, they could counsel us," Fiachna says.

"Brehons!" Connla snorts. "Weren't they the first to flee when the demons arose? Damn the brehons!"

There are mutters of agreement, even from those who don't normally side with Connla. The law-making brehons deserted us when we most needed them and few are in the mood to forgive and forget.

The men continue debating, the women sitting silently behind them, their children sleeping or playing games. On the rampart the lookouts keep watch for demons.

Goll and Fiachna are of the opinion that we should send a small group with Run Fast to help his clan. "It's no accident that he arrived on the same day as the MacCadan," Goll argues. "Yesterday we couldn't have let anyone go. But our ranks have been bolstered. It's a sign."

"*Bolstered?*" Connla almost shrieks, casting a scornful glance at the four men and three women of the MacCadan.

"Connla!" his father snaps, before the hot-headed warrior disgraces our guests. When he's sure of his son's silence,

Conn leans forward, sipping coirm, thinking hard. Like any king, he dare not ignore a possible sign from the gods. But he's not sure this is a sign. And in a situation such as this, there's only one person he can turn to. "Bec?"

I was expecting his query, so I'm able to keep a calm face. I've had time to consider my answer. I believe we're meant to go with Run Fast. That was what the vision meant. The spirit of my mother was telling me to follow this boy.

"We should help," I whisper. Connla rolls his eyes but I ignore him. "We're stronger now, thanks to the MacCadan. We can spare a few of our warriors. I believe Run Fast can find his way back to his people, and I think bad luck would befall us if we refused their plea."

Conn nods slowly. "But who to send? I don't want to command anyone to leave. Are there volunteers…?"

"Aye," Goll says instantly. "Since I argued the case, I have to go."

"I'll go too," Fiachna says quietly.

"You?" Conn frowns. "But you're not a warrior."

Fiachna holds up Run Fast's knife. "This metal is unfamiliar to me. It's tougher than our own, yet lighter. If I knew the secret of it, I could make better weapons." He lowers the knife. "I'll stay if you order it, but I want to go."

"Very well," Conn sighs. "But you'll travel with a guard." He looks around to choose a warrior to send with the smith. There are many to pick from, but he's loath to send a husband or father. So it must be one of the younger warriors. As he studies them, his expression changes and a crafty look comes into his eyes. He points to Connla. "My son will protect you."

Connla gawps at his father. Others are surprised too. This quest is a perilous one. The land is full of demons. The chances of survival are slim. Yet Conn's telling his own flesh and blood to leave the safety of the rath and serve as guard to a smith. Most can't see the wisdom of it.

But I can. Conn wants his son to succeed him. But Connla is largely untested in battle and not everyone respects him. If Conn died tonight, there would be several challengers to replace him and Connla might find powerful allies hard to come by. But if he completes this task and returns with a bloodied blade and tales of glory, that would change. This could be the making of him.

And if the quest goes poorly and he dies? Well, that will be the decision of the gods. You can't fight your destiny.

While Connla blinks stupidly at his father, the teenage twins, Ronan and Lorcan rise. "We'll go too," Ronan says, brushing blood-red hair out of his eyes.

"We want to kill more demons," Lorcan adds, tugging an earring, excited.

Conn growls unhappily. The twins are young but they're two of our finest warriors. He doesn't want to let them go but he can't refuse without insulting them. In the end he nods reluctantly. "Any others?" he asks.

"Me," a woman of the MacCadan says, taking a step forward. "Orna MacCadan. I'll represent my clan, to repay you for your hospitality." Orna is the female warrior I spotted earlier.

Conn smiles. "Our thanks. Now, if that's all…" He looks for any final volunteers, making it clear by the way he asks that he thinks six is more than adequate.

But one last hand goes up. A tiny hand. *Mine.*

"I want to go too."

Conn's astonished. Everybody is.

"Bec," Goll says, "this isn't suitable for a child."

"I'm not a child," I retort. "I'm a priestess. Well, an apprentice priestess."

"It will be dangerous," Fiachna warns me. "This is a task for warriors."

"You're going," I remind him, "but you're no warrior."

"I have to go in case there's a smith in this village, who can teach me to make better weapons," he says.

"Maybe I can learn something too," I reply, then face Conn. "I need to do this. I sense failure if I don't go. I'm not sure what good I can do – maybe none at all – but I believe I must travel with them."

Conn shakes his head, troubled. "I can't allow this. With Banba gone, you're our only link to the ways of magic. We need you."

"You need Fiachna too," I cry, "but you're letting him go."

"Fiachna's a man," Conn says sternly. "He has the right to choose."

"So do I," I growl, then raise my voice and repeat it, with conviction this time. "So do I! We of magic live by our own rules. I was Banba's charge, not yours. She lived here by choice, as do I — neither of us were of this clan. You had no power over her and you don't have any over me. Since she's dead, I'm my own guardian. I answer to a higher voice than any here and that voice tells me to go. If you hold me, it will be against my will and the will of the gods."

Brave, provocative words, which Conn can't ignore. Although I'm no more a real priestess than any of the cows in the fields, I'm closer to the ways of magic than anybody else in the rath. Nobody dares cross me on this.

"Very well," Conn says angrily. "We've pledged an ex-king, our smith, two of our best warriors, a guest and my own son to this reckless cause — why not our young priestess too!"

And so, in a bitter, resentful fashion, my fate is decided and I'm dismissed. With a mix of fear and excitement – mostly fear – I trudge back to my hut to enjoy one final night of sheltered sleep, before leaving home in the morning, to face the demons and other dangers of the world beyond.

THE RIVER

→There are no attacks during the night — an encouraging omen. We depart with the rising of the sun, bidding short farewells to relatives and friends. I want to look back at the huts and walls of the rath as we leave – I might never see them again – but that would be inviting bad luck, so I keep my eyes on the path ahead.

It's a cloudy day, lots of showers, the coolness of autumn. Summer's been late fading this year, but I can tell by sniffing the air that it's finally passed for certain. That could be interpreted as a bad sign – the dying of a season on the day we leave – but I choose to overlook it.

We march east at a steady pace, staying close to Sionan's river. Our boats were destroyed in a demon attack some months back, so we can't cross the river here. We have to go east, cross where it's narrow, then make our way west from there.

The earth is solid underfoot and there are plenty of paths through the trees, so we make good time. Ronan and Lorcan are to the fore of the pack. I'm next, with Orna and Run Fast.

He's eager to move ahead of the rest of us but we hold him back — otherwise he might disappear in the undergrowth like a rabbit. Connla and Fiachna are behind us. Connla's sulking and hasn't said a word since we left. Goll brings up the rear.

I brood upon my reasons for leaving the rath as we march, feeling uneasier the more I think about it. Mostly I chose to leave because of the vision of my mother. But there was another reason — fear. The rath seemed to grow smaller every day. I felt so confined, I sometimes found it hard to breathe. I had nightmares where I was trapped, the wall of the fort closing in, ever tighter, squeezing me to death. If our worst fears come true and we fall to the hordes of demons, I don't want to die caged in.

Is it possible I created the vision to give myself an excuse to leave? I don't think so. I'm almost certain it was genuine. But the mind can play tricks. What if this is folly, if I'm running away from my fears into worse danger than I would have faced if I'd stayed?

If it wasn't a trick — if the vision was real — why would the ghost of my mother send me on this deadly quest? She wouldn't have urged me to risk my life if it wasn't important. Maybe she wants to help me unravel the secrets of my past. I've always longed to know more about my mother, where I came from, who my people were. Perhaps Run Fast can help me find the truth.

If that's just wishful thinking, and my past is to remain a secret, maybe our rath is destined to fall. My mother's spirit might have foreseen the destruction of the MacConn and acted to spare me.

Whatever way I look at it, I realise I left for purely selfish reasons. The MacConn need me. I shouldn't have abandoned them because I was afraid, to hunt down my original people or save myself from an oncoming disaster. I should go back. Fight with them. Use my magic to protect the clan as best I can.

But what if there's some other reason my mother appeared, if I can somehow help the MacConn by coming on this crazy trek? Banba said we should always follow the guidance of spirits, although we had to be wary, because sometimes they could try to trick us.

Ana help me! So many possibilities — my head is hurting, thinking about them. I should stop and give my brain a rest. Besides, there's no point worrying now. We're more than half a day's march from the rath. We couldn't return to safety before nightfall. There's no going back.

→Everybody was quiet during the morning's march, thinking about those we left behind and what lies ahead. We stopped to rest and eat at midday. Ronan and Lorcan caught a couple of rabbits, which we ate raw, along with some berries. After that, as we walked slower on our full stomachs, the talk began, low and leisurely, with Fiachna asking Orna a question about the three-bladed knives she favours.

There were lots more questions for Orna after that. Those from our rath know all there is to know about each other. Orna and Run Fast are the only mysteries in the group, and since Run Fast simply grins and looks away when you ask him anything, that leaves Orna as the focus for our curiosity.

She's had four husbands, children by three of them. She says she likes men but has never been able to put up with one for more than a couple of years. Goll laughs at that and says the pair of them should marry, since he won't live much more than a few years.

"I wouldn't have a lot to leave except memories," he grins. "But they'd be good memories. I had three wives when I was young and didn't disappoint any of them!"

"Except when you lost your eye and kingship," Connla smirks, sending Goll into a foul mood.

"You shouldn't provoke him like that," Fiachna whispers harshly.

"He's an old wreck," Connla retorts. "My father's a king and I plan to follow in his footsteps. I'll speak to the old goat any way I like."

"We're not in the rath now," Fiachna says. "We're a small, isolated group and we need to rely on each other. Think on — Goll might hold your life in his hands one night soon."

As Connla scowls and considers that, I ask Orna about her children. Were they among those who arrived yesterday?

"No," Orna says shortly, gaze set straight, her shaved head glistening in the rain. There are tattoos on both her cheeks – the marks of Nuada, the goddess of war — dark red swirls which suck in the gaze of all who look at them in an almost mesmerising way. "They're dead. Killed by demons a week ago."

"Ana protect them," I mutter automatically.

"Ana keep them dead," Orna replies tonelessly.

"You didn't burn the bodies?"

"We couldn't find them. Demons slipped in through our souterrain and made off with them. They must have been playing in the tunnel. I told them a hundred times never to go down there. But children don't listen."

Her eyes are filled with a mixture of sadness and rage. As a warrior, she won't have allowed herself to mourn. But women can't make themselves as detached as men. Our hearts are bigger. We feel loss in a way men don't. Orna has the body and mind of a warrior but her heart is like mine, and I know inside she's weeping.

→Ronan and Lorcan spar with Orna in the evening as we cross bogland. She knows a few knife feints which are new to the brothers and they practise until they've perfected them. Ronan and Lorcan, in turn, know lots of moves which Orna doesn't and they teach her a few, promising to reveal more over the coming days.

Once warriors were secretive. They kept their techniques to themselves, always wary of their neighbours, knowing that today's friend can be tomorrow's enemy. The Fomorii changed that. Now we share because we have to —

warriors, smiths, magicians. The demons have united the various tuatha of this land in a way no king ever has. A shame we can't join forces and face them on a single battlefield, in fair combat — I'm sure we'd win. But although demons aren't as clever as humans, they're sly. They spread out, taking control of paths and routes, limiting the opportunities to travel, dividing prospective allies. We share our arms, learning and experience with others where possible, but I fear we shan't be able to share enough.

As Ronan and Lorcan spar with Orna, Connla asks Fiachna for advice. He has an idea for a new spear, topped with several sharp fins, and wants Fiachna's opinion. Fiachna listens politely, then explains why the weapon won't work. Connla's disappointed but Fiachna cheers him up by saying if there's a smith in Run Fast's village who can make weapons like the boy's knife, perhaps the two of them can come up with something along the lines of Connla's design.

I chat to Run Fast, asking him again for his real name, where he's from, if he has family. But he doesn't answer. After a while Goll nudges up beside us. "Having trouble, Little One?" he asks.

"He won't tell me anything," I huff. "I'm sure he could – if he can tell us his people need help, he must be able to tell us his name – but he won't!"

"The heads of the touched are hard to fathom," Goll says, rustling Run Fast's hair. "My second wife had a brother like this. He couldn't dress himself, wield a weapon or cook a meal. But he could play the pipes beautifully. In all other ways he was helpless — but set him loose on the pipes and he could play any man into the ground."

"What happened to him?" I ask.

Goll shrugs. "He went wandering one day and ate poisoned berries."

"Berries!" Run Fast shouts, rubbing his stomach. He picks up on certain words every so often and repeats them.

"It's not that long since we last ate," I tell him. "Wait until dinner."

"Berries," Run Fast says again, sadly this time. Then he stamps his right foot several times and looks at me hopefully. "Run fast?"

"No," I groan. "Not now. You have to stay with us."

"Run fast," he sighs, stamping the ground one last time, letting me know that he could race up a storm if I gave him the go-ahead.

Goll laughs. "He's a lively one. You'll have your hands full looking after him!"

"I might just push him into Sionan's river when we cross," I huff.

"We wouldn't be able to find his village then," Goll says.

"I'm not sure we'll find it anyway," I grumble. "How do we know he's leading us the right way? He could have come from a southern tuatha for all we know."

Goll squints at me with his good eye. "You're in dark spirits, Little One. Are you tired?"

"No."

Goll tickles me under the chin until I laugh. "Tired?" he asks again.

"Aye," I sigh. "I'm not used to all this walking. And you go so quickly! I've only got short legs."

"You should have said."

"I didn't want to look like a... a..."

"A child?" Goll smiles. "But you are. And a tiny wee bec of a child at that."

"Just because I'm small doesn't mean I can't keep up!" I fume, quickening my pace. But I've not taken five or six steps when Goll wraps a burly arm around my waist and hauls me off the ground. "Hoi!" I cry. "Put me down!"

"Stop struggling," Goll says and settles me on his shoulders, my legs either side of his head. "We might have need of you later. You're no good to us fit for nothing but sleep."

"I'm fit to turn you into a frog if you don't put me down!" I grunt, but secretly I'm delighted and after struggling playfully for a minute, I settle back and let Goll be my horse for the rest of the afternoon, admiring the view from up high and saving my strength in case I'm called upon to fight demons in the dark.

→We come to the crossing point of Sionan's river late in the evening. The river's narrow here, easy to ford. This is the joining point of two tuatha. A large cashel once stood here, the largest in the province. A couple of wooden roads lead up to and away from the place where the impressive stone fort stood. Many carts used to travel this way and the roads were carefully tended. But the cashel's a pile of rubble now and the roads are in disrepair. We'd heard the cashel had been overrun by demons but hoped the reports were wrong. This would have been the ideal place to shelter tonight.

"What now?" Connla asks, studying the untidy mound which was once the pride of the province. "Cross the river or camp here?"

"Cross," Ronan and Lorcan say together.

"There's no safety here," Ronan says.

"Where demons attack once, they'll attack again," Lorcan agrees.

"And many can't cross flowing water," Ronan says. "We'd be safer on the other side."

Connla nods but looks uneasy. There was never a fort on the opposite side of the river, just some huts where folk of the neighbouring tuath dwelt. They used to greet those who crossed the river and either grant them the freedom of their tuath or turn them back. The huts are still standing but we can't see any people. They might be hiding or they might all be murdered, demons sheltering inside the huts from the sun.

"Come on," Goll says, setting me down and taking the lead. "The sun's setting. Let's get across and find a hole for the night which we can defend."

＊　＊　＊

→There are dugouts tethered to the banks of the river, bobbing up and down. Each holds four people at most. We head for the nearest pair. Ronan and Lorcan team up with Run Fast and me. Goll, Orna, Fiachna and Connla take the other. Lorcan grabs the rope of our dugout and hauls it in. He's almost pulled the boat up on dry land when I get a warning flash.

"Lorcan! No!" I scream.

He reacts instantly, drops the rope and leaps backwards just in time. A huge demonic eel unleashes itself at him, rising out of the boat like an arrow shot from a bow. Its jaws are impossibly wide, filled with teeth which would be more suited to a bear.

The demon snaps for Lorcan's head and only misses by a finger's breadth. It lands hard on the earth and writhes angrily, going for Lorcan's legs. Ronan steps up beside his brother and stabs at the place where the demon's eyes should be. But it doesn't have any. It's blind, operating by some other form of sense.

Orna jumps on to the demon's back and hacks at it with her three-bladed knives, one in either hand. The demon bucks and twists desperately, trying to dislodge her, but she rides it like a pony, digging her heels in, face twisted as she screams hatefully, tattoos rippling with fury.

Connla takes aim and hurls a spear at the beast, down its maw of a mouth. The spear sticks deep in its throat. The demon chokes and slams its head downwards, trying to spit out the spear.

Goll darts forward, grabs the shaft of the spear and drives it further into the Fomorii's throat, twisting savagely. The demon spasms, then weakens. Suddenly the warriors are all over it, hacking away like ants trying to bring down a badger. Fiachna, Run Fast and I watch from nearby.

"Do you think I should help?" Fiachna asks, fingers tapping the head of an axe which hangs from his belt.

"They're in control," I tell him.

And, moments later, the battle's over and the eel demon lies at their feet, covered in the grey blood which previously pumped through its veins, torn to pieces, jaws stretched wide in a final death snarl.

Goll grasps the handle of the spear, yanks it out and hands it to Connla. He laughs and claps the younger warrior on the back. "A master throw!"

Connla smiles sheepishly. "I didn't mean to hurl it down the beast's throat," he says with untypical modesty. "I aimed for the top of its head. But it moved. I got lucky."

"I'll always take luck over skill," Goll says, clapping Connla's back again. The pair grin at each other like lifelong friends.

"I've never fought a water demon before," Orna grunts, wiping her knives clean on the grass. She dabs at the final few drops of grey blood with her middle finger, then rubs it into the centre spots of her spiral tattoos, one after the other.

"They're rare," Ronan says, studying the demon, turning it over on to its back with his foot. "We're lucky it's not night or it would have been stronger."

"Come on," I mutter, glancing around uneasily. "It'll be sunset soon. More will be coming."

That silences everyone. After a quick check to make sure the second dugout is free of demons, we're in the boats and crossing the river as swiftly as possible, everybody keeping one eye on the water, wary of attack from beneath.

THE STONES

→Nobody emerges from the huts as we dock. When we're on dry land, we stare at the huts suspiciously. You're not supposed to enter a tuath without announcing yourself and being guided by one of your own rank. But times have changed. Many of the old laws no longer apply.

"You in the huts!" Goll bellows, in case anyone's alive inside.

Silence.

"Should we go see if anybody's there?" Fiachna asks.

"They'd have answered if there was," Connla says.

"Unless they're scared or sheltering underground," Orna notes.

Ronan points silently at a spot to the left of the huts. My eyes aren't as sharp as his, so it takes me a few seconds to focus. Then I see it — a small arm, probably a child's, lying in the dirt.

Goll sighs, draws his sword and moves to the front of the group. "Let's go," he says gruffly, and we proceed at a forced, nervous jog.

*   *   *

→There's nowhere to shelter, so we don't stop when the sun sets, but keep going, hoping to outpace any demons which catch our scent. I try to persuade myself that we won't be noticed. Only a fool travels at night in these troubled times. The Fomorii won't expect to find anyone out in the open. Maybe they don't even look any more.

A silly, childish notion. But for an hour it seems as though it might hold true. We don't sight any demons and hope begins to grow.

But then we hear a howl of inhuman vibrancy far behind us, but not far enough for comfort. We pause and listen as the howl is answered by others. In my mind's eye I see a group forming, demons and the living dead. They gather around the one who found our trail, sniff the air, lick the earth, quiver with excitement — then lurch forward, to run us down.

"They might be after someone else," Connla says but his words are hollow. We've been discovered.

"Let's pick up the pace," Goll says, expression stern.

Run Fast's head shoots up. "Run fast?" he asks eagerly.

"Aye," Goll says, then grabs the boy as he starts to shoot off. "Not *that* fast!"

→We can hear them, a pack of demons crashing through the woods, snapping off branches, knocking over smaller trees. I've never known demons so excited. I guess, when they attack a fort, it's hard work. It must be frustrating, the scent of prey thick in their nostrils, having to fight their way through, often failing. But out here, in the open, they have only to hunt us down and we're theirs for the taking. They're like dogs after a fox.

We're looking for a place to make a stand, somewhere we can defend. A cave would be perfect. We could squeeze in and fend them off, maybe keep them at bay for the rest of the night, then escape in the morning. But there are no caves, or at least none that we can find.

Goll comes to a halt in a small clearing. Trees have been felled here some time in the last few years. Somebody probably planned to graze animals or build a hut, in the days before the demons came. Goll looks around, assessing.

"Not here," Connla wheezes, face dark from the strain. "Too exposed."

"There's nowhere better," Goll gasps. He points to a mound of logs covered in moss. "We can start a fire. Fell more trees, stake them in the ground and sharpen the tops. Make it hard for the demons to strike all at once."

"But…" Connla looks to the others for support, but Ronan, Lorcan and Orna are already drawing their weapons, preparing for battle. Fiachna has his axe out and is studying the trees. They know it's hopeless, that we're going to die. But what choice do we have? There's nothing to do but draw our lines, wait and face those who will most certainly destroy us. Die as warriors, with pride.

I'm thinking about what spells I can use when a small hand slips into mine. I look round. Run Fast is smiling at me. "Run fast?" he whispers.

"Not now," I sigh.

The boy frowns. "Run fast," he says more firmly.

I shake my head. "We have to stay and fight. Can you fight? Do you know how to—"

The strange boy's fingers grab mine tightly and his face hardens. "Run fast!" he hisses, then points with his free hand. "Worm pups!"

I start to snap at him to be quiet. Then pause. There's a tingling sensation in Run Fast's fingers. Some sort of magic. I look down. His hand is glowing slightly. The boy looks at it too, then up at me. "Worm pups," he repeats, softly this time.

"Goll!" I shout. The old warrior glances at me. "We're leaving."

"But—"

"Don't argue!" I move ahead with Run Fast. "We'll die here. But I think, if we carry on, there's…" I stop, not sure what might lie beyond, but sensing in my heart that it's better than this.

Everybody's looking at me now, torn between hope and suspicion.

"This place isn't much," Fiachna says, "but it's defendable. If we're caught on the run, we're finished for sure. Are you certain…?"

"Yes," I growl. "We have to go. Now. We're dead if we don't."

"But we'll live if we do?" Connla asks dubiously.

"Perhaps."

It's not enough. They don't trust my instincts. They're going to stay. I open my mouth to argue afresh, but then Orna lowers her knives and comes to my side. "I'm with the girl."

"Why?" Goll asks — not a challenge, just curious.

Orna shrugs. "A feeling."

Lorcan taps a few of his earrings with a knife tip. "I don't feel like we'll live if we go, but I'm sure we'll die if we stay."

Goll looks around at the others and asks the question with his eyes. They answer with weary glances and resigned shrugs. "So be it," he says, sheathing his sword. "Bec — lead us."

We run.

→Sweat. Terror. The sounds of chasing demons. Almost upon us. A minute, maybe two, and we'll be forced to stop and fight — stop and *die*.

The trees are thick around us. Impossible to see far. It's dark. *Too* dark. I look up and notice extra branches, scraps of cloth, thatch torn from roofs, all sorts of bits and pieces scattered among the tree tops, linking the upper branches, keeping out the light of the moon and stars.

My stomach sinks. This is a trap! I was wrong. Run Fast *was* sent to lead us to our doom. And we fell for it. I start to shout a warning, even though it's far too late. Then…

We burst into the open and come to a surprised halt. There's a clear circle around us and at the centre — a ring of giant stones. Most are taller than me. Some even tower above the lanky Ronan and Connla. Set in the ground at regular intervals. Ancient, covered in moss and creepers. A place of magic, but magic from a time before ours, the time of the Old Creatures, when this country was the playground of the gods.

The demons are hot on our heels, surging up behind us, their stench foul in the air. "Come on!" Fiachna screams. We fly forward at his call, rushing to the stones, readying ourselves for battle.

We spill past the stones, into the middle of the ring. The stones won't provide much cover but they'll make it slightly harder for the demons to get at us and buy us a few seconds. They won't make a real difference, but you've always got to live in hope. Before you die at the hands of a Fomorii.

Lorcan jumps on to a stone which fell on its side many years ago. He waves his sword over his head, screaming a challenge at the demons which are emerging from the cover of the trees. Dozens of twisted, hideous monsters. One has the body of a bear but the head of a hawk. Another looks like a wolf but its inner organs hang from its limbs. Claws, fangs, blood-red eyes. Nightmares everywhere I look.

The demons advance slowly. I assume they're relishing the moment, prolonging it, toying with us. But then they stop and howl with anger.

As we stare at the demons beating the ground with their fists, or tearing it with their claws, cursing us in their own garbled language, Run Fast steps up behind me, lays a hand on my shoulder and says with a confident little smile, "Worm pups."

→The Old magic is too strong for the demons. They can't come within striking distance of the stones. A few try, over the course of the night, making darting runs, heads low, howling their defiance. Each comes crashing to a halt or is thrown back as if they'd run into a wall.

I wish we knew the magic of the Old Creatures. We could build stone rings like this around every fort. Make the land safe again. But those secrets are long lost. Banba often spoke of the ancient magicians but she knew little about them, except for the tales and legends which she herself was taught as a child.

When we've finished laughing and cheering, we examine the stone circle in greater detail and what we find dampens our newly elated spirits. *Bones.* Some are from animals but most are human, stacked carefully in the centre, arranged so that the heads point west, in the direction of the setting sun. The sun guides the dead to the Otherworld and if bodies aren't cremated, they're usually laid out facing the path of the ever-moving orb.

The bones are more recent than the stones. Many are still dotted with scraps of flesh and hair.

"They must have been brought here after death," Orna says. "To keep the Fomorii from bringing them back to life."

"Perhaps," Fiachna says. "But why not just burn them?"

"Maybe the bodies are part of the magic," Ronan suggests. "The stones might need the power of the newly dead."

"Even if they did," Goll says, "what purpose would it serve? Why drag bodies here just to keep demons from overrunning a ring of stones?"

The mystery puzzles us through the night – nobody can sleep with all the screams of the demons – but it's solved early in the morning. As the sun rises the demons retreat. But they only withdraw as far as the trees which encircle the ring. There, under the shade of the rough shelter, they stop and leer viciously at us, pounding the earth with a terrible, steady, threatening rhythm.

"They worked on the trees," I say, a sick feeling in my stomach. "The people in this area must have sought the protection of the stones every night. It made the demons mad. Then they had an idea. They built a shelter in the trees around the circle. When it was finished, they let the people in one night, then stood guard the next day, trapping them. There was no way out. They died here, slowly, of starvation and thirst."

"Most of the bodies don't have weapons," Goll sighs. "They probably got so used to coming here, they grew lazy.

Didn't bother with weapons, since they were safe within the ring. They couldn't even try to fight their way to freedom."

"And now we're trapped too," Connla says bitterly, shooting me a dirty look.

"It's not Bec's fault," Fiachna snaps. "We'd be dead already if not for her."

"Aye," Connla admits grudgingly. "But I'd have rather died fighting in the open than of hunger and thirst, trapped like a fox in its den."

"You can die any time you like," Goll says. "The demons are waiting. Go pick a fight with them if you want to die quickly."

"Maybe I'll pick a fight with you instead," Connla snarls.

"Men are so childish," Orna snaps before the insults escalate. "Instead of being grateful for this extra day, you're bitter and scrap with each other like dogs."

"What do we have to be grateful for?" Connla shouts. "We're surrounded! We'll die like the others who lie here and our bones will rot slowly, unburied, ignored by the gods."

"Not necessarily," Orna disagrees. "The demons haven't built a wide shelter. And we're not weaponless. If we break through their ranks, they won't be able to chase after us."

"That won't be easy," Ronan says, studying the lie of the land. "There's a lot of space between this ring and the trees. We can't surprise them. They'll see us coming and converge at that point."

"So we separate," Orna shrugs. "We pair off and dart at them from a few directions at once. I doubt if everyone will make it through but some of us should."

"The strongest," Fiachna notes softly, looking at Run Fast and me. "What about the smaller ones?"

"We'll take our chances," I say stiffly, not happy with Fiachna for slighting me. I'm no warrior but I know how to fight and I'm not afraid to die. I want to be treated equally, not as a helpless child.

"If we're going to try that, we need to do it soon," Goll says. "If we can put a full day's march between us and these monsters, they'll never catch up. But if we leave it until later, they'll just wait until dark and give chase again."

"I don't see that we've any choice," Lorcan says. "Hit hard, run fast and—"

"Run fast!" Run Fast shouts. We smile at him but he doesn't see the humour in it. "Run fast!" he yells again. "Run fast!"

"Easy," Goll says, reaching out a hand to soothe the agitated boy.

Run Fast ducks away from Goll. "Run fast!" he insists. Then, before we can stop him, he darts past the safety of the stones and races towards the trees — and the demons.

"Run Fast!" I scream. "Come back!"

He ignores my cry but draws to a halt short of the trees. The demons in that area have bunched together, snarling and drooling, reaching out towards Run Fast, each wanting to be the first to snag him and feast on his flesh.

Run Fast dodges the hands, paws and claws of the demons, then starts to… to… No! I can't believe it. But yes — he starts to *dance*!

It's crazy. Incredible. Ridiculous. But he dances anyway. It's not a graceful dance, or a dance of magic or power. He just hops from foot to foot, clapping his hands, waving them around, grunting a series of off-key tunes.

The demons go wild, infuriated by the display. Run Fast is taunting them, dancing around within their reach, mocking them. They fall over one another in their fury, clutching, grasping, desperate to drag him down and put an end to his insolence. Some even step out of the shade of the trees and lunge at him, risking the burning rays of the sun.

Run Fast dodges them all, leaps here, darts there, dancing all the time. He sets off on a circuit, the demons following him. He comes within range of those who've been standing their ground, keeping an eye or three on the rest of us. As he passes, they lose interest in everything but the dancing boy and join with the rest of their inhuman clan, giving chase, lashing out, spitting poison.

Within minutes every demon is focused on Run Fast, stumbling after him, clashing with each other, fighting among themselves. Demons are never the most logical of creatures. Now they've lost their senses entirely and only care about destroying this dancing thorn in their side. They've forgotten the rest of us.

"I wouldn't have believed it if I hadn't seen it," Goll says, stunned, watching the show with a wide, incredulous eye.

"Look at how he dances away from them," Fiachna murmurs. "He slides through their fingers like smoke."

"There's more to the fool than we thought," Connla says, a hint of disapproval in his expression. He doesn't like surprises, even when they work to his advantage.

"Come on," Orna says. "He's created a gap for us to slip through. Let's not waste it by giving the demons time to regain their senses."

"What about Run Fast?" I ask.

"He'll be fine," Goll laughs. "He'll catch us up later. I think it would take more than all the demons of the land to snare that boy!"

I don't like the thought of leaving Run Fast behind. I study him as he continues to dance around the rim of the circle, teasing and tormenting the demons. As I'm watching, I notice that one of the demons isn't chasing Run Fast. It's standing by itself, ignoring the commotion, gaze fixed on the ring of stones ... on *us*. I can't see very well, but it looks to be a pale red colour and curiously lumpy, as though made of wet clay. And it's not standing on the ground — it's floating.

There's something especially disturbing about this Fomorii. It's not like any other demon I've seen. But before I can move forward for a closer look, Goll slaps my back and points me in the opposite direction, where the trees stand unguarded. "Run like the wind, Little One," he says. "And for Neit's sake, don't stop or look back!"

Then, before I can draw his attention to the floating demon, he barks an order and we're breaking for freedom, heads down, feet kicking up clouds of dust. In the heat of the moment all thoughts, except those of escape, slip from my head and blow away on the cool morning breeze.

THE CRANNOG

→Run Fast joins us nearly an hour later. I thought he'd be quicker than that, and was worrying, thinking about going back for him. When he appears, I see why he was so long — he stopped to pick flowers and weave a necklace out of them.

"Turnips!" he shouts happily, waving the necklace at us.

There's a big group cheer and we surround him, laughing, hugging, exclaiming at the same time —

"That was amazing!"

"I've never seen anything like it!"

"You must be a son of the gods!"

"The demons thought they had us dead but they didn't count on Run Fast!"

Run Fast smiles hazily, unsure of what all the fuss is about. In his head, I don't think leading demons a merry chase counts for much. He's far prouder of the necklace of flowers.

When we're through congratulating Run Fast we set off again, anxious to cover as much ground as we can before nightfall. It's a showery day and we're soon soaked. But that's a minor inconvenience. We'll take any amount of soakings after our unexpected escape from the demons.

→Early afternoon. I've been discussing the ring of stones with Fiachna, wondering how old it was, who built it, what its original purpose might have been.

"A pity they didn't have ogham stones back then," Fiachna says. "They could have told us who they were and lived on through their writing."

"Can you read ogham?" I ask.

"A bit. I learnt it from a bard who couldn't pay me for my work. Can you?"

"No. Banba didn't like ogham. She said magic shouldn't be recorded, that history should be kept alive by word of mouth."

"Perhaps," Fiachna says. "But many stories are lost forever that way. I think…" He stops, eyes narrowing. "Connla!" he calls — the young would-be king has been leading for the last couple of hours. When Connla looks back, Fiachna points to a spot off to the right. "A large, strange hut. I think it's a church."

Everyone gathers around us. I can see the tip of the building now that Fiachna's pointed it out. It's not like any I've seen before but I've heard of its type. A Christian church. I didn't know they'd built any this close to our tuath.

We advance on the church. My insides are tight. It's a feeling I always get when I hear of the upstart religion.

Christians are new to our land, but already it's hard to imagine a time when they weren't here. They've spread as fast as rabbits, bringing their churches and unnatural ways into tuath after tuath, converting everyone they encounter. I've never met a Christian but from what I've heard they're powerful and persuasive, with no tolerance for other ways of thinking. They believe all people should follow their faith, that no gods are real except their own.

The threat of Christians was a major worry for us before the Fomorii came. Even though we were far removed from any of the infected tuatha, we knew we couldn't hope to avoid them forever. From what we heard, they'd converted all of the north and east. It was only a matter of time before their priests came – maybe their high priest, Padraig, would come himself – and then...

Would they convert us too? Would Conn grant them his backing, as so many other kings had, and order us to follow their ways, abandon our gods, adopt their customs? It didn't seem possible. Our religion is old. Our gods are sacred, as real to us as our ancestors. We lead our lives based on ancient, just laws, handed down from father to son, mother to daughter. How could we turn away from all that within a matter of days and become another people entirely?

I'd have said it was impossible, except I knew from the reports that it isn't. While the Christians don't have our understanding and control of magic, they have strange powers of their own. They've come from far across the world, winning over most of those they met along the way. Common sense suggested we'd be no different, no more immune to their persuasive spells than any other clan.

We thought Christianity was the worst disaster that could befall us. Then the demons attacked and we realised there were far greater enemies in the world than the followers of the god they call Christ.

→Creeping up to the door of the church. I sense power within. A dark, throbbing, painful power. It gives me a headache. This church doesn't have the natural feel of our own holy places. It's a building of power but not magic.

We stop at the door of the church, unwilling to enter in case demons are inside. I thought a church would be protected from the Fomorii, like the ring of stones. But as powerful as they are, Christians lack the skills of the Old Creatures, because it's obvious this church has been attacked and demons have been at play.

We can see the mess through the open door. Blood everywhere. Bits of human bodies. A man's head — maybe a priest's — stuck on the tip of a spear set in the centre of the church. Eyelids ripped off, eyes gouged out, demonic symbols scrawled in blood across his forehead and cheeks.

"I've never seen demons do this," Goll says, scratching the flesh over his own lost eye. "They usually strike and kill, make off with the bodies they want, leave the others just scattered around. This is different."

"It's like what we do with our enemies after a battle," Fiachna agrees. "If you add this to the trap they built around the ring of stones, there's only one conclusion. Tiernan was right — they're becoming more intelligent."

I feel sick when Fiachna says that. If the demons start plotting, scheming and fighting like humans, with their extra strength and powers they're certain to crush us all within months.

We stand in the doorway a few moments more, studying the face of the dead man. Then we retreat, spirits dampened, and continue on our trek to Run Fast's home, wondering if we'll find similar scenes of chaos there.

→Late in the evening. Worrying about the night ahead and where we'll stop. It's too much to hope to find another ring of magical stones. We're tired from the march and lack of sleep. If we don't find shelter soon, we're in trouble.

All of a sudden, without warning, Run Fast darts ahead of us. He stops, looks back and beckons hastily. "Bumpy frogs!" he shouts. "Run fast!" Then he tears ahead, disappearing through the trees.

"Looks like our journey's at an end," Connla smiles. "I thought we'd have a much further march than that."

"The gods must be looking down on us," Goll grunts, then catches Connla's arm as he goes to follow Run

Fast. "Careful. Don't forget why we're here. These people are in trouble. There's no telling what we'll find. The demons might have them surrounded, like at the ring of stones."

Connla hesitates, then takes a step back. "What do you suggest? Go in together or send a scout first?"

"Together," Goll says after a second of thought. "To separate is to weaken. But everybody draw your weapons and tread carefully."

When we're all prepared, we advance cautiously, scanning the branches of the trees overhead and roots at our feet — sometimes worm-like demons disguise themselves as roots and snag unsuspecting passers-by.

A couple of minutes later we come to a clearing and find ourselves at the edge of a lake. A crannog has been built on an island in the middle of the water. A small, fenced fort, containing half a dozen huts. There's a sentry post built above the gate, and from the marks beneath it and here on the shore, I think there was once a bridge connecting the island to the mainland. But that's been demolished, probably because of the threat posed by demons. Now you can only get to it by swimming or in one of the curraghs tied up close to the fort's gate.

"Hello!" Goll yells. Echoes, then silence.

Run Fast is hopping up and down, his face alight, reaching out to the crannog as though he can stretch across the lake and stroke the walls of the fence.

"Anybody there?" Goll shouts. When the silence holds, he adds, "We've come to help. Your boy told us you were in trouble. We're here to…"

He draws to a halt, since it's obvious nobody's going to answer.

"It's a ghost village," Ronan says.

"We're too late," Connla sniffs.

"Maybe not," Fiachna disagrees. "They might be sheltering underground, in a souterrain, where they can't hear us."

"You two seem to think people do nothing but cower underground," Connla snorts, nodding at Fiachna and Orna. "Why don't you just accept the simple truth that when nobody answers a call, it means they're all dead?"

"I prefer to hope for the best," Orna says stiffly, "even when I can see just as clearly as you that it's unlikely."

"Smoke bread," Run Fast says bafflingly, leaning over so far that he almost topples into the lake.

"Right," Goll says. "We haven't come all this way to turn back now. If nothing else, the crannog offers a place to rest tonight."

"Unless it's been taken over by demons," Connla says.

"Unless it's been taken over by demons," Goll agrees. "But we have to check. Lorcan, will you swim across and come back in a curragh for the rest of us?"

Lorcan's the best swimmer in our tuath. Even when he was twelve years old, he could beat most grown men in a race. He steps forward now and studies the water, looking for demons. He can't see any but that doesn't mean it's safe — they often hide down deep during the day, to avoid the rays of the sun.

Without saying anything, Lorcan undresses quickly, then dives in and strikes powerfully for the crannog. We watch nervously, Ronan having notched an arrow to his bow, ready to fire instantly if his brother comes under attack.

Lorcan makes it to the crannog unhindered and pulls himself out, pausing only to offer up a quick prayer of thanks to the gods. He brushes water from his stubbly hair — it comes off in rusty red drops, coloured by the blood caked into his scalp. Then he unties a leather-framed curragh and rows across to where we're waiting, hard strokes, one eye on the setting sun.

Lorcan, Goll, Run Fast and Orna cross first. Then Lorcan rows back to pick up Ronan, Fiachna, Connla and me. At the gate I test the air for the scent of demons. It's clear. I don't think there are monsters in the village but I can't be certain.

"Will we try the gate or go over the fence?" Goll asks.

"The gate's open," Fiachna says.

Goll squints, then chuckles. "I was never the sharpest with two eyes, but with only one..." He looks around. "We'll go in fast. Any sign of trouble, retreat to the gate. Based on what we're facing, we'll decide then whether to fight or flee."

Deep breath. Weapons drawn. A signal from Goll. *In*.

* * *

→No demons. No people either. Just a few chickens and lots of blood. While we stand a few paces inside the gate, Run Fast chases after the chickens, laughing. They squawk and flap away from him. With his speed he could catch them easily, but he's only playing with them.

"Do you think they're all dead?" Orna asks, eyes narrow, nose wrinkled against the stench of fresh blood.

"Unless they're hiding," Goll grunts.

"We should check the huts," Fiachna says.

"Aye." Goll points at Ronan, Fiachna, Connla and me. "You four go right. The rest of us will go left. We'll meet in the middle if all's clear."

"What about Run Fast?" I ask.

Goll looks at the boy chasing the chickens. "I don't think he'd be much help."

We set off quickly, each of us aware of the rapidly setting sun. It's almost the time of the Fomorii.

The first hut. Holes have been torn in the walls, so it's easy to peer in. Floor caked in drying blood but otherwise empty. No trapdoor or hiding place. We push on.

The second hut's smaller than the first. A tiny entrance. No holes in the walls. Dark pools of shadows. We stick our heads through the doorway, allowing our eyes to adjust to the gloom. Objects gradually swim into sight. Pots, a small table, a broken chair. Rugs on the floor — there could be a souterrain beneath. We slide in, Ronan first, me last, looking up for winged demons hanging from the thatch. The men search beneath the rugs — nothing. They file out. I'm bringing up the rear, almost through the door, when something breathes behind me.

"*Becccccccc...*"

I stop... turn... eyes wide... heart beating fast. I stare into the shadows. I can't see anything but I know I'm not alone. I want to duck out of the door or call for help but I can't. My tongue is frozen, not with fear, but magic.

Long, terrifying seconds pass. Then, in a blur, claws dart out of the darkness... a twisted face... fiery eyes... a savage mouth filled with rows of teeth... the demon grabs me!

DROST

→Instant reaction — magic. I don't waste time screaming. I bark a spell, my lips moving quicker than ever before. My hands heat up. Then, instead of wrenching my arms away, which is what the demon expects, I grab its claws tightly and try to scorch them to scraps.

It doesn't work. As my hands glow, the claws grasping me glow too. Brighter and brighter, the pair of us, a contest. For several seconds we are locked together, no words, my gaze fixed on my hands and the claws. Then I start noticing details — not claws but *hands*. Smooth flesh, eight fingers, two thumbs. Dark flesh but not demon dark — *human* dark.

I bring my eyes up but I can't see my attacker's face because of the magical glow. A swift inner debate. Then I let the power drain from me. The light dies away. Shadows reform. It takes my eyes a while to adjust but when they do I see that I was right — it's a man, not a monster. And he's smiling.

"Good," the man says. "You have magic – a bit anyway – and common sense. You'll do." Then he brushes past me, out of the hut, and summons the others with a far-reaching call.

"You can stop searching. It's safe. There are no demons here. Now come and find out why I sent the boy to fetch you."

→The stranger's name is Drust and — as we immediately see by his long blue tunic and shaved, tattooed head – he's a druid. After calling us together and telling us his name, Drust doesn't speak for a long time. Instead, he builds a fire and casts a spell to prevent smoke and contain the glow within the crannog, so as not to attract demons. After a while he takes hot rocks from the fire — with his bare fingers – and places them in a pit filled with water. When the water is the right heat, he drops in chunks of meat wrapped in straw.

We sit silently, eyeing Drust suspiciously, waiting for him to speak. I've never seen a druid before. Wandering men of minor magic, yes, but never one of the legendary seers. His tattoos are amazing. They're a map of the stars, but they move like the stars do, slowly revolving across his scalp.

When the meat is cooking to Drust's satisfaction, he stands before us and runs a calculating eye over the group, one by one, judging. His eye seems to rest longest on me but maybe I just imagine that.

We're all tense. We have tremendous respect for druids, but we fear them too. They're human, but something else as well, powerful, with rules and ways of their own. We've heard tales of how they sacrifice children to the gods, breed with demons, build mountains, level raths and divert the course of rivers.

Finally, Drust looks at Run Fast. He smiles at the boy, then clicks his fingers. Run Fast edges over to him like a dog to its master. Drust ruffles the boy's untidy hair, his smile widening. "You did well, Bran," he says.

"Bran!" I gasp. "Is that his name? He never told us. We called him Run Fast because..." Drust looks at me calmly and I come to a halt. There's no menace in his eyes, but no warmth either. He studies me in much the same way that I've studied dead demons in the past.

"Yes," the druid says in an accent not of this land. "It's Bran. He didn't tell you because he's incapable of remembering names." Drust speaks slowly, the words sounding strange on his lips. I don't think our language is his own.

"Is Bran from here," Fiachna asks quietly, "or is he your apprentice?"

Drust raises a mocking eyebrow. "You think I would take an idiot as an apprentice?"

"He's simple but blessed," Fiachna replies. "He has speed and other powers not of normal men."

Drust nods. "Which is why I sent him for assistance. But, touched by magic as he is, Bran's brain can never develop. He would be as useless to me as he was to his own people." He pauses, then adds, "I doubt he came from here originally but this is where I found him."

Drust releases Bran's hair. The boy looks up at the druid,

to see if he's going to pet him again, then slides over to my side and sits beside me. I stroke the back of his hands absent-mindedly while the conversation continues.

"And you?" Goll asks. "Where are you from?"

Drust points in an easterly direction.

"Are you a Pict?" Connla asks. "Drust is a Pict's name."

"I was, as a child, before I became a druid."

The Picts are an ancient people from across the great water to the east. I wasn't aware that any still remained. They're a dying race, killed or absorbed by stronger tribes. Drust must be one of the last of his kind.

Before we can ask any more questions, Drust points at Goll and says, "Are you the leader of this band?"

"No," Goll replies. "We have no leader. But I'm the eldest, so I suppose I can speak for us."

Out of the corner of my eye I see Connla bristle — he probably looks upon himself as the rightful leader — but he doesn't say anything.

"Then I will address my words to you," Drust says. "I'll keep it simple. I am here to end the demon attacks. I need your help. You must come with me."

He stops as though those few sentences are explanation enough.

The flesh around Goll's single eye wrinkles. "You'll need to tell us more than that, druid or no druid," he murmurs. "To begin with, what happened here and where are Run F— I mean, Bran's people?"

345

"Demons." Drust shrugs. "They'd been attacking long before I arrived. Bran's tribe – the MacRoth – were exhausted, close to defeat. Shortly after I came, that defeat finally befell them."

"The demons killed everyone?" Goll asks and Drust nods. "Then why not you?" He phrases it lightly, but it's clearly a challenge. It's unnatural for all to perish except this one stranger. What Goll's really asking is did Drust betray the MacRoth — and will he betray us too?

"They didn't kill me because they couldn't see me," Drust says. "Just as your people couldn't see me when they entered the hut where I was staying. I know masking spells which hide me from sight. If your girl priestess had been more experienced, she'd have seen through my shield. But she is not yet mistress of her arts."

"Why not hide the MacRoth too?" Orna asks angrily.

Drust sniffs. "All magic has its limits. I have the power to mask a handful of people but not sixteen."

"If not sixteen, why not eight?" Lorcan growls. "Or four? Or even one?"

"As your own magician – wet behind the ears as she is – can tell you, magic is draining. A masking spell for several people, maintained over a long period, would have tired me. I need to be at my most powerful if I'm to save all from the threat of the Demonata."

"Demonata?" Ronan frowns. He's been keeping one hand on his bow, ready to swing it round and fire off an arrow if

Drust makes any untoward moves. "Do you mean the Fomorii?"

"They're not Fomorii," Drust snorts. "The Fomorii were brutish humans with just a hint of the demonic about them. The Demonata come directly from what you call the Otherworld. Their powers are pure. They cannot be fought and defeated by human means. Only by magic."

"I think many of the demons we've killed would disagree with that," Connla smirks.

"Familiars," Drust retorts. "Weak, mindless creatures. They've come ahead of their masters, like rats ahead of a mighty plague. When the true Demonata arrive your weapons will be useless."

Our features tighten. We'd guessed that more intelligent, stronger demons were coming, but not that we wouldn't be able to kill them. If this is true, it means the end of all we've ever known and cared about.

Drust cocks an eyebrow, inviting further questions, making it clear that such queries are a waste of his time. Goll pushes on anyway. "So you stood by and let these Demonata kill the MacRoth. We'll return to that, but first tell us—"

"We won't," Drust interrupts. "The MacRoth meant nothing to me, just as you mean nothing to me. My aim is to save this land. If sixteen – or sixty, or six hundred – have to die, so be it. The MacRoth would have perished whether I was here or not. Since their living or dying had no impact on my quest, I kept out of their affairs, just as I'll keep out of yours if I decide you are of no use to me either."

Goll's face whitens with anger but he controls his temper and instead of shouting, he hisses a question. "Tell us how we can be *of use*. If you're so powerful, what are we here for? We came to help people in distress, not a damn druid who has no need of us."

"But I do have need of you," Drust says evenly. "I have travelled far to stem the tide of demons at its source. Such travels are perilous, even for one of my powers. I cannot complete my quest alone. When I set out, months ago, it was with several companions, all of whom fell in the course of our journey. I need new warriors to replace them."

"*Us?*" Connla laughs. "You think *we'll* fight and die for you?"

"If you have any sense," Drust says. "The Demonata are *your* problem. They cannot cross the sea to my land. You and your people are the ones who will suffer if I fail."

"We can fight the demons ourselves," Lorcan says stiffly. "We don't need help from the likes of you."

Drust laughs. His laughter offends us all, but before we can react, he speaks quickly. "You haven't fought the masters yet, only their minions. The demons you've faced – along with the pitiful undead – are merely the first wave. A tunnel has opened between this land and the Otherworld. It will allow demons to enter our realm freely. It's a small tunnel but it's growing. As it grows, larger, smarter, stronger demons will cross. They can roam the land by day as well as night. And, as I've already told you, they can only be killed by magic."

He stops. Our faces are ashen. Nobody can speak, not even the hot-headed Connla. When Drust has measured the impact of his words, he continues. "The druids won't come to your aid. This island had already passed beyond our control — the Christians drove us out. The view of most druids is that it makes no difference whether Christians or demons rule here. In fact many would prefer the Demonata — they hate Christians even more than demons."

"But they'll slaughter us all!" I cry.

Drust's expression is unreadable. "Aye." A pause. "Unless I stop them."

"By yourself?" Connla sneers.

"There's just one tunnel and at the moment it's vulnerable," Drust says. "If the gap between worlds can be plugged, the demons can no longer cross. One man, if he has the power and knows what he's doing, can close the tunnel. I am such a man."

"But why?" Fiachna asks. "If the rest of the druids don't care, why do you?"

"I have reasons," Drust says, lowering his gaze for the first time. "They are my own." His eyes rise again. "Will you help me or not?"

"To do what?" Goll asks.

"Stop the Demonata!" Drust groans. "Haven't you been listening?"

"I have," Goll says, smiling bitterly. "What I mean is, how can we help? What exactly do you want us to do?"

"I must go west," Drust says, "to the coast. There, I can find out where the tunnel is located."

"You don't know?" Fiachna asks.

Drust shakes his head. "I searched for it with my original companions. I thought I could find it by myself. I was wrong."

"How will you find out by going to the coast?" Orna asks.

"That's my business," Drust huffs. "Yours, if you accept the challenge, will be to escort me safely. Say now whether or not you are worthy of such responsibility. If not, I'll send Bran forth again, to hunt for those of a nobler clan."

Connla drives himself to his feet, hand going to his sword, ready to cut Drust down. But at a wave of Drust's hand he stops, frozen. It's a simple halting spell – Banba taught me several like it – but expertly woven. Connla might as well be carved out of wood.

Drust looks questioningly at Goll. The old warrior's unhappy. His distrust of the druid is plain to see and mirrored on the faces of the rest of us. But if what we've heard is true...

"You must come to our rath and tell your story to our king," Goll says. "If he's inclined to provide assistance, he can send more—"

"There isn't time," Drust interrupts sharply. "Come with me in the morning or return to your homes and I'll search for other allies."

Goll sighs, deeply troubled. He looks around for advice.

"I don't trust him," Orna says, making a sign to ward off evil spirits. "But I am not of your tuath. I will follow your lead in this matter."

"We've made it this far," Ronan says neutrally. "We can go further."

"Perhaps he could teach us better ways to kill demons," Lorcan notes.

It's clear the twins like the idea of journeying with the druid and facing extra dangers and demons. They're young and bloodthirsty. They care more about notching up kills than the welfare of the clan.

"I'm of two minds," Fiachna mutters. "Our people will think the worst if we're gone too long. Perhaps one or two of us should go back. Bec, for instance..."

I'm about to protest but before I can, Drust does it for me. "No!" he snaps with unexpected force. "If you stay, the girl stays. Her powers might come in useful. She's weak and undisciplined but I can work with her. She'd be an asset."

"Connla?" Goll asks.

Held by the spell, Connla can't answer, so Drust waves his hand again and frees the warrior. Connla glares hatefully at the druid, then spits at his feet. "I say damn him and all his wretched kind! Where were they when the demons came? We can hold our own without them, as we have since the start."

"And if hordes of demons attack by day?" Fiachna says softly. "More powerful than any we've fought so far? Organised, brutal, unkillable?"

"Why should we believe that?" Connla counters. "He could be lying, just to—"

"The ring of stones and the church," I remind him. I shouldn't involve myself in this without being invited to share my thoughts, but I can't keep quiet. "We've seen the work of clever, cunning demons. It's true, Connla. You know it is."

Connla hesitates, the memories altering his expression.

"It would be a great honour," Fiachna says wryly. "If Drust succeeds, and we play a part in that success, we'll be hailed as heroes throughout the four provinces."

That's the clincher for Connla. If he could help save the entire land, his kingship would be guaranteed. And maybe not just king of our tuath, but of our province. Maybe more — the first high king of *all* the provinces. Many have tried to exercise complete control. All have failed. But still the greedier warriors dream.

"Very well," Connla grunts. "I vote we go with him."

Goll nods reluctantly. "Then it's decided."

"I thought it might be," Drust says with a self-satisfied smirk. Then he turns his attention to the meat boiling in the water and adds a few more hot stones to keep the heat constant.

POTENTIAL

→A quiet night. No attacks. The demons think everyone here is dead, so they've no reason to bother with the crannog. I get a night of deep sleep and so do the others, too exhausted even for nightmares. We all wake refreshed in the morning. Drust's already up. He's prepared cold slices of meat from the night before and hot porridge, which we share in silence in the greyish pre-dawn haze.

Fiachna searches the village for a forge, smith's tools or other weapons like Bran's knife but he doesn't find any. The rest of us go on a quick search too, for weapons or food. We kill the remaining chickens, take the eggs they've laid and some slabs of cured pork. But there's little else worthwhile.

We're ready to go but Drust says he needs to pray first. He finds a place where he can face the rising sun, then kneels, closes his eyes and meditates.

"How long will he be?" Connla asks me.

"Five or ten minutes." Actually, I don't have a clue but I don't want to look ignorant in front of Connla.

"Time enough for a quick shave," Connla says. Filling a bucket with water, he douses his face, takes a small knife, wets the blade and waits for the water to settle. Then, studying his reflection, he scrapes the hairs off his cheeks and chin. Most of the men in our rath grow beards but Connla prefers the smooth look. Goll sometimes teases him about it, says he looks like a girl.

Bran – it's hard not to think of him as Run Fast – watches Connla shave, fascinated. Maybe he's never seen a man shaving before. He pays extra close attention as Connla trims around the sides of his upper lip, careful not to disturb the hairs of his moustache. As he's finishing, cleaning the blade, Bran reaches over, grabs a patch of Connla's moustache and yanks hard. The hairs rip out and Connla howls with pain and surprise.

Bran holds the hairs up proudly, grinning. He thought Connla missed them and was trying to help. But Connla doesn't see it that way. He roars at the boy and swings a fist. Bran ducks, still holding up the hairs. Connla lunges after him. Bran laughs and flees, shouting, "Run fast! Run fast!" Connla chases, cursing foully, drawing his sword.

The rest of us fall about with laughter. We know Connla won't catch Bran — if he was too fast for demons, a human stands no chance. Connla eventually realises this and stops chasing the boy. After hurling a few final curses at him and some more at us, he storms back to the bucket, regards his ruined moustache with a miserable expression, then scrapes the rest of the hairs away, shaving his lip bare.

Bran edges up to me, timidly holding out the hairs. "Giblets," he says, handing them over. I give the boy a delighted hug. Goll claps him hard on the back — the old warrior is crying with laughter.

"I'd keep him out of Connla's way for a few hours," Fiachna chuckles. "He'll calm down later but he'll be in a foul mood for a while."

"Don't worry," I grin, squeezing Bran tight. "I'll look after him."

"Giblets," Bran repeats, stroking the hairs fondly, as if they were petals, making us all laugh again.

→Shortly after the sun rises, Drust stops praying and we depart. Bran trots along beside us, unaware of the scowling Connla's dark looks. I keep the boy close, in case the surly warrior tries to hurt him. I doubt he would, but I'm never sure about Connla. He's a hard one to read. Impossible to know how he'll react to a joke or how deeply to heart he'll take a light insult.

I study Bran as he jogs, smiling at the countryside, squinting up at the sky and birds, perfectly content. I assume he had family and friends in the crannog, all of whom are dead now, but he doesn't seem bothered by the loss. At first I pity him but the more I think about it, pity turns to envy. It must be nice to live like Bran, immune to the pains which the rest of us suffer. Knowing what I know – that unless Drust succeeds, this land will be overrun by unstoppable demons — I wish I could be as empty-headed as the fleet-footed boy.

→Heading due west, we make good time. After a while Drust drops back and walks beside me, nudging Bran out of the way. The druid asks lots of questions about my past, Banba, my training. He wants to know what I can do, how powerful I am. He sneers when I tell him about my remarkable memory — that doesn't interest him. When he asks about my family, I tell him I'm an orphan of unknown origin.

"You've no idea who your people were?" he presses.

"No." I pause. "Do you?"

He frowns. "Why should I?"

I shrug, not wishing to tell him about my vision and the possibility that my mother might have been sending me out to find my original clan.

Drust continues asking about my magic, what spells I know, where my strengths lie. His enquiries fill me with unease. They shouldn't. It's natural for a magician to be interested in the abilities of another. But this doesn't feel like simple curiosity. He seems to be testing me, probing for weaknesses. I recall what he said back in the hut — "You'll do" — and worry burns in my stomach like a fire.

→At midday we take a short rest. Drust sits slightly apart from the rest of us. Instead of eating, he pulls a board out of the bag which he carries on his back. A strange board, the surface divided into an equal number of black and white squares. It's the thickness of the length of my thumb, made of crystal. He sets it down on the ground, then spills small, carved shapes out on to the grass. When he starts to position the pieces on the board, I realise it's some sort of game.

"Chess," Orna says as Drust moves the first piece.

Drust looks up eagerly. "You play?"

"No. One of the slaves in our tuath had a set but it was only played by men. I picked up some of the rules by watching but I don't know them all."

"A pity," Drust sighs. "It's been a long time since I had anyone to test my wits against."

He concentrates. Moves a white piece shaped like a horse's head, then one of the many simply shaped black pieces. Everyone's interested in this new game. We've never seen it in our tuath. Orna explains about the game while Drust plays but it's hard to follow the rules, especially as Orna is unsure of them herself.

"The main aim is to keep your king from being taken?" Lorcan asks.

"Aye," Orna says.

"Why can't he fight?" Ronan frowns. "A king should be a fine warrior, yet the kings in this game seem scared. They hide at the back."

"It hails from a different land," Orna explains. "In some places kings don't fight. They send others to battle in their place."

Angry mutters from the men —

"It's not right!"

"Barbarians!"

"The likes of those wouldn't last long against demons!"

I ignore them and focus on Drust and the way his hands linger over the pieces. Long, slender, unmarked fingers. They move the pieces swiftly, smoothly, from one spot to the other. I get the sense that he could move us just as easily. And maybe already has.

→After lunch, Drust marches beside me again. But now, instead of asking questions, he says, "I can teach you if you're willing to learn."

"Chess?" I reply eagerly.

"No. Magic."

I come to a halt and stare at him as if he'd slapped me. Fiachna and Connla stop behind us, hands sliding to their weapons. I start walking again before they ask what's wrong. Drust keeps pace beside me, waiting for me to speak. Bran's on the other side, following a butterfly. My head's buzzing with conflicting thoughts. I'd love to learn magic from a druid — they can do so much more than priestesses. But men teach boys. Women teach girls. That's the way it's always been.

"I wouldn't teach you all the spells I'd teach a male student," Drust says, reading my thoughts. "There are secrets not fitting for one of your gender, just as you know secrets not suitable for a man. But we could work on your technique. I could show you where you're weak, help you improve and teach you some new spells, those which you deem acceptable."

"But men… girls… it isn't done," I mutter, red-faced at the thought of sharing my spirit with a man, as I must if I allow him to become my tutor.

"Just because something hasn't been done doesn't mean it shouldn't be," Drust says. "I'd prefer a boy to work with, just as you'd rather learn from a priestess. The fact is we have only each other. We can be bold and make the most of this opportunity or we can be prim and let it pass. Bec?"

He waits for my answer. After a long, dry-mouthed moment, I nod clumsily. "I would be… glad to learn… from you."

"Good," he says, then rests his left fingers against my forehead. "Close your eyes and think of the moon. Before we begin, I want to teach you how to clear your head of all the rubbish you've let it fill with lately. Your mind is too much that of a human, not a priestess."

A rush. A buzz. Tingling all over. My head… my body… my spirit… full of… *magic*.

→Four days marching. Four nights spent in the open. We lie down each dusk, singly or in pairs, sheltering beneath trees. Drust comes to each of us in turn, touches us and mutters spells. We have orders not to move during the night, even if we need to empty our insides.

"Go where you lie if you have to," Drust says. "Just don't leave the spot where you settle. The spell will break if you do."

The first night — nothing. No undead or demons. I sleep fitfully, tucked up next to Goll, aware of Drust's magic – the air flickering around me – wondering if it will hold.

The second night, a beast pieced together from several humans stumbles by. It's moaning and scratching at the earth with bone-exposed fingers. Starving, hungry for any kind of flesh, even that of insects. It passes within four or five strides of where I'm resting with Orna. We hold our breath. I feel Orna's fingers slide slowly to her sword. I want to whisper, "No!" but I'm afraid to make any noise.

The undead creature stops. I think it's seen us. Orna hisses. Her hand finds the hilt of her sword. Her fingers tighten.

Then a fox darts out from under a bush and pelts away from the undead beast. It howls and lumbers after the animal, arms flapping up and down.

Silence, broken after a few seconds by Drust. "The only two who didn't reach for their weapons were Bec and Goll. And Goll's asleep." A short pause. I sense his smile in the dark. "Now that you've seen my magic at work, I hope you act less rashly next time. You nearly gave our hiding place away."

We sleep better after that, though at least one of us remains awake at any given time, watching out not just for the undead and the Demonata — but also keeping an eye on the mysterious Drust.

→Under Drust's stern eye, I begin practising magic and learn quickly, feeling my power grow. But I'm unable to make the new spells work. Men's magic is different to women's. We take power from the earth, trees, the wind, sun, moon. The world is charged with natural magic which we channel. We're creatures of nature, and like bees take pollen from flowers, we pluck grains of magic from the land and air around us.

Drust's magic is different. He only reveals fragments of his secrets to me, but he seems to draw most of his power from the stars. Some of it from the sun and moon, but mostly from the heavens beyond.

"Gods are in motion up there," he says to me on the fourth night. Drust sleeps by himself, but tonight he asked me to sleep close by. There aren't many clouds in the sky, so we have a good view of the stars. "Demons too. And the spirits of the dead. They battle, toil, love — like us. But their actions are greater than ours. They inhabit forms hundreds or thousands of times our size."

His eyes are fixed on the stars. From their light I can see the tattooed stars on his head moving slowly. His expression is soft for once.

"When they come here, they come in forms similar to ours," he continues. "This world is too small for them otherwise. But up there…" He sighs. "Male magic comes from the forces generated by the gods, the dead and the Demonata. We've learnt to tap into their power, the way priestesses tap into the roots of trees or the hearts of bears. But the magnitude… the dangers…"

He turns on his side – only slightly, so as not to break the masking spell – and trains his gaze on me. "Man wasn't made to share the universe with gods. Their ways are not meant for the humble likes of us. But we've decoded some of their secrets regardless. Like worms, we've grabbed on to the talons of eagles and learnt some small truths and means of flight. But we can never really fly. We try, and succeed to a certain extent, but the fall is always – will always be – there. To be a druid is to embrace death, dance with it a while and finally fall prey to it. That is why we'll never rule this world. We have the power to bend all men to our whim, but are forever pushing ourselves further, trying to fly higher… and falling."

A silence. His gaze returns to the sky. He looks troubled.

"We could have crushed the Christians hundreds of years ago. They were weak then. If we'd been aware of the threat they posed, we'd have bound their tongues and turned their fingers to stone so they couldn't speak or write. Their religion would have died with them. But our eyes were on the Otherworld, the stars, the gods. We didn't keep watch on the world around us. And when we eventually lowered our heads and studied the waters closer to home, it was too late."

"You could still stop the Christians," I mutter quietly, hoping he won't punish me for disagreeing with him. Drust's a harsh teacher. When I make mistakes, he slaps the back of my head or stamps on my foot or lashes me with a knotted rope. Banba was tough too, but not as cruel as Drust.

"Could we?" Drust sighs. "Some believe it's not too late — even as they retreat from the world of man and hide in caves or deep in forests. I don't agree. Our time has passed. We'll survive in some form or other, I'm sure. But we'll never be this strong or fly so high again."

He says nothing after that, and I know better than to disturb him. Lying on my back, watching the stars until my lids grow heavy and close, I think about his words and try to imagine a world where druids and magic have no place. And I realise, just before I fall asleep, that in such a world I would have no place either.

→Marching. Eyes half closed. Feeling power around me — power from the stars and those who drift among them. Trying to absorb it. Muttering the words of a spell which Drust taught me. I'm holding a small rock. If the spell works, the rock will float for a second or two.

I stutter on a key word and lose my place. Drust's hand instantly connects with the back of my head. "Concentrate!" he snaps.

"I am!" I snap back. It's the seventh or eighth time he's hit me in the last hour. I'm sick of it. "I can't do this stupid men's magic! Teach Bran, why don't you!"

Bran's head rises. He's been walking along just behind us, humming a tune.

"He couldn't do any worse than you," Drust snarls, slapping me again, harder this time. That's it! My right hand comes up. I'm going to slap him back — see what he thinks! But before I can...

"People often say I'm too small to be a smith."

Drust and I look up, startled. Fiachna, who was marching ahead of us, has stopped and is smiling.

"This has nothing to do with you," Drust growls.

"I never said it had," Fiachna replies. "I'm just remarking — people often say I'm too small to be a smith. They think smiths have to be large, burly men who can swing two heavy hammers at once and bend iron with their hands. And most are. But they don't need to be.

"My master was a gentle man. He had a bad leg. He broke it when he was a child and it didn't heal properly. So he never fought. But he made some of the finest weapons imaginable. He knew iron, how to bend it to his will and get the best out of it. He'd always talk while he worked, happily chatting away, seemingly to himself. People thought he was mad but he wasn't. He was talking to the iron, learning from it, easing and teasing it into the shape he wanted — the shape *it* wanted."

"I don't see—" Drust begins but Fiachna talks over him.

"He taught me to work that way too. He never beat me or shouted or lost his temper. I wasn't his first apprentice or his last. He'd take boys on for a while, teach them his ways, observe them, then let them go if he felt they couldn't learn from him." A short pause, then he adds, "Apologies for telling you your business but that might be the best way to teach Bec. Unless you think she can't learn."

"She can!" Drust shouts. "She has potential. I can feel it."

"Then hitting her won't help, will it?" Fiachna says calmly. "My master always said you couldn't beat a skill out of somebody. They had to learn in their own way and time. If you rushed them, you only delayed them. You had to be firm but not cruel. Cruelty is a barrier and barriers slow people down."

"My masters beat me unconscious whenever *I* made a mistake," Drust says and he sounds like a bitter child.

"Did you learn anything while you were knocked out?" Fiachna asks.

Drust starts to roar a retort, then stops and frowns.

"Hard to learn when you're dead to the world," Fiachna says, nodding slowly. Then he turns and starts walking again.

Drust looks at me and catches my smile. He scowls. "I don't like being spoken down to by a smith," he huffs and my smile fades. Then his expression mellows. "But only a fool ignores good advice simply because it comes from an unlikely source. Very well, Bec MacConn. We've tried it my way. Now we'll try it Fiachna's. No more beatings for a few days. If you improve, well and good. If not..." He grins tightly. "I'll have to whip you all the harder!"

I gulp, torn between the relief of the present and the threat of the future. Then I take a breath, relax and start again, drawing in power from the sky, chanting the words of the spell, focusing on the stone, willing it to rise.

AN UNINVITED GUEST

→Another night in the open. No trees, so we sleep in a field littered with rocks.

It's been a day of disappointment on the magic front. Drust stopped hitting me but that's all that changed. I can't get the hang of this new magic. It's too different. I wish Drust would focus on natural magic and help me improve that way. I learnt a lot from Banba but my powers have grown rusty. I think we should work on the type of magic I grew up with.

But Drust is firm. He says he can't teach me the way a priestess could, since he doesn't work that way. And even if he could, he wouldn't.

"You're no good to me the way you were!" he snaps when I question the need to learn new spells. "I need more!"

But what for? Why does he need me? What's he grooming me to do?

→Sleeping deeply. Dreaming of happier days — Banba alive, no demons, safe. Enjoying the dream, but midway through an inner voice whispers, "Wake up." Connla's been guarding us for the last few hours. Now it's my turn to go on watch.

I'm excellent at waking myself. I never need to be called. It was one of the first spells Banba taught me. A priestess has to be able to control her dreams. Otherwise she can cause chaos while asleep.

I'm lying on my back, next to Orna, cloak drawn across my body and over my head. I turn slightly, careful not to break Drust's masking spell. I look across to where Connla is. And see a demon.

For a second I think I'm still dreaming, because the demon doesn't appear to be attacking Connla. It's crouched beside him, bent over, head close to his, as though talking. And when I prick my ears I can hear it whispering.

A drop of rain hits me square between the eyes. I blink — then snap out of my stupor. Leaping to my feet, I roar at the top of my voice, "*Demons!*"

Everyone comes alive in an instant, on their feet, weapons in hands. Ronan notches an arrow to his bow, takes aim and… stops as the demon turns to look at him. I see Ronan's fingers quiver, his face twitch, his eyes narrow. He wants to unleash the arrow but he can't. The demon's controlling him.

Lorcan attacks, sword and axe a blur, screaming a challenge. The demon points with a lumpy, pale red hand. And Lorcan stops too, not frozen in place exactly, but hovering beyond striking distance of the demon, unable to advance.

Goll and Orna are about to leap forward when Drust shouts, "No! Leave him!"

The druid is sitting up. His hands are joined. His lips are moving quickly, gaze fixed on the demon. He looks more purposeful than frightened.

Nobody moves. All eyes are pinned on the demon and the druid. Now that my sight has adjusted and there's time to observe, I get a clear view of the monster. It's tall, with eight arms, roughly shaped hands, dangling strips of flesh instead of legs and feet. Hovering in the air, not touching the ground. Pale red skin, flecked with blood. At first I think it's Connla's blood – I'm sure he's dead – but then I notice scores of cracks in the demon's skin, from which blood oozes, giving the lumpy flesh its unhealthy crimson tinge. No hair. Its eyes are dark red, with a black circle at the centre of each globe. No nose, just two gaping cavities in the middle of its face. No heart either — just a hole in its chest filled with eel-like creatures, which slither over and under one another, hissing and spitting.

The demon cocks its head and smiles sadly at Drust. "You are powerful, druid. The girl too, if she could only learn what you teach her."

Complete shock. I've never heard a demon speak like this, in words of our own. It – *he* – has a deep, sorrowful voice. Not entirely human, but the words are clearly formed. A demon who can speak as a human must also be able to think as a human. Drust's prediction – and our worst fear – has been confirmed.

Then the meaning of his words sink home. He knows Drust has been trying to teach me. He knows I've been failing. That means he can either read minds or…

"He's been following us!" I shriek, taking a step towards the heartless creature.

"Bec!" Drust hisses. "Don't get involved!"

"But—"

"Such sadness," the demon murmurs. "So much pain. A quest doomed to fail. This land overrun by demons. Everybody killed. And all your fault, Little One. Your people will die because you failed them. Imagine the humiliation and guilt."

I tremble, not wanting to believe him. But he sounds so sure of himself, so certain this is what the future holds. There's pity in his voice. I get the feeling he wants to comfort me. As I'm thinking this, the demon extends two arms and nods encouragingly. "Come to me," he whispers. "Seek solace in the embrace of loving Lord Loss."

I move closer to him, gripped by his power and the promise of comfort. The demon – Lord Loss – smiles and nods again. This isn't right. He's making me do his bidding and nothing good can come of that. But I can't resist. I'm filled with a sense of grief and only Lord Loss seems able to help.

Then Drust is by my side, talking quickly. "Use magic. This demon is of the Otherworld, of the stars. He generates power. Take it. Use it. *Fight*."

My body continues forward as though Drust hadn't spoken. But my mind's in a whirl. I'll die if I come within the demon's reach. He'll suck all the life from me and toss me aside, or keep me on as a member of the undead. I try using old magic spells to fight him but I can't move my lips to utter the words.

Drust's warning echoes. The demon is of the stars. He generates power. I recall my recent lessons, the spells Drust tried to teach me, how he encouraged me to draw from the stars, to channel magic from a celestial source.

With my mind, heart and spirit I reach out to Lord Loss. I feel his power, his magic. And I draw from it. I rip it from him sharply, fiercely, filling with it, hair shooting up straight, eyes widening, arms flying out wide.

The demon gasps and rises a few feet higher off the ground. I float too, supported by magic, drawing my power from the sky instead of the earth, becoming part of the world of the air.

I turn my hands palms down. Two large stones rise from the ground, ripping free, dripping soil and pebbles, floating upwards. They stop short of my hands, which I slide behind the stones. I look from hand to hand, stone to stone. Then at Lord Loss. I smile — and *push*. The stones zip towards him.

The demon's arms shoot out and the stones explode into clouds of dust and tiny brittle shards. Everybody ducks to avoid being pierced. Except me and Lord Loss. We remain motionless, supported by the air and magic, staring at each other.

Some of the stone splinters strike the demon's cheeks and open fresh, deep cuts. He doesn't look angry or surprised. Just sad.

"Such potential," the demon sighs. "What a waste. To die so young, when you could achieve so much…"

"Begone!" Drust roars, getting to his feet, linking his right hand with my left. I fill with even more power than before. I feel like I could reach up and quench the stars themselves. "Go or fight!" Drust shouts.

"Fight?" the demon chuckles. "I could destroy you both without even nearing my limits." One hand starts to point at us. Then stops. The demon lowers his arms. "But where would be the sport in that?" he murmurs. And then he turns smoothly and drifts away into the darkness of the night.

Just when I think he's gone, there comes a call from the shadows. "You stole from me, Bec. You took magic which was not yours. Pain will come of that. And great sorrow. And death." A teasing pause, then he adds, "It starts tomorrow."

Then he really is gone, leaving behind silence, confusion… and terror.

→Connla's alive. He rises when the demon leaves. Pale and shivering. He says he was asleep until my shout, that he couldn't move when he woke, held in place by magic. Drust checks to see if the demon has fed from him but can find no marks on the warrior's flesh.

I'm not interested in Connla or why Lord Loss was whispering to him in his sleep instead of killing him. I have time only for magic. I've never felt this powerful or so alive. The world looks and feels completely different. I can see as if it's day. The stars are brighter than a full moon, shining through the cover of the clouds, pulsing, multicoloured. And they're connected! I couldn't see it until tonight but now it's obvious. The sky's like a giant system of roots, each star linked. The lines between the stars are veins of magical power. The sky is alive. I can draw magic from it, just as Banba taught me to draw from a tree or a stag.

I reach out with my mind and suck in power. I want it all, the whole of the sky, every bit of magic it has to offer. I can be a goddess, capable of changing the world with a click of my fingers. I can...

"No," Drust says softly. I look down and see that his hands are on either side of my shoulders but not touching me. His eyes are as dark as the sky is bright. "You must stop."

"Why?" I whisper, continuing to draw strength from the stars.

"You won't be able to contain so much power. Your body will unravel. You'll die."

"I can hold it together," I sigh. "With this much magic I can do anything."

"No," he says firmly. "It will destroy you."

I don't want to believe him. I don't want to stop. But I can see the truth in his expression. He's not a jealous teacher intent on holding me back — he's a worried ally trying to save me. Reluctantly I pull back and cut off the seductive flow of power from the stars. The world dims around me. I become human again.

Drust's hands close on my shoulders and he squeezes warmly. "You did well," he says.

"I did it," I reply, hardly able to believe it now the moment has passed. "I made the magic work. *Your* magic."

"Yes." He doesn't let go. He looks troubled. "I've never seen someone make the leap from novice to adept so swiftly. The demon said you stole magic from him. The power that involved..."

"I didn't mean to steal," I say quietly. "Is it a bad thing?"

Drust shakes his head and smiles thinly. "No. Just unexpected." He releases me. "Now, let's get everybody settled down and restore the masking spells. There may be other demons nearby who might not be so willing to retreat as Lord Loss."

"Do you know what he was?" I ask. "Why he could speak? What he meant about death and sorrow coming tomorrow?"

"We will talk about him shortly," Drust says. "First the spells. You can help me cast them this time. Listen carefully, then copy what I do." And he shows me. And I try it. And it works. Easy.

→"Lord Loss is one of the more powerful Demonata," Drust says. We're all lying close together. It's late in the night but nobody can sleep, not after what we've so recently witnessed. "He's a demon master."

"You said they couldn't come through yet," Fiachna notes.

Drust nods thoughtfully. "When the first demon master forces its way through the tunnel, it will widen. There will be a flood of demons more powerful than those who roam the land now, eager to get in on the killing while there are humans left to kill. They'll be savage, unformed, monstrous. We'll know when they are here — the screams of the dying will fill the air.

"I don't think Lord Loss came through the tunnel, or that he crossed any time recently. He could speak our language. Even the powerful demon masters cannot do that without much practice. I believe he has been here for many years, walking among us."

"How?" Orna gasps. "The demons only started coming last year."

"No," Drust says. "Some came before that. There are ways for humans to summon them. They can never stay for long. They usually kill recklessly, then slip back to their own foul realm. But this one seems at home here…" He falls silent, then says, "Much of our knowledge of the Demonata comes from the Old Creatures. They walked the land once. This was their world. They instructed the early druids, told them about demons, taught them how to fight. But they did not teach us all that they knew. Perhaps they couldn't, since they were gods and we were only humans.

"As far as I was aware, demons could not roam this world freely unless a tunnel was open. That is what the Old Creatures taught us, and we have seen evidence of that in the many centuries since they withdrew from our company. But I see now that there are exceptions to that rule. Lord Loss must be one of them."

"Are you sure he was a demon?" Goll asks. "He looked more like a Fomorii to me, judging by the old legends."

"He was definitely a Demonata," Drust says. "But he is different to most. The majority revel in bloodshed. The masters are like the weaker demons which you've seen — crude and wild, interested only in slaughter. Lord Loss appears to be more cultured. Cruel rather than brute. He could have killed us but he didn't. Instead he spoke of sport and future suffering. He—"

"The stones!" I blurt out. I'd been thinking about him trailing us by day, moving among us at night, when an image clicked into place. "I saw him at the ring!" When the others look blank, I tell them about the demon I saw when we were trapped within the circle of magical stones. "There was one who didn't pay attention to Bran when he was running around and dancing. He was by himself, floating in the air, watching the rest of us. It was Lord Loss. He's been following us since then."

"But why?" Orna asks.

"*Sport*," Drust replies, face dark with worry. "I think this demon is as vicious as any of the others, but he feasts on the agony of humans instead of their blood. Sorrow excites him. He must have sensed the promise of pain when he saw you and has been following ever since, waiting for the misery to start."

"Then it will be a long wait!" Goll huffs. "I won't be played by a demon. Now that we know he's here, we can fight him."

"Maybe," Drust says gloomily but his eyes are dark and I can see the embers of fear in them.

CHILDREN OF THE DARK

→We march at the same pace as before, but anxiously now, aware of the demon's warning that death would strike today. We're tense, prone to snap at the slightest irritation. When Connla passes a simple insult about Goll's blind eye late in the morning, Goll responds by criticising Connla for falling asleep while on watch. The pair almost come to blows and have to be separated by the rest of us.

Ronan and Lorcan are the calmest. The brothers have little fear of death. This is just part of the big adventure for them. I think they're half-hoping we *are* attacked, so they can kill more demons.

My lessons continue throughout the day. I was afraid the magic would desert me when the sun rose, that I wouldn't be able to draw upon the power of the stars. But Drust teaches me to ignore the state of the sky and draw from it regardless of whether it's day or night.

"The stars hide but are always there," he says. "We're weaker in the day but not as weak as demons. Most of them can't draw from the stars at all while the sun shines, but we can."

Since I made the breakthrough, I've come on like a child who's taken her first step and is now toddling everywhere at high speed. I find it easy to move objects — stones, branches, even Bran. I make him rise while we're resting, move him a few strides across in the air and set him down without him even noticing. That tires me but it doesn't exhaust me and I recover quickly.

Drust says I'm one of the strongest at doing this that he's ever seen. I ask if there's a limit to what I can lift and move. He says there are always limits but he has no idea what mine might be. I suggest trying to uproot a tree but he says it's too soon for so ambitious a test.

I'm not as accomplished in other areas. I learn how to create fire and hold it in my hands, either as a torch or to use as a weapon. But my flames are pitiful flickerings, nothing like Drust's solid columns, and they singe my fingers.

I develop protective spells, like the one we use to mask ourselves at night. But these are more complicated, designed to shield me from physical assault. If they work correctly, a demon won't be able to harm me with its claws or teeth, only with magic.

There are spells to protect me from magic too, but they're even harder to learn. I make a small amount of headway with both sets of spells. Drust is pleased with my progress, but it's tough work and leaves me feeling drained and grumpy.

"What about spells of attack?" I ask in the afternoon, thinking of the night ahead, worrying about the dangers we'll face.

"Survival is our only concern right now," Drust says, then looks around. We're not close to any of the others, except Bran, who walks behind me like a faithful hound. Drust lowers his voice. "You must think only of your own well being if we're attacked. Don't put yourself in danger, even to save another. I need you, Bec. Your people need you too. Don't waste your life trying to save someone who isn't important."

"You don't want me to fight?" I ask archly. "You want me to stand by and let my friends die?"

"If you have to," he says.

"I can't. I won't. Not unless you tell me what you want me for."

Drust shrugs. "I'm offering you good advice. Ignore it if you wish. Now, let's work on a different type of spell. This one gives you the appearance of a giant. It will frighten off certain demons."

And he says no more about why I'm so important to him or why he wants to keep me alive when he's happy to stand by and accept the slaughter of everybody else.

→Lessons cease a couple of hours before sunset, to give myself and Drust time to recharge and prepare for any battles we might find ourselves involved in. I spend the time until dark wondering what Lord Loss will throw at us.

Hordes of demons? An army of the undead? Maybe they'll burrow at us from beneath the earth or drop on us from the sky. How powerful is the demon master? Drust doesn't know. There's no way of telling, not until we've studied the heartless beast in action.

The others are nervous too, even Ronan and Lorcan now that night is almost upon us. They're not afraid of death but of being taken by surprise and dying in disgrace. Oddly enough, Connla seems the most assured. He was edgy earlier but now walks cockily, urging us on, telling us not to worry. He's acting like a king, which isn't unusual, but he's doing it in the face of danger, which is strange. Maybe he's finally growing into the leader his father always wanted him to be.

Half an hour before sunset, Drust halts on top of a hill and says, "Here."

Goll looks around. "Are you sure? We can be seen from all directions."

"If Lord Loss plans to guide demons to us, he'll find us no matter where we are," Drust responds. "At least up here we can see them coming. And the exposure is good for Bec and me. We can draw strength from the stars easier at this height."

As the others make camp I ask Drust if that was true or if he was just saying it to give Goll confidence. "It's true," he says. "High places, with no trees, are ideal for magicians who absorb power from the heavens."

"But won't this place favour the demons too?" I ask.

Drust shrugs. "Best not to think about that."

When everyone's ready, Drust and I cast masking spells. The spells won't count for much if Lord Loss reveals our position to other demons, but they'll protect us if strays wander by.

→Time passes. It rains heavily, then eases, though the sky remains clogged with clouds. Nobody speaks. I realise after a few hours how hungry I am. We were so concerned with finding a good spot for the night that we never thought to hunt or pick berries. Oh well, too late now. I'll just have to wait for morning — and hope *I'm* not eaten before then.

→Midnight. You can always tell, even when the moon and stars are blocked out. I want nothing more than to curl up and sleep. It's been a long day, coming on the back of a sleepless night. Hunger adds to my tiredness. But I dare not shut my eyes. There's no telling how swift the demons will be if – when – they attack. Seconds of grogginess could spell the difference between life and death.

→Later. A few hours shy of dawn. I've been dozing, despite my desire to remain awake. Halfway between the worlds of dreams and flesh. A dangerous state, open to the threat of both realms. Banba always told me to sleep or stay awake, never hover betwixt the two.

A cry in the darkness jolts me out of my half-sleep. It sounds like a child but it can't be — we passed no villages earlier, and no child would dare wander the world by night, not in these troubled times.

I look around. Everyone's awake. All eyes are focused on the spot from where the sound came. Ronan's bow is aimed, an arrow ready to fly at its target the moment he sights one.

"Don't move," Drust whispers, just loud enough for all to hear. "The spells are still intact. This might be nothing to do with—"

"*Motherrrrrr…*" comes a cry, clearer this time. A girl's voice. Full of pain and grief.

"*Help us… motherrrr…*" A different voice, this time a boy.

"*So cold… motherrrr…*" A third child, also a boy. He sounds younger than the other two.

"What is that?" Lorcan asks, nervously tugging at his earrings.

"I'm not sure," Drust answers. "Only demon masters can mimic human voices. And the undead don't retain the power of speech. Perhaps Lord Loss is manipulating a lesser demon."

"*Motherrrr… hold usssssss…*" The girl again. Her voice sends shivers down the back of my neck. I want to run to her and wrap my arms around her, even knowing she can't be human. She sounds young, scared, lost.

"I don't like this," Goll mutters, his eye darting left and right, trying to pick out figures in the darkness.

"They might be real children," Fiachna says. "The demon could be using them to trap us."

"No," Orna says, and there's a tremble to her voice. "They... I..."

"*Motherrrr!*" the elder boy cries, as if in response to Orna's voice.

Orna stands. "No!" Drust barks, but she ignores him and takes a step forward, hands clasped over her breasts, face torn between terror and delight.

Something moves in the shadows. Three shapes advance. Drust curses, then creates a ball of fire and sends it floating down the hill, to illuminate the creatures. Three children are revealed, stumbling forward. Undead. Their bodies are in good condition, most of the limbs are attached, the flesh isn't ripped to pieces, heads on necks. But they're definitely not living children. They move sluggishly and one boy's missing an eye, the other both its ears, the girl some fingers.

"My children," Orna croaks, and although I was cold with fear already, now I turn to ice.

Orna takes a second step down the hill.

"Orna!" Goll hisses. "Stop! They're not your children! It's a trick!"

"But they are," Orna says. Tears are flowing down her cheeks, a warrior no longer, all woman now — all mother.

"It's a glamour," Drust says softly. "They're probably the bodies of other children disguised to look like yours."

"No," Orna says. "I'd know my young loves anywhere."

"*Cold… motherrrr…*" the youngest boy moans.

"*Lonely… motherrrr…*" the girl wails.

Orna takes a third step.

"They'll kill you," Fiachna says. He gets up, breaking his masking spell. Moves towards her, hands outspread. "If you go to them, they'll slaughter you, like the demons slaughtered them. It doesn't matter if they were your children. They're the Demonata's now. They're Lord Loss's." He shouts, scaring us all, "You're out there, aren't you, demon lord? Watching this and grinning, aye?"

No answer, except more cries from the undead children.

Fiachna closes on Orna and reaches for her, to lead her back to safety. Before his fingers touch her, she leaps away from him and draws a knife. "Stay back!" she snarls. Fiachna blinks and lowers his hands. Orna looks at the smith pitifully. "They're my children," she whimpers. "I can't leave them. They're calling me."

"*Motherrrr!*" all three wail at the same time.

"This is madness," Goll says, stepping up beside Fiachna. Orna points her knife at him. Goll glares at her with disgust — but with sympathy too. "Put your weapon away and come to us. You'll see the folly of this in the morning."

"But they're my—"

"No!" Goll shouts. "They're nothing except walking lumps of rotting flesh! Look at them, woman! Look with your eyes and brain, not your heart. Your children are dead. Accept that. Let this vision pass."

"But what if... maybe they could..." Orna's shoulders slump. Tears fall more freely. Fiachna moves towards her again. Goll stops him and shakes his head — *wait*.

"Can we lift the spell?" I ask Drust. "Remove the glamour so she can see them as they really are?"

"No," Drust says shortly. "She's seeing with her heart now, not her eyes. No magic I know can combat a self-powered spell like that."

"I could shoot one of them with an arrow," Ronan says, squinting as he takes careful aim.

Orna growls like a wild animal. "You'll die on that spot if you do!"

"Let her go," Connla laughs cruelly. "If she's so desperate to mother demons, who are we to stop her?"

"*Bricriu!*" Goll roars, the foul curse for a meddler. Connla only smiles.

"Please, Orna," I mutter, trying another approach. "I need you. You're like a mother to me. Let *me* be your daughter. I couldn't bear it if you left."

Orna's eyes soften and she smiles. "You're a good girl, Bec. And I love you, almost as much as I loved... *love* my little lost ones." She shakes her head ever so slightly. "But you're not mine. They are. And they're calling me."

"But—"

I get no further. In an instant, taking us all by surprise, she leaps away and is racing down the hill towards the three undead children, who raise their arms and croon with delight.

Fiachna starts after her but Goll trips him. As he rises angrily, turning on Goll, the old warrior sticks his hands out, palms upwards, the sign for peace, then says softly, "Macha help her."

The fury fades from Fiachna and he turns to watch, along with the rest of us. "You should have let me go," he murmurs. "I might have caught her."

"No," Goll replies. "She was too far ahead and too desperate."

Orna reaches the children and stops. I expect them to attack but they just stand there, staring at her, arms outstretched, waiting for her to hug them. For a moment I wonder if we were mistaken, if these *are* her children and mean her no harm. But then Drust nudges me and points to the right, further down the hill. I spot the outline of Lord Loss, inhuman eyes fixed on the woman and children, wicked smile visible even from here.

Ronan fires an arrow at the demon master, then another, but both stop short of their target, as though they've struck an invisible wall. Lord Loss doesn't even glance in our direction.

Orna kneels, extends her arms and draws the children in close. I see their faces, alight with evil glee. The eldest boy gently, lovingly brushes the soft flesh of her neck — then sinks his teeth into it. Orna stiffens but doesn't cry out. The girl latches on to the warrior's upper arm, chewing at it like a dog with a bone. The youngest boy's head sinks beneath

Orna's shoulders. He rips her tunic open. I can't see from here, but I know he's suckling, drawing blood instead of milk.

Orna's arms tighten around the children, hugging them closer. She hums a tune women sing to send their young to sleep. I gasp with horror when I hear that and turn away from the awful sight of the undead boys and girl feasting on the living flesh of their *mother*.

Fiachna squats beside me and grabs me tight, letting me bury my face in his chest. "There there, Little One," he coos. "She's happy. She thinks she's back with her children. We should all be lucky to die so willingly."

"But they're not!" I cry. "They're not her—"

"I know," he whispers, stroking the back of my head. "But she thinks they are. That's all that matters."

Although I've turned my back on the carnage, I can't block out the sounds of ripping flesh and the occasional painful hiss from Orna or moan of satisfaction from the undead beasts. Even when I cover my ears with my hands, I hear them, or imagine I do.

After a while the others turn away from the sickening sight, one by one, ashen-faced, eyes filled with regret, stomachs turning. Even cruel Connla, who gave up on her before anybody else.

The only one who doesn't turn away is Bran. The boy remains sitting where he awoke, watching silently, head tilted to one side, frowning curiously, as if he's not entirely sure what's happening and is waiting to see if this is a game with an unexpected, amusing finale.

Eventually, since I can't bear it, I walk over, turn him around and sit beside him. I lean against the simple boy and keep him faced away from Orna, allowing her the humble dignity of dying in private.

FAMILY

→We leave first thing in the morning, pausing only for Drust to set Orna's remains aflame, so she can't return to life as one of the undead. Often demons take the bodies of their victims with them. I think Lord Loss made the children leave Orna so her bones and last few scraps of flesh could further unnerve us.

We march in silence, all thoughts on Orna and how she went willingly to her monstrous death. Is her spirit with her children now in the Otherworld or is it doomed to wander this land for all time, lost and damned?

Even Drust is sombre, leaving the lessons for later, proof that in spite of his stern appearance, he too is human, with the same emotions as the rest of us.

→The ground has been getting rockier the further west we proceed. Fewer trees, no fields of crops, not many animals, no raths or crannogs. But people live here, or did at one time, since there are remains of many dolmens and wedge tombs. Most of the dolmens have been knocked over, the stones scattered, the bones they housed burnt to ash. And the seals of the wedge tombs have been broken, either by demons or humans. If we were to go into the tombs, we'd find charred ash or the sleeping undead. I don't think any of the dead in this land lie whole and in peace any more.

→In the afternoon we come to a small village of beehive-shaped stone huts. It's an old settlement, with only a crumbling short wall surrounding the perimeter. The huts are in poor condition, some fallen in on themselves. At first I think it's a ghost village, all the people dead or fled. But then I spot smoke coming from a few of the huts and hear a woman shouting at a child. We look around at each other, surprised to find life in such a hostile, vulnerable environment.

"Humans or demons?" Fiachna asks.

"I'm not sure." Drust sniffs the air. "There's a scent of something inhuman, but…" He smells the air again, eyes narrow slits. "There are humans too. Peculiar."

"Should we avoid it?" Goll asks.

Drust thinks a while, then shakes his head. "We need to rest. We've had little sleep recently. We must seek shelter."

"But if there are demons…" Goll mutters.

Drust glances up at the sky. "It's a long time until sunset. We should be safe. And I'm curious. I want to know what these people are doing here — and how they've avoided being butchered by the Demonata."

*　*　*

→There's a narrow gateway into the village but we climb over the wall in case the entrance is set with traps. There are animals within, scraggly sheep and goats. They scatter when they see us, bleating loudly.

A boy sticks his head out of a hut, a sling in one hand. He starts to shout — he thinks some animal has entered the village and scared the sheep and goats. Then he sees us and his shout changes from one of anger to one of alarm. "*Strangers!*"

Within seconds two men, three women and three children – two girls and the boy – are in front of the huts, spears and crude swords to hand, facing us. We hold our ground, weapons raised defensively. Then Goll gives the order for us to lower our arms. He steps forward, right hand held palm up, and shouts a greeting.

One of the men meets Goll halfway, face creased with suspicion, eyeing us beadily. The pair have a quick, hushed conversation. At the end, Goll turns and nods us forward, while the man returns to his place among the others.

When we're all together, Goll makes our introductions. The man who met him then tells us they're the MacGrigor. His name is Torin. The other man's Ert. The women are Aideen, Dara and Fand. We aren't told the names of the children.

"They're on a quest," Torin says. He's a short, muscular man, dark skinned. "They want to stop the demons."

One of the women — Fand — laughs. "Just the eight of them?"

"One is all it takes," Drust responds.

"We don't have much respect for druids here," Ert says, spitting into the dirt at Drust's feet. "Your kind aren't as powerful as you pretend to be. We had dealings with your lot before and they failed us."

"Failed you in what way?" Drust asks with cold politeness.

"We'll talk of that later," Torin says, frowning at Ert. "For now you're welcome. We won't turn you away. However, we can't feed you, so if you want to eat, you'll have to hunt." He squints at the sun. "I wouldn't wait too long."

The woman called Aideen points to a pair of huts near the wall, both in poor condition. "You can stay there," she says. "You'll be safe if you don't wander."

"We'll call for you later," the third woman — Dara — adds.

"Thank you," I mutter when the men don't respond.

"Our pleasure," Aideen replies. She starts to turn away, then stops and stares at me. "Girl," she commands, "come here."

I step forward cautiously. Aideen reaches for me sharply and I draw back from her cracked nails, readying myself to bark a spell. She spreads her fingers to show she means no harm, then smiles crookedly. I stand still while she cups my chin and tilts my head back.

"What is it?" Torin asks.

"Her face…" Aideen murmurs, turning my chin towards Torin.

The man frowns. "She looks like… but she can't… Girl! What's your name? Where are you from?"

"Bec," I tell him. "I'm from the rath of the MacConn."

"Are you of them?" Torin asks. "Is your mother of the clan?"

"My mother's dead," I answer softly. "Nobody knows who she was or where she came from. She died not long after I was born."

"Aednat's child!" Aideen gasps, her fingers tightening on my chin. "She must be!" I tingle with shock when she says that. The face of my mother forms quickly in my mind and for the first time ever I have a name to go with it.

"You knew my mother!" I cry.

"She was my sister," Aideen croaks.

"Then this is where I'm from? This was where my mother lived?" When Aideen nods wonderingly my head spins and my heart leaps. "Why did she leave?" I yell. "What happened? Who was my father? Is he still alive? Do you–"

"Enough!" Torin interrupts. He's glaring at me — the news that I'm of his people hasn't pleased him. "We must think on this. We'll talk about it tonight."

Then he heads back inside the large stone hut, waving at the others to follow, leaving us to stare at one another uncertainly and make our way to the smaller huts to set up camp for the night.

* * *

→My head's still spinning. I'd almost forgotten about the spirit of my mother beckoning me west, and the notion that maybe she wanted to help me unlock the secrets of my past. Inside I never really believed I'd discover the truth about my family — it was a childish dream. Yet here I am, in the most unlikely of places, suddenly confronted with her name and the promise of my history.

Aednat. As soon as Aideen said it I *knew* it was my mother. Maybe it's the magic that makes me sure, but I think I would have known even if it had happened before my new power blossomed. But her name is all I know. Who was she? Why did she live in this wilderness with the others? And why leave her family to bear me in loneliness and die so far from home?

I want to ask the questions *now*, find out the answers immediately. I want to rush to the large hut and demand the truth from Aideen and Torin. But this is their home, meagre as it is, and it would be disrespectful to speak out of turn. If their wish is for me to wait, then wait I must — no matter how frustrating that is.

→Ronan and Lorcan hunt for food in the hours before sunset. Game is scarce in this rocky wilderness but the twins return with two hares, a crow and a cub fox. Fiachna, Bran and I pick berries and wild roots while they're gone. It makes for a fine meal. There's even some left over, which we offer to Fand when she comes to fetch us shortly after sunset.

"We have our own food," she says curtly.

As we're walking to the largest building, there's a ferocious howl from one of the huts in poor repair. The warriors in our group draw their weapons immediately but Fand waves away their concerns. "It's nothing," she says.

"That was a demon," Goll growls, not lowering his sword.

"No," Fand says. "It was my brother."

We stare at her with disbelief. She sighs, then strides towards the hut where the howl came from. We follow cautiously. At the entrance, Fand crouches and points within. We bend down beside her. Dim evening light shines through holes in the roof. In the weak glow we see an animal tied by a short length of rope to a rock in the middle of the hut. It's human-shaped but covered in long thick hair, with claws and dark yellow eyes. It snarls when it sees us and tries to attack, but is held back by the rope.

"*That's* your brother?" Goll asks suspiciously.

"His name is — was — Fintan," Fand says.

"What happened to him?" I ask, staring uncomfortably at the yellow eyes. Disfigured as they are, they look disturbingly similar to mine. "Is he undead?"

"No." Fand stands. "We'll tell you in the main hut. Come." When we hesitate, she manages a thin smile. "Don't worry. You're safe here. Fintan and the others are tied up tight."

"There are more like this?" Ronan says.

"Four." Fand pauses and her expression darkens. "For now."

She goes to the largest hut and ducks inside. One last glance at the creature chained to the rock — it looks like a cross between a wolf and a man — then we follow, gripping our weapons tight, watching the shadows for any sign of other, unchained beasts.

→It's crowded inside the hut, with all five adults, the three children we saw earlier, two younger kids — one just a babe — and us. The MacGrigor are poorly dressed — most of the children are naked — and scrawny. Dirty hair, rough tattoos, cracked nails, bloodshot eyes.

"They've seen Fintan," Fand says when we're seated, after a few seconds of uneasy silence.

"Good," Torin grunts. "That saves some time." He collects his thoughts, glances at me, then tells us their sorry tale — *my* tale.

Several generations ago their ancestors bred with the Fomorii. They thought the semi-demons were going to conquer this land and threw in their lot with them. When the Fomorii were defeated, the MacGrigor were hunted down and executed as traitors. But some survived and went into hiding.

"Though if they'd known what was to come next, I think they'd have stayed and accepted death," Torin says bitterly.

Some of the children of the human-Fomorii couplings were born deformed and demonic, and were immediately put to death. But most were human in appearance. These lived and grew, and for many years all was well.

"Then the changes began," Torin sighs. "When children came of a certain age — usually on the cusp of adulthood — some transformed. It always happened around the time of a full moon. Their bodies twisted. Hair sprouted. Their teeth lengthened into fangs, their nails into claws. The change developed and worsened over three or four moons. By the end, they were wild, inhuman beasts, incapable of speech or recognition. Killers if left to wander free."

The affected children were slain, while the others grew and had children of their own. They thought they were safe, that they'd survived the curse — but they were wrong. Some of the children of the survivors changed too, and their grandchildren, and those who came after.

"It strikes at random," Torin says. "Sometimes four of five children of any generation will change, sometimes only two. But always a few. There's never been a generation where none of the children turned."

The family sought the help of priestesses and druids in later years, when their treachery had been forgotten and they were free to live among normal folk again. But no magician could lift the curse. So they struggled on, moving from one place to another whenever their dark secret was discovered, living as far away from other clans as possible, sometimes killing their beastly young, other times — as here — allowing them to live, in the hope they might one day change back or be cured by a powerful druid.

"It's no sort of life," Torin mutters, eyes distant, "waiting for our children to turn. Having to feed those who've fallen foul of the curse and look upon them as they are, remembering them as they were. I'd rather kill the poor beasts, but…" He glances at Fand, who glowers at him.

"And Bec?" Fiachna asks, sensing my impatience, speaking on my behalf. "Her mother was of your clan?"

"If her mother was Aednat, aye," Torin says. He looks at me and again his face is dark. "Aednat had six children. All turned. When she fell pregnant for the seventh time, years after she and her husband, Struan, had agreed not to try again, Struan was furious. He couldn't bear the thought of bringing another child into the world and rearing it, only to have to kill it when it fell prey to the ravages of the moon.

"Aednat argued to keep the child. She thought she might be lucky this time, that the gods would never curse her seven times in a row. She was old, at an age when most women can no longer conceive. She thought it was a sign that this child was blessed, that it would be safe. Struan didn't agree. Neither did the rest of us."

"Some did!" Aideen interrupts bitterly, but says no more when Torin glares at her warningly.

"We decided to kill the child in the womb," Torin continues gruffly. "That was Struan's wish and we believed it was the right thing to do. Struan took Aednat off into the wilds, to do the deed in private. But none of us knew how much Aednat wanted the baby. She fought with Struan when they were alone. Stabbed him. I don't think she meant to kill him, but—"

"My mother killed my father?" I almost scream.

"Aye," Torin says, burning me with his stare. "She probably only intended to wound him, but she cut too deeply. He died and she fled. By the time we discovered his body, she was far away. We followed for a time, to avenge Struan's murder, but lost her trail after a couple of days. We prayed for her death when we returned. I'm pleased to hear our prayers were answered."

I rear myself back to curse him for saying such a mean thing, but Fiachna grabs my left arm and squeezes hard, warning me to be silent.

"Of course the girl's not our business now," Torin says heavily. "She's of your clan, not ours, so we can't tell you what to do with her. But she's a cursed child, from a line of cursed children, and the spawn of a killer. She's at the age when the moon usually works its wicked charms. If you let her live, the chances are strong that she'll change into a beast like Fintan. If you want my advice—"

"We don't," Goll snaps.

"As you wish," Torin concedes. "But when the moon is full, be wary of her."

He falls silent. I'm panting hard, as if I'd been running, thinking of the kind, weary face of my mother, trying to picture her killing my father. Then I recall the boy-beast in the hut and imagine myself in his position. I wish now that the past had remained a secret!

"What about the demons?" Drust asks, maybe to change the subject to stop me brooding, or maybe because he has no interest in my history or Torin's grim prediction. "Don't they ever attack?"

"No," Torin says.

"Even though you're poorly defended and they could butcher you any time they pleased?"

Torin shrugs. "There were other families living near here. They'd been forced out of their tuatha for various reasons and settled in this wasteland. The demons killed them last year. We've seen the monsters pass from time to time and they've seen us. But they leave us alone."

Drust nods. "Then it wasn't a Fomorii your ancestors bred with. It was a true demon. Some of the Demonata fought alongside the Fomorii. Many demons don't attack their own, especially if there are pure humans to kill. You're kin to them, so they spare you — for now at least."

"We've heard talk of the Demonata before," Torin says. "Other druids – those we went to for help – spoke of them. They told us the curse was demonic and that was why they couldn't help." He leans forward. "I don't suppose *you* know any way to…?" He leaves the question hanging.

Drust thinks about it a while, then says, "A demon master might be able to lift the curse. But I know of no human – druid, priestess or any other – who has the power to remove such a blood stain."

"You mean the demons could cure us?" Fand says sharply.

"One of the more powerful masters, perhaps," Drust says.

"Do you know where we can find one?"

Drust starts to respond, to tell them about Lord Loss. Then he stops and shakes his head. "The demon masters have not broken through to this world yet. When and if they do, they will be easy to locate. But I doubt if you will be able to convince them to help — by nature they are not inclined to be merciful."

We stay talking a while longer. I ask questions about my mother and father, what they were like, how they spoke and lived. But Torin ignores my queries and speaks sharply whenever Aideen or Fand tries to answer, changing the conversation. I consider using magic on him, to make him tell me what I want to know, but Drust reads my thoughts and growls in my ear, "This is neither the time nor place for magic. Control yourself."

When the MacGrigor have told us some more of their sad history and how they eke out a living here, Drust speaks of our quest, of the tunnel which has opened between the demon world and this, and his plan to close it. But he says nothing of how he hopes to pinpoint its location or why he's leading us to the western coast — the end of the world.

When it's time to sleep, we return to the two stone huts set aside for us and make ourselves comfortable. It's been both a revealing and frustrating night for me — I've learnt some of my history but not all. There's so much more Torin and the others could tell me, but Torin hates my mother for betraying the clan, killing her husband and deserting them. And, since she's no longer here for him to hate, he hates me in her place. He'll never tell me about her or allow the others to.

Before I lie down, I remember the conversation after the revelations about my past and ask Drust why he didn't tell Torin about Lord Loss. "If they could find him, they might be able to persuade him to help," I note — figuring, if I could play a part in curing them of their curse, they'd surely tell me more about my parents.

"Aye," Drust says archly. "But all we know about Lord Loss is that he likes to follow *us* around. If we told them that, they might try to hold us here, to use as bait."

"But there are more of us than them," I point out. "We're stronger and better armed. You and I have magical powers. They couldn't force us to stay."

"Probably not," Drust says. "But it's safer not to take the risk. This way, they have no need to delay us and no conflict can come of it. The MacGrigor – or their descendants – will have to track down and petition a demon master another time."

So saying, he rolls over and falls asleep, not even bothering to cast any masking spells, certain of our safety here in this bitterly charmed village of the damned.

THE SOURCE

→I spend a few tortured hours thinking about my parents, Aednat and Struan, and the tragedy which separated them and brought me into the world. Torin called me a cursed child and he was right. I'm doubly cursed. The curse of my clan and the curse of being a killer's daughter. Surely, of all the current MacGrigor crop, I must be the most likely to turn into a monster.

I worry about it for hours, imagining what it would be like to lose control of my mind, feel my body change, become a beast like the one I saw earlier. I thought death was the worst thing I had to fear but now I know better. With worries like these, I doubt I'll ever be able to sleep again. But eventually tiredness overcomes even my gravest fears and I drift off into a fitful sleep, one filled with dreams of wolf-girls and dead children.

→I awake late in the morning. The others are already up but most have only risen within the last hour so I don't feel too guilty for sleeping in.

I expect them to treat me differently now they know the truth of my background and the threat of what I might become. But it quickly becomes clear that they think of me no differently than they did yesterday. I suppose there's too much else to worry about. After all, what's one potential half-demon when judged against the hordes of genuine, fully-formed Demonata we might yet have to face?

Ronan and Lorcan have caught another hare, which Fiachna roasts on a spit. Along with the leftovers from the night before it provides us with a filling meal to start the day. Again we offer to share it with the MacGrigor, but again they refuse. They have too much pride to eat from another's fire.

When we're finished, they point us in the easiest direction to the coast, then wave us off. Aideen looks like she wants to wish me well but she dare not speak kindly to me in front of the glowering Torin. I wish I could stay here and work on Torin, earn his respect and love. But even if he wasn't so hostile to me, I'm part of a quest, and although it's shrouded in secrecy and I'm deeply suspicious of Drust's reasons for helping us, it would be wrong to quit now. Perhaps, if I survive, I can return and seek a place here in my true home — even if it's only so that they can chain me up with others of my kind if my body starts to change.

One of the wretched wolf-humans is howling madly as we leave, as if it senses a kindred spirit and is singing to the beast I might one day become.

I think about the MacGrigor – my family – as we set off, wondering what will happen if we fail and the Demonata overrun the land. Will these poor excuses for humans be all that remain of our people? Will they alone be spared, kept alive because of their poisoned blood, the only human faces in a land of twisted demons?

My lessons resume as we march. I practise the spells which Drust has already taught me and learn some new ones, like —

How to hold my breath for ten minutes.

How to make my fingers so cold that anything I touch turns to ice.

How to create an image of myself, to confuse a human or demonic foe.

How to sharpen a rock using only magic, to fashion a crude knife or spearhead for those times when magic alone might not be enough.

I'm amazed at how swiftly I'm developing. Under Banba it would sometimes take me a week to master a new spell. Now I'm mastering some in minutes, almost before Drust has finished explaining how they work. And although they tire me, they don't drain me and I recover rapidly.

Drust is surprised too. He keeps commenting on how fast I am, quicker to learn than anyone he's ever taught, how deep my magic runs. At first I think it's flattery, designed to keep me happy and stop me thinking about the MacGrigor.

But as the day wears on I realise he's actually worried about my progress.

"What's wrong?" I snap as for the twentieth time he mutters darkly about my skills. "Aren't you glad that I'm learning quickly?"

"Of course," Drust says. "Any teacher would be pleased to pass on so much with such little effort. But it's not natural. Of course *all* magic is unnatural. We bend the laws of the universe to suit our needs. Each student is different, learning in a unique way, developing unlike any other. But there are similarities... learning steps all must climb... patterns they share.

"Except you." His eyes are heavy. "When we started out, you were like any student. Slow to learn, stubborn to abandon your old ways, gradually opening yourself up to a new world of magic. Now you're nothing like that. You've changed in every imaginable way and I'm not sure what to think of it."

"It's not that strange," I mutter. "Once I perfected my first spell, it was easy. I just had a hard time getting started."

"No," Drust says. "There's more to it than that. I..." He hesitates, then says it. "I want to look inside your mind. I want to join spirits with you and see what inspired this change."

I go very quiet. I shared my mind and spirit with Banba many times. It's part of the teaching process. I thought I'd have to do the same with Drust, but there'd been no mention of it until now. Sharing one's spirit is a personal, private thing. To do it with a woman is hard, but to share with a man...

"It won't be easy for me either," Drust says quietly. "If you refuse, I won't force you. But I have good reason for asking. There's something unsettling about your growth. I suspect I know what it is. But I need to go within your mind to be sure."

"Can't you just tell me?" I groan. "Why all this need for secrets?"

"Druids and priestesses are creatures of secrets," he says. "We live in worlds of mazes and mysteries. Secrecy is part of who we are and how we live. It should be enough for you when I say I need to do this. My reasons are unimportant. You either trust me or you don't."

I want to pull a face and say that I don't, to annoy him. But his worry has set me worrying too. Now that I think about it, I realise no apprentice should advance this far, this fast. Banba told me ignorance is the greatest danger any magician ever faces. If you don't know yourself intimately – your powers and the magic you wield – sooner or later you'll fall victim to forces of the unknown.

"Very well," I sigh. "But I don't want you rooting around inside my head too long. Find what you need, then get out. If not, I'll fight."

Drust nods, smiling wryly. Then, without slowing, he takes hold of my left hand and directs his thoughts towards me. I feel his presence immediately, as if he'd opened a door into my mind and stepped through. His magic washes into me, seeping through my skin. Most of it is directed through his fingers but it comes from other places too — legs, chest, head. His power is like a cloud wrapped around me, swallowing me, tasting and testing me. Soon it's as if there are two people sharing one body. My thoughts are his, my past, my dreams, my magic.

I stiffen but don't stop walking. Movement gives me a notion of separation. I'm still aware of my individual self, who I am, who I was, who I hope to be. If I stop, I'm afraid Drust will become me and I'll lose myself to him completely.

He presses further into my mind, searching, exploring the well of my magic. He's already deeper within me than Banba ever got, discovering truths which nobody knows, my secret wishes and desires, my hopes, loves and fears. And still he doesn't stop. He keeps going, working on the part of me that is pure magic, dragging himself down towards my core, deeper and deeper, searching…

Something flares within me. I feel a bolt of lethal power shoot towards Drust. I know it will kill him upon contact but I can't stop it. It's coming from a place I can't control, that I didn't know was there. The bolt flies straight at Drust, increasing in power. It's going to kill him! It will blow him apart! It –

Suddenly, he isn't there. Contact has been broken. He throws himself away physically, mind following, disappearing from my thoughts, crying out in pain, but not the sort of pain that accompanies death.

I cry out too and drop, head on fire, screaming, feeling the bolt of power explode into nothingness, tearing at the rim of my mind but not damaging me, not like it would have damaged – destroyed – Drust.

Bright lights. Stars. Then a red haze. When it clears, everyone's around Drust and me. Concerned for me, wary of the druid. Ronan and Lorcan have him at sword point, even though he's rolled up into a ball and isn't moving. Connla's behind them, testing his own sword's edge, eyes flicking from one twin to the other. Fiachna's studying my face, rolling my eyelids up, making sure I'm all right. Bran is close by, anxiously chewing his lower lip.

"I'm fine," I mutter, pushing Fiachna away — my skin is more sensitive than it's ever been. His touch is painful.

"What did he do?" Ronan asks, positioning the tip of his sword by Drust's throat, ready to slice it open and end his life the second I give him an excuse.

"Put down that sword," Connla growls, unexpectedly coming to the druid's aid. "Don't harm him."

"I will if he's hurt her!" Ronan snaps.

"He didn't," I gasp. I want to lie down and rest, but I'm afraid they'll kill Drust if I don't speak up. "We were… working on a spell. It went wrong. He was trying to help me, not harm me."

The others look relieved, except Ronan, who looks annoyed at being denied his kill. They sheathe their weapons. Goll asks how long it will take for Drust to recover and when we'll be ready to continue. I tell him I don't know and ask them to leave us alone for a while. When they're out of earshot, I slide over next to Drust and whisper, "Can you hear me?"

A long pause, then a very shaky, "Aye."

"What happened?" I hiss.

Drust rolls on to his side and stretches out slowly. There are burn marks on his right hand, ugly welts. There are red lines etched across his temple too, as though flames had shot up from his hand to his head.

"I was right," he croaks.

"About what?"

"The source of your magic." His fingers twitch and he winces. It hurts but I lean forward and cast a healing spell on his hand. As the worst of the redness cools away, Drust looks at me, no gratitude in his eyes, only doubt. "Magic exploded within you when you fought Lord Loss."

"I know. I reached in and stole power from him."

Drust shakes his head. "No. That's not the whole truth. He gave it to you." I frown, not understanding. "Lord Loss let you take from him," Drust explains. "More than that — he extended his magic towards you. He reached within you and struck at the… the flint of your spirit, for want of a better term. He created the magical sparks and fanned them into life. You're powerful because he wants you to be — because he lit the flames of magic inside you."

My face whitens. "You mean the magic… my spells… that's all because of *him?*"

"Aye."

"But why?" I cry. "Why would a demon give power to a human?"

"I don't know," Drust says. "But I do know this. I thought you were my apprentice, but you're not — you're Lord Loss's."

And the suspicion in his eyes cuts to my heart as if he'd stabbed me in the chest with a knife.

THE EMIGRANTS

→We make slow progress in the afternoon, hampered by bad weather, having to climb lots of hills and Drust's injuries. I hurt him with the blast of magic. He got out of my head just in time, but even so he took a hammering. He casts healing spells when he's able, but movement is still painful.

There have been no more lessons. Drust has kept clear of me, walking close to Goll and Fiachna, bringing up the rear of the group. I don't blame him. I'm suspicious of myself too. There's no telling what Lord Loss got up to inside my skull and heart. Maybe he planted spells of destruction and I'm doomed to betray my friends and kill them all.

They should be told of the threat I pose but Drust has said nothing and I lack the courage to tell them. I don't think they'd kill me but trust would be impossible. They'd cut me off. I'd be their friend no longer — merely a possible enemy.

So I walk in silence and keep my fears to myself, wondering if and when the animal within me will burst forth — either the magical animal of Lord Loss's making or the beast of my MacGrigor heritage.

*   *   *

→It's late afternoon when we sight the sea. Dark blue, with white, choppy waves smashing against the rocks of the shore, roaring like a monster. It stretches as far as the eye can see. I hoped I might glimpse the shores of Tir na n'Og from here, the legendary land which lies somewhere between this place and the Otherworld. But if it's out there, as the legends claim, it lies beyond the sight of normal folk — and magical folk too.

We stop atop a hill and marvel at the vision of the sea. Even Drust wipes a hand across his brow, then stares at the horizon with wide, childlike eyes, as though he can hardly believe it's there.

"A thing of wild beauty," Goll murmurs, smiling as the wind whips at his beard and hair. He strokes the flesh of his blind eye. "I saw it as a young man. I had perfect sight then. But it's just as wondrous seen with a single eye."

"Where does it end?" Lorcan asks, looking left and right, then straight ahead.

"Nobody knows," Drust says, his first words of the afternoon. "Some say it goes on forever. Others that it comes to the edge of the world and drops away into nothingness. A few even claim that by some form of magic it leads to the other side of the world, that if you were to sail all the way across, you'd wash up at the lands to the east. But nobody really knows."

"And Tir na n'Og?" Fiachna asks. "Is it out there?"

Drust shrugs. "Perhaps. There are…" He pauses, sniffs the air, looks west. "We will soon find some who believe they know where Tir na n'Og lies. You can ask them. They might be able to provide clearer answers than me."

On that curious note, Drust starts down the hill, angling gently southwest, to a point further along the coastline. The rest of us cherish one last long look at the sea. Then we follow, reluctantly abandoning sight of the great expanse of water, eagerly awaiting the moment when we come within view of it again.

→Night is close when we spot them. We've been walking along the edge of the coast for an hour, stumbling often on the strange, flat, cracked layers of rock underfoot. The strength of the sea can be felt first-hand here. The wind, the spray, the tremors in the ground from the pounding of the waves. I'm amazed the land has stood up to the battering for so long. I always knew there was power in the earth, but it must be much stronger than I imagined to resist such a relentless foe, day after day, night after night, year after year.

We're all focused on the sea, watching the waves rise and crash, no two alike. In some places, where they strike, they rise up in huge plumes like smoke, spreading their drops far in a fine mist. It's like a moving painting of never-ending designs. Because of this extraordinary show, we're almost upon the travellers before Lorcan – at the front of the group – glances up and realises we're not alone.

"People!" he shouts, halting abruptly and pointing ahead. Squinting – because of the spray – I spot a procession of twenty or thirty figures, heading to a large boat bobbing up and down in a relatively calm cove.

"Demons?" Connla asks, standing on his toes, as if that will help him see better.

"No," Drust says, passing Lorcan without slowing.

"Humans?" Goll calls after him.

"Not as such," is Drust's response.

We look at each other uncertainly, then shuffle along after the druid.

→The travellers are creatures of legend. Impossibly towering giants, the height of three or four men. Tiny, stick-thin people who might be the meddlesome leprechauns of myth. Slender, graceful, pointy-eared fairies. Weeping, pale-faced, dark-eyed, terrifying banshees. Others who look more like demons than humans. Druids and priestesses too. All are part of the procession, winding their way to the boat, where others like them are patiently waiting, seated or standing, all looking west.

"Morrigan's milk!" Goll gasps, making a sign to ward off evil. Then he stops, confused, since although these are obviously beings of magic, they don't have the look or feel of wickedness.

The walkers have their eyes set on the path or boat. One of the druids happens to look up and spot us. He breaks off from the others and comes towards us. As he draws close, Ronan nudges over to Drust and whispers, "Is he a threat?"

"No," Drust says. He has stopped and is waiting calmly for his fellow druid, arms folded across his chest.

"Who are they?" Fiachna asks, studying one of the burly, brutal-looking giants. We've heard stories of these fierce warriors of the past, part god, part human. But ancient stories are sometimes hard to believe. They grow in the telling over the generations. Things get exaggerated. I always assumed the giants of lore were simply large but otherwise normal warriors. Fiachna and the others thought that too. We were wrong.

"They are beings of lessening magic," Drust says in answer to Fiachna's query. "They came after the Old Creatures and flourished for a time on the magic of the past. They're leaving now. The magic of the Old Creatures has almost faded from this earth. Those it nurtured can't survive without it. Their time here is finished. They go west in search of Tir na n'Og or death." His eyes are sad but also filled with longing. He wants to go with them.

"Do they flee from the Demonata?" I ask quietly.

"Not necessarily," Drust says. "Most have come from distant lands, some from the other side of the world. They leave to escape the Christians and other new religious groups. The world has changed and will change more in the centuries to come. Old magic is no longer dominant.

Those who practise it have no place here. They leave before the magic disappears completely, to avoid an undignified end."

"Why don't they fight?" Goll asks.

"They did. But only a fool continues to fight when it's clear the battle is lost. Everything has an end. This is the end of great magic and those who belong to it."

The other druid reaches us and stops. He nods to Drust, who nods back. Then he casts a curious eye over the rest of us. "Do you seek a place on board our boat, brother?" the druid asks.

"Nay," Drust replies. "I am here on other business."

"There won't be many more boats this year," the druid says. "This might be the last before spring. If you miss this one…"

"I have work here," Drust says.

"This is a dangerous land," the druid notes. "Several of our kind have fallen on their way to this point. If you wait and the Demonata triumph within the next few months, there might never be a boat again."

"My work involves the Demonata," Drust says. "If I am successful the boats will continue to sail."

The druid raises an eyebrow. "You have set yourself against the demons?"

"Aye," Drust says steadily.

"A perilous undertaking. You do it to keep the path to the west clear for those who will follow?"

"No," Drust smiles. "We should all be so self-sacrificing, but most are not and I am no exception. I do this for personal reasons."

The druid returns Drust's smile. "Whatever they are, I wish you luck. If you can close the tunnel between this world and the Demonata's, boatloads to come will praise your name in the lands west of here… or in the lands of the dead."

Both druids look at the boat and those boarding it. Only a couple remain on the shore now, untying the ropes which hold the boat in place. It's unlike any boat I've ever seen, long and narrow, tall poles sprouting from the middle to hold large sails. It's hard to see how it stays afloat.

"What of your companions?" the druid asks, looking around, his gaze coming to rest on me. "Do they seek sanctuary with us? There are a few places left. If they wish to take their chances, we can give them berth."

Drust glances at me, then speaks to the others. "If you want to go, I won't stop you. But I might have need of you in the days and nights to come. Remember — if I fail, your people will pay the price."

"Tir na n'Og," Goll whispers, his good eye sparkling as he studies the boat. "To go there now… to live forever, having come this close to death…"

"It would be a just reward for an honest life," Fiachna says softly. "You should go, old friend."

Goll's lips part. He breathes out the word, "Aye." But then his face hardens and he barks a laugh. "No. Tir na n'Og's for the beautiful and magical — not an ugly old warhorse like me! Anyway, what would I do there for all eternity? Play hurling with giants?" He turns and winks. "Ten years ago, maybe. But I'd feel like a fool if I went now. And what if they find nothing but sea? I've been on those waves before — and never as sick in all my life!"

"Anybody else?" the druid asks politely. He's still looking at me, a small frown creasing his forehead.

"I would give much to hunt in the fabled forests of Tir na n'Og," Lorcan sighs dreamily. "But I can't abandon my clan, not until the demons have been defeated or I lie dead. Next year, if we succeed, I'll return and ask for passage then."

Goll nudges Connla playfully. "How about you, young king? We know how vain you are. In Tir na n'Og you'd keep your looks and never grow old."

Connla sneers. "Give up a kingship here to be a peasant there? I think not!"

"You sound very certain of your kingship," Goll murmurs. "Do you know something we don't?"

Connla flushes. "Of course not. I was just… I mean…" He coughs and glares at Goll. "I don't have to explain myself to the likes of you!"

"Peace," the druid says before the pair start to argue in earnest. "If you do not wish to travel with us, I must take my leave. Night is almost upon us and we mean to depart before the demons attack — they come here often, the braver monsters, in search of rich pickings."

"We have delayed you too long already, brother," Drust says, bowing. "Go, and may the grace of the gods go with you."

"Our thanks — and may the gods bless you in your honourable quest," the druid says. He returns the bow, nods at the rest of us, then makes his way to the boat. The creatures holding the ropes untie the last of them as he approaches. By the time he reaches the shoreline the ropes have been cast off and the boat is drifting away from the land. The druid increases his pace and jumps to the deck of the boat, propelling himself through the air with magic. He waves to us before settling down and facing the bow, which points like an arrow straight at the setting sun.

We watch as the boat moves off, sails rising smoothly, catching a magical wind. The boat shoots ahead at an incredible speed, leaving hardly any wake, a speck on the horizon within minutes, then – to my eyes at least – gone.

There's a long, thoughtful silence. All eyes are on the dimming sun, scanning the point where sea meets sky, straining for one final glimpse of the boat and its cargo of giants and fairies.

Then Goll shatters the mood by clapping Drust on the back. "So, druid," he drawls, "where shall we cast for tonight? Your friends are safe from the demons and undead at sea, but we're somewhat exposed out here, aye?"

Drust looks around, blank-eyed for a second. Then he focuses. "Aye. It would not do if we were caught in the open.

We will be safe further down the coast — there is a place protected by rare Old Magic — but we must move fast if we are to get there before night."

"Can't we stop and cast a masking spell?" I ask.

"No," Drust says, starting forward, faster than he'd been walking earlier. "You heard the warning — demons come here."

"Demons are everywhere," Fiachna says.

"Aye," Drust agrees. "But only the brave go where beings of magic congregate. And a brave demon is usually a powerful demon. I wouldn't trust our spells to hide us from their gaze. Now march and save your breath — if we fail to make our destination in time, you might need to fight tonight, and the monsters you lock arms with will be fiercer and harder to kill than any you've faced before."

THE GEIS

→The day is in its final stages when we come to a cliff high above the sea. We've been climbing for the last half hour, out of sight of the waves. Now we stop, stunned by the new view. The cliff drops straight beneath us, as though the land had been cut away with a godly knife. I take an instant step back, terrified I'm going to fall. Most of the others retreat instinctively too.

But Drust isn't afraid. He breaks into a smile and points towards a row of cliffs, jutting out into the sea like gigantic fingers. It's amazing scenery. Even Goll hasn't seen anything like this — he was further north when he came to the coast as a young man. We gawp, astonished.

"There," Drust says. "The third jutland from the end — that's where we're going." He looks at the sun, then the land around us. "We should be fine. Demons don't like the throb of Old Magic and usually avoid it. But let's not tarry, just in case."

We push on, moving downhill now, following the coastline. Seagulls are settling in their nests for the night, cawing and screeching. Some rabbits watch us from a safe distance. Even further beyond the rabbits, a small, rugged pony grazes alone. I can't see it lasting long by itself out here in the demon-pillaged wilds.

At the foot of the dip there's hard, level ground. It's possible to crawl forward on your stomach and look down directly over the edge of the cliff. Drust doesn't pause – he's not interested in the view, intent on reaching the third jut of land – but the rest of us can't resist the opportunity to gaze upon the sea from such a spectacular viewpoint. Lying on our stomachs, we wriggle forward to the end of the world and a sight that surpasses any I ever dreamt about in the past.

Unbelievable. With my chin resting over the edge, and the rest of my body hugging the cliff edge for dear life, it's as if I'm suspended in mid-air, looking down at the sea as a bird or god must. I see the heads of seagulls nestled in the rock. The white of the waves as they batter the base of the cliff, visible even in the dim light of the advanced dusk. The rolling, crashing sounds. The scent of birds and salt.

The urge to throw myself over the edge is strong. To die so beautifully, so perfectly… to fly for a handful of seconds… become part of the sea, dashed against the rocks until I'm nothing, then swept away to the Otherworld in the company of fish, mermaids and all the other creatures of the deep…

I ignore the suicidal urge, but it's difficult. I suppose people who live along the shore grow hardened to this call of the sea. But it's dangerous for land-dwellers like us. When I look up, I see misty expressions on the faces of the others, which prove I'm not alone in my desire to cast myself off.

But there's something else in those expressions which I feel too — triumph. Though I'm tempted by the call of the sea, I resist. It can't claim me. In a way I'm stronger than the waves and I feel good about that. Smug, even.

We remain lying on the ledge for what seems a long time but is probably no more than a few minutes. Connla's the first to crawl back and stand up when he's a safe distance from the edge, where the wind can't catch him and whip him over. Ronan rises next, but closer to the edge than Connla, not afraid of the whirling, whistling wind.

The pair head after Drust. A minute later Goll follows and that's the signal for the rest of us to retreat. Bran's the last to leave, laughing as he gazes down, pointing at seagulls and waving as though he knows them. I call to him to come with us but he doesn't move. Annoyed – I've now had my fill of the sea – I double back, grab his legs and reel him in.

"Come on," I snap as he tries to squirm back to the edge. "We have to follow the others. It's not safe here."

"Eggs boiled leaf," Bran says, nodding to show that he agrees. But he looks at the edge one last time, regretfully, before rising, linking his hand with mine and jogging after Lorcan at the rear of the main pack.

We've almost caught up with Lorcan when the demons attack. They burst out of the earth like savage worms, a dozen or more. Multi-limbed. Many have several heads. Claws like branches on a tree. Mouths full of fangs. Gibbering and howling — familiar demon sounds.

Most attack the main group of Fiachna, Lorcan and Goll. A few go for Ronan and Connla. One lumbers after Drust, far ahead on his own. And one surges at Bran and me.

I reach inside and draw upon my magic, forgetting in the heat of the moment that it's the magic of the Demonata, unable to worry about what I might unleash. Lips moving quickly, I fill my hands with fire, then blow flames at the demon, which has two heads — one of a bear, one a fox. The demon screams and falls. Bran laughs and leaps over the flailing demon, then leaps back again, playing with it as if it was a skipping rope of fire.

Drust's demon is almost upon him when he flicks his right hand, casting a spell. The demon flies over the druid's head, then off the cliff, falling to its death on the rocks beneath, hollering hatefully all the way down.

The others are battling, swords and axes flashing, hacking at demon flesh. Drust starts back to help, then pauses and stares inland. I follow the direction of his gaze and spot a figure in the distance, hovering above the earth. There's no mistaking him, even in this poor light — Lord Loss. Something that looks like a dog is jumping up and down beside him.

Drust hesitates, then races along the cliff, heading for the jutland where he said we'd be safe, leaving the rest of us to fight and, if we lose, perish.

I curse the druid, then wade in to where Lorcan, Goll and Fiachna are struggling with the demons. The ground around them is slippery with blood, littered with demon limbs, chunks of flesh, even a head or two. But still the demons press on, driving the warriors and smith towards the edge of the cliff, seeking to push them over.

I touch the back of a leathery demon about twice my height. It looks down at me and laughs. I say a word and the nails of my fingers instantly lengthen, digging deep into the monster, piercing its skin, bones, inner organs. The hellish creature chokes, blood gurgling up its throat. My nails burst out the far side of its body. I say another word and jerk my hand away, snapping free of the nails, leaving them buried within. The demon collapses, shudders, then goes still.

Another of the demonic pack sees what I've done. It screeches and hurls itself at me. No time for magic. I drop to my back, stick my legs up and halt the demon's charge with my feet. It swipes at me with a clawed hand. Barely misses my eyes. I point at its face. Words leap from my tongue and its head explodes, splattering me with blood and bits of bone and brain.

Rising, turning to deal with a third demon, I hear a human scream from further away. No time to check it out. A bull-headed demon is on top of Fiachna. It's bitten a chunk out of his left shoulder and is trying to latch on to his throat. I dive at it, grab its mouth, put my face close to its pink, cracked lips and breathe out.

A mist flies into the demon's mouth. It coughs, tries to snarl at me but can't. Because the mist has thickened and clogged its throat. It can't breathe. Some demons don't need to breathe but this one does. It falls away, scratching at its neck, eyes bulging as it suffocates.

Goll and Lorcan force the final demon over the cliff, pushing it off, only just avoiding a lashing tendril which threatens to drag them over with it. They glance around, make sure we've dealt with all the monsters, then rush off to help Ronan and Connla. Bran and I follow just behind.

When Goll and Lorcan stop short I fear the worst. But running up, readying myself to cast more spells, I see the demons fleeing, Connla standing proudly by the cliff's edge, sword raised, bellowing colourful curses after the monsters. We approach uncertainly. Connla beams at us, his blade grey and green with demon blood. "Cowards!" he laughs. "They didn't have the guts to fight! I ran them off! Did you see how fast they—"

"Ronan," Lorcan interrupts, scanning the area. "Where's my brother?"

Connla sighs. "They forced him over."

Lorcan stares at Connla, then walks to the edge of the cliff and looks down. The rest of us hang our heads, the joy of victory already forgotten. There's a lump in my throat that makes breathing almost as hard as it must have been for the demon I choked to death. I flash on images of Ronan fighting, hunting, laughing, flicking blood from his long, curly hair as he raced from the pack of demons who first pursued us. He would have wanted to die this way, fighting, but that doesn't make his loss any easier for me to bear.

"He fought bravely," Connla says. He probably means to comfort Lorcan but he sounds patronising, as though talking to a child.

"Did he fall before or after the demons ran?" Goll asks.

"Before, of course," Connla frowns. "They forced him over. He was close to the edge. He never stood a chance."

"Yet they left you alone?" Goll doesn't phrase it as a challenge but it's hard not to interpret it as such. "They killed Ronan, then ran?"

"They saw I wasn't such an easy touch," Connla snorts. "They got lucky with Ronan, but when they tangled with me and realised they were out of their depth, they ran for their miserable, demonic lives." Connla's face hardens and he looks at each of us in turn. "You don't seem too pleased," he mutters darkly.

"It's strange," Fiachna says uneasily. "Demons don't fight that way. To catch a person in the open... outnumbering him... night just beginning... then running off..."

"What are you—" Connla starts to roar.

"Enough," Lorcan stops him — and the rest of us too. He turns from the edge of the cliff, face strained but resigned. "Ronan's dead. That's the end of it. I don't care why the demons ran. There will be no arguments, not at a time like this."

Goll and Fiachna look down uncomfortably. Connla too. "He didn't die through any fault of his own," Connla says. "They took him by surprise. It was just bad luck that he was so close to the edge. I would have saved him if I could."

Lorcan nods slowly. "Luck will always turn against a warrior in the end. You have nothing to answer for." He looks off into the distance, to where Drust is still running, closing in on the jutland. A light flares in Lorcan's eyes. "That coward, on the other hand..."

He sets off after Drust at top speed. I share a worried look with the rest of the group, then hurry after him, afraid of what will happen if he catches up with the druid in this dark mood.

→Drust has reached the jutland by the time we get to him. A long stretch of cliff sticking out into the sea, grass growing thickly along the top, blowing ever easterly from the winds coming in from the west. He's sitting in a spot in the middle of the jutland, hunched over against the wind, his chess set on the grass in front of him, studying the figures.

"You!" Lorcan shouts, striding up to the druid. Drust doesn't look up at the furious teenager. "You abandoned us and left us to the demons! What do you have to say in defence of yourself?"

No answer. Drust is fully focused on the chess game.

Lorcan's axe is in his left hand. He raises it, his youthful face twisted with hatred. I want to stop him but I dare not interfere. And, to be honest, part of me loathes Drust for running out on us and wants to see him punished.

Connla roars a warning and reaches for his knife, to intervene, but before he can, Drust says quietly, "You cannot harm me here. You will suffer if you try."

"Suffer this!" Lorcan screams and brings his axe down.

The head of the axe melts. The handle turns into a shaft of fire. Lorcan yells with pain and drops it. I blink dumbly — this is the work of magic, but it didn't come from Drust. It seemed to come from the earth itself.

"Violence is not permitted here," Drust says and he looks up. "If you try that again, you'll die."

Lorcan snatches for his sword with his unharmed right hand. Stops and curses. Kicks the smouldering remains of his axe and turns away, disgusted.

Drust looks around at us, meeting our accusing gazes without any hint of shame. "Lord Loss orchestrated the attack. He set the demons in place, knowing we must pass this way. I thought it was an ambush, so I fled for my life, as I was duty bound to. I see now it was merely a cruel game but I was not to know that at the time. I acted correctly."

"What are you talking about?" Goll snarls. "Ronan died. It was no game."

Drust shakes his head. "If it had been a real ambush, they'd have jumped *me*. Having trailed us this far and listened to our conversations, Lord Loss must know what our plan is. If he truly wished to stop us at this point, he'd have killed me. The rest of you don't matter. That was why I ran. I couldn't let myself fall, not this close to the end."

"Fancy words, but it boils down to the same thing — *cowardice*," Fiachna says.

"You may call it that if you wish," Drust says coolly. "But I told you from the start that your lives meant nothing to me. You've helped me come this far, and so served a noble purpose. I'm grateful for that but it makes you no less insignificant in the greater scheme of things."

Goll laughs bitterly. "I bet you didn't have many friends when you were a child!"

"Druids don't need friends," Drust replies, then regards his chess set again.

I study the jutland uncertainly. Night is upon us and I can hear the howls of the demons that Connla ran off. And Lord Loss is still out there. I feel exposed, open to attack. "Are you sure we're safe?" I ask.

"Aye," Drust says. "This is a place of Old magic. No lesser demon can set foot here. A demon master can, but like us, they can commit no violence on this soil."

"Thank the gods for small mercies," Connla sniffs. "Are there more places like this along the coast, where we can shelter in the coming nights?"

"No," Drust says. "But we would have no need of them

even if there were. This is the place I have been heading for. It's the end of the road."

Then he gives his attention over fully to the chess game, leaving us to stare at the grass, the drop on either side, the sea which stretches off into the distance — and wonder what exactly he brought us to this desolate place for.

→Night darkens. Black clouds blow in off the sea, unloading their rain on top of us. I'm glad of the rain at first – it washes the worst of the blood from my face and neck – but its appeal quickly fades as a chill sets in. To combat the rain and sharp, bitter wind, I create a fire using magic and we huddle around it, capes and cloaks pulled over our heads, shivering from the damp and cold.

I've treated Fiachna's wounded shoulder, but it's a nasty purple colour. I'm not sure I cleaned out all the demon's poison. It doesn't look too dangerous at the moment but I'll be keeping a close eye on it.

Lorcan is silent and distant, thinking of his dead brother. There's not much you can say to a warrior when a loved one dies. Death is something all warriors learn to embrace. It's part of their trade. At least Ronan died in battle. Lorcan will miss him but life must go on. There's no benefit to be had from weeping or wailing like a woman or a child.

Drust continues with his game, head bent over the board to shelter it from the rain, moving figures around slowly, after much deliberation. Maybe this was his aim — to escape to a place where he'd be protected, safe to play his games of chess all night and day in peace.

After an hour the rain eases and moonlight breaks through the clouds. We should be grateful, but now that we can see more clearly, we spot Lord Loss hovering near where the jutland starts, watching us intently.

With shouts and cries, we scramble to our feet and the men draw their weapons. Goll starts forward, roaring, then halts, remembering what happened to Lorcan's axe. He lowers his sword and studies Lord Loss nervously.

The demon master ignores the old warrior and tilts his head sideways for a better view of Drust. He seems fascinated by the game the druid's playing. He drifts closer. Something moves near where his legs end in long strips of flesh. I recall the dog-like creature I saw earlier. Peering down, I see that it has a large dog's body, but its head is long and curiously flat, a dark green or brown colour, with evil yellow eyes. And it has human hands instead of paws. A woman's hands.

Lord Loss passes Goll. The dog demon starts to follow, then stops, growls and retreats a few steps. Drust was right about this place being out of bounds for lesser demons.

Lord Loss drifts to a halt close to where Drust is sitting. We surround him, suspicious yet captivated. We've never been this close to a living demon for such a long period of time, free to study him at will. It's a strange sensation. I feel the magic around him, lightly crackling, not that different to the power Drust and I create when we cast a spell. Except his magic is constant, never changing.

Finally the game ends and Drust begins rearranging the pieces.

"What is that you play?" Lord Loss asks, his voice laced with sorrow.

"Chess," Drust says and peers up. "You don't play?"

"No."

"A pity."

"But I would like to learn."

Drust pauses, surprised. "Do demons play human games?"

"No," Lord Loss says. "But this interests me. I have never seen it before. And the board… there is magic in it."

"This board is unique," Drust says, smiling proudly. "My master told me it is the original Board, a gift to us from the Old Creatures. My people have guarded it for many centuries, and others of magic protected it before the druids. Long ago, one of its owners fashioned a game to play on it, to pass the time. He crafted the pieces which have developed into what you see now, and so the game of chess came into being."

"Then the board was not created for the game?" Lord Loss asks.

"No."

"What was its original purpose?"

Drust shrugs. "Nobody knows. As you noticed, it is an artefact of magic, but we have never been able to unlock its secrets."

"Perhaps I could," Lord Loss says.

"Perhaps," Drust agrees, then smiles. "Some other time."

"Why not now?" Lord Loss asks eagerly.

Drust's smile spreads. "That's not possible. You have to leave."

"I do not," Lord Loss frowns.

"Aye," Drust says. "You do." He raises a hand and Lord Loss drifts backwards.

"What's happening?" the demon master shouts, trying to stop but unable to.

"A minor spell," Drust chuckles. "I tire of having you hound our trail. This will keep you at a safe distance for a while."

"No!" Lord Loss roars. "You have no power over me! You're just a human! You cannot command a demon master!"

"Normally, no," Drust murmurs. "But magic works differently here. I am able to do things on this jutland which I could do nowhere else — and you are helpless to resist, since this magic is more mine than yours."

Lord Loss's features darken and eight arms extend outwards. I feel power build within him, directed at Drust. Then it stops suddenly as he realises what will happen if he strikes in anger.

"You are very clever," the demon snarls, drifting further away. "But once I'm back on normal land my powers will be mine again. I will wait. And follow. And next time I will kill."

Drust shakes his head. "The spell won't last for long, but it will hold for a few days, no matter where you go." He crooks a finger at Lord Loss and the demon master stops. "But I can break the spell now, if you wish to bargain."

"Bargain with what?" Lord Loss spits.

"Information," Drust says. "Tell me why you follow us. Why you laid the trap but did not kill me. What's in this for you?"

"I feed on the sorrow of others," Lord Loss says stiffly. "I follow you because I know misery is your destiny. Your suffering brings me pleasure."

"No," Drust says. "This land is full of suffering. I don't believe you'd pick us at random, out of all the thousands of tortured souls, for special attention."

Lord Loss shrugs and smiles. "What other reason could there be?"

"You interfered with the girl," Drust says. The others look at me questioningly but I avoid their gaze. "You filled her with magic of your own. Why?"

"I like her," the demon gurgles. "I wanted to help."

"Answer me honestly," Drust growls, "or I'll banish you."

"Actually, I don't think you will," Lord Loss purrs, then points an arm at Goll. Abruptly, unwillingly, with a startled roar, Goll turns away from the rest of us and runs.

For an awful second I think Lord Loss plans to run him over the edge of the cliff. But then I see he's more cunning than that — he's making Goll race to the mainland, where the dog demon is yapping with delight, ready to tear Goll to pieces on a patch of ground where there's no magical protection.

"Goll!" I scream and try to stop him with magic. But I can't find a way to unlock Lord Loss's spell.

"Release me," Lord Loss says. "Immediately. Or the human dies at the hands of the ever-faithful, ever-vicious Vein."

"No," Drust says.

"You must," Lord Loss growls, "or I'll send the others to their deaths too."

"No," Drust repeats.

"Very well," the demon master sneers. "Vein! Destroy him!"

The dog demon barks and howls, leaping around, jaws snapping open and shut. Goll's almost at the mainland. A few more seconds and...

Suddenly, Bran is in front of the old warrior, by the side of Vein, patting his knees, whistling as though calling to a tame dog and not some demon half-breed. Vein leaps at Bran. Lord Loss laughs. The rest of us gasp with horror.

Then everybody's jaw drops as the dog demon licks Bran's face, before rolling over on to her back and offering her stomach to be tickled.

"Vein!" Lord Loss bellows. "Stop that! Kill him!"

The demon ignores her master's call and whines with pleasure as Bran scratches under her chin. He's giggling, playing with her as he would with any normal dog, making cooing sounds and uttering the odd insensible word or two.

Lord Loss can't believe it. Nobody can. But then Fiachna laughs out loud and soon all of us are laughing, pointing at the boy and the dog, and Goll standing beside the pair of them, having come to a stop at last. We double over, tears of mirth streaming down our faces. Even Drust is smiling.

Lord Loss doesn't see the funny side of it. He glares at the dog demon, then the rest of us. When his eyes eventually settle on Drust, he snarls and says, "What manner of thing is that boy?"

"I'm not sure," Drust chuckles. "I knew he'd been blessed with some special form of magic but I never guessed he was this powerful. It seems he can charm any creature he wishes. And maybe that's only one of his lesser gifts. Who knows what else he might be capable of?" Drust's smile tightens. "Maybe he can kill a demon master."

Lord Loss quivers but I'm not sure if it's with fear or outrage. "You have humiliated me," he hisses.

"Aye," Drust agrees cheerfully.

"You will pay for that." Seven of Lord Loss's arms come up and he points at each of us. "I place a geis upon you. A curse to destroy you all. Whether you succeed in your quest or not, none of you will know anything but misery for the rest of your pitifully short lives."

"Your geis doesn't frighten us," Drust snorts. "Now begone — and I don't want to see you again any time soon."

He waves his right hand and Lord Loss peels away as though blown by a strong wind. He shoots off the jutland, managing to grab his dog as he flies past, yanking her away from Bran by grabbing her snout. Vein gives a muffled howl. Bran's hands stretch out after the dog and he waves goodbye. Soon the pair vanish from sight, separated from us by Drust's spell and the darkness of the night.

On the jutland we carry on laughing, delighted to have thwarted the demon master. But there's an edge to our laughter. A demon's geis is nothing to sneer at. As happy as we are, I'm certain that each of us is inwardly pondering Lord Loss's curse and wondering what sort of a price we might ultimately be made to pay for our meagre victory.

OLD CREATURES

→Drust is still playing chess. The rest of us are gathered around the fire. Now that the danger has passed, my clansfolk discuss the conversation between Drust and Lord Loss and I feel eyes settle on me suspiciously. Finally Fiachna asks the question which is on all their tongues. "What did Drust mean about Lord Loss interfering with you?"

I sigh miserably. "My magic has grown faster than it should. I've leapt from being a poor apprentice to being almost as strong as Drust, with the ability to be a lot stronger — because of Lord Loss. He reached within me and gave me power. Thanks to him, I'm able to do things which nobody of my limited experience should be able to."

"Why would he do that?" Goll asks gruffly.

"We don't know," I answer honestly. "We'd be fools to think he did it to help but we can't see how my being so strong can be a drawback. Unless…" I gulp, then say what I've been thinking since Drust revealed the truth about my powers. "Unless he left a secret spell behind. Maybe, when

I'm powerful enough, a force will explode inside me and destroy everything around me."

"A demon in the fold," Lorcan growls bitterly, with venom born out of the loss of his brother. "We can't harm her here, but I say we take her back to the mainland and slit her throat before—"

"Peace," Goll hushes him.

"But—"

"Peace!" Goll says again, harshly this time. Then he smiles at me. "I don't believe that, Bec. I've known you since you were a baby. You wouldn't hurt anyone, intentionally or otherwise. If the demon master thinks he can use you to harm us, he's wrong."

Tears spring to my eyes. I haven't cried since I was a very young child — tears are for the weak — but the warmth of Goll's words unleashes a spring within me and soon my cheeks are wet with warm, salty water.

"Goll's right," Fiachna says, putting a thumb to my cheeks and wiping some of the tears away. "We have nothing to fear from you, Bec."

"Of course we don't," Connla agrees, stunning us all by giving me a quick hug. Then he looks pointedly at Lorcan.

The teenager pulls a face. "If that's how you feel, I won't argue. But I'll be keeping an eye on her, especially when there's a full moon, because there's the threat of her turning into a wild beast too, in case you'd forgotten. And if I ever think she's going to act against us..."

"...you'll tell us and we'll have a calm chat about it," Connla finishes sternly, in the authoritative tone of a true king. "Understood?"

Lorcan bares his teeth, but then nods roughly and turns away to sulk. I don't blame him for this unusual show of hatred. It's hard when you lose one you love, even if you're a warrior who isn't supposed to let sorrow affect you.

Bran shuffles up beside me a few seconds later, stares at my damp cheeks, touches them with a finger, then tastes it. "Stony," he declares mysteriously, then lays his head on my shoulder, closes his eyes, smiles and goes to sleep.

→Some hours later, having finished another game of chess, Drust packs the pieces and board away, sets his bag down and rises. "Bec," he summons me. I gently move Bran's head and go see what the druid wants.

"It's time," Drust says, looking down at me solemnly.

"For what?" I frown.

"I've been waiting for the tide," he answers cryptically. "The level is correct now. But it won't remain that way for long. We must hurry."

"I don't understand. What...?" I stop. Drust is taking off his robes. Soon he's naked. I've seen many naked men – a lot of warriors fight the old way, stripped bare – but Drust looks different in the flesh. His nudity is unsettling, as if I'm seeing an aspect of him I shouldn't.

"Hey!" Goll grunts, getting up. "What are you–"

"Stay back," Drust says, eyes flashing. "Bec and I must go for a while. But we'll return shortly."

"Go where?" Fiachna asks. He's standing beside Goll now, as is Lorcan. Connla watches us with mild interest, lying on his back. Bran still sleeps.

Drust nods towards the edge of the cliff. "Old Creatures reside beneath our feet. They are maybe the only true beings of Old Magic left in the world. They can tell us where to find the tunnel between this world and the Demonata's. Now stay back and keep quiet — this is a delicate business and we need to concentrate."

Drust faces me again. "Remove your clothes," he says, and though I feel uneasy, I do as he commands. "We're going to walk to the edge of the cliff, then step off. Before that, we'll cast two spells. One will let us hold our breath for several minutes. The other will keep us warm — the water's extremely cold."

"But… the fall… I can't swim… the rocks…" I stammer.

"You have nothing to fear," Drust says. He takes hold of my right hand. "I'll be with you. I'll guide you. As long as you cast the spells correctly and don't panic, you'll be fine."

"But how will we get back up?"

"Climb," he says, then laughs at my incredulous expression. "It's easier than it sounds. Trust me. You're no good to me dead. I'll not see you come to harm."

"You left me for the demons tonight," I mutter.

"Aye," he agrees. "But I thought I'd perish if I went back for you. It was better that one of us survive than none at all. But I need you, Bec. If you'd died, I'd have had to search for another apprentice."

"Why?" I ask. "Why am I so important to you?"

"You'll find out soon," Drust promises, then turns to face the edge of the cliff. "Will you do this with me? Take my word that the future of your land and people rests upon it?"

I don't want to. But we've come too far, faced too many dangers, and lost too many friends to stop now. I start walking, Drust beside me. We mutter spells, warming ourselves, holding our breath and extending it. Behind us the others watch – except Bran – unsure of what to expect.

We reach the edge. The waves are rough below, smashing into the rocks of the cliff, tearing themselves to pieces along the length of the jutland. It looks like the mouth into the Otherworld. Only a fool could stare down and not feel fear. And only someone far beyond ordinary foolishness would even think for a moment of leaping into that roaring, forbidding abyss.

I look up quickly at Drust, starting to unlock the breathing spell, to tell him I've changed my mind, this is madness, I'm not going to do it. But before I can, Drust hops forward. His fingers are tight around mine. He drags me after him. I fall. The land disappears behind me. I plummet into darkness… violent roaring… into terror and certain death.

* * *

→The fall doesn't last as long as I thought it would. A couple of seconds, surely no longer. Then the collision. Our feet hit hard. We shoot underwater. My teeth shake in my jaw, threatening to snap loose and burst up into my brain. Even with the warming spell, the water is colder than anything I've experienced.

Dark down here, much darker than the night world above. We slow. Water presses tight around me. I feel the swell of the waves. Inside my head I see myself being smashed against the rocks. I start to panic, to kick defensively against the rocks – which must be close – breaking for the surface so I can scream.

Drust's fingers squeeze mine. Pain forces me to ignore the cold and dark. I try to wrench my hand free but Drust squeezes again. Then a light flares and his face is next to mine. His eyes are furious, warning me to stop struggling, to obey his commands.

I go limp and Drust relaxes his grip. The light is coming from his right hand, flames glowing dully despite being underwater. That's a spell I don't know. I wonder if I could do it. While I'm wondering, Drust looks around, then moves slowly through the water. He's not swimming exactly, although his legs kick out softly behind him and his right arm sways to the left and right, guiding us.

A shoal of fish glides by, either not seeing us or unworried by our presence. I watch them swish past, amazed, taking a moment to reflect on the strange twists my life has taken, the marvels I've become part of. So easy to take it for granted, but this is something no normal human was made to see. The world of magic has blessed me with wonders and it's only right to stop every now and then to appreciate them.

Then — rock. The cliff, studded with shells, draped with seaweed, jagged and immense. Drust is heading straight for it. Coming up fast. He angles downwards. It looks like we're going to hit the rock and be torn to shreds, but at the last moment I spot a hole — the entrance to a tunnel.

We're swept through the mouth of the tunnel. I'm not sure if magic propels us or the thrust of the tide. We pass along smoothly, protected from the walls by the water and Drust's spell. The light in Drust's hand fades, plunging us into total darkness. For a while there's just the rush and noise of the water. I don't feel afraid. It's oddly comforting. It reminds me of when I was born, entering the world through the tunnel from my mother's womb.

Then there's a glow ahead of us. Seconds later we're out, shot into a pool of comparatively warm water. We float to the surface, where Drust pushes me on to land and crawls out after me. He touches my lips and nods. I stop the breathing spell and draw in a lungful of fresh air, shivering from the chill of the water.

Drust stands and offers me his hand. Clutching it, I let him draw me to my feet. He smiles at me when I'm standing, then places a hand on my left shoulder. Heat flares within me and I dry quickly. Drust releases me and looks up. I follow his gaze and gasp.

We're in the middle of a huge cave. I can't see the roof, it's so far above us. All around are thick stone pillars... twenty... thirty... more. And on each pillar — *something*.

I can't think of any other word to describe them. Slowly shifting shapes of coloured light, taller than ten men stacked one on top of the other, the colours changing as their shapes twist and swirl, casting a dim light which illuminates the massive cave. There's magic in these shapes, strong magic, but unlike any I've felt before. No... that's not true. I *have* felt it a couple of times. In the ring of stones when the demons were repelled. And earlier tonight when Lorcan's axe melted.

"What are they?" I whisper.

"Old Creatures," Drust whispers back. He's smiling strangely, gazing at the lights as a child might regard a new toy. "The magicians of the ancient past. The creators of land, life, maybe even the gods. Some say they came from the stars. Others that they *are* the stars, or at least their worldly forms."

He walks forward, then around in a slow circle, studying each pillar and shape. Most of the pillars boast scores of old etchings, but not like those found on ogham stones. These are long, complicated signs. If they represent words, the language must be much more complicated than ours.

"Nobody knows how many there were," Drust says as he walks. "Maybe thousands. This world was theirs. A playpen… a breeding ground… an experiment? We can only guess. Most have moved on, taken their magic with them, returned to the stars or wherever they came from. Or maybe they've died. We're not sure. The Old Creatures communicated openly with our ancestors, but they've been silent for several generations.

"Many druids mourned the passing of our original masters and begged them to stay, to help us protect this world from the threat of the Demonata, to teach us more of the wonders and magic of the stars. But even the Old Creatures must obey the laws of the universe. And those laws state that for everything there is a time. Nothing remains unchanged forever."

He stops before one of the shapes and stares up at it. Reaches out, then draws his hand back, fingers twitching.

"I was told that when the final Old Creature leaves this world, all life will fade, all lands will fall, everything will turn to dust and blow away in the savage winds which will lash the world in their wake. But I don't believe that. I think if they created this world and all its beings – especially us – they created it with love. Maybe they've created others, and will create more worlds later, a string of them throughout the universe. They give birth, help us through our infancy, then move on, leaving us to our own devices, maybe returning in the far-off future to see how we've fared. One day our descendants might be like them — mothers and fathers of worlds and life…"

He trails to a halt. His words are strange, hard for me to understand. I've never heard anyone speak of such things before. My head's spinning as I try to see the universe as Drust imagines it, speckled with beings greater than gods.

And then one of the shapes – or all of them together – speaks.

"Why Have You Come?"

The accent is all the accents I've ever heard. The words are both lyrical and flat. Loud and soft. Coming from within my head and all around. Warm and comforting. No malice or threat. Only tired curiosity.

"To seek answers," Drust says, bowing his head. "I know it's bold to ask, to disturb you when you wish for peace, but—"

"—These Are Troubling Times," the voice finishes. A pause. "The Demonata Have Crossed. We Were Not Aware Of It. But It Was Not Unexpected. They Have Always Been A Threat And Always Will Be. The Battle Between Demons And Humans Must Be Fought Over And Over, Until They Defeat You."

"Or we defeat them?" Drust says hopefully.

"No," the voice says. "The Demonata Are Creatures Of Pure Magic. Their Power Is Beyond That Of Humanity. That Is Something No Force Can Change. In The Past We Protected Humans And Prevented Demonic Incursions. But

We Must Move On. We Cannot Stay And Repulse The Demon Hordes Indefinitely."

"But you can help us stop this current assault," Drust groans, voice laced with more than a hint of desperation. He looks up and his eyes are red. I realise he's crying. "You can show me the location of the tunnel entrance. You can tell me how to close it."

Another pause. Then the voice says, "Our Time Here Is Almost At An End, But While We Remain, We Will Assist, As We Always Have."

One of the shapes contracts and changes colour, becoming green, brown, grey, blue. It takes on the form of land, only much smaller than real land. I haven't seen one of these before but I know what it is. "A map," I mutter.

"Aye," Drust says, studying the map eagerly, reading it in ways I cannot. To the right there's a shining dot, the size of my smallest nail. "That's where the tunnel entrance lies?" Drust asks.

"It Is."

"That's not so far." Drust looks excited. "We can be there in eight or nine days if we march hard."

"Indeed." The map changes and the shape resumes its original, ever-shifting form. "But You Do Not Have Such Temporal Luxury."

Drust frowns. "What do you mean?"

"The Demonata Gather," the voice says. "We Can Sense Them Now That We Have Focused. They Press And Rip At

The Fabric Of This Universe. In Two Days And Nights The First Demon Masters Will Cross."

Drust's face turns a sickly grey colour. "No! They can't! Not when we're so close! We have to stop them! You must help us!"

"We Cannot," the voice says. "We Are Confined Here And Our Powers Are Fading Fast. From This Place, In Our Condition, We Cannot Speed You On Your Way."

"But…" Drust drops to his knees. "We're damned then? There's no hope?"

"There Is Always Hope," the voice answers. "You Have Two Days And Nights."

"But we can't move that quickly, even with magic," Drust complains.

"You Must Find A Way," the voice says. "Or Perish."

Drust nods bitterly, getting his emotions under control. When he addresses the Old Creatures again, he speaks neutrally. "If we make it in time, we can close the tunnel?"

"You Can," the voice says. "But You Already Knew The Answer To That Question."

Drust looks sideways at me, then licks his lips. "Aye," he croaks. "But I hoped… I thought there might be other ways."

"No," the voice says. "There Is Only One."

"So be it," Drust says, even more stone-faced than usual. "Will she suffice? A demon master worked a charm on her. She has not been warped by his touch?"

"No," the voice says. "Actually, Without It She Would Not Have Been Suitable."

Drust looks puzzled. "Do you know why–" he begins, but I interrupt before he finishes, unable to hold my tongue any longer.

"Pardon me," I say, my voice trembling, "but how can we close the tunnel? What's my part in this?"

"Quiet!" Drust snaps. "You have no right to speak! This place is–"

"Peace," the voice cuts in gently but firmly. "All Who Come Before Us Have The Right To Be Heard. The Girl Has Asked A Question. It Will Be Answered."

"But I only brought her to make sure she was pure!" Drust shouts. "She has no–"

The rock beneath our feet shudders. It's all the warning Drust requires. He closes his mouth and hangs his head.

"The Tunnel Between Your Universe And The Demonata's Has Been Created By A Human Magician," the voice explains. "He Must Be Eradicated For The Tunnel To Be Closed, But That Spell Requires A Sacrifice."

"A human sacrifice?" I guess.

"It Is More Specific Than That. The Killing Of A Human Would Not Generate The Power Necessary To Destroy The Tunnel. A Magician Must Be Slaughtered In Order For The Spell To Work." The voice pauses. Drust looks up at me with haunted – but firm, unapologetic – eyes. "A Druid Must be Killed," the voice concludes, "Or A *Priestess*."

TAMING THE WILD

→The Old Creatures fall silent and I get the sense that they won't talk to us again. Drust senses it too and prepares to leave in a hurry without asking any further questions. Once we've recast the breathing and warming spells, he takes my hand – without looking me in the eye – and we jump into the pool, sink, then return through the tunnel. I thought we'd move slower this time, because the force of the water is against us, but it's exactly the same as before.

Shooting out of the tunnel, we rise to the surface, where we hang, bobbing up and down with the swell of the waves. I don't break my breathing spell — the water is still foaming over my head. With his free hand, Drust points at the cliff face. I think he's mad – there's no way we can make the cliff safely or climb it even if we could – but I don't argue as he guides us towards it, opposing the pull and cut of the waves.

We move on the surface of the sea as we moved below, propelled by magic, not swimming, but gliding like seabirds across the surf. The wind and waves lash us angrily, as though enraged by our ability to defy them.

Closer to the lethal screen of the cliff... closer... almost upon it. One more sweep of a wave and I'll be able to reach out and touch it.

We come to a stop and hang calmly in the water, rising and falling with the swell of the waves, but not moving towards or away from the cliff. Drust puts his free hand on mine and moves it forward until I make contact with the rock. He then nudges my other hand up beside it and releases both at the same time. As soon as he lets go, the wind and waves bite at me, trying to rip me loose. I cling to the cliff by my fingertips and scream, shattering the breathing spell.

Then Drust's arm is around me and he's shouting in my ear, "Climb! Keep going! Don't look down!"

"I'll fall!" I shriek. "I'll drown!"

"You will if you don't climb!" he bellows, digging his chin hard into my neck.

Since I've no choice but to climb and risk death or stay and die for certain, I push my left hand up, searching for a handhold. After a second or two I find one and rest a moment, face turned away from the spray of the waves. Then I move my right hand up. My feet follow automatically, scrabbling for toeholds.

Drust keeps his hand on me, steadying me by placing pressure on my shoulder, then my back, my bottom, my legs, finally my feet. When I move out of reach, he shouts at me to stop, then climbs up after me until we're level. Then it's my turn to lead again.

That's how we progress, a small stretch of cliff at a time, dragging our way up, defying the angry howls of the sea, disturbing seagulls in their slumber. Drust only uses magic when I slip, to keep me hanging in the air momentarily, so that I can grab hold of a piece of rock again.

I look down once and immediately wish I hadn't.

"We'll never make it," I sob, feeling my strength ebb away, certain I'll collapse soon, not even able to keep myself going with magic.

"We will," Drust replies stubbornly, then pinches me to get me moving again.

→Finally, when I've started to think this is a nightmare from which I'll never awake, we make it to the top and friendly hands pull us over the edge of the cliff, then carry us to our clothes. Fiachna has to help me slip into mine — my fingers are too numb to grasp and manipulate the material.

They ask what happened, where we've been, how we survived, what we saw. They were sure we'd drowned. Their excitement at finding us alive makes them babble like children.

Drust ignores the questions and pulls on his robes. I ignore them as well, too exhausted to provide answers. When we're fully dressed, the clothes deliciously warm on my cold-blue skin, Drust tells the others we need some time on our own. He marches me along the cliff to where a jutting rock shelters us from the wind. Settling behind it, Drust starts a fire using magic, makes it expand so the flames are three times their normal size, then sits staring into the heart of the blaze, saying nothing.

"Why didn't you tell me?" I say eventually when I'm warm enough to speak.

"I couldn't," he replies. "You wouldn't have come with me."

"I might."

"No. You wouldn't have trusted me. Nor would the others."

"So you were going to keep it secret?" I snort. "Not tell me until we got to the tunnel, then kill me without asking?"

"Aye." He looks at me sideways, torn between arrogance and shame. "That's part of the reason I was so hard on you to begin with. Yes, I needed to bring your magic out — you weren't powerful enough the way you were. But I also didn't want to get close to you because I knew I'd have to..."

He stops and looks at the fire again.

"Was there another magician with you when you first set off?" I ask.

He nods. "An apprentice. No grown druid would accompany me. As I told you before, they have no love for Christians and will be quite pleased if the Demonata take over this land. But I found an apprentice who was born here, whose family still live on these shores. He was happy to lay down his life if necessary."

"*If?*" I sneer. "You told him it might not be?"

Drust blushes. "I said there might be other ways. It wasn't a total lie. Until I asked the Old Creatures, I still hoped…" He trails off into silence.

"Is it truly the only way?" I murmur after a while.

"So the Old Creatures said," he sighs.

"They couldn't be wrong?" He shakes his head. "Then we must go there and you must kill me," I mutter, and his neck practically snaps as his head lifts sharply.

"What?" he gasps.

"If that's the only way to close the tunnel, we must do it."

"You mean you'll let me…" He stops and scratches his head. "Why? Now that you know, you don't have to come. You can flee, sail for safe lands to the east. With your power, you could become a priestess of high standing or even a druid. There's never been a female druid, but you can control male magic, so perhaps you'd be the first. You don't have to stay — or die."

I stare at him as if he's insane. "But the tunnel would remain open," I say slowly. "The demon masters would cross. They'd kill everyone, then make them walk around as undead slaves. I can't let that happen."

"Even if it means your own death?" Drust asks.

"Of course." I frown. "Why do you ask me this? You feel the same way. Otherwise why come on this quest and risk your life?"

He shifts uncomfortably. "My reasons are not the same as yours. These aren't my people, so I don't really care whether they live or die. And I never planned to perish. The risks were high but I hoped – still hope – to get out of here alive. But if *you* go on, it's to certain death, one way or the other. How can you do that?"

"How can I not?" I reply simply. "One life is nothing when measured against thousands. I'd give it a dozen times over to save the lives of those I care about."

"And those you don't know, who mean nothing to you?"

"Aye."

Drust chuckles darkly. "A teacher of mine once said we druids knew nothing of ordinary people, that we'd been apart from them so long, we couldn't understand them any more. I didn't agree, but I see now that he was wiser than me. Your way of thinking is opposite to ours. No druid would throw away his life to save others. Some let themselves be sacrificed when they believe it will lead to greater power in the Otherworld. But I know none who'd offer themselves as you have."

"Then they're fools," I tell him. "A single person is nothing. Only the clan matters."

Drust shakes his head again. "So different," he mumbles, then looks at me with fresh respect. "Very well, Bec. Our quest continues, even though I believe it's doomed and we won't make the tunnel in time. But if we do, you know what must be done?"

"Aye."

"You'll accept my guidance, follow my orders, let me kill you?"

A short pause. Then, softly but firmly, "Aye."

"You are a true hero." He smiles wanly. "Now get some sleep, little girl. We must leave as soon as possible, but we're in no condition to march tonight. We'll wait for morning, then make our way east as quickly as we can."

"Is it all right if I sleep with the others?" I ask.

"You're tired of my company?" Before I can answer, he grunts, "Of course. They're your people. Spend as much time with them as you wish."

"Thank you." I rise and make my way around the rock, bowing my head against the wind. As I round the rock there's a noise, like hooves skittering over grass. I glance up but the wind and rain are in my eyes and it's a few seconds before I can see clearly. When I look, there's nothing nearby. I don't worry about it as I tramp back to camp – nothing can harm us here – but I wonder. Because if it wasn't my imagination, it was probably just a rabbit or fox. But it might have been a human — one who could move very, *very* fast...

→When I'm back with the group, I ask Bran if he was listening to what Drust and I were saying. The boy smiles foolishly, as he normally does, and gabbles a few meaningless words. I feel uneasy about it as I settle down to sleep. Then Bran snuggles up beside me for warmth and murmurs, "Flower," under his breath as he folds his arms around me.

I laugh at myself, misgivings vanishing. It probably wasn't Bran I heard when I was coming back, only a wild animal.

And even if it was him, what of it? We've nothing to fear from Bran. What harm could a poor, innocent, muddled boy like him do?

→Drust addresses us early in the morning. He says the location of the tunnel has been revealed to him but doesn't mention the fact that I have to be sacrificed to close it. Then he outlines our main problem.

"The tunnel lies to the east of your village," he says. "A march of at least a week, probably longer. But we only have two days and nights. Then the demon masters will break through and we're finished. It will be too late to repair the damage."

"Then we've lost," Goll says softly. "We came too late."

"Probably," Drust agrees. "But we have to try. We'll push on as quickly as we can. Run in bursts. Use boats or rafts on rivers and streams where possible. And pray to the gods that the demons encounter some unexpected delay."

"What about magic?" Fiachna asks. "Can't you use that to make us go quicker?" He's had a hard night. The demon poison from the bite has spread and the whole of his upper body is an ugly purple colour. He has the shakes and is sweating badly. I tried to cure him, without success. I asked Drust if he could help but he said this wasn't something he had any knowledge of.

"There are spells which would allow us to run much faster," Drust says. "But they're incredibly tiring. They'd let us push our bodies to their limits, but we could easily pass those limits without knowing and drop dead. If it was a matter of a day or two's march, I'd risk it. But the distance is too great. When we're closer, we'll gamble. But not now."

"What if you cast the spell on only a few of us?" Lorcan asks. "We could provide rides for the rest of you."

Drust blinks. "Use you as horses?" he says, astonished.

"Why not?" the teenager shrugs. "We'll die anyway if the demons break through. Bec and Bran are too small, and Fiachna's in no shape to carry anyone, but the rest of us could—"

"Not me!" Connla barks. "I'm not running myself dead for that damn druid!"

"You'd rather perish at the hands of demons?" Goll asks coolly.

"I won't—" Connla starts to shout, then stops and growls. "I mean, I'd rather take my chances with the monsters. I trust them more than this one. You know where you stand with demons."

"You're a fool," Goll says bluntly, then faces Drust. "Even without our *young king*, Lorcan and I could carry you and Bec. And Bran could keep up, the speed he runs at. It means leaving Fiachna behind, but he'll probably die soon anyway." He grins bleakly at Fiachna. "Sorry for being so blunt."

"Don't worry about it," Fiachna wheezes, grinning back.

"Maybe Lorcan doesn't want to carry me," I say quietly, recalling his outburst the night before.

Lorcan grumbles something, then raises his voice but keeps his eyes lowered. "I was upset about losing Ronan. I reacted savagely and said things I didn't mean. I beg your pardon."

"You don't need to," I smile.

Lorcan looks up, returns my smile, then squints at Drust. "Well? Will it work?"

"I'm not sure," Drust says and does some quick calculations. "We could cover maybe half the distance in a day if we did it your way — but only if you ran non-stop, which would certainly mean your deaths."

"Never mind that," Goll snorts. "If we get you halfway, it leaves you with a three- or four-day march. If you walk by night as well as day…"

"We still won't be quick enough," Drust mutters. "Bec and I could use magic to run faster after you died, but we'd have to rest often, to arrive fit enough to cast our spells. It would take at least two days, making three in total. The demon masters will have crossed by then."

"But we've more hope this way," Lorcan notes. "So we'll have to chance it. Aye?"

"If you're willing to make that sacrifice," Drust says slowly, "then… aye."

"You're mad," Connla sneers. "You'll kill yourselves for nothing instead of doing the wise thing."

"And what's that?" Goll enquires with all the sweetness of a bat's bite.

Connla points west. "We're on the coast, fools! Find a boat. Set sail. Get out of here before the demons slaughter you all."

Goll shakes his head. "I never had a high opinion of you but I wouldn't have expected this. Flee when there's a chance to save those we left behind? Run when there's a war to be fought? I don't believe you're of our people. I think Conn reared a changeling."

"Is that so?" Connla growls, drawing his sword. "Well, watch closely, old man, while this changeling rips your guts out and—"

"Run fast!"

The shout jolts us all. Bran roared it at the top of his voice, which is louder than anyone expected. Lorcan, who was closest to him, has covered his ears with his hands and is grimacing.

The strange boy from the crannog is glaring at us, hands on hips. "Run fast," he repeats, stiffly this time, looking from one of us to the other like a brehon passing judgement on a pack of bickering complainants. Then he points at the scraggly pony in the distance — it survived the night — and says, in a tone which brooks no argument, "Bubbly!"

Then he takes off, running as swiftly as he can, becoming a fast-moving speck within seconds. We stare after Bran, bewildered, then at each other. The heat of the moment has dwindled away and those who were arguing look embarrassed.

"Where do you think he's going?" Fiachna asks of no one in particular.

"That boy's a mystery even to himself," Drust answers, then sighs and looks at Lorcan and Goll. "But we can't wait here to wonder about him. If we're to set off as agreed, it's best we start now. If both of you are still sure…"

Goll and Lorcan nod. Drust beckons them forward. I see his lips move as he begins to cast a spell.

"Wait." I step between the warriors and Drust, my eyes on the far-off form of Bran. "I think we should leave it a while."

"Bec, I know you care about us…" Goll begins but I shake my head.

"It's not that. I think Bran has a plan. He can help us."

"How?" Drust frowns. "By being *bubbly*?"

"I don't know. But my instinct tells me we should wait. We can march but we shouldn't cast any spells. Not until we see what Bran's up to."

"And if he's up to nothing?" Drust asks. "If he's simply running around for the sake of it, or because we upset him? If he never returns?"

"I can't answer that. I don't know. I just think it would be a mistake to use our magic now."

Drust studies me in silence, troubled. The others are staring at me too, but it's clear from their expressions that they'll leave this decision to the druid.

"So be it," Drust huffs, then laughs. "I must be as mad as the boy, but I'll go with your instinct. We'll leave the magic for a while. I'm not setting a time limit but if I start to feel he's a lost cause, that's that. Agreed?"

I nod reluctantly and mutter a quick prayer under my breath that I'm not wrong about the brain-addled Bran.

→We make good early progress, me riding piggyback on Lorcan. But Fiachna finds it hard to keep the pace. It's clear we'll have to leave him behind soon, to die alone in the wilderness. My heart weeps at the thought, as I remember my childish dreams of putting magic behind me and becoming his wife. But dreams are dreams and reality's reality. Few, if any, of us are going to survive the next few days. We can't be foolish about this. If Fiachna can't keep up, he must be abandoned.

As I'm thinking that, Fiachna stumbles – Goll has been half-supporting him – then slumps to the ground and rests, massaging his neck, which is pure purple. "I'm finished," he says quietly. "Leave me."

"We could… if you want…" Goll mumbles, touching the hilt of his sword.

"No." Fiachna smiles weakly. "I'd rather lie here, watch the clouds drift across the sky and die in my own, natural time. It's peaceful."

"But the pain?" Goll enquires.

"Not so bad," Fiachna says. "It was worse in the night. The fire's turned to ice. It still hurts but I can bear it."

"Very well." Goll salutes the blacksmith. Lorcan salutes too and so does Connla, though his salute is quick and disinterested.

Drust spreads his hands over Fiachna. "I will pray for your spirit. And, if we succeed, I'll tell people of your bravery and the debt they owe you."

"Thank you." Fiachna coughs, then shudders.

I kneel beside him. A few weeks ago I would have fought not to cry. But now I let tears flow freely. I don't care how I'm supposed to behave. I'll miss Fiachna dreadfully and I want him to know that.

"I could… if there's anything… I wish…" I can't find suitable words. In the end I abandon speech, throw my arms around Fiachna and kiss him fully, a kiss between a woman and a man. It's the first time I've ever kissed someone this way. It will also probably be the last.

Fiachna smiles when I break the embrace. "I had my eye on you for a few years, Little One. If you hadn't been a priestess…" He touches my left cheek with cold, trembling fingers. "Perhaps in the Otherworld?"

"I'll pray for it," I sob, then rise and stumble away, wiping tears from my cheeks, not looking back for fear I'd crumble completely and beg to stay with him. There's no time for that. He must die by himself on this miserable day if we are to press on and prevent many more from dying soon after.

I hear Lorcan ask, "Do you need a weapon?"

Fiachna replies, "No. I have my knife. If I'm not dead by nightfall, and the demons come, that will take care of the job."

Then I'm gone. The others soon come after me – Connla among them, although I half-expected him to part from us here – our ranks lessened by the fall of yet one more much-loved friend.

→An hour later. Jogging steadily. Silent, thoughts heavy, wondering if Fiachna has succumbed to the disease yet or is still clinging on. Then noises from the far side of a hill. Like the growing sound of thunder, only coming from the ground, not the sky. We look around, puzzled. Then Connla gasps, "Horses!"

Moments later they appear, galloping over the hill, seven of them. Six are bareback. On the seventh, a rider — Bran! He laughs as the horses surge around us and come to a stop. He hops off and beams, pointing to the steeds. "*Bubbly*," he says proudly. "Run fast!"

"I don't believe it!" Goll howls with delight.

"Will the spells work on them?" I ask Drust quickly.

"Aye." He smiles softly with wonder. "And they can run much quicker than we could. We'll be able to rest them every few hours and still make great time."

"Enough?" I ask. "Will we get to the tunnel before…?"

"Possibly," Drust says. "But let's not waste precious minutes talking about it. Mount up!"

As Goll puts me atop one of the smaller horses – I've never been on one before, so I'm nervous – and the other men mount theirs, Bran looks for Fiachna.

"Drust," I call, then nod backwards. "Could we…?"

"There's no point," Drust says as kindly as he can. "Whether he dies on the ground or on horseback, he'll surely die, if he hasn't already."

I think about that and how hard it would be to bid Fiachna farewell a second time. I nod sadly, shedding a few fresh tears.

"Do you want a horse?" Goll grunts at Connla.

The arrogant warrior stares back haughtily. "Why wouldn't I?"

"I thought, from what you said earlier, you might have other plans. You don't need a horse to get to the coast or hunt for a boat."

Connla sneers. "I never said I was leaving. I simply said it would be the wise thing for the rest of you to do. I'm not one for running away from a challenge." And, with Goll staring at him in disbelief, he leaps up on one of the horse's backs and sits there regally, looking calmer and more relaxed than any of us.

Drust works his spell – I help, once he's demonstrated on the first horse – and moments later we're off. The seventh, riderless horse runs along behind us, but we're going too fast for it, sped along by magic. It soon gives up and turns aside to head back wherever it came from, leaving us to charge across the land ahead of even the jealous wind.

THE FINAL DAY

→We move so fast, it's as though we're not really part of the world. The horses push on at tremendous speeds without appearing to tire. It's only when we stop at Drust's command that they sweat and pant, trembling from exhaustion. We rub them down to warm them, find water for the beasts to drink and let them graze for a while. The others are keen to continue but Drust says we mustn't rush the horses.

"I'm keeping a close eye on the time," he snaps, irritated at being questioned. "This is *my* quest. I'm the one who knows what we can and can't do, when to race and when to rest."

While the horses are grazing, the druid approaches me. "I want you to ride beside me when we remount," he says. "I'm going to teach you the spells needed to close the tunnel."

"Why? I thought you were going to cast them."

"I am. But if anything should happen to me..."

"The Old Creatures said it would only work if a magician or priestess was sacrificed."

Drust sighs. "Aye. But if the worst comes to the worst, you might as well try it on one of the others. Cast the spell – it's complicated but I think you'll be able to master it – then pick someone for sacrifice…" He hesitates, gaze flickering over my friends. It comes to rest on Bran.

"No," I say instantly.

"He's a kind of magician," Drust says. "Of the four, he'd be most suitable. You'd stand a better chance with him than—"

"No," I say again. "Goll or Lorcan would give their lives willingly – maybe even Connla, though I doubt it – but Bran wouldn't understand. He couldn't make a choice. I won't kill someone who doesn't know what's being asked of him."

"I'm not so sure he wouldn't understand," Drust murmurs. "But if he didn't, wouldn't that be for the best? You could do it quickly, mercifully. He needn't even know what's happening."

I shake my head stubbornly. "If I have to, I'll ask one of the others. But I won't murder Bran."

"Even knowing the consequences if we fail?" Drust asks menacingly.

"Even then," I mutter. "There are certain things we should never do. Otherwise we'll become like the demons — mere monsters, best suited to the dark."

Drust shrugs sourly. "As you wish. If luck is with us, it won't come to that. But I thought I'd make you aware of your options. Just in case."

He rises and shouts at Bran to gather the horses — though they obey us when we're on their backs, they revert to creatures of the wild when left to graze and only Bran can get close to them. Soon we're off, racing through a forest, Drust riding beside me, teaching me the spells which will hopefully destroy the tunnel between this world and the Demonata's.

→We rest several times over the course of the day. The third time, one of the horses collapses and dies. I ride with Bran after that, my hands loose around his waist. I can tell he enjoys having me behind him by the way he tilts his head back to nuzzle my cheek.

We stop for nightfall. This time Lorcan and Goll don't question Drust's judgement, but it's plain from their worried expressions that they think we should press on. Drust sees this, and though he scowls, he takes the time to reassure them. "We made excellent progress today. If we rest the horses tonight, we can push them hard tomorrow and arrive at the tunnel by afternoon. If we continued now, they'd die before dawn, leaving us to walk — we wouldn't make it on time."

Many demons pass us during the night, snuffling and snorting, more than I've ever seen before. It must be because we're so close to the tunnel through which they cross. It's hard masking the horses from the demons, but Bran gathered them in a small circle before dusk and dozes in the middle of them, waking whenever one stirs, shushing them, keeping them motionless.

I don't sleep. I can't. This is probably my last night alive. It's horrible, lying here, shivering with cold and fear, knowing what's to come, thinking about death and all that I'll lose. Why couldn't I have fallen in battle, killed quickly, no time to worry about the Otherworld and what I was leaving behind? This waiting is worse than death itself.

I have moments of doubt in the middle of the night, when the world is a lonely place. I could run. Desert with Connla. I'm not sure why he's stuck with us this long. He could have left when we were at the coast or when Bran brought the horses. He said he wasn't one to flee a challenge but maybe it's just that he fears running by himself, with no one to watch his back. If I said I'd go with him, I'm certain he'd jump at the chance. With his strength and standing, allied to my magical abilities, we could be a mighty pair. Set ourselves up as rulers of some far-off tuath. Connla a king, me a priestess-queen. All-powerful.

It's tempting. I know my duty and I believe my suffering will be brief, that I'll find peace in the Otherworld. But in my heart I'm a young girl, afraid of the darkness of death, wanting to grow up and see more of the world, taste more of life. I cry quietly to myself, thinking of the terrible sacrifice I must make, the joys I will never know, the love I'll now definitely never find. Part of me wants to slither across to Connla, put my offer to him, then leap on a horse and ride out of this nightmare as fast as I can.

But I don't. Duty wins out over fear in the end. I can't stop the shivers or the fast beat of my heart, but I can wipe away tears and hold my ground. And I do. I hate the prospect of dying and I'm more afraid than I ever thought I could be. But if this is my destiny… if it's what the gods ask of me… so be it. Better to die for my people in my own land than rule in another and suffer a lifetime of cowardly guilt.

→Many of the demons return in the hour before dawn, some bearing trophies of their battles with humans — heads, limbs, torsos, sometimes children who are still alive, kicking and screaming in terror. It's hard to ignore the cries of the young but there's nothing we can do without giving our position away. If we did that, the demons would attack in great and unmerciful force and we'd all perish.

"They'll be the last," Drust whispers, his eyes hard. "After tomorrow, no more will die at the hands of the Demonata."

"You promise?" I ask, my fears and doubts causing me to question him, desperately searching his face for a hint of the lie that would provide me with an excuse to bail out.

"I promise," Drust says calmly. "It won't be easy, but having come this far I'm sure we won't fail." He pauses. "You're still prepared to…?"

"Of course!" I snap, pretending to be offended by the notion that I might have had second thoughts.

He lays a gentle hand on my right knee. "It will be quick. It won't hurt. You have my word."

I shrug as if that was the furthest thing from my thoughts, then listen to the demons crashing by and try to drown out the echoes of the children's screams.

→Day. The order of the world restored. My final sun. Fittingly, it's obscured by heavy grey clouds. I've heard that clouds are rare in some lands, that the sun shines all day in a clear blue sky. But surely those are fanciful tales, told for the amusement of the young. This world was made to be cloaked in grey. It wouldn't feel natural if the sun shone brightly all the time.

Drust examines the horses and declares one of them unfit for the trek. We let it go and after a few mumbles from Bran it wanders off to find a good grazing spot. Perhaps it will be the only survivor of our group this day.

Before we leave, Drust makes a final speech, looking around slowly, his gaze lingering on each of us in turn, first Connla, then Lorcan, Goll, Bran and me.

"I've acted as if I don't care about you. In the beginning it was true. You were figures for me to manipulate, like pieces on my chess board. I didn't care if you lived or died. I couldn't afford to.

"But I've changed. I wasn't aware of it happening but it did. I think of you as friends now. You've been loyal and brave, putting the welfare of others before your own, risking all on the strength of my promise to rid this world of demons.

"So I say to you now, as friends — you can leave. Only Bec and I need go on. If our plan works, there won't be any battle. If something goes wrong and we have to fight, the chances are you won't make much difference against the masses of demons. You can step aside and return home without any shame or guilt."

He stops and awaits the men's response.

"A gracious offer," Goll says warmly, "but I'll stay. I want to see how it finishes, so I can tell those in our tuath and bask in the glory. I've always wanted to be part of a legend!"

"Me too," Lorcan says. "Besides, I want to kill a few more demons before you banish them from our land. For Ronan."

We all look at Connla. "I'm going nowhere," he says quietly, defiantly.

Drust smiles. "True warriors one and all." He puts a hand out and, one by one, we touch it, until all of us are joined, even Bran, who squints at the hands as if he expects a trick. "To the end," Drust says simply.

"To the end," we repeat.

"Of the demons!" Goll adds and we laugh.

Then we mount up – Drust rides with Bran, while I sit behind Lorcan – and set off. Our final journey. Our final challenge. My final day.

*   *   *

→Working on the spells of closure. Not one spell but several. Spells to join split rock back together, move earth, seal magical gaps. The most difficult spells I've ever tried to learn. Even with my vastly expanded powers I have trouble mastering them. My tongue trips on the words. Despite my perfect memory, I get the order wrong and muddle them up.

Drust doesn't lose his temper. He repeats the spells over and over, making me slowly practise the words and phrases which are particularly difficult.

"This is helpful for me too," he says as we take a short break. "I've never cast these spells before. It's good that I get the order straight within my mind and the words clear on my tongue."

"If you… if I have to replace you," I say. "When do I make the sacrifice?"

"You'll know when the time comes," he says. "The spells will direct you. There is no single right moment. These spells react to the threat which the caster faces, so they're different each time. Even as you're uttering them, they'll change. As long as you keep the original spells clear within your thoughts, and don't stumble, you'll be fine — the new spells will carry you along."

"And if I make a mistake? Should I stop and start again?"

"No," he says quickly. "Once you start, you must continue. If you say a wrong word or stutter, don't stop. Push on and hope the error wasn't important. There will be forces working in opposition to our magic. Once the Demonata realise what we're doing, they'll set themselves against us. The spells will protect us – I hope – but if they break down, a second is all it will take for our enemies to destroy us."

I wish he could be more encouraging, but this is a time for the truth, however troubling it might be. So I listen. And repeat. And hope that I'm never charged with the task of having to do this. Because I'm not only unsure whether or not I'd be able to get the spells right — I also don't know if I could bring myself to take up a weapon against one of my friends and kill him.

THE WORLD BENEATH

→The tunnel. The rent between this world and the Demonata's. The passageway for demons. The source of the nightmares.

We're here.

It's an hour or so before sunset. We've set the horses free and are on our knees, hiding behind bushes, studying the scene. A hole in the ground ahead is the focal point. The branches of the trees around it are thick with strips of cloth, bits of wood, bodies of the dead. A solid ceiling, like the one around the ring of magical stones where we sheltered earlier, in what feels now like a separate age.

Beneath the cover of the trees — hordes of demons. Most sleeping. Some fighting, playing with dead bodies, eating. Every disgusting shape and shade imaginable. Some undead too, but not many.

"We'll never get through them all," Goll whispers.

"I could create a diversion," Lorcan suggests. "Attack at one side and draw them away. The rest of you could sneak in while they were dealing with me."

"No," Goll says. "That wouldn't work. Maybe Bran could dance and lead them astray."

"Run fast," Bran says, nodding vigorously.

"Too many," Drust mutters. "Not all would be lured away."

"Magic?" I ask. "A masking spell?"

Drust nods. "That's our best hope but we can't count on it. These are superior to most of the demons we've faced. They're some of the more powerful demons who have crossed, placed here by their masters to guard the opening."

"Then they might see through the spell," I note.

"Aye. But we'll have to risk it. We'll cast a strong spell over you, me and Bran, then advance. Goll, Lorcan and Connla can attack at the same time, at different spots, to create distractions."

"Sounds good to me," Goll says. "How about you, my fine young…?" He stops, brow furrowing as he stares at Connla. The vain warrior has cut the flesh of both his palms and is daubing his cheeks and forehead with blood, quietly muttering words which could be either a spell or a prayer. "What are you doing?" Goll asks suspiciously.

Connla finishes the spell or prayer, then smiles. "A bit of added protection."

"That won't help," Drust says.

"We'll see," Connla chuckles, casually glancing over the top of the bush at the demons. "Well, I'm ready. Make up your minds, tell me what you want to do and on we'll go."

Drust regards Connla with uneasy surprise. Some warriors are never afraid going into battle, but Connla isn't one of them. Yet here he squats, more at peace than anyone, looking like a man with nothing to lose or no notion of losing.

"You understand what we're discussing?" Drust asks. "If you fight, you'll die. It will take time to cast the spells of closure. The demons will kill you while we're at work."

"Just worry about your magic, druid," Connla laughs. "Leave us to handle the fighting."

"A man at last," Goll remarks wryly, then faces Drust. "So the three of us will attack the demons while you, Bran and Bec forge ahead on your own?"

Drust hesitates, then abruptly changes his mind. "No. Some demons may have orders to stay by the entrance in case of an attack. It might be better if we don't give them advance warning. We'll stick together and push on as a group. If they see through the spell, Bec and I will make a dash for the hole and the rest of you can fight then."

"We won't let you down," Connla says grandly.

Drust and I concentrate and draw upon our magic. The night's rest has done me a world of good, even though I didn't sleep. I feel power bubbling up inside, stronger than ever. When I cast the masking spell, I add a few twists to it, improvising, improving on the spell which Drust taught me. The druid feels the strength of the new spell. He's surprised, but follows my lead, and we carefully wrap our small group safely within it.

"The spell will trail us," I tell Drust when we're finished. "We won't need to maintain it as we walk. We can focus on the task ahead."

"How did you manage that?" he asks, slightly jealous.

I shrug. "It just came to me."

Drust sighs. "Such promise. There's so much you could do, maybe more than any magician has ever done. I wish…" He stops and steels himself. Checks that everybody has a weapon to hand (except simple Bran). Then we push through the bush and enter the camp of the Demonata.

→The spell holds. We edge through the demonic ranks, carefully stepping over tentacles and twisted limbs, ignoring the stench of rotting human bodies and the even fouler smells of the demons. Most are larger than any who attacked our rath. They look fiercer and stronger. I don't think we would have survived an assault by this lot. Yet these aren't the strongest Demonata, only the more worthy servants of the demon masters.

Until this moment I didn't truly believe the demons would overrun the land. I was inwardly sure that my people would fight hard and win in some places, repel the demons, hold their own. Now I know I was wrong. If we fail and the demon masters cross, all will fall in quick succession. Depending on how fast the demons move, this entire land could be a steaming pile of ruins, broken bones and decaying flesh within a week.

Bran studies the demons with interest, smiling at some of the more hideously deformed monsters. Connla casts a cool eye over them, acting unimpressed, as if they were a flock of scraggly sheep. Everybody else looks at them with disgust and fear.

A four-headed, red-skinned demon stirs and looks right at me. I freeze, certain it's seen through the spell. But then it belches, spits out a chewed-up hand and lowers its head again. I step over the half-dissolved, bile-speckled hand and fight to keep my stomach quiet as we pass the dozing monster.

Close to the hole. It looks like a natural rip in the earth, though the area around it has been torn at and dug up, to enlarge the mouth. No demons rest close by — they keep at least six or seven paces away from the hole.

We slip through a space between two misshapen demons and enter the clearing. Drust walks to the rim of the hole and looks down. I step up beside him and see a long shaft angling down, deep into the earth. Unnatural heat billows from it. I want Drust to start the spells here, close the tunnel from this point, not lead us down that shaft to whatever horrors lie beneath.

But Drust points down, as I knew he would. He makes sure we all understand, then lowers himself into the hole, searching for handholds, descending into the darkness of the pit. I go next, then Bran, Lorcan, Goll. Connla brings up the rear.

BEC

The rock is hot to the touch but bearable. Lots of holds. Easy to climb. The shaft turns to the left after a while. Pure darkness around the bend. I pause, look up at the overcast but beautiful, human evening sky one last time, then slide across into eternal, demonic night.

→We climb for five minutes, ten, slowly feeling our way down. I could cast a lighting spell but Drust hasn't, so I don't think I should either. I'm expecting the descent to last for ages. But a few minutes later we hit level ground and are soon standing in a huddle, not sure what to do next, afraid to continue in case we're on a platform overhanging a deadly drop.

"I'm going to feel ahead with magic," Drust whispers. "You try too. Explore with your mind. Try and determine where we are and what lies ahead."

I close my eyes – not that it makes any difference in this place – and send out mental feelers. But I'm not very good at this type of magic. I get the sense of a large space around us – a cave, I think – but I can't be sure of its exact size. And I've no idea what the ground is like underfoot, whether it's solid, breaks off into nothingness after a few feet, or is littered with traps.

Fortunately Drust is more accomplished at this than me and a minute later he sighs the contented sigh of a man who has finally found what he's been looking long and hard for. "It's all right," he says, excitement in his voice. "We're here."

Light flares dimly in his left hand. Slowly, he lets it grow and expand, filling his palm and then rising to hang in the hot air above us. It lights up the entire cave, revealing a site of beautiful wonders and a wretched terror.

The wonders — V-shaped, glistening formations of a substance not quite rock. Some reach up from the floor, others hang from the ceiling. All sorts of sizes. Water drips from the tips of some of the overhanging shapes, to splash over the floor of the cave or one of the uprising V's. In some places it's as if the shapes are reaching for each other, growing towards one another.

There are other formations stretched between the floor and ceiling, some huge, others tiny bulges. And an underground waterfall to our right, the water appearing as if by magic from high up the wall, vanishing through a crack in the rocks underneath, flowing on to who knows where.

This is what I imagine the Otherworld or Tir na n'Og to be like. It doesn't feel as if it belongs to our world. It's so quiet – except for the noise of the waterfall – and peaceful. I feel like if I fell asleep, I could snooze for a hundred years and not be any different when I awoke. Time doesn't touch this cave — or if it does, it touches it softly, slowly, subtly.

But then there's the wretched terror, which is almost impossible to comprehend. And difficult to describe.

There's a hole – the start of the tunnel – in one of the walls of the cave. And around and within it, the head and warped body of a man. The head hangs just above the hole, limp, its neck jutting out of the rock. Its body is spread out around it, mixed in with the rock, part of the wall. An arm far off to the left. A leg farther down to the right. The chest and stomach torn open, surrounding the hole, some inner organs visible inside the mouth of the tunnel.

At first, I think it's a trick of the rock formation, that the head has been stuck there to emphasise the strange nature of the hole. Then I think that the body just adorns the outside of the rock, that bits and pieces have been stuck on or crammed into cracks. But as we move closer, drawn to it in silent fascination and horror, I see that isn't right either.

The body *is* the rock. Somehow the two exist together, occupying the same space. It's as if the rock melted and the man stepped into it, coming apart as the rock grew hard again around him. It must have been a painful way to die. Was he sacrificed? Did demons melt the rock and then –

The head bobs up and its eyes flicker open. I stifle a scream. There are gasps all around me. Goll, Lorcan and Connla raise their weapons automatically.

"No," Drust says, signalling for calm. "It's all right. He can't harm us."

"Don't be… so… sure," the man in the rock croaks.

"Balor's eye!" Goll exclaims. "It speaks!"

"What is it?" Lorcan asks. "What manner of…?" He stops, eyes narrowing. Takes a step ahead of everyone, gazes at the face for a long moment, then looks back at Drust. "Druid, what spell is this? That face is *yours*!"

I don't understand what he's saying until I look again and see that the face hanging from the rock is very similar to Drust's. Stubbly hair. Agonised eyes. A fuller beard. But *his* shape, *his* mouth, *his* expression.

"His name was Brude," Drust says quietly, eyes locked with the man's. "My twin brother. A druid like me."

"Brotherrrrrr," the man who once was – or still is – Brude sighs, then chuckles creakily. "You have... come... to witness... the glory?"

"Brude hated Christians more than most," Drust says, ignoring the question. "I was never sure why."

"Because... they... corrupt," Brude hisses, eyes filling with fury. "They... change... that which... should not... be changed. They... destroy."

"He decided to fight them," Drust continues. "He sought a way to defeat them. Magic failed him. So did brute force when he tried to organise an army to lead against them. In the end he resorted to..." He trails off into silence for a moment, then speaks again, louder this time. "He opened the tunnel between our world and the Demonata's. Invited the demons to cross. He's responsible for all the savagery and deaths. He's the one we must stop if we are to close the–"

"That's why you came!" I cry suddenly. "The other druids refused to help, but your twin was the cause of the invasion. You felt guilty. You couldn't bear to let so many people die because of him."

Drust nods slowly. "We were like two parts of the same person when we were children. If he cut himself, I hurt. When I was happy, he laughed. That changed with time, but the bond was always there, linking us, binding us. What he's doing is wrong. Christianity can't be fought — and even if it can, it should be fought by human means, not demonic. I couldn't stand by and let my brother – my own flesh and blood – commit such an atrocity against the entire human race. I had to stop him."

"Not such a noble cause then," Connla snickers. "You didn't rush to our rescue because you cared for us, but because you didn't like what your twin was up to."

Drust shrugs. "Do my motives matter? I came. I wish to put a stop to the madness. That should be enough."

"Can't... stop," Brude growls. Now that I'm closer I can see his heart, beating slowly within the wall, the rock pulsing along with it. So he's not just alive within the rock — the rock is alive too.

"It has to stop," Drust says. "This is wrong, Brude. The Demonata will destroy everything. They won't stay on this island — they'll find a way to cross the sea and spread throughout the world, killing all in their path."

"Good," Brude gurgles. "I want... them to. Except... our kind. The druids will... stand firm. We won't... fall. The weak... will perish. The strong... will remain. The way it... should be."

Drust shakes his head. "Even the druids would fall in the

end. The Demonata don't share, or even rule. They consume. All would fall to them — human, priestess, druid. All."

Brude sneers. "If so... so be it. Better a world... of demons... than one... of Christian stain."

"This is pointless," Goll grunts. "We could stand here arguing forever and not get anywhere. Will I chop his head off at the neck and have done with it?"

"That won't stop him," Drust says, moving closer, breaking eye contact with his brother to motion me forward. "Brude's spirit is infused with the rock. He has become part of the tunnel between worlds. He is beyond physical harm. We can only kill him by closing the tunnel."

"Then do it, quick, and let's be out of here," Lorcan says, eyeing Brude uneasily, tugging nervously at his earrings, one after the other.

"*You* are a... twin too," Brude says bitterly. "I can... tell. What would you... think if... your brother... spoke of killing... you?"

"If I was in your place, I'd say he had every right to spill my blood," Lorcan answers stiffly.

"You lie," Brude snarls. "Twin should... never raise a hand... against twin." His snarl turns to a smile. "But... in this case... I don't think... it will come to... that. I smell... a friend... among my... foes. *He* will... protect me."

Goll frowns. "What's he talking about?"

"Ignore him," Drust mutters. "He's mad. Let's push on and—"

A cry of pain stops him. It's Lorcan. As I whirl, the teenage warrior falls to the ground, clutching his chest, blood pouring out around his fingers.

"Demons!" Goll shouts, turning sharply, sword raised. He stops, bewildered. There are no demons in the cave behind Lorcan. Only Connla — with a blood-red knife and a killer's smile.

Before anyone can react, Connla races to the cave entrance and roars up the shaft, "Demonata! Hurry to my side! There are enemies in your midst!"

Goll curses vilely and starts across the cave. But then we hear the sounds of demons pouring into the hole above and scrambling down the shaft. Goll stops, not sure what to do.

Drust ignores the chaos above us. He steps up, so he's almost face to face with his twin, then speaks to me from the side of his mouth. "I'm going to start the spells. When I complete the first one, we'll be able to enter the tunnel, where I'll finish the rest."

"What about—" I begin.

"No time!" he shouts. "Ask them to fight and buy a few seconds for us, and pray that's enough."

His lips start moving at an unnatural speed and his hands come up, glowing a dark blue hue. Brude curses him but Drust ignores the foul insults and carries on with the spell.

I turn my attention to Connla and Goll. Connla is standing by the side of the entrance, whistling merrily, cleaning under his fingernails with the tip of his bloodied knife. Goll has helped Lorcan back to his feet — Connla must have missed the young warrior's heart because although he's wounded fatally, he isn't dead. Bran stares at the blood on Lorcan's chest, head cocked sideways, not sure what to make of it.

From the shaft come screams of outrage. The demons must have piled down too fast, too many of them, and jammed. But the blockage can't last long. They'll be upon us in a minute or so, I guess.

"Why?" Goll roars at Connla. "We'll all die now!"

"*You'll* die," Connla replies smugly. "Not me. I've cut a deal with the demon master, Lord Loss."

"The night when he was talking to you!" I gasp, remembering our first encounter with Lord Loss, finding him crouched over Connla, whispering.

"Aye," Connla smiles. "I wasn't asleep. He came to me. Told me everything, of Drust's quest, his real reason for coming, what would happen if – when – he failed. For my cooperation he promised great power. In the new world I will be a high king, in command of all those whom the demons choose to spare."

"Weren't you listening?" I cry. "They won't spare anyone!"

"Of course they will," Connla laughs. "Every master needs slaves."

"Did Lord Loss actually say that?" I ask.

"Not directly, no, but it was implied."

"You're an ass!" Goll spits. Then he squints at Connla. "What do you mean by *cooperation*? What did you do for the demon?"

"Information," Connla murmurs. "I told him about you all, your pasts, your strengths and weaknesses. I told him about Orna's children — that's how he knew to fetch them. And then there were the services rendered…"

From the sounds in the shaft, the jam has cleared and the demons are moving forward again. Time's almost up. I glance desperately at Drust but his lips are still moving and he hasn't stepped forward.

"Be quick!" Goll shouts at Connla. "They'll be on us in seconds and I don't want to die without knowing the full extent of your treachery."

"Very well." Connla grins at Lorcan. "*I* killed Ronan — I pushed him off the cliff." Lorcan tries to curse but his face twists with pain and he only doubles over and grunts. "And Fiachna," Connla continues, laughing at me now. "Lord Loss gave me a pouch of poisoned powder. I rubbed it into Fiachna's wound after he'd been bitten by the demon, when everyone was asleep or preoccupied. I–"

Whatever he was about to say is lost as the first demon crashes through the entrance into the cave. It falls on its face but is up in an instant, head swivelling, searching for the source of danger. It spots Connla, takes a step towards him, then sniffs the air, pauses and turns its gaze on the rest of us, leaving the smirking traitor alone.

The demon bounds forward, shrieking. Goll meets it solidly, drives his sword through the tip of its head, then kicks it into the path of those which are following.

Lorcan shrugs off his death and lays into the demons with his sword, pushing forward, keeping one hand over the hole in his chest to stem the flow of blood.

Bran dances around the cave, over, under and around the demons spilling into it, confusing and enraging them, doing what he can to draw their attention away from the rest of us — and especially from Drust, still muttering his spell in front of the abusive Brude.

I reach within, call upon my magic and unleash it. I set a demon on fire. Make another's eyes pop. I drive one mad by squeezing its brain — in its madness it attacks those around it.

The spells come quickly to my tongue, power flowing through me, building up and dispersing through my fingers, lips and eyes at a frightening speed. I make one demon's stomach explode. I cause a host of the V-shaped formations overhead to snap free and fall, killing several demons in the process.

But it isn't enough. More come. An endless flow. Streaming into the cave. Lorcan has disappeared under an avalanche of monsters. I see one of his ring-pierced ears fly high into the air — my final glimpse of him. Goll's stomach has been ripped open and half his face clawed away. He fights on but it's hopeless. I can't save the old warrior. Bran is still going strong, fast and agile as ever, but what good is that?

I catch sight of Connla, moving among the demons like a master through a pack of hounds. Many growl at him suspiciously but when they smell his blood they leave him be. He's laughing at the carnage. Angling for Drust, twirling a knife, preparing to kill the druid. I start a spell to make his brain melt in his head — but then I have a better idea.

A moving spell. I cast it quickly and Connla flies across the cave, colliding with the wall beneath the waterfall. He falls heavily, then sits up, wincing but otherwise unharmed, shaking his head as water cascades over him.

"You'll have to do better than that!" he chortles, wiping water from his eyes.

"I don't think so," I retort.

He frowns at my tone. A demon standing close to him, with a head that's mostly human except for an extra eye in the middle of its forehead, sniffs at Connla uncertainly, then hisses with delight. Its mouth opens wider than any human's — row upon row of dagger-like teeth and two forked tongues.

Connla stares at the demon, confused. Then he realises — the water has washed the blood from his face! A moment of panic. He tries to cut his palms again, to redaub his cheeks. But the demon's upon him before he can restore his protective spell. It bites at his face. Catches his lips. It looks as though the pair are kissing — until the demon rips free, tearing Connla's mouth away, leaving him to fall, gibbering madly, and be set upon by a handful of other savage demons.

"Hah!" Goll shouts, taking great pleasure from Connla's savage death. "That'll teach him! Well done, Little One!"

Then a demon knocks the old warrior's legs out from under him. He falls. Demonic bodies fill the space around him. And the one-eyed ex-king who was like a father to me – who gave me my name – is gone.

Alone. No time to mourn. The demons are closing in, ignoring the dancing Bran, focusing on me. I lash out at them with every spell at my disposal, wreaking havoc. But I can't kill them all. They're getting closer. Almost upon me. Any second now, one will lurch within striking distance and then –

A hand grabs the neck of my tunic. I'm hauled backwards. I cry out, but the cry's cut short by the V of the tunic digging into my throat. I land hard on the ground. Scrabble to my feet, trying to clear my throat, to cast a spell, to take at least one more demon down with me before...

I stop. I'm in the gut-studded tunnel. Drust is beside me. The demons are at the mouth, howling, reaching for us, lashing out with all their force and fury — but not connecting. Unable to break through the invisible barrier which separates Drust and me from them.

"A positive start," the druid says. He smiles quickly, then half-closes his eyes and moves down the tunnel, muttering the words of the next spell.

I laugh hysterically and pull faces at the furious, thrashing demons. But then I recall the deaths of my friends and my crazy humour passes. I look for the bodies of Goll and Lorcan but I can't see through the demons crowded around the mouth of the tunnel. There's no sign of Bran either, but I'm sure he's safe — daft as he is, he leads a charmed existence. I don't think any of these demons can harm him.

I sigh heavily and wipe tears from my eyes, thinking about Goll and Lorcan, all the good times and adventures we shared. Then, putting soft thoughts behind me, I make myself hard, turn my back on the demonic chaos and set off after Drust, readying myself for a swift, victorious death.

THE SACRIFICE

→The walls of the tunnel are hot and fleshy, both to the look and touch. By the glow coming from Drust's hands I can see more of Brude from here — more than I want to. Almost all the bits inside him – the bits of a person which are supposed to remain hidden – are obscenely revealed, pulsing, bubbling and gurgling within the transformed layers of rock.

Brude screams at us as we invade the tunnel of his body, his voice only just audible above the bellowing and mewling of the demons. He curses us, threatens a violent end, warns us to turn back. When that fails, he tries to win us over with promises of power, long lives and protection from the Demonata.

We ignore him and proceed, Drust chanting words of powerful magic, me following obediently, awaiting his command.

→Brude's voice fades as we move down the tunnel until it's nothing more than a low murmur. The walls around us change too, hardening, becoming more like real rock, although with small lines running through them — I think they're veins.

I expect Drust to stop, complete his spells and make the sacrifice. But he keeps moving, slow but sure, following the path of the tunnel as it curves and dips ever lower. I want to ask why he doesn't end it here, so he can get out quickly if successful, before the walls close around him. But I dare not interrupt while he's casting the spells, for fear I'd break his concentration, shatter the web of magic and free the demons to hurtle down the tunnel after us.

→Eventually, the tunnel leads us to another cave. This one's smaller than the first, with none of the spectacular formations. Most of the floor is covered by a pool of water. An island of bones juts out of the middle of the pool. In the centre stands a large rectangular stone which reminds me of the ring of Old stones where we sought shelter from the demons.

Drust stands by the edge of the water, observing the stone, for several minutes, muttering more spells. Then he stops and looks at me, smiling tiredly. "A lodestone," he says. "A reservoir of ancient magic. Very powerful. We think the Old Creatures used stones like this to mark the position of our world, so they could find their way here from the stars. The Old Creatures have drained most of the remaining lodestones of their power, but they either missed this one or deliberately left it charged for one reason or another. Brude found it and used it to open the tunnel. We'll turn it against him now."

"Is it safe for you to stop?" I ask nervously, glancing back up the tunnel.

"For a moment," Drust says. "The spells I've cast are at work on the walls of the rock, Brude, the…" He nods towards a point beyond the island. Staring hard, I see the mouth of a second tunnel in the rock on the far side of the pool — but the walls of this tunnel are made of red webs and strips of flesh.

"That's the tunnel to the Demonata's world?" I ask.

"Aye. On their side a demon master has undergone a transformation like Brude, creating that tunnel. The lodestone links the pair. It's been absorbing magic from Brude and the demon master, uniting their forms, slowly knitting together the fabric of the two tunnels. The lesser demons have been able to squeeze through during the process. When the tunnels become one, the masters will be able to follow their servants to our world. If that happens, mankind is finished."

"What if a demon comes through when you're casting the rest of your spells?" I ask.

Drust pauses. "I won't be able to stop. You'll have to fight it." He runs an eye over me. "Are you all right?"

"Yes." I lick my lips, mouth dry from the heat of the tunnel and cave. "Goll and Lorcan are dead. Connla too. I removed his protective spell. The demons killed him."

"Good," Drust grunts. "And Bran?"

"I don't know. He was alive when we entered the tunnel, but there were so many demons…"

"If I make it back, I'll look for the boy," Drust promises. "If he's alive, I'll take care of him."

He straightens, casts his tiredness off and steps into the water, starting on the next set of spells. I stare at the island of bones for a second – impossible to tell if they're human or demon, or a mix of the two – then step in after him. Despite the heat of the cave, the water's cold, but not as cold as the sea was. No need for a warming spell. I wade after Drust, eyes on the lodestone and bones, morbidly wondering if he'll leave my bones there, on top of the pile, when he's done.

→The water's shallow, no higher than my lower thigh. It doesn't take us long to reach the island. When we're there, Drust climbs up on to the mound of bones. The bones are brittle and many snap under his feet. He takes no notice, continues with the spells, clambering his way over to the lodestone, beckoning me to follow.

The glow in Drust's hands has changed from blue to a pinkish red. The bones – especially the skulls – look as though they're aflame. I try to keep my eyes off them as I crawl to where Drust is kneeling, hands stretched out on either side of the lodestone, ready to clasp it when the moment's right.

As Drust casts spells, I move slightly to one side of him, so I have a clear view of the tunnel to the Demonata's universe — I want plenty of warning if a demon comes through. But the monsters on the other side don't seem to be aware of the threat, or else they can't cross quickly. Nothing stirs. No shadows or sounds.

I find myself thinking about the bones and lodestone. Who set them here? The stone was put in place by the Old Creatures, but did Brude stick the bones underneath it? Have they been left by demons? Or are they the work of the Old Creatures too? Did they sacrifice people to create this place of magic, as Drust plans to sacrifice me?

Despite my unease, I can't help studying the skulls, wondering if these people were killed on the surface or if they died down here. Were they volunteers? What were they thinking in their final moments? Did they go bravely to their deaths, as I hope to, or did they crumble at the end and scream for mercy?

Drust's voice rises, disturbing my thoughts. His hands close upon the lodestone, drawing gradually closer as he slips deeper inside the intricate web of spells. I listen to his words, and though they're hard to decipher – he's speaking so quickly! – after a while I catch a few of them. He's on one of the final spells. It won't be much longer. If I want to offer up any last prayers for myself, I'd better do so now, before –

Drust cries out. His hands fly wide apart, then dart to the small of his back. My eyes shoot down and I spot a dagger sticking out of his flesh, handle quivering, buried to the hilt. I whirl, summoning magic, expecting Connla or a demon.

But it's neither.

It's *Bran*!

The boy stands at the edge of the pool, arm extended — he threw the knife. His face is curiously blank.

My heart leaps. Has Bran's innocence been an act all along? A spy in our midst, playing us for fools, waiting for the ultimate moment to strike? Impossible! Nobody could have been that convincing an actor. But there he stands, hand outstretched, dagger buried in Drust's back.

Drust topples aside and sees Bran. He yells with astonishment, then groans with pain. I falter. I want to unleash a spell, drive the boy – the killer – back, destroy him if I can. But it's *Bran*! I can't hurt him, not until I'm sure, not unless –

"Why?" Drust gasps.

Bran blinks. He frowns at Drust, then looks at me — and bursts into tears. "Flower!" he cries. Starting forward, he wades sluggishly through the water, arms flailing, displaying none of his customary lightness of movement.

"Bec!" Drust croaks. "Stop him!"

"No," I sigh, letting the spell die on my lips, understanding by his tears what has happened. "It's all right. He won't do any more damage."

Bran makes it to the island of bones, wailing and sobbing. He throws himself at me, yelling "Flower!" again and again. I catch him, let him bury his face in my chest, and hold him as he weeps, stroking the back of his head, murmuring quieting words.

After a few seconds I look over his head at the wounded druid. "He heard us on the cliff," I whisper. "He knew you planned to kill me. He couldn't let that happen. In his own crazy way he loves me. He hasn't done this to sabotage your plans — he did it to save *me*."

Drust grits his teeth with desperate anger. "The idiot! Doesn't he know what will happen if–"

"No," I interrupt calmly. "He doesn't. I'm his friend, maybe the one person in the world he feels close to. He only knew that he didn't want me to die. Don't blame him. He couldn't control himself."

Drust's expression softens. "Aye," he chuckles. "I think you're right. It's not much comfort to us, but…" His eyes flick to the lodestone. He reaches for it, then winces and remains lying on his side. "I can't do it, Bec."

I go cold. "You must!"

He shakes his head. "It's not too late – the spells will work if resumed quickly – but Bran has wounded me deeply. I haven't the strength to continue."

"You must!" I shout again. "You have to try! Don't just lie there and give up!"

"I'm not talking about giving up," he smiles sadly. "*I* can't complete the spells — but *you* can."

"And sacrifice Bran?" I ask quietly, dreading the answer.

"No, you fool," the druid snaps, more like the Drust of old. "Why kill two when one's already half dead? I'm finished. Even if I could cast the rest of the spells, I'd never make my way back to the surface. You need to take over, complete the spells, then slit my throat and let my blood flow over the lodestone."

I stare at him stupidly.

"There's no time for gawping," he growls. "I'll last a few more minutes with luck, but not much longer. Do it, Bec. Say the spells. Kill me. Spare your people the wrath of the Demonata. Then save yourself and Bran."

That final word jars me into action. Bran's risked all to rescue me. I can't repay him by stranding him here, to perish at the hands of the demon masters when they come. Unwrapping his arms from around my shivering frame, I push him back, smile to show everything's all right, then shuffle up beside Drust.

"What do I have to do?"

"Do you know where I stopped?" he asks.

"No."

"You must," he insists. "You have a perfect memory. Cast your thoughts back."

It's not easy but I force myself to focus. I pick at the strings of my always reliable memory with nimble fingers. Recall the spell Drust was chanting, the place where Bran interrupted him. "Got it," I mutter.

"Continue from there," the dying druid says. "Spread

your arms. Embrace the lodestone as you finish, then launch into the next spell. It should be a clear run from there."

"And the sacrifice?" I ask. "When…?"

"You'll know," he vows.

One deep breath. A quick glance at the tunnel to the Demonata's universe to make sure nothing's barging towards us. I begin.

→The words come easily. There's great power in this cave. I sensed it as soon as I came here – even before, when I was on the surface – but it's only when I open myself up to the magic that I feel the full extent of it. This stone has been filled with some of the most potent magical power imaginable. I believe I could do anything I set my mind to if I tapped into the lodestone long enough.

I finish the spell, then grab the stone with both hands. I mean to start the next spell immediately, but the rush of power from the lodestone catches me by surprise and the words stick in my throat. It's incredible, as if all the magic of the stars was rushing into me. I can see the universe, the entire night sky. I could reach out if I wanted, leave this world, go and explore the stars with the Old Creatures. This land suddenly seems insignificant, hardly worth bothering about. With this much power I could create my own worlds and people to inhabit them. Not a priestess, not a queen — a *goddess*.

Fate whispers to me. Asks me to accept a new destiny, travel a fresh path, blaze a godly trail. I don't ever have to know fear again, pain, want. I don't even have to die. All I need is to reach out and...

"Rainbow," Bran whispers, touching my left forearm, gazing at me seriously.

I feel the power rush into Bran through my flesh, then out of him again. It's not that he can't hold it — he just doesn't want it. The promise of the stars doesn't interest the boy. He cares only for me. If he could express himself with words, I think he'd say something like, "All the power in the universe means nothing if you can't be with the one you love." And he's right. What's the point of becoming a goddess if it costs the lives of all those I care about? I don't want a world of worshipful slaves, just a village of welcoming friends.

I smile at Bran, nodding slowly. He smiles back and releases my arm. I focus, close my eyes, shut out the seductive temptation of the stars and cast the next spell.

→A wind develops as I progress, a hot, biting, swirling wind. It gusts in a circle around the island of bones, gathering speed and power. Drust and Bran huddle up to the lodestone, not touching it, but wriggling in as close as they can, sheltering from the unearthly wind.

Screams. At first I think it's the sound of the wind. Then I realise they're coming from the tunnel which links this cave to the realm of the demons. The Demonata know what's happening. They can sense their gateway to this world collapsing. But all they can do in response is shriek hatefully at the herald of their ill fortune.

The spells race off my tongue. I'm barely aware of what I'm saying. I was foolish to worry about making a mistake. The spells are almost chanting themselves. I don't think I could stop even I wanted. I'm not in control now. The magic is.

I draw to the end of another spell, lick my lips, open them wide to start on the next… and stop. It's time. Only one spell left. And that comes after the sacrifice.

Drust knows too. He hauls himself up without having to be told. Smiles crookedly at me. "Live long, Bec. Live well."

I don't answer. I can't. My next words can only be words of magic. I can't break the sequence of spells.

Drust limps around to the other side of the lodestone. He leans forward, so his chin is directly over the rock. Then he tilts his head back, offering his throat. I let go of the lodestone with my right hand and press the nail of my index finger to the flesh of his throat. I smile at him, a tear trickling from my left eye. Then I swipe the magically hardened and sharpened nail across.

Blood gushes. The lodestone is soaked. It absorbs, then thirstily gulps the blood. Drust trembles but doesn't fall away. I can't see his eyes, only his throat. I'm glad of that. He remains upright, feeding his blood to the stone, held up by magic or sheer willpower — I'm not sure which.

And then, as the stone flashes with a blinding yellow light, Drust slumps.

No time to grieve. With a bellow of triumph, I roar the words of the final spell. The lodestone quivers. The cave shakes. The wind howls to a climax, ripping the outer layers of bones off the island, threatening to pick loose Bran and me and dash us to death against the walls. But before it can…

Release.

The wind roars up the tunnel – Brude's tunnel – increasing in strength as it tears through the druid's form. It fills the cave beyond, then explodes up the shaft and billows outwards at an unnatural speed, in all directions, scraping every demon and undead spirit free of the earth. It's like a giant wave, washing away all things demonic in its path, carrying them tumbling and screaming to the very edge of the land, not stopping until it reaches the sea, where it pauses for one long, dreadful moment… then sweeps back, drawn to its source, this point. After that it will drag its demonic prisoners back to their own world and crudely dump them there.

I don't wait for that. Magic has brought understanding. I know that when the last of the demons has been blown back to its own land by the final gust of wind, Brude's rock-infused bones will follow, then the tunnel will close, the rip between worlds will heal — and anyone still here will be crushed by rock or trapped underground to die slowly and horribly in the darkness.

ESCAPE

→Trying to race to safety. Hindered by the wind, which is returning to its source, blowing fiercely against us, a gale in the tunnel. And not just the wind — it contains all the demons and undead which it's captured. They swirl and tumble through the air, smash into us, knock us over, send us sprawling, threaten to drag us back to their world with them.

Abandoning our efforts to stand, we lie on our stomachs and crawl, side by side. But even this would be impossible if we were normal, since the wind – and its captive demons – fills the tunnel.

But we're not normal. We're beings of magic and I use that power to protect us. I draw from deep down and around me, using the magic in my body and the walls of the tunnel, creating a barrier around us. It doesn't keep out the wind, but most of the demons bounce off it without harming us. Most, not all. Sometimes a limb, claw or fang breaks through and bundles us over, bruising or cutting us.

Bran was laughing when we started up the tunnel — he thought it was great fun. He's not laughing now. Blood coats his face – I can see him in the glow of the light I created to guide us – and his right arm hangs uselessly by his side, snapped in two or three places.

I'm in no better shape. I have to pause frequently to wipe blood from my eyes. A few of the toes on my left foot have been ripped off — I don't stop for a close examination. The tunic on my back has been torn to tattered shreds and much of the flesh underneath too.

I ignore the terrible pain. Battle against the savage wind. Shrug off the blows of the beastly demons. And drag myself ever further up the tunnel, towards the promise of escape and life.

→Crawling. Panting. The demons hitting us more often as my power dwindles. The closing spells took a lot out of me. I was all-powerful clutching the lodestone, but now I'm the weakest I've been in a long time. It's a struggle to move, never mind cast spells. I want to abandon the shield and divert all of my strength to my flesh and bones, but I'd be swept away within seconds if I did that, and Bran beside me.

Part of me thinks about letting Bran go. It's hard enough protecting myself. If I halved the problem, I'd stand a better chance of getting out alive.

I turn a deaf ear to the treacherous thoughts, gasp as nails dig along the length of my spine, then strengthen the shield around us. At the same time I let the light die — it didn't require much power, but every last bit of magic might count in the end. I don't want to fall just short of the exit because of some unnecessary ball of light.

Impossible to tell in the darkness how much further there is to go. Forcing our way on, the wind deafening, demons striking freely. I can't maintain the shield. I now use magic to root us to the floor when we're struck and on the point of being blown away. Quick bursts instead of extended spells. Dangerous – if I'm knocked unconscious, we're doomed – but I don't have the strength for anything else.

How long is this damn tunnel! We came down so quickly — or was that a trick of my mind? What if it has somehow extended, if Brude caused it to double or triple in length to spite us? Is that possible? I don't know. I choose to believe it isn't. Otherwise despair will consume me and I'll certainly fail.

Onwards by slow, painful, bloody, hard-fought-for patches. So sore and weak. Struggling to breathe. Every spell dug up from the deepest depths of my spirit. Thinking each time I cast one, "This is it. The last spell. I can't do any more." But constantly surprising myself, finding a smattering of power here, a glimmer there.

Barely aware of Bran, sticking by me doggedly, patting my arm every few seconds to reassure himself that I'm here. Poor Bran. He didn't ask for this. The rest of us understood the risks. Did he? No way of knowing. He can comprehend some things, but how much did he really know of what he was letting himself in for? I listen to him panting, heavy and fast, and…

The thought dies unfinished.

I can *hear* him panting. But I haven't been able to hear anything since we started crawling, because of the roar of the wind and screams of the demons. I raise my head and realise the wind has died away. It's over. Which means…

Panicking, I find another burst of magic and create light again. It flares around us, blinding after the darkness. I shut my eyes against it, then force them open and stare ahead desperately, expecting to find nothing but rock, the pair of us buried alive, to die beneath the earth in a ready-made tomb.

For a moment I think we're lost, that we've won the battle but surrendered our lives in the process. My heart sinks. I ready myself to sob with terror.

But then — a gap! The exit still exists and we're close to it. The walls are just walls now, no traces of Brude's veins or guts. But they're grinding together, the mouth of the tunnel tightening and closing. There's enough space for us to get out but there won't be for much longer. We have to *move!* — *fast!* — *now!*

"Bran!" I gasp, struggling to my feet. So weak, near the end of my resources. But one last surge. One final effort. Then we'll be safe. We can sleep. Recover. No demons. We'll have all the time we need.

"Bran!" I shout, dragging his head up. He looks around, dazed, defeated. Then he spots the opening and cries out with fresh hope. He leaps up beside me, stumbles, then finds his feet and lurches forward, taking my hand, gurgling happily.

We reel towards the exit, a pair of barely living, impossibly weary spirits. The hole in the rock continues to close, but at the same regular pace. If we keep moving as we are… if we don't collapse… if we don't give up…

We'll make it! I don't want to let myself hope too strongly – that might tempt the gods to act against us – but if we can maintain our slow, steady stagger, I'm sure we'll –

Something clatters into my back. I fall, crying out with pain and surprise. Teeth lock around my right leg and bite through to the bone. I scream and try to shake my attacker loose, but can't.

The light fades. But in the dimness I catch sight of my assailant — Lord Loss's pet demon, Vein! The one with a dog's body, strange long head and a woman's hands. She's gnawing at my leg. The pain is dreadful. I scream again, kicking at her with my free foot, to no effect.

Then Bran's by her side. He tries to tug the demon loose. When that fails, he kneels beside her and murmurs desperately, stroking her head, smiling shakily. After a few seconds Vein stops biting, lets go and yaps at Bran with delight, falling under his spell as she did before.

As soon as I'm free, I freeze out the pain, leave Bran to deal with the demon, and turn and focus on the gap. My insides harden. The delay's ruined us. The hole has been narrowing steadily. We're not going to make it, even if we pick up our pace. I search within myself, digging deep for magic, going to the very core of my spirit, trying to find enough power to propel us forward and shoot us to safety like a pair of arrows fired from a bow.

But it isn't there. I'm magicked out. Enough for one last minor spell perhaps — definitely no more.

Sorrow overwhelms me. I feel madness coming on. But I force it back and turn my gaze on Bran. He's still playing with the dog but his eyes are flicking from me to the hole. He knows it's closing. He knows I can't make it in my condition. He also knows that at the speed he can run, he could abandon me and escape.

But he won't. He's going to stay with me, protect me from the demon, keep me company as the gap shuts and seals our fate.

"Bran," I sob. "You have to go." He just smiles. "Bran! You must!" Again the smile. He won't leave. He'll be my faithful friend forever. He'd rather die by my side than skip free without me.

I return the smile. "Very well," I sigh and reach out a hand. Bran takes it, expecting only my touch. But what he gets on top of that is the last of my magic. A swift, improvised spell. I reach into his mind and send an image into his thoughts, of the hole, him dashing out of it, racing through the cave and not coming back. And then, with all the magical force I can muster, I yell at him — "*Run fast!*"

He shoots off. Running without meaning to, roaring with surprise and fright. He flies up the tunnel, leaps through the hole and keeps on going, a temporary slave of my magic. I wave after him sadly, letting out a long, shuddering breath. Alone at last — and damned.

→ I expect Vein to attack again, now that Bran's gone, but she doesn't. I hear her growls, close to where I'm stranded, but for some reason she leaves me be.

Watching the hole in the ever-fading light. It's the size of a baby now, closing all the time. Narrower and narrower, until there's barely room to fit an arm through. I'm thinking about quenching the light before the hole shuts – this is just torture – when a face suddenly appears.

It's Bran. The spell has passed and he's come back. He wants to get through, to be with me. But the hole's too small. He punches it, pulls at it, slips his fingers into the gap and strains with all his might — but it's no good. The rock continues to grind together. The hole gets smaller, the width of a finger now.

At the last moment, Bran presses his mouth up to the hole and roars with raw pain and loss, at the top of his voice, "*Bec!*" It's the only time he's ever uttered my name. Anyone's name. His anguished cry stabs at my heart and tears spring to my eyes. I open my mouth to shout his own name back, to offer whatever small shred of comfort I can… but then the rock closes all the way and a fierce rumbling drowns out the echoes of Bran's cry.

I stare at the solid rock. My mouth closes. The light fades. Darkness.

FULL CIRCLE

→Lost in the all-enfolding shadows, I pull myself forward, away from Vein — she's stopped growling — towards the place where the hole used to be. I wonder if the rest of the tunnel will close the way the hole did. Impossible to tell in this total, unearthly darkness. Probably better that way. Banba used to say that knowledge was strength, and for the most part she was right. But in this place knowledge only means more distress and pain.

Struggling forward, weeping softly, steeling myself against the bite of Vein's teeth, sure she's playing with me, waiting to jump on my back when I least expect it. Why didn't she return to the Demonata's universe along with the rest of her kind? How did she remain? I'd have made it to safety if she hadn't attacked. I'd be in the cave now with Bran, laughing at our close escape, mourning the deaths of Drust and my friends, looking forward to…

No. Forget such thoughts. They can only torment me. I didn't get out. Vein delayed me just long enough. I'm trapped here now. Accept it. Take comfort in the fact that it won't be for long.

My left hand touches rock. The end of the tunnel.

I press an ear to the rock, in case I can still hear Bran. But there's nothing, not even the rumbling sound. Not as warm as it was either. The rock is cooling quickly now that it's rid of the druid Brude.

Maybe, if Vein isn't here – if she's been sucked back to her own realm a little later than the others – I can rest. Return to the lodestone. Recharge. Then force my way out. Break a hole through the rock with magic and…

Light behind me. A green, low, throbbing light. And a sad chuckle.

I turn slowly, already knowing what I'll find.

"Poor little Bec," Lord Loss says, floating not far away from me, flesh as lumpy as ever, coated in a red sheen from the blood oozing out of the cracks in his skin, the hole in his chest filled with those wriggling eel-like creatures. He's holding Drust's bag and a couple of his hands are rooting through the contents, stroking the chess board stored within.

Lord Loss drifts closer. I spot Vein behind him, sitting to attention, eyes hot with evil delight. The demon master picks a piece out of the bag and gazes at it. "All alone," he sighs, looking at the chess piece but speaking to me. "Friends dead or cut off. No way out. If only you'd known it would end this way. Maybe you would have stayed in your rath. Or perhaps you wouldn't have used up all your magic on the lodestone."

"We won," I snarl. "We beat you. We sent all the demons back."

"Really?" Lord Loss's crimson eyes widen and he drops the piece back into the bag. "Then what am *I* doing here?" He grins when I can't answer. "Poor Bec. You know so little of the universes. I didn't come to this world through the tunnel. I was wandering your land long before Brude set about his ignoble task. Your wind – impressive as it was – had no claim on me. I was too powerful for it."

"You weren't so powerful when Drust banished you from sight," I sneer.

Lord Loss's features twitch. "I grant you that one. But I wouldn't be so boastful if I was in your position. That spell of Drust's was clever but costly. Remember my geis?"

"I'm not afraid of a demon's geis," I tell him.

"You should be," he replies, face darkening. "Humans should never mock a demon master. We make perilous enemies. I might have let you live if you hadn't scorned me. I liked you, Bec. I gave you some of my magic. I was looking forward to watching you mature."

"Why *did* you give me the magic?" I ask, curiosity winning out over fear. "We wouldn't have been able to close the tunnel if you hadn't."

Lord Loss smiles smugly. "I am a sentinel of sorrow. I feed on the misery of humanity. I cherish this world and its sad, pathetic, pain-struck humans. But if my fellow Demonata had been able to come here at will, they would have destroyed it. Demons are vulgar, wrathful creatures. They would have murdered every human in sight, swiftly, leaving no survivors, and in a short few years I would have had no more subjects to play with. I couldn't let that happen, could I?"

I stare at him with disbelief. "You betrayed your own kind! You tricked them! You gave me power so that I could close the tunnel!"

"Of course," he chuckles. "I couldn't act too obviously — I don't want hordes of Demonata screaming for my head — but by slyly interfering, providing you with the means of stopping Brude, I was able to secure peace for this world, thus preserving my mortal minions of misery."

"But…" My head's awhirl. I can see it all now. "Connla was working for you. That's why he protected Drust whenever he was threatened."

"My wolf in the fold," Lord Loss laughs. "I let him kill some of the others for sport but warned him not to let any harm befall you or the druid. He forgot that at the end and summoned the demons to butcher you all. He almost ruined everything. I'm glad you dealt with him, though I would have preferred to do it myself — I'd have made him suffer much more."

"Why use him at all?" I cry. "Why set him against the rest of us if we were working towards the same goal?"

"Pain," Lord Loss says, his smile growing. "I knew he would create discord and unhappiness, delicious misery for me to relish. I was having so much fun." His smile fades. "Until the druid banished me."

The demon master clicks his fingers and Vein trots over. Lord Loss tickles the demon's head with one of his eight twisted hands. "You could have walked away from this," he whispers. "Your death serves no purpose. You'd have been more interesting to me alive. Misery would have followed you — I could sense it. I'd have been there, trailing you, delighting in the sorrow you both suffered and caused.

"But that can't be. In my fury I cast a geis. I made a solemn vow. And now, as a creature of my word, I must make good on my promise."

He drifts away from me. The green light fades slowly. Vein stays where she is. Other demons join her. A score or more. Monstrous creatures, misshapen, one with fire for eyes and the body of a baby, another covered in scales like a fish, another a giant insect with a knife-sized stinger in its tail.

"My familiars," Lord Loss whispers, disappearing from sight in the lengthening shadows. "They have more fleshly appetites than me."

"No," I whimper, cringing against the wall. "Please don't do this. I'll do anything you ask. I'll..."

I stop and catch myself. Remember who I am, my heritage, my people.

"Damn you then," I growl as the light fades away to the

dimmest of glows, even the light in the sockets of the demon with fire instead of eyes.

"Goodbye, Bec," Lord Loss calls softly.

"Damn you!" I shout again, throwing it after him as a challenge.

The last light flickers out and everything turns black.

Silence for a moment. Then a snicker. A growl. The sound of claws and fingers scuttling forward. I relax against the rock, resigned, not crying or begging. I want to die with dignity, like a true priestess or warrior. The sounds come closer. Hissing. Crackling. The grinding of teeth and fangs.

I lay my head against the wall. Stare up into nothingness. Try to be strong.

Fingers touch my damaged legs. Claws and tendrils explore. Soon I'm being mauled everywhere, pinched, stroked, sliced. Their breath is both hot and cold on my face as they crowd around me. I imagine their savage jaws, twisted faces and sharpened fangs.

I tremble, then grit my teeth hard, determined not to give Lord Loss the satisfaction of crying out. "I won't scream!" I tell myself. "I won't! I won't! I–"

Teeth and fangs bite into my flesh, every part of me at once. Nails dig in deep, burrowing through to my guts. Hands worm inside me and pull bits of my innards out, scraping at my skin from the inside. I'm being torn apart. The pain is unbearable. I lose control. My mouth shoots open. My senses dissolve. My brain goes wild. The last thing I hear, before madness and demons consume me, is the tunnel filling with my anguished, uncontrollable death howls.

Screams in the dark.

CELTIC TERMS AND PHRASES

ANA — *pronounced Ay (rhymes with play)-nah* — the mother of all the gods.

BALOR'S EYE — *Bal (rhymes with Hal)-or* Balor was a one-eyed giant, one of the Fomorii.

BANSHEES — the souls of dead women who wail loudly when somebody is about to die.

BREHONS — *breh-hons* — lawmakers, an early type of judge.

BRICRIU — *brick-roo* — a troublemaker.

CASHEL — *cash-el* — a stone fort.

CATHAIR — *ka-hair* — a round fort, surrounded by a stone wall.

COIRM — *kworm* — an alcoholic drink

CRANNOG — *kran-ogue (rhymes with "rogue")* — a fort built on an island in the middle of a lake.

CURRAGH — *cur-ah* — a small boat, like a canoe.

DOLMENS — *dole-mens* — tombs made of three upright stones, set in a pyramid-type shape, capped by a flat stone. Normally, one person would be buried beneath them or their ashes might be left in them.

FOMORII – *Fuh-more-ee* – an ancient tribe, reputed to be part demons.

GEIS – *gesh (rhymes with mesh)* – a curse.

HURLING – *her-ling* – a traditional Irish sport, the fastest team game in the world. It's played on a rugby-sized pitch, fifteen players per side. Each player has a stick which ends in a curved, flat head. They use it to hit a small, hard leather ball about, and score goals and points by hitting it into their opponent's goal or over the bar.

LEPRECHAUNS – *Lep-reh-cawns* – the Little People of Irish legends.

MACHA – *Mack-ah* – a war goddess.

MORRIGAN – *More-ee-gan* – a war goddess.

NEIT – *Net* – a god of war.

NUADA – *Noo-dah* – a war goddess.

OGHAM STONES – *Owe-am stones* – stones with lines cut into them – an early form of writing.

PICT – *Pick-t* – an ancient tribe from Britain.

QUERN – *kern* – a bowl.

RATH – *raff* – a round fort, surrounded by a wooden fence.

SEANACHAIDH – *shan-ah-key* – a storyteller or poet.

SIONAN'S RIVER – *Sun-un's river* – River Shannon.

SOUTERRAIN – *soo-tur-ane* – an underground tunnel, often used to store food and drink or as an escape route.

TIR NA N'OG – *Teer na nogue (rhymes with rogue)* – a mystical land where people never got sick or grew old.

TUATH – *chew-ah* – a county.

TUATHA – *chew-ah* – counties.

WEDGE TOMBS – tombs in which lots of stones are stacked side by side in the shape of a wedge, then topped with large flat stones.

NAMES

AIDEEN – *Aid-een.*

AEDNAT – *Aid-nat.*

AMARGEN – *Am-are-gen.*

BANBA – *Bon-bah.*

BEC – *rhymes with deck.*

BRAN – *rhymes with man.*

BRUDE – *Brood.*

CERA – *Keerah.*

CONN – *Kon.*

CONNLA – *Kon-lah.*

DARA – *Darr-ah.*

DRUST – *Jrust.*

ENA – *Ee-nah.*

ERC – *rhymes with perk.*

ERT – *rhymes with hurt.*

FAND – *Fond.*

FIACHNA – *Feek-nah.*

FINTAN – *Finn-tan.*

GOLL – *rhymes with doll.*

LORCAN – *Lor-can.*

MACCADAN – *Mac-Cad-an.*

MACGRIGOR – *Mac-Grig-or.*

MACROTH – *MacRoff.*

NECTAN – *Neck-tan.*

NINIAN – *Nin-ee-an.*

ORNA – *Or-nah.*

PADRAIG – *Paw-drig.* This refers St Patrick. (The book is set in Ireland in the middle of the 5th century AD when St Patrick was converting Ireland to Christianity.)

RONAN – *Row-nan.*

SCOTA – *Scow (rhymes with low)-tah.*

STRUAN – *Strew-an.*

TIERNAN – *Teer-nan.*

TORIN – *Tore-in.*

Look out for

THE DEMONATA

Volumes 5 and 6

DARREN SHAN
THE DEMONATA VOL. 5 & 6

Blood
Beast &
Demon Apocalypse

Digging a hole through to
your world July 2011